DINARZAD'S CHILDREN

DINARZAD'S CHILDREN

An Anthology of Contemporary Arab American Fiction

Edited by
PAULINE KALDAS AND
KHALED MATTAWA

THE UNIVERSITY OF ARKANSAS PRESS

Fayetteville

2004

Copyright © 2004 by The University of Arkansas Press

08   07   06   05   04   5   4   3   2   1

Designed by Liz Lester

∞ The paper used in this publication meets the minimum requirements
of the American National Standard for Permanence of Paper for
Printed Library Materials Z39.48-1984.

LIBRARY OF CONGRESS CATALOGING-IN-PUBLICATION DATA

Dinarzad's children : an anthology of contemporary Arab American fiction /
edited by Pauline Kaldas and Khaled Mattawa.
p.   cm.
Includes bibliographical references.
ISBN 1-55728-781-3 (pbk. : alk. paper)
1. American fiction—Arab American authors. 2. American fiction—
20th century. 3. American fiction—21st century. 4. Arab
Americans—Fiction. 5. Short stories, American.
I. Kaldas, Pauline, 1961–   II. Mattawa, Khaled.
PS647.A72D56   2004
813'.010892705—dc22
2004019344

CONTENTS

ACKNOWLEDGMENTS

Our sincerest thanks goes to everyone who has supported this project, especially Lisa Suhair Majaj and T. J. Anderson III.

Thanks also goes to Alyssa Antonelli and Amelia Boldaji. Their dedication and attention to detail helped us to bring this book to life.

Our appreciation goes to the University of Arkansas Press, especially Larry Malley, for his encouragement and belief in the importance of this book.

Credits

"My Elizabeth," by Diana Abu-Jaber, was originally published in the *Kenyon Review* 17 (Winter 1995).

"And What Else" and "News from Phoenix" copyright 1990 by Joseph Geha. Reprinted from *Through and Through* with the permission of Graywolf Press, Saint Paul, Minnesota.

"Stage Directions for an Extended Conversation," by Yussef El Guindi, was originally published in *Mizna* 3.3 (2001).

"Fire and Sand" copyright 2003 by Laila Halaby. Reprinted from *West of the Jordan* by permission of Beacon Press, Boston.

"Edge of Rock," by May Mansoor Munn, was originally published in *Ms.* 3 (October 1992).

"The American Way" and "The Hike to Heart Rock" copyright 2000 by Frances Khirallah Noble. Reprinted from *The Situe Stories* with the permission of Syracuse University Press, Syracuse, New York.

"Oh, Lebanon," by Evelyn Shakir, was originally published in *Flyway* 7 (Fall–Winter 2002).

"How We Are Bound," by Patricia Sarrafian Ward, was originally published in *Ararat* (Autumn 1996).

"Arabic Lessons," by David Williams, was originally published in *Flyway* 7 (Fall–Winter 2002).

INTRODUCTION

In *The Thousand and One Nights,* Shahrazad saves herself by telling stories to distract her murderous king and husband, Shahrayar. To assure her survival, the legendary narrator asks that her sister Dinarzad accompany her. It is Dinarzad who asks for a story on the first night and on subsequent nights. She says, "Sister, if you are not sleepy, tell us one of your lovely little tales to while away the night, before I bid you good-bye, at daybreak, for I don't know what will happen to you tomorrow." With that invitation Shahrazad begins. The 1001 tales end with Shahrayar falling in love with Shahrazad. The tales transform him, allowing his imagination to seek out other means of dealing with life's complex issues. Shahrayar renounces his promise to marry a virgin each night and kill her the following morning. But the tales end without a clear sense of what happened to Dinarzad. Central as she was to the structure of the tales, she disappears into silence.

In some ways, the lives of Arab Americans have been similar to that of Dinarzad. Though Arabic-speaking immigrants have been coming to the United States since the late nineteenth century, it is only recently that their fellow Americans have become aware of them. With the events of September 11, the seemingly oxymoronic term "Arab American" began to rattle easily off the lips of pundits and news reporters. This attention has perpetuated acts of hostility that, though never highly publicized, have occurred with every crisis in the Middle East, beginning with the American hostage crisis in Iran in 1979. However, on the positive side, in some parts of the country Arab Americans are beginning to be touted as a political block or a group to be consulted on issues related to multiculturalism or foreign policy. For better or for worse, Arab Americans have arrived.

As Alixa Naff has noted, the silence surrounding Arab American lives may have been because many among them "assimilated themselves out of existence." Arabic-speaking immigrants who came in the early decades of the twentieth century were adamant about blending in. Practical concerns induced this. Parents told their children not to speak Arabic so as not to hinder their English. Arab Christians, when churches of their own denominations were not available, joined their neighbors in worship. Many claimed they were Greek or Italian to better pass as European Americans. At a certain period in the United States, to be Arab was merely bothersome. And so Arabic-speaking immigrants identified themselves as Syrians, and later Lebanese, but upheld certain traditions within their own households because it was what "Arabs" did.

By the 1960s being Arab became embarrassing to some. Narratives by Arab Americans available at the time reflect that embarrassment. Salom Rizk, in his *Syrian Yankee,* never mentions that the language he spoke at home was Arabic. Upon returning to Lebanon for a brief visit, the narrator describes his own people in the most derogatory terms and is relieved when he at last leaves them to their misery. William Blatty's *Which Way to Mecca, Jack?* is filled with so much self-hatred that it is a truly painful read. The narrator, in his longing to be an Irishman, in his derogatory portrayal of his mother, and in his acceptance of racist stereotypes, provides a testament to the pressures exerted by American mainstream culture on the non-whites living within it. Yet by the late 1960s, the devastating effects of the 1967 Middle East war, the subsequent Arab bashing that resulted from it, and the general greater interest in minority rights propelled by the civil rights movement prompted some people of Arab descent to claim their ancestral links. It was in that era that the term "Arab American" was coined and became more accepted among Arabic-speaking immigrants and their descendants. Arab American political organizations came into being. Publications were started; exhibits of Arab art and translations of Arab literature ensued.

The years after the late 1960s saw a flourishing interest in ethnic identity politics. With that, a sea change began on the American cultural scene. African American authors became major "American" authors, Asian American writers published widely, and Latino writers gained a wide readership. Arab Americans, a small but significant minority, were conspicuously absent from these developments, at least in prose genres. On the other hand, poets such as Samuel Hazo, Sam Hamod, D. H. Melhem, and Jack Marshall have been publishing since the 1960s, and hence there came into being such a thing as Arab American literature. There was, nonetheless, uncertainty about the usefulness of the label, about what kind of light such identification would shed on one's work. During those decades, Arab American writers, and Arab Americans in general, were in a sense like their ancestor Dinarzad, helpful to the dialogue about a new American culture but generally unheard.

The reasons for the absence of Arab American narratives are complicated. For decades, Arab American writers have relied almost exclusively on the lyric poem as their preferred medium. In recent decades Arab American poetry has flourished. Arab Americans Naomi Shihab Nye, Samuel Hazo, and Lawrence Joseph are among the most accomplished poets on the American poetry scene. The 1990s produced a slew of Arab American poets, including Hayan Charara, Nathalie Handal, Walid Bitar, and Suheir Hammad. However, the Arab American narrative has been quiet, possibly due to the sense of isolation Arab American writers felt even within their own community. The lyric poem afforded them a way to speak as individuals to individuals, and a way to affirm that they were speaking for themselves even when their poems contained the concerns of multitudes around the world.

In shying away from fiction and prose narrative in general, Arab American writers may have wished to exert greater control over the representation of their community. The narrative elements in their poetry were mediated through the exertion of the poet's subjectivity that lyric poetry has traditionally demanded. However, in the last few years, emboldened with a sense of urgency and confidence as well as a deeper ethnic and feminist consciousness, Arab American narrative has begun to emerge. Critic Lisa Suhair Majaj writes:

> It is noticeable, for instance, that the growing emergence of a body of feminist Arab American writing corresponds with a shift toward prose writing, fiction as well as nonfiction. It is as if the turn away from nostalgic celebration toward more rigorous and self-critical explorations mandates a move away from the lyric compression of poetry toward the more expansive and explanatory medium of prose.

The 1990s saw the publication of Diana Abu-Jaber's novel *Arabian Jazz;* Elmaz Abinader's memoir *Children of the Roojme;* and a groundbreaking anthology, *Food for Our Grandmothers: Writings by Arab-American and Arab-Canadian Feminists,* edited by Joanna Kadi.

Fiction, however, still presented both practical and ethical challenges. The American publishing establishment has created a formula for success for ethnic writers, particularly women. By inference, this formula is best described by critic Lisa Sanchez-Gonzalez in her critique of some Puerto Rican feminist novels. She writes,

> For the most part, a certain simplistic trope permeates these texts—the island (Puerto Rico)—represents outgrown, retrograde communal and family values, while in the final instance "America" (that is, any area of the mainland United States unpopulated by Boricuas) is celebrated as the utopia of the mature female protagonist's liberatory exile.

Arab American writers were wary of this modus operandi. They innately refused it even when their texts provided lacerating critiques of male chauvinism in Arab and Arab American cultures. Unlike Rizk and Blatty before them, they were aware of how any criticism of Arab culture could perpetuate negative stereotypes, thus shrinking Arab Americans' sense of freedom, not enlarging it.

When some authors tried to provide a "balanced" portrait, other dynamics came into play. Diana Abu-Jaber notes that while she was trying to publish her first novel, *Arabian Jazz,* some editors wanted to take the word "Arabian" out of the title. Others wanted to change the characters' names so they would not seem alien. When Arab characters appeared to be normal, or universal, it was felt that the American book market could not handle it. Understandably, when the only option, in Dennis Lee's words, is "to collaborate further in one's extinction as a rooted human being," it seems natural that a "drastic and involuntary stratagem of self-preserval" ensues whereby "words [go] silent." And the reluctance to tell our stories continued.

Other elements may have provoked this sense of unease. While some Arab immigrants arrived in the United States as refugees, the vast majority came for economic betterment. Except for refugees from Palestine and Iraq, their countries were not shut away from them, and so they could not put them behind. And while most Arab immigrants who first started coming to the United States are from minority groups in their countries, they were for the most part thoroughly integrated into their societies and were in most cases the oldest cultures in their homelands. Understandably, Arab American lives are haunted by a deep sense of nostalgia. This longing resonates even more loudly when coupled with being unwelcome within the host culture—the stereotype of the Arab remaining one of the few racist images that can still be portrayed with unchecked abandon. With their place of origin still beckoning and their place of relocation continuously wincing at their presence, Arab Americans have lived on unsettled ground, biding their time, waiting to be invited to tell their stories.

The silence could not be kept for long. Even before the September 11 events brought the American public's attention to the existence of an Arab American community, Arab American writers had presented their stories to the public, albeit on an individual basis. While this anthology distinguishes itself by focusing solely on Arab American fiction, other anthologies of Arab American literature, such as *Grapeleaves: A Century of Arab-American Poetry* (1988), *Food for Our Grandmothers: Writings by Arab-American and Arab-Canadian Feminists* (1993), and *Post Gibran: Anthology of New Arab American Writing* (1999), have helped increase readers' interest in Arab American writing. Post—September 11, the invasion of Afghanistan, the extralegal treatment of Arab Americans, and the war on Iraq must be considered turning points not only for the community but also for the larger American public's awareness of this community's existence. Arab Americans could not try to engage the world and remain anonymous. Even those who wished to remain in the shadows were sought out. The unsympathetic sensibilities of some individuals, like those who targeted Edward Said and blacklisted pro-Palestinian or antiwar activists, required solidarity, coalition building, and adequate responses. Also, those with sympathetic sensibilities wanted to know the Arab American world better.

The stories in this anthology are in a sense a double coming out.

While literary through and through, these stories are nonetheless testaments to the humanity of a heterogeneous and complex group of people. They attempt to familiarize the average reader with Arab culture and its presence in the United States, with its positive and negative aspects. Furthermore, that Arab American writers trusted themselves enough to write their stories indicates their sense of confidence in their skill. Shedding their reluctance to let us into their private worlds, they have found ways to tell their stories without being co-opted; these stories are neither acts of betrayal nor acts of eulogy that sing uncritical praise. More ethnically and politically conscious, the current generation of Arab American writers sheds a more critical light on issues of heritage, gender, nationalism, and assimilation within the Arab American community.

Finally, many of these stories, quite a few of which are written by women, are testaments to a well-honed feminism. Keeping their silence for a long time, Arab American storytellers have learned a great deal from their African American, Asian American, and Latina sisters, the American Shahrazads who have sustained the integrity of their communities through their stories, letting the outside world into their world and providing a sense of community for their kin. As hostilities remain to blaze between U.S. policy leaders and the Arab world, the mission of Arab American writers can only be daunting. The feminist sensibility that permeates these stories assures us that a primary focus on justice and inclusiveness will continue to guide Arab American writers in their endeavor to chronicle the lives that surround them. The children of Dinarzad are facing their own crises. They are obligated by their art to tell their stories well, and their sense of integrity demands that they tell them in truth. We think they succeed in both.

HOW WE ARE BOUND

PATRICIA SARRAFIAN WARD

I

Madelaine called her daughter's name, but Shereen had not yet returned from her errand to the Dairy Mart. The apartment was silent but for the television humming with low voices. Madelaine pressed her knuckles to her eyes, agitated by what she had dreamed. It had been almost an hour since Shereen left, she calculated, because the program had changed. She sat up, plucking at her shirt to separate it from her damp skin. It was impossible to stay awake on hot days like this. She went to the kitchen and opened the refrigerator, stood there for a few moments breathing in the cold.

She considered calling Shereen's friend Jenny, who worked at the Dairy Mart, but Jenny always wanted to talk, or ask strange questions. The day Shereen had introduced her, Jenny had confessed dramatically that she wished she had been born a Palestinian. Shereen's father, Amin, had been enraged after this unfortunate introduction. "What sort of idiot is she?" he asked. "What else does she wish? That she was a starving Ethiopian? A piece of shit in New Delhi?" Madelaine felt sorry for Shereen, as sorry as she felt for herself, friendless in this country. She had told Amin: "Leave her alone. She needs some sort of companionship. Look at me, all alone."

"You could become friends with Zeina."

"She's a zero-on-the-left." Not only were Zeina and Adel obsessed by money ("In America, this is how it is," they would say in that explaining voice, as if she and Amin were fools), but they had fled the war too early. They knew nothing and here they were, pretending to be experts on everything. "He's my brother," Amin would say, but Madelaine saw with her inner eye the burn-mark of shame from helping Adel with accounts he needed no help with, from tending the cash register in "emergencies" when Zeina and Adel disappeared for one or two hours.

Madelaine lit a cigarette and sat down by the telephone. She pictured Shereen leaning on the Dairy Mart counter talking with Jenny, and endured a tinge of jealousy. In Lebanon they used to sit and talk for hours on the balcony. Now Shereen spoke to other people, students she met at the community college, and she wore jeans with holes in them. Madelaine felt her daughter's slow separation like something unraveling inside her. They should never have left home, just as her dreams kept telling her. They could get rid of the renters, move back. A loose thread snaked away from the carpet and she pushed it underneath with her toe. The smell of this apartment was offensive. They had been here almost a year and no matter what she cooked, no matter how much she washed the floors with lemon-scented soap, that American odor remained, of sagging hardwood floors and linoleum that curled away from the walls.

"Jenny?" she said as soon as she heard the Hello. "Let me speak Shereen."

"*To* Shereen, Madame Nasrallah. Shereen left *eons* ago."

Amin rang up an American woman's purchases: three bags of Arabic bread, a jar of imported molasses, tahini, black olives, falafel mix. What a mish-mash. He hoped she did not think these ingredients should find their way into the same meal. He waved good-bye and called out in Arabic, "God be with you," and she smiled nervously over her shoulder, as if he had cursed her. Amin watched through the window as she placed the bags in the trunk of her car and then walked around to the driver's side and climbed in. Ribbons of heat rose from the asphalt. The woman edged her car out of the lot, her turn signal blinking inanely at the empty street.

The television was always on in the back of the store and the weatherman was saying a record high had been attained. He pointed to the yellow sun, the big red *H* (for Heat, Amin thought), and his arms made grandiose motions as he recited the temperatures. "It's a Doggie

Day," the weatherman announced smugly. *Doggie Day* appeared in large, dripping letters across the screen.

"What this country needs is a civil war," Amin grumbled, goading the same old argument.

"You and your war. I wonder about you. You need help, to think people need a war." Adel spoke lazily from the stool in the corner. Amin saw that his brother's willingness to argue had been dulled by the heat, that it would take more to get a fight going.

Zeina shouted from the kitchen: "What I always say is this: why did you come here if you didn't want to? Go back if you hate it so much!"

Both men flinched at the sound of her voice, glancing quickly at each other to share the irritation before settling back into their stand-off. Amin knew exactly the progression of this argument and the eventual desolation he would feel. They were right. He had chosen to leave. He had given in to fear after fourteen years of courage, when Aoun had announced his maniacal war against the Syrians and it seemed that the whole country would crack open from the bombs and crumble into the sea. Who was he to complain about this country? But Adel probably wished *he* had been the one to stay behind instead of running away because of his wife's hysteria. Amin wanted his brother to admit, just *once,* that he missed Zghorta, he missed Jounieh, that he wished he had not abandoned the war. He wanted to break open the surface of things and reveal the truth of his brother's disdain for what it was, a hatred for the self. Amin glanced at his older brother, who gazed back with half-closed eyes, a bit dangerous, a look he had had since he was a child.

It was too hot for this. Amin felt, as always, the inborn hollowness of his attacks, the central weakness. His mind fumbled with things he might say as he wet a paper towel and started wiping the counter. The telephone rang.

"Lebanese Bakery and General Goods," Adel intoned, then handed the receiver to Amin.

When Madelaine explained that Shereen had left the Dairy Mart at five fifteen and now it was after six, Amin said, "Don't worry. This is America. You worry too much."

"What's the problem?" Adel said when he hung up.

"Shereen's not home on time."

Zeina appeared, wiping her hands on her apron. Her waist-length dark red hair was piled on top of her head. She was a beautiful woman, and Amin often thought, *If only she would shut up.*

"She crushes that girl!" Zeina announced. "She's twenty years old! Uf!"

Amin thought, *What do you know about children,* then quickly looked down. "She should come back when she says she'll come back."

"Maybe she has a boyfriend," Zeina said, winking.

"There's time for boyfriends," he said lamely, and Zeina huffed at him.

"Men always think there's time if it's their *daughter.*" She slapped her hands together once. "Time goes like that." She looked Adel up and down. He was cleaning his nails with a piece of twisted paper. "What are *you* doing? Maybe you should go to the beauty parlor and get a pedicure too, why not."

"Maybe you could give me one," Adel said blandly, but Amin detected the suggestive tone beneath and turned away. Zeina whispered something and Amin bent his head, continuing to wipe the counter, the back of his neck hot as if the words had singed his skin.

After calling Amin, Madelaine sleepily removed her clothes and lay down in her slip on the bedcovers because there was nothing else to do. Amin was right, there was no need to panic. Shereen had probably run into some friend from the college, but usually she called. The Salvation Army fan rattled in the window, and a warm breeze floated across her skin, across this body that over time had lost significance and was somehow no longer attached to her. She stared at the jutting angles of her hips and kneecaps, the cracked toenails, and she thought as she had often thought over the past months, *I am rotting from the inside out. I am rotting with remembrances like garbage.* Then she let in the nostalgia with a rush of anxiety like a door gliding open: the summer *sabhiyyehs* in Zghorta with the sounds of water running from the taps and the laughter of women cooking; the cool stone walls of Byblos; the blinding white pavements of the beach complexes in

Jounieh. The memories collided with one another, tumbling into her mouth and opening it with a groan. Madelaine clung to her imagination, wringing the pain from her system. Her body trembled during this exorcism and the tears boiled under her eyelids, and Madelaine could not stop thinking, *I am a cadaver.* Then, as the memories subsided and her losses trickled away, she once again heard the silence of the apartment, the silence of breathing in an empty room.

Amin came home at seven. He opened the downstairs door and was at once engulfed by the thick, hot air locked in the stairwell. He checked the mail, noticing in a distant way that usually Shereen collected it and here it was, still on the floor even at this late hour. The two bolts clanged open upstairs, and then Madelaine's shrill voice rang out: "Shereen?" and he paused halfway up the stairs.

"Did you see her?" Madelaine cried.

Amin checked his watch. She had been gone for at least two hours. The Dairy Mart was only a fifteen-minute walk.

"Didn't you drive her route, Amin?"

He shook his head. Madelaine pushed her hair back from her forehead. She looked bewildered. Her kohl was smudged.

"Were you crying?" he asked.

She stared at him, shaking her head, until he understood that this was not what mattered.

Amin drove, but he did not see her anywhere, and cars honked behind him because he was driving at only fifteen miles per hour and the speed limit was twenty-five. "Asshole," a man shouted as he screeched past. Amin thought, *In Beirut you would have been shot,* but he knew that was not always true, and he sensed the mocking presence of his own ineptness like a person sitting beside him.

It was seven thirty, and the sun would not set for another two hours, and now Shereen was exactly two hours late, an odd coincidence that Amin fixated on when he checked his watch in the Dairy Mart parking lot. He searched between the Coca-Cola and Marlboro posters and glimpsed Jenny behind the counter, working the cash register. She was wearing a purple turban-like headdress, and her long curly red hair exploded from beneath it. A few moments later, a young man emerged smacking a pack of cigarettes against his palm. Amin looked around the parking lot, half-expecting to see Shereen appear and wave, but instead he saw the faded parking lines and oil stains, the napkins and candy wrappers pushed up against the curb, the graffiti on the pay phone, and he was taken by the fear that there was something to be known here, something in the strangely desolate vision of this parking lot, but whatever it was remained hidden.

Amin got out of the car. Then he unlocked the door in case Shereen turned up. As he walked toward the entrance of the store, he realized how stupid that was because why would she get into the car? The illogic of his thinking stabbed him with panic.

Jenny grinned. "Hi, Mr. Nasrallah."

Amin always felt like squinting, her appearance was so bright. A round green pin on her shirt said "Pray for Palestine." He managed a smile and said, "Have you seen Shereen?"

She frowned. She shook her head. "I told Madame Nasrallah. She hung out for a few minutes, bought a gallon of milk, and then left."

"A gallon of milk," Amin repeated.

Jenny stared at him; then she walked to the window. Amin saw she was wearing cut-off jeans and that there was a large mole on her thigh. Shereen would not wear shorts, at least not that short. When Jenny turned around and started saying something, for the first time Amin felt a closeness to her, a craving for her voice like the craving for Shereen's. He nodded without hearing what she said and left.

Amin walked. He walked with his eyes exploring every part of the road, the empty chairs on porches, the darkening side streets. When he reached the intersection halfway home, he stopped. The street continued down the gentle curve of the hill and then flattened out, and the two-family house where they lived was visible from here. Amin waited, unable to leave this position, because now it seemed that if he just stood here, Shereen would appear from maybe this direction, or from one of these houses, but nothing happened. He stared at this neighborhood that was muted and ugly in the heat, the sodden air smelling of narrow, wasted front lawns, melting asphalt and wooden houses. Farther down the block, two people swinging plastic bags swayed along the sidewalk, hips touching. The light changed twice with no traffic passing before Amin turned back.

He parked across the street from the house. Madelaine made a brief appearance in the window. Amin climbed the four steps onto the front porch, fumbling with his keys. He had mixed all his keys from Lebanon with those that were American, to prove that one place is like any other, one key just like the next.

"Hallo," the old man said from next door.

Amin nodded at him. For the first time he wondered what this old man had accomplished with his life, what did he think he was doing, sitting all day on a chair looking at the street.

At eight thirty Amin called the police but they told him Shereen had to disappear for twenty-four hours and it had only been three, really, and not even that. Amin left the telephone feeling insulted. Madelaine took one of the kitchen chairs to the balcony and sat down, her eyes fixed on the quiet scene below.

"Madelaine, it's fine," Amin said from the doorway, but her heart had been snatched upward and clamped into a cold, hard place whose taste crept into her throat and mouth. She was thinking of the dream she had had earlier in the day, during her nap after Shereen left. It had been about Lebanon. An olive tree had stood by itself in a field, and she was approaching it with little time left. Her hand produced a knife and the branches began to fall away without sound; a great sadness accompanied this necessary action. When the last branches dropped to the earth, Shereen was revealed, crouched like a spider in the heart of the tree. Madelaine had seized her and pulled but Shereen had clung to the bark, her brown eyes shining like wet stones.

Now Madelaine struggled to remember other dreams, perhaps from the night before, to find clues, but all she saw were branches dropping to the earth and Shereen's fingers and toes gripping the center of the tree. The bitterness of knowing that had they stayed in Lebanon none of this would be happening felt its way around her, closing her in like armor.

Amin stepped back into the living room, looked around helplessly.

Until now, he had relied on Shereen to watch over Madelaine. If Shereen's stories about Jenny or summer school did not make her laugh, or if the English lessons Shereen patiently gave her became too frustrating, sometimes Amin would challenge her to trick-track contests and let her win. Now he retreated. He recognized the inward expression on his wife's face, the eyes as impenetrable as those of a blind person. He paced the living room, stopping at the window every few minutes to check the street. In the immobility of dusk, the buzz of the streetlamps sounded malevolent.

"I'm going to call Adel," he said.

When she heard him speaking into the telephone, she looked over her shoulder and saw the plumpness of her husband, the thin hair, and thought, *You can't handle anything.*

II

"The police are right. She's not *missing* yet." Adel searched through the paper bag he had brought and pulled out a Ziploc of *ma'-moul*, Madelaine's favorite. Zeina nodded emphatically at his words. He strode into the kitchen, returned with a plate that he set on the coffee table. Madelaine thought, *He went into my kitchen,* while Adel arranged the pastries in a pattern of circles, as if they were expecting visitors.

"Dates *and* walnut," he added, and sat down.

Amin sat with his arm around Madelaine's shoulders. She smelled of sweat. He had seen this face during the war, that crumpled look of fallen resistance. Amin repelled the urge to lash out at her, tell her to snap out of it. He gripped her shoulder, shaking it gently every now and then, aware of Adel's curious eyes.

"Madelaine, you must eat something," Zeina commanded. "You must take care of yourself better. You're so thin." She propelled the plate of *ma'moul* a few inches in her sister-in-law's direction. "Is there anything I can get for you from the kitchen?"

Madelaine thought of the tabbouleh Shereen had helped her to prepare earlier. She shook her head. She hardly ever went anywhere alone, but now she was imagining walking up the street, toward the Dairy Mart, walking in the darkness. She stared at her legs, trying to communicate with them.

"What should we talk about?" Amin offered.

"No politics," Zeina moaned. "If I have to hear about the Syrians one more time, *yay.*" She flicked the subject away with her hands. Amin chuckled.

"I don't think she's coming back," Madelaine said, as if apologizing for something, and then she stood up and left the room. They heard the front door open, then her footsteps going down the stairs with odd spaces of silence between each step, like the walk of someone who has been struck.

"She's really overreacting," Zeina told Amin. "Is something wrong with her?"

Amin suddenly wanted to confess that Madelaine had been this way for years now and he was losing his ability to help her, but he caught Adel and Zeina in a shared, impatient glance. He closed his eyes, opened them again. He went to the window, found Madelaine standing on the sidewalk, staring up the road. She turned, looked the other way. Then she retreated from view, and he heard her footsteps creaking up the porch stairs.

When she came in, she scowled at Zeina and said, "You were right all along. Maybe we should never have left Beirut."

"What were you doing?" Amin could not keep the resentment out of his voice. He thought, *It's just like you, to collapse right away.*

Madelaine sat down. Her legs had betrayed her by stiffening and refusing to walk. *You want to go away in the dark?* they had chastised. *You fool.* The harmless, empty street remained with her, the muggy smell of trees and smoke from someone's grill.

"How do you live here?" Madelaine said, and Amin groaned, covered his face with his hands. "How do you live here without going mad?"

"Look, we want to help," Adel said. "Let's not argue." Then he added, "She can't have just disappeared."

"What do you know about disappearing?" Madelaine said.

Zeina sucked in air. "Are you going to torture us with stories again? We all have pain."

"I tell you, Madelaine," said Adel, snapping a glance at his wife. "She has a boyfriend. That's what happens in America."

"What boyfriend? Show me the boyfriend."

Amin gestured at Madelaine to be quiet. "Adel, you don't understand."

"I don't understand," Adel repeated belligerently.

Madelaine stood up, started to walk from window to window, her hands holding each other behind her back. Zeina watched her.

Amin wanted to say, *It's our whole history you don't understand,* but it seemed absurd to say such a thing now, in this shabby, foreign apartment. There was nothing here to grasp, to point at, that would lead them backward in time. Even the shape of the room was wrong: it was too small, the ceilings too low. The floors creaked whenever he walked through this place, as if refusing his right to dominate them, and the glass doorknobs he had not yet tightened would spin loosely in his palm. Amin felt now that if he moved at all, he would break apart the structure of this place with his own, because he did not fit. Beyond Madelaine's thin, stiff frame, through the window, he became aware of the breadth of silence, of the evening carrying on without them. He inhaled deeply, but the vast isolation stayed. He wanted to cross the room and grasp his wife, shake her. *She will come home.*

"Well? What don't I understand?"

Amin caught a note of greed in his brother's voice. *He wants to fight now. He wants to know everything so he can crush it under his feet.*

Amin said, "Why did you never come back?"

Zeina sneered. "What? Go back to that shithole?"

"So you wanted to come back." Amin pointed at Zeina. "It was her."

Adel closed his eyes. "Only fools want to go live in a war."

"A war?" Amin laughed. "What about this? Look at this." His voice shook.

"What's 'this'? Nothing has happened." Adel threw his hands up and looked around the room to beg that this one point be agreed upon.

Amin waited a moment, examining his brother's face. Then he said, "You left your country, Adel. You could have come back any time."

"I have no country."

"Don't be ridiculous," said Zeina.

A silence inserted itself between them. Zeina leaned forward and examined the *ma'moul*. She selected one, bit into it with one hand cupped under her mouth. Amin thought about how she had spent all day making these pastries in the back and he had helped at the end, sprinkling them with powdered sugar, moving along the trays beside her. Now some of those pastries, destined for sale, were in his living room. Zeina's lips were flecked.

"In Beirut, I had more than I'll ever have here," he said.

"You have your life here," Zeina countered.

"I had my life there," Amin said stubbornly. "You think I appreciate becoming someone who sells bread? I was an *accountant*." He paused, but no one said anything. "You know what's funniest about it? The girl Jenny, Shereen's friend, she wants my job. She told me, 'When you quit, will you recommend me?' She wants to be around the *mana'ish* and the *fatayer*. She probably thinks they'll transform her into a Palestinian, or at least a Lebanese like us, the next best thing."

Madelaine was imagining Shereen's room, the secrets that might be there that would explain where she was. "We should never have moved here," she said quietly. "It was cowardly. After fourteen years."

She leaned her forehead against the window. She willed her mind to empty itself but it clung to its life of nostalgia, so she started to wander through the rooms of the home she had lived in for her whole marriage, and with a hollowness opening wider and wider in her chest, she felt the exact sensation of cool bare floors, the precise temperature of marble counters, the perfect shape of a piece of tile that had slipped out of place and had stayed on the kitchen window-sill for years. She heard from a distance the voices in the room rising and falling, and struggled to stay away from this new place.

"You think you're martyrs. You could have left years ago," Adel was shouting.

"You mean, I could have become a bread seller years ago."

"You have no respect for me. Listen to yourself."

Amin shrugged this away. "I do. In fact, I've decided. What do we need with this stupid country? We're going back," he announced triumphantly.

Madelaine stared as he sat up and nodded at her. "What's wrong with you?" she said. "How can we go now?"

III

At seven thirty in the morning Amin and Madelaine were still sitting straight up in bed, his hand covering hers. They had called the police twice more and a policeman had visited briefly with a notepad. Madelaine could still feel his presence, which had brought such crashing hope into her, such strength, until the questions Amin translated for her (*Has she ever gone off before? Does she have a boyfriend? Is she pregnant? Any friends she'd be visiting?*) had settled into a stone in her chest. They were supposed to go to the downtown police station at around nine.

Zeina was asleep on the couch, Adel on the floor on cushions. Madelaine went to the bathroom and washed her face. She kept her eyes away from Shereen's room. In the kitchen Amin gestured her to the chair. "You sit down," he whispered. "I'll make the coffee."

He searched for the Nescafé. Madelaine pointed. Her skin was crawling with tiredness but her mind felt clear and somehow cold. She was irritated by Amin's kindness, Amin who never made the coffee. She wanted him to stop.

He tried to block her gaze with his shoulder, hunching over a little.

"You need to put more," Madelaine said as he was about the replace the lid on the jar, and Amin's hands stumbled so that the coffee spilled onto the counter. He started crying though he knew he should not for Madelaine's sake, but he thought maybe, just maybe, if he gave in to this then Shereen would appear and his punishment would end. He could not even remember what he had been doing around five fifteen the day before, the time when Shereen left the Dairy Mart. How could he not remember?

Madelaine wet a sponge and cleaned the counter. On a shelf just above it were jars with the labels Shereen had made for her: *burghul, zaatar, foul, riz, fasoulia*. Madelaine started wiping the lids, replacing each jar so that the labels were facing out. Amin stood back, hands hanging by his sides.

"Can I make you food?" Zeina asked from the doorway.

At eight thirty Madelaine and Amin drove to the police station. On the radio the announcer said today would be another scorcher. Madelaine searched the streets, her eyes dry and gritty.

Detective Jeremy Brown was young, which Amin immediately latched onto as a sign that Shereen would be found very soon, because after all someone young would not yet be immune to their fears and therefore would work harder.

Amin and Madelaine sat down on wooden chairs opposite Detective Brown. Madelaine stared at the birthmark on his cheek. It was a dark purple, a formless blotch on a face that otherwise was curiously handsome and benign. The blond hair on his arms stood out against the tan skin. She felt a terror rising in her.

She tapped Amin's arm, said in Arabic: "He's too young. Look at him. They gave him to us because we're immigrants. They don't care."

Detective Brown looked up from the forms he had been reading, perhaps the forms filled in from all their telephone calls, and nodded at each of them. He said, more gently than the policeman of the night before, "Now, your daughter's name is Sherry, is that right?"

The sound of that useless word, *Sherry,* a word that meant absolutely nothing to Madelaine, squeezed from her the last of her remaining strength so that she bent all the way over until her forehead touched her knees. She looked at the inch of concrete floor between her feet. The land of America opened in her mind, a vast gray place of secrets and hidden things, and then some words, faintly surprising, revealed themselves to her: *We are bound to this place.* Madelaine saw herself walking and walking, trying to open up the concrete, bending over the smallest crack and tearing at it.

"No," Amin said. "Shereen. Sher*een.*"

The New World

SUSAN MUADDI DARRAJ

It was a small apartment, comprising the second and third stories of the rowhouse; the first level was a flower shop, run by an Italian widow and her spinster daughter. On Siham's first day in the apartment, they had brought up a coconut custard pie, slightly browned on top. It had also been her first week in America, so they gave her a red rose as well. Mrs. Donato spoke with a heavy accent, which reassured Siham about her own. But Carla, the daughter with the penciled eyebrows, emitted negative vibes that Siham could not explain.

The floors of the apartment were what Nader called "hardwood"—dark, polished slats of wood, side by side like slumbering children. She'd never seen floors like this; back home in Jerusalem, all the homes, even those of the very poor, were made of stone. The most democratic of building supplies because there was plenty of it. People only used wood to create heat and to make furniture. Whenever Nader was at work, Siham liked to put on her socks and slide across her new "hardwood" floors like an ice skater. Hopefully, Philadelphia had a real ice rink, because she'd never seen one of those either, except on TV.

Nader worked all day, five days a week, with his friend George, who owned a food truck and catered to the businesspeople in the city. They stood at Sixteenth and Market Streets, crammed together in a metal cart, one frying the steaks and the other bagging the soft pretzels, from six A.M. until late in the evening. Nader always came home smelling like grease, his thick mustache limp with the steam that filled up their cart. She missed him terribly during the day and offered to work with them like George's wife had done before their daughter was born, but he said that his wife was a lady and he didn't want her to get dirty. "What about George's wife?" she asked, but Nader said that she had lived in a refugee camp and was used to the dirt. It was an unkind comment and it bothered Siham, because she liked Layla. Siham's father had taught her to treat everyone kindly, and he had stitched the wounds of poor villagers without taking money and without making them feel indebted (even though her mother huffed in frustration when they themselves sometimes ran out of milk and eggs). Siham liked to think that she had inherited his open heart, and she told Nader many times not to speak that way. After all, Layla was also struggling to learn English and to get used to living here. Her little son had just died and her daughter was a handful, so Siham tried to stay in touch with her.

In every other way except this, Nader was perfect. Once a week, he stopped at the general store on Ninth Street on his way home and bought her a present. Once it was a black satin scarf, embroidered with blue leaves on silver vines. Then a tube of her favorite lipstick, Revlon's Toast of New York. It used to cost her sixty shekels, or fifteen dollars, in Jerusalem's finest drugstores. Here, in America, it was only six dollars at Eckerd. The most amusing thing he'd bought was a Barbie doll, the most American doll of all, who could do everything from astrophysics to zoology, all with her long blond plastic hair perfectly coiffed. The most thoughtful thing was a personal date book to keep her appointments, though for now those would be things like "Monday: Clean windows and dust ceiling fan" and "Thursday: Shine floors and do English exercises." She practiced her English like a religion; Nader had bought her a primer and an Arab-English dictionary (yet another present) and she studied it for at least an hour every morning.

Anticipate.

Expect.

Wait. I wait. You wait. He/she/it waits.

One August morning, she sat on her green sofa, a used one from a consignment store. She was embroidering a small coin purse for herself, using the black and red design of the Palestinian villages. Her English book lay open on the armrest and she read the sentences aloud.

The phone rang, a not unwelcome disturbance. Siham slid across the floor to it, nearly colliding with the end table, eager to practice her English with another person. Hopefully, it would be one of those telephone survey people so she could get at least ten minutes worth.

"Is Nader home?" The voice was a woman's, but deep and smooth, like the chords of a lute.

"No. May I please take your message?"

"Who is this?"

"I am his wife."

"His wife!" Pause. "No, thanks. I'll try calling later."

Siham slid the phone back into its curved cradle. Not hearing the familiar "click," she picked it up and replaced it firmly. Later that evening, Nader told her not to think about it again. "If it's important, she'll call back. But I don't know who she is."

"But she used your first name. That means she knows you."

"*Habibti,* in America, that's what they do. These telephone people, they don't use 'Mr.' and 'Mrs.' anymore. You'll get used to these little cultural things. It's how they get you not to hang up right away." But she knew it wasn't.

She looked up a new word in her dictionary that night. Suspect. I suspect. You suspect. He/she/it suspects.

Siham enjoyed exploring their new neighborhood, taking long early-afternoon walks through South Philadelphia. The streets were neatly arranged. Perfectly organized, like a grid. Numbers ran north and south, names ran east and west. Or was it the other way around? She and Nader lived on Ninth and Passyunk, in what they called the Italian Market. Layla rarely visited because the crowds were too much for her to handle with her young daughter. Siham found everything at the Italian Market, from tomatoes to fresh coffee beans to bath towels sold by everyone from leathery Vietnamese women to Sicilian men with mustaches like Nader's to young Irishwomen with green eyes and their reddish-blond hair in tight braids. Some of these Philadelphians were immigrants like her, and others were the children of immigrants, with an entire generation to adjust.

Sometimes, the Italian Market reminded her of the Old City quarter of Jerusalem, full of men yelling out the prices of vegetables and women peddling their crafts, their embroidered pillowcases and blouses. They even targeted tourists with photo frames and wall hangings that said in embroidered English, "God Bless Our Home" or "Home Is Where the Heart Is." In Jerusalem, she could bargain with the peddlers. In fact, they were insulted if you did not engage them on some level of negotiations. It was in stark contrast to the culture of the Italian Market, where the price was set. She knew because she'd tried to talk the fruit man down to two dollars. "Hey lady, no bargaining! This is already a bargain, aai-ight?" Nader claimed that her ability to bring prices down in the Khan al-Zeit bazaar was what had won his heart.

She was examining the leather wallets at the stand next to the entrance to the Dome of the Rock when he approached. They each bought a wallet, although she paid eight shekels and he paid fourteen. As Siham walked away, Nader called after her, "How did you do that?"

She did not answer. So he asked, "Can you come shopping with me? I have a few more things to buy today and I could use your help."

Siham took one look at his pleated trousers, linen blazer and shiny, lace-up shoes and kept walking. Ignored him, who was so obviously, as she'd thought, one of those returning American Arab nouveau riche. He probably sold bananas on the city streets in America but made himself look rich when he returned home to visit the "old country." Sickening. Especially when the richest man in the "old country" only made about 800 American dollars a month. Her own father, a doctor, made a mere 625 dollars.

She entered one of the coffee shops and sat at a small table in the corner, reading her newspaper and sipping the bitter Turkish qahwa from the small, enameled cup. The boy shot in the riots yesterday had died last night. There were expansions planned for six more settlements, four in the West Bank. The Boutique Shahrazad was announcing another sale on evening gowns.

"May I join you?"

She looked up and saw Mr. Linen Jacket bent slightly over her table, staring eagerly at her.

"No."

With a chuckle, he sat down anyway. He ordered coffee for himself with an imperious wave of his hand. The other men in the café stared at them curiously, stopping their conversations to see who was this Amerkani sit-

ting with the eldest daughter of Doctor Abdallah al-Medani. Siham stood up and left.

What an ill-timed first meeting! she thought to herself now. She'd dismissed him as a self-centered piece of fluff who had become lost among the casinos and dance clubs of America. Thank God he'd sought her out, asked people about her. He came to her parents' house and entertained her family by bringing boxes of sweets, giving her little sister Nadia rides on his shoulders, and by singing—he had such a deep, wonderful voice. He especially charmed her mother. One month later, after he and his family had formally asked for her hand in marriage, Siham applied for a visa to the States. Nader had recently become a citizen himself, so she filed happily as "spouse of U.S. citizen." They were going to wed. To marry. I marry. You marry. We marry.

She strolled toward Ellsworth Avenue and entered the lobby of the Lebanese Maronite church. Inside, Siham saw the two old Lebanese widows who volunteered. Polishing pews and vacuuming the dark, wine-colored carpets. Giving their free time to God, good hearts. They reminded her of her mother, who walked around all day in her housedress, attacking dust in every corner of their home. She and Nader had talked about sponsoring her entire family to come to the States, because the economy was slipping faster than before and people couldn't even afford doctors. One of the ladies kissed the image of the Virgin Mary as she dusted the base of the statue. Siham lit three candles, driving the slim, white tapers deep into the sand pile. One for her family, especially her mother, back home. One for Layla, to help her overcome her grief and to have another child soon. The third one for Nader, to keep him safe.

As she walked home, she thought how Nader would smile indulgently at her "voodoo," as he called it. When they'd first moved in to the apartment, she'd immediately set about sprinkling chrism on each wall. Mrs. Donato had nodded approvingly when she heard about the incident. "A good, good girl. Fears God," she'd said. But all Nader had wanted to do was make love in their new bed, though Siham had insisted on first driving a small nail in the wall so that she could hang a charm above their heads. It was a blue glass stone, with an eye painted on it, a charm that hung in every home in Jerusalem. "To ward off the Evil Eye," she announced proudly, as Nader tugged at her arm, pulled her down.

She entered the flower shop and headed for the back stairs, the only way to get up to her own apartment. It would be this way until the landlord decided to make a separate entrance. But Siham didn't mind so much. "Hello, Mrs. Donato," she said to the black-haired, elderly woman sitting at the counter, arms folded across her chest and eyes closed.

"Hello, *bella*," she replied, her eyes snapping open. She didn't miss a beat.

"I did not mean to awaken you, Mrs. Donato."

"No, no, *bella*. Iz OK." Mrs. Donato beckoned to her daughter, who was at the other end of the shop arranging flowers in a basket. "Wait, wait for Carla. There is a woman here before. Blondie woman."

"A woman?"

"Wait for Carla. Wait, she tells you."

Carla approached them with two lilies in her hands, the long stems coiled like serpents. "Hi, Siham. How are you?"

"Fine, thank you very much."

"How is Nader?" she asked, a curious glitter in her brown eyes.

"Fine. Your mother, she said about a woman?"

"Yes, there was a woman here about an hour ago, looking for Nader. A tall, blond woman. Red suit, linen, with black heels. Looked a little younger than me, maybe forty or forty-five years old."

"What does she say?" Siham interrupted Carla's flood of description. She liked Carla's mother, but Siham was wary of this woman who was obviously very smart but who thrived on gossip, like her old aunts back home. A woman who never missed a single detail or a gesture or a look.

"She asked if Nader Jundi lived upstairs. I said yes, he does, with his new wife." Carla casually snapped the heads off the lilies and Siham watched a lone, white petal float to the floor. "She asked how long you'd both been married. I said, 'I don't know,' but that you had moved in together last month."

"Does she—did she leave a message?"

"No, she just left. Didn't even say thank you. Tossed her head and walked out."

"Thank you, Carla. I will see you later." Siham headed upstairs, a sick feeling creeping into her belly.

"*Bella,* have some coffee with us," Mrs. Donato called out behind her.

"No, thank you." She scaled the steps three at a time. Before she shut the door firmly behind her, she heard Mrs. Donato yell at her daughter for ruining the flowers.

She asked Nader about it, of course. Her father used to say, as he furrowed his shaggy brows, that his daughter had been aptly named. Siham meant "arrows" in Arabic. Straight to the target. No deviations.

Nader was visibly startled; his eyes widened like white disks. Especially when she told him of her feeling that it was the same woman who had phoned the day before. "It was probably an old friend, *habibti,* from work or something," he said reassuringly, though he didn't stop tapping his foot through the rest of dinner. That night, their lovemaking knocked the blue stone off the wall. It rolled along the headboard and, before she could grasp it, shattered into fragments on the hardwood floor.

Siham heard nothing about the blond woman for the next month. Nader's work schedule became more intense, and he came home more often with sagging shoulders, but more bills in his wallet. "We're getting a lot of business because of the nice weather. Everyone wants to come out and buy lunch and get out of their offices." She could tell he was grateful for the work, because he sighed less heavily when he wrote checks for the bills at the beginning of the month. To pass the time, she began English classes at the community college. Her professor told her that she was one of the most advanced students in the class. She'd better be, she thought, after all her own self-tutoring.

By October, the leaves on the occasional tree in South Philadelphia began to change colors. The trees in Jerusalem were mostly olive trees and they didn't change colors, as she tried to explain to Carla, w! ⟩

didn't seem to care. Their leaves just curled up like shrimp and died, pulled away from the branches by the harsh wind that whipped through and wrapped around the hills. The leaves of trees in Philadelphia were different. One day, she slipped two leaves, a yellow one and a red one, into an envelope and mailed them to her youngest sister, Nadia. She also described Halloween to her, how goblins, witches and even a bizarre purple dinosaur came to the flower shop and the other places along the Market for candy.

In November, she found a way to help Nader pay the bills. She invited Carla and Mrs. Donato up to the apartment for tea one evening after they'd closed the shop. They praised her embroidery skills. It was not a rare talent for Palestinian women—Siham had been taught by her grandmothers—but Carla and her mother seemed deeply impressed and made a proposal. Siham gave them a pair of sofa pillowcases that she'd stashed away in a chest to put for sale in the shop. They sold the next day and the Donatos took orders for three more sets. "You make 'em, we'll sell 'em," said Carla, handing her thirty dollars that evening. "I'll just take a 10 percent cut. People snap them up when you say that they're handmade." Siham only requested that they hide her work from Nader when he passed through the shop on his way up to the apartment after work. She wanted to save the money and surprise him with a gift.

Thus, the extra bedroom on the third floor of the apartment became Siham's embroidery and study room. The floor was covered with yards of cloth and dozens of spools of thread. Tightly wound ribbons of red, wrapped rivers of yellow, and coils of green. They were rainbows in her hand that she could unfurl at will. Her English books were stacked in a corner underneath the sole window in the room. A lonely, stuffed chair stood in the middle of the room, next to a halogen lamp. Her only desk was her lap. This room would be a nursery one day. They had decided to start trying soon.

She was sitting one November afternoon in this room, listening to a Miles Davis cassette tape. It was part of her effort to be infinitely more American, like watching reruns of *Cheers* and making hamburgers. She would conquer jazz music just as she had the others. She heard Carla's familiar tap on her door downstairs and she ran down to get the mail. The bundle, which grew daily as she and Nader became more "established" (and thus more susceptible to circulars and junk mailings), sat on the top step, where Carla left it every day. There was one letter in particular, addressed only to Nader, in a woman's slanted, looped script. The J of their last name was decorated with a large loop at the top. The return address had no name, only the street name and zip code. 1012 Chestnut Street, Philadelphia PA.

She took it upstairs to her embroidery room and placed it at the foot of her chair. She resumed her work, shaping a flower pattern on the black background of the cloth. It would be a wall hanging for a woman from Queen's Village. Occasionally, she glanced at the letter, wanting to open it, but she was an American wife now and they were cool about these things. No suspicions. A marriage was a friendship in America, not a spy operation. Miles Davis played "My Funny Valentine" over and over, at the request of the rewind button, until six P.M.

"Here," she said, handing Nader the letter. She made no other acknowledgment, just left him alone with it and went into the kitchen to heat up yesterday's leftover spaghetti. Mrs. Donato's recipe, which Nader loved. He came in as she was setting the table. The letter was not in his hands; she made a mental note to check the wastebasket later. "Anything interesting?" she asked.

"No, just an old friend who wanted to say hello." His voice was steady and casual and he kissed her cheek with his usual lingering sweetness. He even lit a candle and placed it on the table between them as they ate. It was only his incessant foot-wiggling under the table that confirmed Siham's suspicion. When she couldn't find the letter the next morning, neither in the wastebasket nor in his pants pocket, she decided to visit Chestnut Street.

It took her forty minutes of brisk walking and she realized that she'd worn bad shoes for such exercise. She also noticed that, as city blocks streamed slowly by her, the sidewalks displayed less litter. The brick of each building front was cleaner and each door frame had a fresh coat of paint. Several windows opened to little plants on their sills. The storefronts became fancier, as did the names. Gone were places like "Mike's Deli" and "Geno's Steaks." Here, there were only salons, cafés and food markets that advertised themselves as "gourmet." The sidewalks were red brick, not tan cement blocks, separated by tufts of grass trying to break through. The men on these streets wore dark suits, not blue jeans, and the women got thinner with each block.

She approached 1012 Chestnut Street, a three-story house that was attached to the other homes on the block. A "rowhouse," as Nader called them, like their own. She had had a difficult time understanding this concept of homes attached like the links in a chain. When Nader had shown her the front of their building for the first time, she'd shown delight.

A puzzled Nader had asked, "You really like it?"

"Of course!" she'd answered, pointing to Washington Avenue on her left and Federal Street on her right. "This whole building is yours—you must have been right about America! You really can do well here." He'd laughed for several minutes before explaining that only the top two floors of the single unit in front of them were theirs. "It'll be a few years before we own a big house, but it'll happen in time," he'd said.

But 1012 Chestnut was nothing like their tiny apartment above the flower shop. 1012's white front steps, edged by a beautifully carved stone rail, descended elegantly to the sidewalk. The door, made of dark wood, featured a round brass knocker in its center, like an eye. Like the Evil Eye painted on her blue stones. She stared up at the windows, awed and suddenly sad. A glimpse of a blond head looking out of the second-story window sent her walking back. She hummed "My Funny Valentine" all the way home to calm the frenzied beat of her heart.

She spent the rest of the day studying her verbs.
I hide. You hide. He/she/it hides.
I lie. We lie. They lie.
I cry. You cry. He/she/it cries.
I cry.

Their six-month anniversary was December 3rd, three weeks before Christmas. Nader had carefully planned a surprise, which included an early dinner at a Lebanese restaurant on South Street (where Siham was impressed to see that most of the clientele were not Arabs but Americans) and a concert in Atlantic City. The headliner was Siham's favorite Arab singer, who rarely ever performed in Palestine. Her sisters would get a long letter about this.

As they drove to Atlantic City in their two-door Nissan, Nader explained that many Arab singers held concerts in the States. "When I was single, I would go to a concert, when I could afford it, with some Egyptian guys I worked with," he said. "We always hoped that we'd be attending these affairs with wives on our arms one day. I imagined taking my dream girl out for a romantic dinner, how she looked, how she spoke. And then I saw her outsmarting a leather vendor in the bazaar in Jerusalem!" They laughed and he reached for her hand in the darkness. He kissed the tips of her fingers gently, then lingered on her palm. "I'm so happy."

"Me, too." She truly was. She was also relieved that she had not refused his proposal. It was a risk, to marry a man who had spent so much time in America, but a lot of girls in Palestine did it. To get out of the country, to try their lives and their luck across the ocean, they married. Layla's husband had even been born here and barely spoke Arabic, although Layla was starting to teach him. One-month, even one-week engagements were not unusual, but Siham had never imagined she'd do it. How could you know about a man's past? she used to argue. Unlike Jerusalem, where gossip lines kept everyone updated on their neighbors, someone could hide an entire life, conceal so many secrets behind America's veil. Even though Nader's family was originally from Jerusalem and had been sufficiently "checked out" by the al-Medanis, how could she trust him immediately? She had always claimed that she would get to know her fiancé for a long time, at least three years, before they married. Well, she was simply doing the "getting to know" part after the wedding.

"I'm so lucky to have you, Nader," she said, turning to look at his face, highlighted in short intervals by the lights along the expressway.

He kept the wheel steady with his left hand and wove the fingers of his right hand through hers. "When we first met, you *hated* me. I know you did. I thought you'd never agree to marry me, but I had to try."

"So you charmed my family to death? Good strategy."

He took his hand away to switch lanes, then surrendered it again. "I just wanted you to like me so badly. If that meant flowers for your mother and American whiskey for your father and uncles . . ."

"And candy and chocolates for my sisters, and perfume for my aunts," she continued. "That's what really got me. One day, Nadia walked into my room with chocolate all over her mouth and told me I had to marry you—or else she would!"

"Really?"

"Yes." Siham smiled to herself. All she'd heard from her mother was that a man was coming to the house to meet her, with the intention of eventual marriage. *He was an Amerkani, she'd said to her confused and bewildered daughter. Siham had immediately suspected the brazen Mr. Linen Blazer from the bazaar last week and, sure enough, he strode into their living room the next evening, his arms laden with gifts, hair freshly combed and linen blazer newly ironed. He told jokes, did impressions of celebrities, and discussed the importance of family. He engaged her directly in conversation and seemed thrilled that she could hold her own when it came to culture and politics. He liked the fact that she was studying literature at the university.*

After Nader left, her father called her into the kitchen and asked her opinion of this tall, dark, smooth-faced Arab from America. "You would have to live in America with him," her father had warned her. "In a city called Philadeelpheea." One month later, he walked her down the aisle of the Greek Orthodox church. June 3rd.

Now, six months later, she was beside him, on the way to a concert at the seashore. She would make sure this marriage lasted forever. Lasted happily. She clutched his hand even tighter, twisting her fingers between his in the way that she'd seen Carla twist the necks of the lilies.

Carla came up to the apartment one Thursday morning, three weeks later. It was almost Christmas and Siham had all the windows open, trying to infuse the rooms with fresh, cold air before she began to decorate. She had two red stockings on which she planned to embroider their names. She'd considered writing in glitter, but glitter would eventually wear off. She and Nader had bought a tree last night and she had yards of silver garland that she couldn't wait to use.

"It's like a freezer up here," Carla grunted, rubbing her arms. "I brought you two more orders for pillowcases, both black cloth, and this." She handed her 140 dollars. "From the last batch."

"Thank you, Carla." Siham rolled the wad of twenties and put them into the pocket of her cardigan. She purposefully didn't count them, knowing that Carla would pick up on it and her eyes would flash. She had such a temper, this one, so unlike her mother, whose smile was all gentle curves. A patient smile. She had probably developed it over the years.

"Carla, I am making tea. Would you like a cup?" She could also be patient and kind. Why not? She was feeling good.

"Yes," Carla said, seeming startled, probably because Siham had never invited her to stay unless her mother was also there.

"Please sit down." Siham indicated the large, green sofa in the living room and went to the kitchen. She poured two cups, set them on the tray with the sugar bowl and came out to find Carla standing underneath the wedding picture on the wall.

"Your dress is beautiful," Carla said. "Very traditional, with that full skirt and the long train. Very . . . well, bridal."

Siham gazed up at the portrait. She and Nader stood before the white stone wall that formed the back of her parents' house in Jerusalem. The Dome of the Rock, with its golden cupola, was visible in the background. Though she thought her own face looked pale and washed out by the whiteness of her dress, Nader's face blazed like the sun. Dark olive skin, the color of the inside of an almond shell. Black brows that could look fierce when he was tired or irritated, but always masculine. She only had to smooth them with her index finger to reveal their gentleness. They framed large, caramel eyes that were always soft, that had emanated only love for the last three days, since she told him that she was pregnant.

"You know, I almost got married," Carla said, stirring lemon into her tea and perching on the edge of the sofa. "I had a fiancé many years ago. An Irish guy from Northeast Philly."

Siham noted the way that her hair curled softly at her neck. How her hands were slender and her fingers long, how her cheekbones sat high up in her face. Yes, a man *could* have loved her once.

"He worked at a dry cleaning and tailoring shop with his parents.

When we got married, his parents said they were gonna retire. They were old, you know. David was their youngest of eight kids. They wanted us to take over the store, because I knew how to sew and handle customers."

"What happened to him?" Siham asked, making a mental note to look up the word "retire" later.

"He cheated on me. Got another girl from his neighborhood pregnant." Carla drained the last of her tea. "I refused to marry him after that. But I never married anyone else." She smirked, closing off the softness that had been subtly creeping into her face. "My mother said I'm just stubborn, that I didn't want to give anyone else a chance. But that's my decision, I said, right?"

"Yes, of course. I am sorry for this happening to you."

"I'm not." Carla stood to leave. "Just proves you can't really trust men." She arched her painted eyebrow meaningfully in the direction of the wedding portrait. "Thanks for the tea." Her dark eyes glittered and Siham shuddered.

Later that night, when Nader was snoring softly, Siham rummaged through her wooden storage chest until she found what she wanted. She crept downstairs to the living room and taped a small, blue bead, painted with the Eye, to the back of the portrait. She would have to find another, a larger one, to replace the one above her bed. How could she have left that precious space unprotected for so long? She climbed back into the bed, shivering.

She had seen the Evil Eye itself today, sipping lemon tea on her sofa.

It was not enough. The Eye worked its evil the very next day, assuming the shape not of a black-haired, meddlesome spinster, but of a tall, slim, blond woman. Powder-blue suit, collarless jacket with a scalloped neck. Siham didn't understand why she focused on this detail, but she did. Maybe she'd known already, from the moment she heard Mrs. Donato's voice calling her down, she'd known it would be this woman with hard, rounded calves and pale brows. Sitting calmly in a chair in the flower shop, looking like Attorney Barbie.

"Hi," she said, standing up. She was tall, too, which made Siham feel even smaller. "Are you Nader's wife?"

"Yes. My name is Siham al-Jundi." Thank God she'd at least had the foresight to put on lipstick and style her hair. "Can I help you?"

"I need to get in touch with Nader, to collect some money he owes me. I've tried to reach him several times, but it seems like he's avoiding me and I can't wait any longer."

"Money? For what?"

"Well, that's really between Nader and myself," replied Attorney Barbie, her voice brusque and dismissive. "When do you expect him home?"

"Maybe in an hour." Siham was acutely aware of Carla's glittering, inquisitive eyes staring at them from behind the counter. She felt even more minuscule and tiny next to this living doll, this American dream.

"I will return then. Please tell him to expect me." She slung her purse over her shoulder and headed for the door.

"What shall I tell him your name is?" Siham called after her.

With a weary sigh, as if it hurt to speak, she said, "Just tell him that his first wife came by to see him."

Siham refused to allow Nader to bring Homewrecker Barbie upstairs to the apartment. "Talk with her down there," she said when Mrs. Donato's voice summoned him. Nader squeezed her hand apologetically and descended to the flower shop.

All the while that he was downstairs, she could only think that he had brought the evil in himself. With his lies, his guilt. He had explained it, of course. He had even cried with her a little. After he'd graduated from the university, they were going to deport him, he said. He'd needed a green card. So he got married, like a business deal. She'd done him a favor, but he still owed her two thousand dollars that he didn't have.

But had they been lovers? No, he insisted, so adamantly that she believed him. "She wouldn't have an Arab in her bed. Just in her third-story room, for the promise of six thousand dollars," he said. The third story of the house on Chestnut Street, in case the INS checked up on them. He'd even paid her rent during those three years, in addition to the money she wanted. Two months after their official divorce, he'd returned to the old country and spent the remaining two thousand dollars on his wedding. His "real and mean-ingful" wedding, not the sham one of almost four years ago.

Siham sat at the window in her embroidery room, looking down at the sidewalk below. She had 850 dollars in an envelope, tucked beneath layers of fabric and spools of thread in her craft box. She'd wanted to use it to buy a new crib, a changing table and a rocking chair to put in this room. This room in which she had lined the Barbie dolls on shelves, that would soon be a nursery. She hoped the baby would be a girl, and she had found a beautiful set of baby fur-niture in the Sunday circular, an ashy-colored wood with brass details on the drawer handles.

A blond head appeared below and turned right heading down Ninth Street, probably toward her beautiful and elegant home. She was abandoning the numbered streets for one with an elegant and thoroughly American name. Only Americans named their streets after trees, instead of after presidents and wars and prophets. She probably wouldn't walk; she'd hail a cab along the way or maybe get into her expensive car.

He would come upstairs now, probably with a rose that he'd bought from Mrs. Donato. He would be climbing the steps, hoping that the gift would make her smile. And she would smile, as genuinely as she could stretch her lips, and she'd say that she understood. That it would take a while to forget it, but they had to think about the baby now. Then she'd hand him the envelope with the money and ask him to never mention this again. She would not tell him about the nurs-ery set, just quietly toss out the picture in the circular.

And she would call her mother and ask her to mail a few more blue stones, at least three. She had to be more careful from now on.

A Frame for the Sky

RANDA JARRAR

In a New York café a few months ago, I sat and read through an old volume of poetry, full of wonder at how as a young man—even before my life in distant America; before my fascination with clouds, the endless questioning at airports, the many hours I've spent on trains, my pining for my mother, the deaths of thousands a few blocks away from my office; before I began to think of the worst days of my life—I'd identified with the verse: "don't tell me I'm a cloud at an airport, for all I want, from my country which fell out of the window of a train, is my mother's handkerchief, and reasons for a new death." It's as though those lines had forecast a future in which I was sure I would one day reside.

The third-worst day of my life was July 21, 1991. I was in a New York hotel room, waiting for a phone call from my old boss in Kuwait. I remember the sun was halfway down in the clear summer sky, its rays sneaking into the room. I'd spent the last of my money to come to New York to secure a decent project for the architecture firm in Kuwait since it had recently been "liberated" and the Iraqis driven out. I'd borrowed money to pay for an extra ticket so I could bring along my eldest son, who was usually a source of good luck; my father had once dubbed him the human equivalent of a bashoora moth since he always flitted in and out of sight, and when you could get him to sit still some good news would consistently arrive. He was barely fourteen years old, and was now sitting on the hotel's dirty carpet wearing a black bowler hat he'd bought from a street vendor and reading an upside-down map of Manhattan.

The phone rang and I answered it. My old boss simply said sorry, over and over again, and when I asked him why he was sorry, he said, you will not be allowed to return to Kuwait. I asked him why not; after all, I wasn't just anybody, I'd literally helped build that country, put in my blood, and spent time away from my family for it. Then he said, but your people supported the bastards, and so the government won't let you in. I discovered later that almost four thousand Palestinians were expelled or banned from re-entering Kuwait due to the PLO's support of Saddam Hussein's actions.

I hung the phone up and allowed myself to cry. I released only a single tear, which rolled down my nose and dried at my mustache. My son asked me what had happened, and I hated the world, because I had to tell him he would never see his home again.

"Do you remember the Iraqi invasion?" I said, realizing it was a stupid question.

"You mean, August 2nd, 1990, less than a year ago?" he said, full of sarcasm. "Yeah, Baba." It turns out that was the worst day of his life.

"Well, because I'm Palestinian . . ."

"I know, Baba. I was listening in on the whole conversation. So we're never going home!" He looked down at the map and tapped his thumb against Central Park.

"You know your cousin Ihab?"

He nodded, and laughed.

"Well, you know how the women he is supposed to marry always leave him the day of the wedding?"

"Yeah, except Majdoline; she left him three days before."

"OK," I said. "See how he always loses his fiancées? Well, that's how we are with homes. Our family, since time immemorial, loses a home and the country around it every few decades. It's part of our legacy."

"That sucks!" he said.

"What is this 'suck'?" I said.

"It's an American expression, Dad."

"Don't call me Dad."

He took it the way I did when I was told, as a seventeen-year-old, on the second-worst day of my life, that I would not be allowed to return home for some time. Now that I think about it, the circumstances were eerily similar; I was stuck in a pension in Jordan, shortly after the 1967 war. I'd awaited phone calls from my family for a week, and finally my father called and calmly told me that I would not be allowed to re-enter the territories for a while. Soon, the pension was flooded with refugees, men of every age, and I spent the rest of the year smoking cigarettes with them and planning my escape into Egypt, where I wanted to go to college. I worked a few odd jobs to pay my room fees and buy cigarettes and bread. Once a week, I met with fellow young Palestinian men, and we drank Arak and wrote poetry, and then printed it in a flyer which I posted all around Amman halfway through the night. I feared that the glue I'd used to roll up the flyer and that had stayed on my pants would give me away, but no one noticed, since, in the wake of that war, they were all too busy being angry and ashamed.

That 1991 afternoon in New York, after receiving the exiling call, I looked at myself in the mirror and saw short black hairs all over my face, which was paler than ever. I shaved and we walked to the Empire State Building, and once we reached the top, I watched the city and drew my breath. I was in New York City. I was among some of man's most beautiful modern architecture. My son pointed to the World Trade Center towers and asked me, what do they remind you of? This was a silly game we'd played since he was little; I'd take him to my office and show him the plastic models of future buildings, ask him to look at them and guess what they reminded him of; one in particular was abstractly shaped like a fig tree. That day, I looked hard at the buildings and couldn't really guess, and that's when he lifted his hand in front of my eyes in a victory sign, his forefinger covering one building, and his middle finger covering the closer building. "They call it a peace sign in America, Dad," he said, and it was the first of many lessons in language and perspective that he would give me.

The next day, I headed to the Cesar-Pelli–type firms in midtown, looking for a job. I was immediately turned down from the first three places I went to, and was told that I needed papers and that they weren't hiring anyway. I headed toward the firm I'd been working with that week to secure a project for the Kuwaiti company, and stood on the street corner of Fifth and Seventeenth, waiting for the company's partners to come down for lunch.

My wife was waiting in Alexandria, Egypt, in our beach apartment that I'd bought in her name a few years before. I thought she still had no idea about our non-return to Kuwait, but now I remembered the way she'd scanned the house when we'd left it, heading toward the Iraqi desert on our way into Jordan; she'd looked at it with somber finality, the same way she'd looked at her mother's grave when we'd finally visited it. My wife is the daughter of a Nasserite officer who retired early from the military to manage a silk-manufacturing factory, and so she is infinitely more practical than I.

I wondered what our lives would be like in America. We'd lived here once before, in the late seventies, but that was before the children (although she was pregnant), before the responsibilities that now rain so constantly on our heads. That time, we were young, her hair was longer, I had sideburns, and we wore polyester shirts and bell-bottoms. I drank more than I do now, I smoked cigarettes, I still had a mother, and no interest in staying away from the Middle East for longer than a year. We saw *Saturday Night Fever* the night it was released, and appreciated it more than the others in the theater, because we didn't have to wait two years for it to be brought into Egypt, or stand in line at the Rialto only to see it all chopped up. We called our friends in Alexandria the night after we saw it, and told them we weren't calling from a Centrale calling center but from our regular home phone, then described to them the phenomenon that was Travolta. I bought *Playboys* and was nauseated at the first viewing, but packed them for friends back home. I went to museums and saw dinosaur bones and art that came from my birthplace and had, like me, been transported all the way over here and given a strange name ("Canaan"), a practical name ("Levantine"), any name ("Phoenician"), anything other than "Palestinian." Shortly before we left, we had a daughter here, and I saw her name in English around her wrists. In the mornings, I fought with waitresses who took my drink order by asking, "Sir, would you like tea or coffee?" And I would say, Tea and coffee. And the waitress would say, "Sir? Would you like tea or coffee?" And I'd say, Tea and coffee, and she'd say, "No, tea or coffee," and I'd say, Both: tea and coffee, and she'd say, "You cannot have tea and coffee, you can have either tea . . . or coffee," and I'd say, I would like tea and coffee, miss, and she'd say, "Well, it's either tea or coffee," and I'd finish it by saying: Well, in my country we have tea with breakfast and coffee after breakfast, so I want tea . . . and coffee! My wife was present once during such a debacle, and explained to me that I only had to say that I would pay for both, and it would clarify everything right away. Sometimes I envied her apartment upbringing, her nannies and her education. Would she want to live in America?

When the partners swung through the revolving doors, their eyes immediately darted toward me, and one of them yelled, "Coming to lunch with us?" We walked a few blocks in silence, reaching a street corner where the red crossing light read DON'T WALK. David asked me if I was planning my return to Kuwait, and I told him about my old boss's phone call.

"That's awful!" he said. "What will you do now?"

"Well," I said, and the yellow crossing sign read WALK, "I was hoping you'd give me a job." That's when David, my future best friend in America and an incredible architect, turned to me in the middle of the crosswalk and with a huge smile said, "You're hired!"

Now the question remained: would my wife want to part with Egypt forever and come to America?

"Of course I would!" she screamed into the phone when I called and gave her the good news, and she began packing what little we had. That afternoon, my son and I walked around the East Village and looked at brownstones, fantasizing about living in one. I was staying in America. I was to build a new home. In a few years, my children and I would be American. I wanted to record this moment inside my mind, to remember forever the day I—a Palestinian boy with a pity-passport and a third-rate education who'd spent the past year getting rejected from Egyptian firms and who'd just been officially disallowed from returning to yet another country—was hired by a top firm in midtown Manhattan; wanted to etch it into my memory. I looked all around me but found no impressive image to latch onto, so I leaned my head back and looked up into the sky and recorded, white square inch by white square inch, the shape of a single and immense cottony cloud which floated in the otherwise *fairuz* sky.

Moments later my son asked, his just-broken voice anxious, "But if we are like cousin Ihab and if we make America our home, does that mean we're going to lose our home here too? That there will be a war here, too?"

"Of course not!" I said, but I wasn't too sure.

In the next few weeks, my wife and our other children arrived, and we set up our new home a few miles north of the city. In those days, I wished I could call my mother and tell her about what I was experiencing.

The day my mother died was the absolute worst day of my life, full stop. My sister called me in Kuwait from the West Bank, and told me on the phone that she'd gone: she repeated the word "rahat," over and over again, and I gripped the receiver, pondering that verb, thinking about its roots, and then its variations: the words "ruh," soul, and "reeh," wind. I didn't want to face it. So she'd gone, like that. I wept in front of my children, I refused my wife's embrace. I thought of the way mother cooked eggplant, and how her head, which she never covered, would always part with a single black hair, dispatching it into the sauce, and how that hair would always find its way to my dish, into my mouth; and just when I thought I'd reconciled with the fact of never tasting it again, I screamed, unspooling all of my sorrow. So Mother is gone from this world? I said, marking an X in the air with my finger. None of my children knew my mother.

Nobody really knew Mother; she spent most of her days away from us, and when she was present she rarely conversed. Her favorite thing to do was to spread cold cream on the pale skin of her face, and to tell my father what to do. We discovered as we grew older that, as a young child, she was told her mother had died with her father, and so she was raised by her aunt. She told me once the story of the worst day of her life: One morning, one year before her marriage to my father, she was lowering a bucket into her aunt's well when she heard her own mother's voice. She dropped the bucket and heard its faint thud, then turned and saw what she thought was her mother's ghost. With some effort, my grandmother assured her that she was human and not a visitor from the land of the djinnis, and my mother ran to the house, hating her for the rest of her days. Grandmother's explanation for Mother's perceived abandonment, an explanation which was yelled through the rifts of a wooden door while Mother cried on its other side—that my mother's father was killed by enemy fire during the days of the war, that her mother had to remarry or be left on the street, and that she'd left my mother with her aunt for her own good—was met with Mama's utter coldness and an obstinate refusal to forgive. I am not sure if this was the source of her angry composure during my entire childhood, her selfish aloofness, the gulf of distance she placed between us, her children, and herself; I only know she gave each of us a generous morsel of these attitudes, which we all carry in ourselves—selves which reside in nine different countries—to this day.

So her loss is one of the things I think about constantly in America. My years here have passed like a metro-north express train speeding through a small local station. I have subscriptions to the *New Yorker,* which I never read, and the *New York Times,* which I read front page to back page on my one-hour commute into the city. On Saturday nights, I used to watch *Saturday Night Live* with my children, and even began a list of Jewish men that my daughters would be allowed to marry, but it still looks like this:

1. Adam Sandler
2.

Whenever I visited my children's schools, I would stare in wonderment at the carpeted classrooms, the pay phones in the wide hallways, and laugh out loud. I imagined my younger self, a student in a two-room schoolhouse where the windows—the ones that weren't broken, anyway—flapped up and down with the wind which, during West Bank winters, came in like cold knives. My name was always posted "First" on the wall outside, and now I saw my kids' names on what Americans call the "Honor Roll." When I went in to ask for their ranks, the counselors looked at me as though I were insane, their eyes nervously fixed on my dark mustache.

On the trains, I look outside and see white houses flying by, green trees and suburbia sinking away as the projects rise up and the graffiti takes over like ivy. Inside the trains I see American women putting on makeup and fixing their clothes, their feet stuffed into small high heels. I think about this feminism I am always hearing about, and wonder why a feminist would wear so much makeup it would need its own seat belt, a suit so ugly just to look like a man, and then heels, all the while subjecting other riders to her preparation. I want to see a skit on *SNL* about a woman who brings her own showerhead, a razor, and a small shower curtain into the train, showers and shaves her legs, then when she's done, plugs in a hair dryer and styles her blond mane.

My sisters have never taken a train to a job in their entire lives. They were "hired" as wives by the age of fifteen, and left our house forever. Some of them married when I was too young to remember, but the others I still have a vivid image of, standing against a white-washed wall in the village and marrying someone at least fifteen years older than themselves. My twin sister was the only one who—we hoped—would not be subjected to this, and when I was in America on a one-year internship, she wrote me letters begging me to send her here. I arranged something for her at a local community college, but when I sent for her it was too late; she'd married, on the worst day of her life, a jeweler, and given up on her dreams. After his death, she told me how he used to look at her as though through an appraisal lens, constantly judging her worth.

In 1994, shortly after the signing of the Oslo Accords, I suggested, during a meeting with the partners, that we build something on the West Bank.

One partner joked, "Why, so it can be bulldozed a few years from now?"

I didn't think it was funny, and I insisted, but the closest I could get to the West Bank was a college hall in Beirut.

During basketball season, nothing would take me away from the television screen. I'd watch Olajuwon and Jordan battle, sure that only in this country could a man fly like that. During a Rockets game in '95, I heard a thud in my front yard, and reluctantly went outside to see what it was. Lo and behold, my eldest daughter had pulled a Jordan, "flying" out of her second-story window and into a stranger's car, which was now speeding away. I went back and turned off the game; then my wife and I frantically called all our friends looking for her. The next day, she didn't reappear until six A.M. She wouldn't tell us where she'd been, or apologize for her flight, and so, as they say here in America, I kicked her ass.

The fourth-worst day of my life was two weeks later when I had to call in sick to work, wear a suit, and go to court. My daughter had brought charges against me for hitting her, and the cops had come to the house looking to handcuff me. After I pointed out to them that I had a perfect record, and that there was no need, they agreed, drank a cup of weak coffee, and left. But there was still the matter of the state against the dad. I couldn't understand her anymore. When I saw old pictures of her, her hair long and brown, body small, I knew who she was, but this lunatic with a head of short curls, a nose ring, and enough anger to fuel a second intifada was a stranger to me.

As we sat on the wooden benches awaiting the judge's verdict, I instinctively asked her, "What happened to you?"

She turned and sucked her teeth, then actually said, "You did."

Had I really been the one who had changed? I never used to believe in change; in fact, I was once convinced that John Lennon and Paul McCartney were singing about me in "Across the Universe." But then Mother died, and I believed with all my heart that life is about change, that the only thing that doesn't change is the fact of change. Had America changed me? Or had I not allowed it to change me, holding onto what I thought was my True (= Arab) identity, while never meeting with other Arabs, and was that really a bad thing?

When it was time for my son to go to college, I wrote his college essay for him. It turned out to be an essay about me, about my inherent sense of aloneness, which I've guarded like the nomad's water canteen. If I try to remember when it was that I first felt alone, I can only say that it started even before language. I could blame our land, the unnamed and desolate, raped, green and rocky fact of it. I could blame my mother, whose demeanor I inherited, and who never cared for me as a child—so much so that I cried at my sister's wedding, thinking my own mother was getting married and leaving me forever. Or can I blame myself? In any case, I remember, as a child, hiding in our mattress closet for hours, waiting for someone to come look for me, and when they didn't, I stayed there and thought about how I was not wanted, and when it was time to sleep and they found me among the mattresses, my eyes swollen with tears, they doted on me like a long-lost kitten, but their attention arrived too late, and did nothing to ease my sense of aloneness. When I began to smoke cigarettes—hiding the pack in my twin sister's red heels that she never wore—I would sit on the green hill by Em Hisham's house and blow rings into the sky, thinking not of how small I was, but of how small the sky was, wishing I could frame my best smoke ring in it.

My son ended up writing his own college essay, and upon reading it, I wept because I finally felt vindicated for coming to America. My son had written a better essay, and in an English I could only dream of commanding. In the summer of 2000, shortly after he left, an official letter arrived in the mail announcing that it was time for me to be sworn in as an American citizen.

I drove to the capital on a day that could easily have been either my best or my fifth-worst; my Americanness has brought me nothing but feelings of ambivalence. Next door to the capital there was a church with the funny sign "exposure to the Son prevents from burning." I hadn't prayed in two years, had skipped fasting for five, but still considered myself a Muslim, even though I was now wearing my only pair of jeans, and a shirt with red and white stripes and a blue patch with white stars on its shoulder. When I answered the test questions about the American government, I thought of how all governments reflect their societies and religions . . . or was it vice versa?

At home, my father was the boss of our house and the head of the table; our Arab leaders were "democratically" elected and were presidents for decades at a time; our God was a masculine, lonely and only God, ruler of all. Each circle was a microcosm of another. "In America, the government is split into three branches," I wrote in an answer box, "the executive, the judicial, and the legislative"— the same way the Christian God is split into the Holy Trinity, I thought, but didn't write.

When I took my oath, a deep sadness shook inside me; I'd promised to keep my allegiance to the American government and no other. My blue passport had a handsome black and white photograph of me; its pages were blank, and I was already eager to fill them.

A trip came soon enough. The sixth-worst day came less than a week after my becoming an American citizen, when my brother called to tell me that my father had died. I boarded a plane to Israel, which I'd never before done, and by the time I'd passed "security" and arrived in the West Bank, my father had already been buried, and my brother was in the hospital, facing death. I gave the hospital administration my credit card and slept on the cold floor for three days, until my brother was healed. The Israeli doctor called me into his office, and asked me if I was American.

"I am now," I answered, and felt like I was lying, like a troop of Haganeh officers would jump out from under the doctor's desk and take me away.

"Where do you live?" he said.

"In New York," I said.

"I saw your address," he said, tapping my card against his table. "I used to live three blocks away from you, on Hassake Road."

I said nothing.

"Your brother will be all right," he said.

That night, after hailing half a dozen taxis—all of them refusing to take me to the West Bank—one taxi driver agreed, and we rode out of Israel and to the cemetery where my father was buried. I tipped the driver and walked to the gate, which was shut and locked. I jumped it, and the hem of my pants tore, then, when I landed on the other side, got dipped in mud. I found my father's grave and I read the *fateha* on his soul, and when I thought about him, how hurried he was in life—he'd always repeated that he didn't have enough time to do everything he wanted—a verse came to mind: "In autumn, he will die like a fig / shriveled, sweet, and full of himself. / The leaves dry out on the ground / and the naked branches point / to the place where there is time for everything." Ironically—and this was a story he loved to tell—my father almost died at age five when he was drowning in a local pond, but was thankfully saved by a neighbor who was a Jew. In

1998, during one of my several short visits to the West Bank since my immigration to America, and while the entire family—his nine children, thirty-two grandchildren, thirteen great-grandchildren—were gathered in his home for a feast, Father, who was slowly becoming senile, had looked at all of us for a moment, then yelled, "If it weren't for that Jew . . ." and so it felt befitting that Amichai would help me in farewelling him.

I then went to my mother's grave, which was sixteen years older than my father's, and was across the cemetery, and I read the *fateha* on her soul and wept.

Since my status as an American and an orphan, the second intifada has broken out, all my children have left the house, my wife has gotten a job, my entire mustache has gone gray, and, on the seventh-worst day of my life, those fingers pointing up in a peace sign at the tail end of Manhattan have crumbled. Everything continues to change in my world. A few hours after the attacks, I stood at St. Vincent's Hospital, the left sleeve of my shirt rolled up, thinking, every ten years, there's a new asshole, a new fucking maniac.

One recent afternoon, my son came in to visit and told me he was writing stories now. We went for a walk and I wanted to tell him all about my world, my childhood in the two-room schoolhouse, how when I was seventeen I was stranded in a Jordanian pension, why I fell in love with his mother and his mother's country, how worthless I felt after the Gulf War, that I've always felt alone, how afraid I am now that, because we are Arab Americans, we might again be like cousin Ihab (who, incidentally, is still single), how much I miss my mother, how much I want to take care of my family. But then, I look up at the sky and I see it, white square inch by white square inch: the same exact, immense, single cottony cloud floating in the otherwise turquoise sky that I'd seen in the East Village years before.

So instead, I say, "I have an idea for you. You should write a story about a man who looks up and sees the same exact cloud he'd seen ten years before. The same exact one."

"And then what?" he says, jogging ahead of me.

"And then nothing. That's it." He jogs away and I am left there, alone, building in my mind a frame for the sky.

Lost in Freakin' Yonkers

RANDA JARRAR

New York, during the summer of '96, sees its highest temperatures on record, and it is toward the end of this summer that I sit, my enormous pregnant belly to accompany me, on an 80 percent acrylic, 20 percent wool covered futon. I look over the tag again, and under the materials it says, made in ASU. So I'm sitting on the futon, sweating—we have neither an air conditioner nor a fan, and our window is held up by an embarrassingly huge copy of *Dirtiest Jokes Volume III*—and wondering: should I marry my worthless boyfriend? and: was the tag maker dyslexic? I quit worrying and start to masturbate, reminding myself that the pregnancy book says that in the last trimester the mother is "at her sexual peak," and that each strong orgasm brings her closer to real contractions. How totally unfair this is, considering I can hardly reach my own crotch.

The phone rings, and it's my mother calling from a pay phone, wondering if she should make the Ninety-sixth Street imam wait much longer.

"Don't bother," I say. "Tell him to forget it, tell him to go home."

"Why, *habibti*? Come on, do the conversion, and get married. We're all waiting for you." She sounds unconvinced and hurried.

Who is "we"? I imagine that Mama has picked up a few Hell's Angels and a couple of squeegee boys for witnesses on her way into the city.

"He's not even here," I say. "He's not converting. I don't want him to convert. He'll be a shitty Muslim, and a shitty husband too."

"Oh, it's not about shitty Muslim or no shitty Muslim. Come, *yalla*, let's get this finished. Conversion, marriage, boom, boom, two stones with one pigeon, do they say?"

Leave it to an Arab to mangle an idiom beyond recognition, and to double the called-for amount of stone.

"Sorry, Mama, he's at a bar getting shit-faced. Just go home before Baba gets suspicious."

"Final, that?"

"Yes. Sorry. Bye."

The sun goes down (incidentally, something my boyfriend James rarely does) and the Saturday is wrapping up and I haven't seen James's face since the day before. I decide to get up and call the bars.

"Hey, Vinnie."

"Hi, Aida. He ain't here."

"All right. How's Maureen?"

"She's great."

"Yeah? OK, Vin, bye."

"Sorry, Aida."

Click.

"Tony, you seen James?"

"Naaah, Ai, but why you don't come down here no more?"

"I'm seven months pregnant, Tone."

"Oh, yeah, good fer you."

Click.

Well, then I guess I'm going down to the bar. I beg my mother-in-law, who sits on her stoop three blocks away and chain-smokes mint cigarettes all night, if I can borrow her Cadillac. She shows me her nails; she's just had them done at the nail salon.

"What's that a decal of?"

"It's a Christmas tree, what're you blind? I had sharp eyes when I was your age!"

"Yeah, yeah, yeah. Keys."

I get into the Cadillac and adjust the seat. I can probably steer with my tummy at this point. I stick my head out of the window and say, "Isn't it too early for Christmas?"

"It's never too early to celebrate the Lord's birthday," she says, crossing herself. "We're getting the lights and the garlands this weekend."

"I bet you are, you fucking psycho," I say when the window is up, the air conditioning on high and aimed directly at my face. Mama says she knows a handful of people who have been paralyzed this way.

I get to Phil's Tavern just before closing. This is where I met James, the man who is ten years my senior. I go inside and stand by the door, scanning heads. I find him less than a minute later, talking to a blond girl with makeup so thick she'd have to claim it at an airport.

When I met James, I'd just gotten off my shift, was drinking my first beer, and he was on his eighth. A cigarette butt had accidentally started a small fire in my hair; he put it out by slapping my head over and over again. This seemed to foreshadow the nature of our entire relationship, and I should have known right then that this is not a person to have a child with.

"Hey, asshole," I say, "wanna introduce me to your friend?"

"Shit . . . honey . . . are we havin' it?"

"No, two months to go."

"All right, fuck me, then, what are you doing here?"

I punch him in the nose. He calls me a stupid Ay-rab and punches me in my eye. I kick his groin and go back to the car.

Let me explain a little. So I was eighteen, just finished a year of college, and found out I was pregnant. Naturally, I told my mother; unfortunately, I told her in the middle of Interstate 95. She slammed on the brakes and parked the car right in the middle of the highway.

"What? *Na'am yakhti?* What's that, sister? You're pregnant? I knew it! I knew it!" she said.

"Mama, pull into the emergency lane, please!" I said.

"Ass! You big, stupid ass! I should've sewn up your pussy the last time we were in Egypt!" she said.

"Excuse me?" I said.

"Hey, get the fuck out of the road!" said a man in a Jeep.

"You were gonna sew up my pussy?"

"Who is this pimp? Where did you find the bastard? Aren't you at an all-girls college?"

"Wait, I'm still stuck on the sewing-my-pussy-up-in-Egypt-last-summer part."

"Your father's going to shoot you. No baby for you, no baby for me. You'll both be killed, finished, peace be upon you," she said.

"You're in the middle of the fucking road, you spic!" a pasty woman in a van said.

"I am Egyptian!" Mama yelled after her, and gave her the arm.

"You seriously thought of sewing up my pussy?" I said.

"You will have an abortion, *yalla*, right now." She checked her mirrors and restarted the car, speeding ahead.

"I will not!" I said.

"Yes, you will. Women have them every day, and I'm not ready to be a grandmother."

"I'm not ready to be a mother, but that's not stopping me," I said.

"*Ya sharmoota*, you slut!" she said, and parked again, this time in the emergency lane.

"I'm going to finish school—everything will be fine, just the way it was, but with a baby."

"You're so naive, you schew-bid, schew-bid girl." Mama was crying, and I felt like shit. Literally. I bent over and hurled all over the yellow stripe in the road.

I didn't tell Baba face to face. Mona, my only Arab girlfriend, came to my dorm room the day I left him a note, penned in my best Arabic, explaining everything. I'd taken the train to his office in midtown and left the note on his desk. I knew that if I left it at home someone would get hurt. Mona said it was the perfect thing to do, that it was what she did when she came out to her father as a gay man and told him she was going to be a full-time transvestite.

"Did he ever get over it?" I asked her, drinking milk through a carton.

"Oh, no, honey," said Mona, whose real name is Munir. "He left my mom and married another woman, said maybe she'll give him straight sons."

"Oh," I said, and threw up all over Mona's fabulous D&G skirt.

My father took it better than Mona's. Having always quoted me poetry, on every occasion, he was not going to stop doing it now. The note he sent back said,

> Ibnati Aida,
> Each river has its source, its course, its life.
> My friend, our land is not barren.
> Each land has its time for being born,
> Each dawn a date with a rebel.
> If you have the child, we will no longer be your family. You will be dead to us forever.

Holy shit, I said out loud after reading it. I can't believe it. Darwish? Infuriated, I took the train north, to our house. I sat by a window and watched the streets fly by. Flagship Road, Mary Lane, Raymond Street. What did it mean? Was I supposed to be the land, or the rebel, or both? I didn't know; I couldn't care. I didn't understand that there are different ways to love, and this was the only way Baba knew how to love. When the train stopped, I got off and walked the thirteen blocks from the station. When I arrived at the door, I stopped and looked at the doorknob. How many times had I turned it to leave? How many times had I stood here after coming home from running away? It was spring then, and fireflies were floating all around, as if taking pictures of me on this momentous day. Four years in America, no traceable accent, no one would guess I'm Arab, and people mispronounce my name. The house was white and small, the people inside threatening to turn away for good. And inside me, there was life. I turned the knob and took my shoes off at the door, saw Mama reading the *Ahram* she gets from the Indian guy's stationery store. I hugged her and she shook her head, and got up to go into the den with me. The den: wood paneling, fireplace, Americana par excellence. Baba switched the TV off.

"You sent me a poem?" I said. "I'm pregnant and you quote me Darwish?" I was shaking with fear.

"You're fucking pregnant. Who has the right to be enraged? Not you, my dear."

It was final. Baby = no family = no money for college = I am dead. No baby = family back. I didn't want this family anyway, so I chose baby.

It was a hard trimester. There were no easy mornings. My awakenings were filled with a pressing need to race to the toilet and unfill my insides.

"Jeez, Ai," James would say, peering into the bathroom. "Jeez, hon, you gonna puke the whole kid out if you keep doin' that."

"Why am I here?"

"What's that, cutie? Why you here? 'Cause, you pukin' the whole kid out. I'll make you a waffle, come on."

I didn't need a waffle. I didn't need to be sitting here, hugging this toilet and not needing a waffle, at eighteen, while my friends were home in their dorms recovering from a newly bought, PCP-laced ounce of weed. I needed to be not dead. I needed Baba and Mama to want to know that I was hugging a toilet, not wanting a waffle and not wanting to be dead.

When you're disowned, your mother becomes your secret lover, calling from pay phones, visiting at odd hours and for short bits of time; and your lover becomes your mother, has to take care of you now that she's gone. It's been hard getting used to, and besides, my so-called lover is a drunk and not very motherly.

The bastard is broke, and on weekends, when he's supposed to be home, he has to work odd jobs to pay the bills. This includes delivering flowers, which I usually do for him, since he's allergic to their smell. I sit in the delivery van with him, watching tears run down his face, his eyes bloodshot, his face smelling like rubber because he drank so much the night before. He loses the flower job one Sunday when I refuse to go with him since he'd refused to engage me in the bringing-contractions-closer process of oral sex.

The night I have to bail him out of jail for public intoxication and battery, my best friends Shoshanna and Mona are crying: "Fuck this, Aida, let's just go. You have to leave this asshole!"

I want to explain to them that I need this, need to keep going to school and have a father for the kid, need to be able to tell the God, on the day of judgment when I crawl out of my grave and I'm all alone and shards of sky are crashing down on me, that look, dude, I tried.

Once a week, I go to the Laundromat down the street and bargain with Jackie, who has an entire row of gold front teeth, to do my laundry for two dollars. She usually settles for two dollars and a bottle of OE, which I can never buy her since I'm underage. While waiting for my filthy industrial-mechanic boyfriend's uniforms to wash halfway clean, I sit in the nail parlor and let the old ladies play with my curls, paint my toenails, which I can no longer reach, and give me five dollars if I make them Turkish coffee and read their fortunes. They have a hot plate and I bring my own old-school copper coffeepot and pretty soon invest in demitasses from Yaranoush, the Armenian store on Central Ave., and have my own fortune-telling business going.

"Oh, Ai, tell Joan what you told me about the man in Flo-o-orida," Mrs. Leibowitz says, punctuating words with her very long and fake nails.

"Aida, you goin' to services, honey?" someone asks on a Friday, and Mrs. Leibowitz or Mamie the Widow says, "Oh, shut your mouth, the girl's a moselem, she don't go there!"

Eventually, Jackie sticks her head in and says, "Yar filthy clothes done finish, now, chil', go home and git some rest!"

I walk home with the bag on my back, a baby in my tummy, and a ton of shit going on inside my head.

He is drunk in his sleep, he is drunk in the afternoon. He is drunk at work, he is drunk while we make love, he is drunk when he throws a dictionary at my belly and causes me internal bleeding. He is drunk when I am in the hospital waiting for a diagnosis from a doctor who scans my DOB and shakes her head. He is drunk when I tell him the baby will be all right.

That night, I have to drive home, and I look over at him when we are stopped at a red light, see his Adam's apple dance, up, down, his eyes shut, his brown forehead covered in sweat. This is it? I ask myself, hating the government and financial aid rules, my reproductive system, his big dick, my father, and mostly, my God. Not just

God, but the God, the one who wrote the book resting in the car-door pocket on my left, the book that my boyfriend erroneously skims from left to right, the book that provides Guilt big enough to make me want to marry this ape with several mental illnesses which he does not plan on getting cured of anytime soon. Just then, the light turns green, a sign from the God, I decide, that yeah, this is it.

James had no idea how broke we were, he claims five days after the hospital bill comes. I pick up the phone and call the college library, ask them if I can come in and work. When he finds out that I got the job, twenty-five hours a week at $6.50 an hour, he puts his hand on my shoulder and winks. I say to him sweetly, *Habibi, ibn il-sharmoota ya khawal. Yarab tmoot.*

What's that mean, baby? He wants to know, and I lie, It means I'll love you forever and ever.

So I take the stupid job at the library, and like I said, it's summer, and he's driving out to fucking Jers every day, which means I have to walk to the stupid job at the library. It's a lovely stroll, I must say; here are my favorite moments:

a. Getting mugged at knifepoint right at the corner of Fleetwood and Gramattan and having to give the kid my backpack, which contains three interlibrary loan books by Latifa al-Zayyat, all in Arabic. He must have felt like one lucky motherfucker.
b. Stepping in broken glass while wearing my ugly pregnant-girl sandals.
c. Stepping in dog (or human) shit while wearing my ugly pregnant-girl sandals.

I tell James the walk isn't worth it, and he says I should watch my step more. I say, "Yeah, that's easy for you to say, you don't have a three-by-two-foot addition to the front of your fucking body."

"You're right, hon," he says, one hand on my thigh and the other holding a Bud. "But I can't afford to not work in Jers, although I did get a weekend job at the scrap-metal yard." He leans over and kisses my lips. His lips are soft and wet, and the more I look at him, the more fine the asshole seems. His eyes are a brown that always shocks me because it seems too light for his complexion. His hair, which is always five weeks too late for a cut, curls up in gorgeous black bunches. We make love, or I should say, achieve the impossible, what with the three-by-two-foot obstacle. The whole time, I'm yelling, *Habibi, ibn ilshar-moota ya khawal. Ya rab tmoot,* and the idiot is moaning, Yeah you hot Arabic princess baby I love you too.

While I'm in the shower, the door has to stay open because I am growing at an alarming rate. He is shaving at the sink, which is the size of a small notebook, and I am attempting to wash my nether regions.

"I'm not Arabic," I decide to inform him.

"What, you fucking lied about that, too?"

"No, you moron," I say. "I am not a fucking language; if you must, you can call me Arab. But never Arabian or Arabic."

"Yeah," he says, shaving his dimpled chin, "all right, so you ain't a horse or a language. Got it."

I tell him I love him, and I really mean it, and that I need a showerhead thing because I can't reach my pussy anymore.

He starts to come home from the scrap-metal job with a lot of cash. I don't know how he's getting it, but we have more than just a jar of peanut butter in the fridge. He says he finds metal everywhere and the boss gives him money for it.

"Where do you find this metal?" I ask him.

"Everywhere, shit, there's metal all over the place. If people only knew."

"What kind of metal?"

"Like tire rims, metal from old roofs, metal window frames, metal metal, anything."

"And how do you get money from it?"

"I go around and pick it up and then I take it to the scrap yard and Mikey gives me cash for however much it weighs."

"He goes by weight? Like gold?" I say, shocked.

"Yes, like gold. Now will you get me a beer?"

Then there are long weeks when we have no money again.

"It's because there's no metal anywhere, they must've caught on, those fucking bums," he says, staring off into the distance . . .

well, not so much into the distance since our living room is no bigger than a tuna can. I think the beer in his calloused palm is a Pabst.

I get hungry every two hours. The baby inside me is a ravenous and costly little fucker; selfish like its father. The women at the parlor feed me, saying, "Eat! Eat! You're eating for two now!" And I say, "Yes, but one of them is 160 pounds and the other one is 5 pounds. Why does it need to eat so much?"

During those moneyless weeks, I make enough cash at the nail parlor for the laundry, a bag of potatoes, and a bottle of ketchup. I peel the potatoes at the kitchen table, which James made out of wood and cinder blocks, and then fry them in a pot. I eat them on the floor on a thick layer of newspapers, along with a bottle's worth of ketchup, and three vitamins. On Halloween, completely broke, and not fitting into any of my clothes, I go into a Sears changing room, put on a maternity outfit, leave my jeans and holey t-shirt, and walk out of the store, like that. I walk three miles to the college's library, look up "Arab" and "American" and "Women" and "Fiction" on the computer, find nothing, then go into the girls' room and weep into cheap toilet paper, wondering what I am supposed to be doing now. Defeated, I read *Beloved,* and when I'm done, it's already nearing midnight. I put a quarter in a pay phone, dial my own number, no one. Bastard. I decide, fuck it, walk home, if someone mugs you they mug you, it's Halloween, call a cab, fuck a cab, I'm walking, if I die I die, and for the first time, I want to die, I was dead to my family anyway, I should just die, die, die.

On the way home I pass fellow students partying in their dorm rooms and wonder if they can tell that I'm dead. Or that I'm pregnant. The last professor I had thought I was just "large." Like a fat ass. I can tell some people don't want to ask when I'm due, in case I'm just fat. It always sucks when you ask that and then the woman looks at you in horror and runs for a place to hide, to cry, to eat a chili dog.

I'm home, and when I open the door, I am greeted by a gigantic mound of candy piled high on the kitchen table. When I look closer, atop this mound is a video camera with wires sticking out of its base. "James," I scream, "what the fuck is this shit, *yilan abuk ibnil-sharmuta ya khawal ya rab tmoot?*"

And that's when he tells me the story about the movie theater in Bonville: the neighboring town, where I go to college, is considered so safe (read: white) that people leave their doors unlocked and their businesses unattended.

This is how James, my apish, barrel-chested thug of a man, once drunkenly walked into my dormitory lounge and literally swept me off my feet. It is also how, tonight, after consuming ungodly amounts of Guinness and weed, he walked into the Sony theater downtown, "through the back door, which was not only left unlocked but AJAR" (he stresses this word; I think he's proud of himself for knowing it), and in less than half a minute, shoved all the candy that was behind the counter into a garbage bag. On his way out, he happened to notice the video camera mounted on the wall. At first he lifted the garbage bag up and yelled desperately into the camera, This is for my pregnant wife! But on second thought, figuring he might get caught, he walked up to the camera and ripped it out of the wall.

"I'll get a lot of money for it at the scrap-metal yard," he says, kissing me.

Calmly, I say, "Never mind the fact that you should have robbed their cash registers and that you should sell the camera at an electric store, not the fucking metal yard . . . you do know that you're on a videotape"—here, and for extra emphasis, I form a rectangle with my fingers—"somewhere in their back room, don't you?" He pretends not to hear me, and instead thrusts a box of candy at me and asks, "Juju?"

On the Saturday before I am scheduled to go in for a cesarean (unlike me, my child is not in the habit of doing everything early), I take James's keys to go to the Laundromat and get his clothes for the last time without a baby in tow. Jackie is there, and she winks at me, says, "Good luck, chil'," and hands me the bag.

I get in the car and back up, right into a woman's Oldsmobile.

"Holy shit!" I say, and jump out of the car.

"It's a-rye!" she says, snapping her gum. "It's my stupid boyfriend's car anyhow. Fuck 'm! Don't worry about it, hon." She gets in her car and drives away.

A cop comes up to me and shakes his head. "All right, I saw that, and you're lucky." He is gorgeous, all eyebrows and lips.

"I'm sorry, I'm having a baby tomorrow and I'm a little nervous," I say.

"No worries. Here's a dollar, go get yourself a bagel and come back when you're ready to drive." He points at the diner next to the nail parlor. I realize that all the girls are standing outside the parlor, talking about the accident.

"What happened, hon?" they ask.

"Nothing, Mrs. Leibowitz, small accident. I'm getting a bagel."

"Look at my nail, Aida!" says Mamie the Widow, sticking up her middle finger. I see the profile of a black man. "MLK day, it's comin' up!"

When I get back in the car, after eating a bagel and drinking two not-allowed cups of coffee, I back up, and this time, hit a blue truck. A burly man jumps out.

"Yeah, and where were you goin', huh? Fuckin' backin' up like a rocket, and where to? Look at this freakin' thing, it looks like Beirut in my truck now, look at my truck, ah, jeez . . ."

"I'm sorry, sir, I'm having a baby tomorrow . . ."

"She's havin' the baby, did she say?" the women at the parlor yell.

"Yeah, she's also gettin' a ticket!" yells the cop, walking back toward me.

" . . . please, I'm broke, I'm having a kid," I tell the cop, then turn to the man, who has a mustache and looks eerily similar to an Egyptian comedian. "And you, sir, your truck's not so bad . . . I live with a drunk . . . and my parents disowned me . . . I haven't seen my mother smile in over a year . . . I haven't seen my father, period . . . and I have these bags of potatoes and I fry them and eat them on newspapers . . . why on newspapers? Because, because my husband throws dishes at me when he's drunk . . . he's always drunk . . . and in my entire life every man who's claimed he loved me hit me . . . and I had to read those old Jewish ladies their fortunes every Shabbat for weeks and lie about their impending deaths . . . and there's not a single book by an Arab woman in my college library, so please cut me some slack, willya?"

Mrs. Leibowitz and Mamie aren't sure what I've just said, but it sounded like a good speech, and they start applauding, making the rest of the women standing outside the strip mall clap, too.

"It's my fuckin' boss's truck," the man says, then looks away. "The man's a bastard. All right, I'm going thataway, and you go thataway."

"Once again, a lucky girl," the cop says. And he doesn't give me a ticket.

That night James and I go for a walk and buy dinner: a kid's cone from Baskin-Robbins. We lick it together and hold hands.

"I can't believe I'm having a baby tomorrow. A baby, James. I'm giving birth to an American citizen. It better not look too much like you."

"I'm sorry we ain't got no money, sweetie," he says. We're standing at the intersection of Fleetwood and Gramatan.

"This is where I got mugged," I tell him.

"Sons of bitches," he says. "If I was there, honey, it woulda never happened. I woulda killed that bastard for puttin' a knife up to you." He strokes my hair, which is getting oranger every day.

"You're right," I say angrily. "It would've never happened because you're huge and no one would think of mugging me if you're here." I look away from him, and into the distance. He must think just then that I'm sick of him, that if I have to eat another Juju I'll leave him, that I don't really love him anymore, because he asks, "What's wrong?" his voice shaky.

"What about that?" I say, pointing at what it is that I'm looking at in the distance. "Think of how much that thing weighs . . . how many groceries we could buy if we could sell that!"

There is a long silence, and at last he says, "Honey, that's a lamppost!"

And just then, I realize that we won't last, that we can't possibly, but that he's so fucking cute, and he makes me laugh, and there's Skittles and Junior Mints and a showerhead massager at home waiting for us. He holds my hand, keeps his eye on the street for me since I am wearing the ugly pregnant-girl sandals, and we walk off into the Yonkers sunset, licking our $1.37 kid's cone.

Oh, Lebanon

EVELYN SHAKIR

She'd had three husbands, and she held four passports. Her English mother had given birth to her in London, and there she'd stayed until the age of three. When the mother died of a brain tumor, her father sent for her in Lebanon. Two passports accounted for already and perhaps three marriages. Failed attempts at finding mother love.

All her growing-up years, she lived with her father and with her stepmother, who was kind enough, and with their children, of whom she was more fond than not. The family spent winters in Beirut, her father refusing—war or no war—to be driven from a city as much a part of him as his own breath. And, except for the year a militia camped in their country house, they still spent summers in the mountains. Like many well-off Muslims (and as long as roads were open), they sent the children to French nuns for schooling. She was the only one they sent to Anglicans. "On account of her mother," they explained to friends, who got teary-eyed and said, "How beautiful!"

Her father was stubborn and knew what he knew but was also progressive and very rich. So when she showed him catalogues from American universities, he saw no problem. Felt, in fact, a tinge of pride. Just never noticed she was desperate to escape.

In her first semester at Wellesley, she met a junior at MIT, a black Jamaican, who soon became husband number one. Her father, not that progressive, refused her phone calls, deleted e-mails, and burned her letters without opening them until eventually she gave up. He'd change his mind one day, she thought, and then they'd see who wouldn't talk to who.

When the Jamaican boy graduated, she dropped out of Wellesley to go home with him to Kingston. His family was skeptical. "And who may you be?" they as much as asked her, thinking to themselves, "white trash." But when he explained about the father's millions and the English mother, they said, "Well, that's all right then," and waited to see if she would put on airs.

The first weeks, she was tentative, but soon she fell in with the rhythms of the place—calypso, reggae, the spirit of her in-laws' teasing. When she held her own, giving back as good as she got, they were content, just as she was beguiled by green sea, lush hills, breezes perfumed with pimento and frangipani. She brought home carvings from the outdoor markets. She lined the walkway with driftwood scavenged from the beach and conch shells sold by boatmen in the harbor.

"Are you bored?" her husband asked when fifteen months had passed. "Do you miss your friends?"

"You must be joking," she said. "I could live here forever."

As soon as she said it, she knew it wasn't true. By now, her in-laws worried her, doting on her in a half-ironic way, expecting something in return she couldn't muster. But it was fear that finally turned her against the island. Each day, news circulated of shoot-outs on the street and gangland executions; the murder rate, the papers said, was third-highest in the world. When the mayhem got close to home, her brother-in-law stabbed outside his garden gate, she'd had enough.

Her husband added bars to the two windows where they were missing and bought new double bolts for every door. It didn't matter, she was still afraid. At night, she tossed and dreamed of Beirut, rockets turning night to day, a teenage sniper ogling her from the roof across the street. Nearby, what had been an apartment building. Now just a grid of tattered cubicles, naked, taken by surprise. Then taken over—rats scurrying, squatters camping behind plastic sheeting, a militiaman stirring coffee over a coal brazier or hanging out wet skivvies. And yet you could emerge after laying low all morning in a shelter and know you were safe again till nightfall. In Kingston there was no moratorium.

"I can't live this way," she told him. He answered that away from Jamaica he would be a dull knife, an empty pod, a dry leaf.

Cambridge had nearly sucked the marrow out of him, but, at least, he'd known it wouldn't last forever. He tried to blot out her fears with sex. Made love to her before leaving for work each morning and again as soon as he got home. The more he fucked her, the more he wanted to. Wrapped himself around her all night, and if she stirred at all, he only held her tighter. Even when she slept, he was whispering in her ear, how he adored her golden skin, her green eyes; was bewitched by her breasts, her belly, and this, this! He ran his hand over the hot, wet place.

"I love you madly," she said. "But that has nothing to do with it." And so ended marriage number one. Though not before she'd gained passport number three.

Back in Boston by way of Canada, she ran through two more husbands in short order, each time thinking she'd hit pay dirt. One a middle-aged professor she'd studied philosophy with at Wellesley, who looked at her young body and couldn't believe his luck; the other a beautiful young man from Santa Fe, with red lips and Navajo blood. After three years of marriage but no children, she'd left the professor for the beautiful young man. No more listening to the old fart worry the subtext out of her most casual statement. Excused forever from faculty parties that she'd scowled her way through, nursing soda water with a slice of lime and a growing list of grievances against the man who had trapped her in this facsimile of life.

After their wedding, the young man was as cheerful and charming as before. She found she wanted to please him, the only ways she knew—in bed and at table—and gave thought to both, reading books and calling on imagination. Hoping for his smile, she felt the way she had the day she'd gone shopping for a car, and, through the luck of the draw, he was her salesman. She'd bought a hatchback on the spot, agreeing to the wrong color because she would not disappoint him. On their second anniversary, he announced that he was walking out, not for another man—which had been her secret dread—but for a forty-year-old woman with money who wanted him for his body and told him so. He'd reported it with pride.

As the young man was kissing her good-bye, she asked him to fuck her for good luck, and he obliged. Taking his time, plumbing for the sweet spot, coaxing her to pleasure so deep, she knew he would never leave her.

"Margo would kill me if she found out," he told her as he pulled on his trousers. "But I wanted to give you something special to remember me by."

She had to stop herself from saying, "Thank you."

Two months later she turned thirty, and depression took her by surprise. Her youth was gone, frittered away on men who had, each in his own way, been wrong for her. And what was to stop it from happening again since her own judgment had never yet guided her right? Now she understood why her uncle had arranged marriages for her cousins Mona and Aisha. It was an act of love. She used to be proud that her father was not old-fashioned, but now she was angry at his neglect. And when she remembered how easily he'd released her to drift on her own across an ocean, she was astonished.

The fact was she'd been a babe in the woods here despite watching American movies all her life. You had to be born to it, she thought. American girls were shrewd. They knew how to play the game and win the prize of living happily ever after or something closer to it. But she'd done impulse shopping. Without stopping to think, she'd said yes to anyone who popped the question. As if they were inviting her to a movie and would bring her home after a late-night cappuccino. As if it would be rude to say no.

For the first time since she'd left Lebanon, she thought of returning, an American passport (number four) like a gold nugget tucked in her pocket. No war now to scare her away. But it was too late. In Lebanon she would be reduced to a dirty story, perhaps already had been. She knew her father would not let her enter his house, for fear the neighbors would think that he had forgiven her shamelessness.

"But what have I done?" she argued with him in her head. "I haven't been loose, I haven't slept around." She thought of calling on the Jamaican boy to bear witness she'd been a virgin on their wedding night. He could vouch for her, like the blood-stained sheets mothers had hung, in the old days, from the window of the bridal chamber.

It came to her with a pang. Now that she was single again and meaning to stay that way for a long time, what would she do for sex? "Never mind that," she scolded herself. "What will you do with your life?" She had money to live on for a while, a small bequest from her English grandmother. But that would run out, and meanwhile she couldn't sit home and do nothing.

In Jamaica, the idea of taking a job had never occurred. Her professor husband would have liked her to have a career, as a lawyer, for instance, or an architect or even an associate dean. But not to demean herself and him by clerking in a store or doing temp work in an office. "What are my options?" she asked him. "I'm a college dropout." He didn't have to be reminded. The only question was how to explain to his friends. Finally, he arrived at a formula. "She's a free spirit," he said.

The beautiful young man didn't care or even remember whether she had a college degree, and he was glad to have her bring in a few dollars any way she could. But now, thinking back, she rather liked the ring of *free spirit*. It called to mind a girl she'd admired at Wellesley, who wore filmy dresses and multiple rings in her earlobes and danced with abandon. Maybe here was something to thank the professor for, an insight, a romantic read on herself. "Don't be an idiot," she told herself and signed up for an accounting class at the nearest branch of the state university. She could see now that Wellesley, too, had been a mistake. History of art and Russian novels in translation when she should have been learning how to make money and cut a figure in the world.

After just one hour with a guidance counselor, she was on her way. The woman had drawn a road map for her, checking off little boxes on a pre-printed form. That sheet of paper set her mind at rest. Something tangible, something to explain why she was sitting in this classroom and not that one. Next semester she'd enroll full-time, and in just three years—if she went summers—she'd have her bachelor's in hand and an MBA. And then, it seemed, the world would be her oyster. Now that she had a destination, she studied hard. True, the work bored her silly, but that's how she knew it would cure what ailed her.

One important matter settled, she turned her mind to the other. In bed at night, after masturbating, she thought again about marriage.

Because the problem, she decided, was not with wedlock but with her choice of husbands. No recipe would come out right with poor ingredients. Back in Lebanon, her stepmother's housekeeper had taught her to snap the pointy tip of okra to test for freshness and sniff a honeydew for ripeness. But no heart-to-heart from anyone about sizing up a man. Not that she remembered. Or had she just not listened? She could turn to friends for leads—she had a few nearby, going back even to her student days. But with three husbands notched on her belt, she was embarrassed. She'd hate listening to their coy laughter. "Why don't you give it a rest?" they might say.

What she needed was another sheet of paper with more little boxes to fill in. And someone who made a living putting two and two —or rather, one and one—together. Someone who would study her like a book, then pull Mr. Right out of a database while she stood by, feet to the ground, hormones in check.

In the Sunday paper she found what she was looking for, on the same page as the personals. Which, out of curiosity, she skimmed. Under the heading "Men Looking for Women" were the wish lists of the single, widowed, and divorced, all advertising for females who were *thin* (or *trim* or *slim*) and yet *curvaceous*, beautiful *inside/outside*, and always younger. In return, the men offered a summer of fun or dangled the prospect of *LTRs*. One saw himself as a knight in shining armor seeking "a damsel worth jousting for"; another as a sea captain "scanning the horizon for a mermaid."

"Oh, please," she thought, anger welling up inside her.

When she met with the woman from the agency, she spelled out what she wanted—a sober assessment and rational match. "A man my parents would approve of," she explained, leaving it at that. "Good for you," the agent said, pulling a six-page form out of her slender briefcase. "I wish all our clients had your attitude."

The first man referred to her was described as three parts Lebanese, the great-grandson of immigrants from Tripoli in the north. Her heart fell, she was looking for a fresh start. Still, she could see the logic. He turned out to be dark, slight, and with features that reminded her of her cousins. Thick hair, small ears that lay close to his head, a serious gaze. Altogether, more attractive than she'd allowed herself to hope for. He liked her looks, too—she'd seen his eyes light up when he first spotted her wearing the carnation they'd agreed upon. Mutual attraction. If things turned out, that would be the icing on their cake.

On their first date, they met, as the agency advised, in a public place. From City Hall Plaza, they strolled over to Quincy Market and found an ice-cream shop with tables outside, each shaded by a royal blue or tangerine umbrella.

"Let's go for blue," he said.

"Let's," she agreed, pleased that he noticed color, though, truthfully, the tangerine had caught her eye.

After ordering sundaes, strawberry for her, hot fudge for him, they were quiet for a bit. No getting around it, she thought, it was awkward, this calculated assignation. She wanted to break the silence, to put them both at ease. But then she saw he was already at ease, one tanned arm thrown over the back of his chair, his gaze taking in the tourists and shoppers passing on the periphery of the café. She looked, too, trying to guess what he saw that prompted his look of contentment. The flow of colors and shapes, she thought; the balloons, the afternoon sunshine. Or maybe just his sense of being at home. It took an almost-Lebanese to remind her of her exile.

When she turned back, he was facing her, his arms crossed and resting on the table.

"You look happy," she said.

His smile broadened. "I am. I'm happy you're Lebanese."

"What difference does that make?" She was startled, and the question came out more sharply than she'd intended.

"It makes all the difference in the world," he said as if stating the obvious. "In my family, we've lost our Arab culture, and I'm the only one who cares."

"Poor you."

He laughed. "Poor them."

She liked it that he didn't take offense. Liked it, too, that he said "Arab." Some Christians in Lebanon—and he was Christian, she knew—refused that label. She was not a practicing Muslim. Even her father, for all his store of sayings from the Hadith, had never been devout. In fact, her own mother—his first wife—had been Christian. And she, his daughter, had married two Protestants and a Catholic, following in his footsteps. Someday she'd point it out to him, the family resemblance. Still, she could never spend her life with someone who looked down on Islam or thought that "Arab" was a slur. She remembered her former sister-in-law—the professor's sister, it was—who had instructed her always to introduce herself as *Phoenician* or, if she must, as simply *Lebanese*. A warning finger raised. "Don't say *Arab*." "Why not?" she'd asked. "It doesn't sound very nice," the sister-in-law had explained.

"Have you ever been to Lebanon?" she asked him. "Or to the Middle East?"

He shook his head. "No," he confessed. "I'm overdue." Then after a moment, "Way overdue."

She rushed to the rescue. "Well, it's a distance."

"Sure, but you can bank on it—I'm going to get there soon."

Did he think she was his ticket?

She imagined returning to Beirut with a Lebanese American husband in tow. Imagined her father's pleasure because now she'd finally done it right. "You were sick with a fever," he would say, "but, praise Allah, you are well." He'd throw a party, the whole family would come, three generations of uncles and aunts, and cousins. There would be long tables laden with food. Maaza, first, of every sort—hummus and baba ghanouj and tabbouleh, olives, sprigs of green thyme, pickled eggplant; then main dishes of chicken with rice, rolled grape leaves, and *kibbee;* then pastries, sweet and sticky, stuffed with nuts or cheese and flavored with orange-blossom water. Finally, Turkish coffee meted out in tiny porcelain cups. She licked dreamily at the back of her spoon. The round of relatives (taking their cue from her father) would all come up to her husband with an embrace and kiss him on both cheeks. They'd want to know in what town or village his family had its roots and inquire about his great-grandmother's family name. "You are one of us," they would say, reclaiming her at the same time.

"Now *you* look happy," he said, calling her back to the present.

"Do you speak Arabic?" How that would thrill the family.

"About three words. But I have this fantasy, I guess you'd call it." She waited to hear.

"It's set in the future. I'm walking down a street in Beirut. Name one."

"Hamra."

"OK, I'm walking down Hamra Street with my son—let's say he's seven or eight. And we get lost. I'm assuming that could happen pretty easily."

"Well, maybe."

"*Leave it to me, Dad,*" my son says, and the little guy goes up to this man with a white beard and a fez—do they still wear them?"

"Not today."

"OK, this man without a fez—and asks directions. In Arabic, you see, because my kid's been learning and he's fluent. Before you know it, the old gentleman invites us to go home with him to lunch. We meet his wife—she's a great cook, by the way—and his children and grandchildren. *My house is your house,* he says, and we become like part of the family. When my kid grows up, he marries the prettiest granddaughter."

She laughed. "And lives happily ever after."

"He's a good kid, he deserves it. But first"—and he was laughing now, too—"I have to find a wife to teach my kids-to-be the ABC's of Arabic."

She looked past him at a cluster of tourists settled on a bench. One teenager in a Bruins t-shirt poked another playfully in the shoulder. Beside them, a young woman in a sundress lifted a plump little girl onto her lap and kissed the top of her head.

"Listen." He leaned forward, his small, shapely hands stretched toward hers. "Don't think I'm trying to rush things. I just want you to understand where I'm coming from, and"—he smiled sweetly— "I want to know all about you." She was busy twirling her bracelet of twisted gold around her wrist. "So we can figure out if I fit your bill and you fit mine." He waited for her to look up at him. "I mean, what are we talking here? This is for life. At least that's what I have in mind, and you said—or they told me—that you were thinking along the same lines."

At first, they saw each other twice a week, then three times, ice cream again or coffee or lunch. They took in art galleries on

Newbury Street, an afternoon concert at Mrs. Jack Gardner's Palace, feeding time at the aquarium. One day he coaxed her onto a Duck Tour. They sat high in an amphibious vehicle that ferried tourists through the downtown streets. Pedestrians looked up and grinned. "Quack-quack," they teased. "Quack-quack," the tourists called back. "It's true," she thought, "Americans have no dignity." Just then he tugged her hair playfully and mouthed a silent *quack*. "Oh, why not?" she thought, and soon she was carrying on with the rest. When they rolled down the bank and splashed into the Charles, she caught her breath.

"Like it?" he asked.

"Wonderful!" she said.

Another day he led her through the South End neighborhood where the early Lebanese families—people like his ancestors—had moved in almost a century ago and then moved out in the forties and fifties to lose themselves in the suburbs. He stood with her in front of the townhouse that had once been home to the Lebanese Syrian Ladies' Aid Society, of which, he explained with pride, his father's grandmother had been a charter member.

She knew of Kahlil Gibran, of course? Knew his book *The Prophet*? She nodded. Well, when Gibran died, if she could believe it, he'd been waked in that very building, his remains brought up by train from New York for a funeral Mass at the local Maronite church. Though one priest, hearing that Gibran had refused last rites, wanted to bar the door.

"When the funeral cortege went by, people all along here"—he pointed up and down the street as if he owned it—"they fell to their knees."

"How do you know these things?"

"I told you, I'm interested. I read, I talk to people."

Some time after the funeral—but this she already knew—Gibran's body had been shipped to Lebanon and carried high up the mountains for burial in his native village of Besharri. Because that's the way he had wanted it. He'd wanted to go home.

"I know Besharri," she announced. She had passed through it many times. To visit Gibran's grave? "No, not that," she said. But on her way to the ski resort higher than Besharri, higher even than the cedars. Driving her Citroën along a narrow road, all hairpin turns and sheer drops down to ancient monasteries.

"Someday you'll show me," he said with such assurance that she could picture the two of them, hand in hand like children, exploring caves where Maronite Catholics had hidden for protection. Could imagine his lean arm around her waist, in front of chains those same Catholics once used to restrain the mad and the possessed. On a damp September day in Boston, she leaned closer, then caught herself and stepped away.

By mutual consent, they avoided close quarters and stayed out of each other's apartments. Making a point of not getting physical, no more than an arm offered and taken, or triple kisses when they said hello or good-bye. Right cheek, left, then right again—Lebanese style. "I feel so pure," she said once, and they grinned at each other. Being responsible had them both on a high.

Still, all the time now he was popping up in her thoughts. In bed, of course, when she hugged her pillow to her chest and tried to remember the rough soft feel of his cheek. But also at school, breaking her concentration in the middle of statistics class or crisis management or macroeconomics. She'd be staring at a pie chart in a textbook, and suddenly there he was, darting across the page, happily dodging cars to come to her side of the street. If she fixed her gaze on the professor, she saw him instead. He was saying, "Yes?" and opening his eyes in surprise at something she'd told him, turning it over. In class sometimes she'd raise her hand to answer a question, but it was his approval that mattered. It warmed her to remember how she'd stumbled into it one day. "I think that's what I'd do," she'd said in an offhand way, and, without missing a beat, he'd declared, "Well sure, that's because you're a good person." She guessed he was the good person. If she fumbled in her purse for a tissue or a cough drop, she'd remember his wallet with his little brother's picture inside.

Four weeks into their courtship, he told her, "I feel comfortable with you." It was early evening, for a change, and they were sitting at an outdoor café in Harvard Square. Dusty trees overhead, disreputable sparrows pecking at crumbs on the ground, in front of him a Sanka, in front of her an espresso, and between them, on a square of wax paper, the last of a corn muffin.

"It doesn't bother you my family is Muslim?"

"I love it your family is Muslim."

She forced a laugh, not knowing how to take that. "You love it? That's nice," she said, pouring more sugar into her coffee and stirring it slowly. "Mind telling me why?"

"Because it makes you that much more authentic. A card-carrying Arab. I love that. In fact, I want you to take me to a mosque, I want you to teach me. Maybe I'll convert. Would you like that?"

"I don't think so," she said.

"I've been thinking that if your ex had converted"—he spoke gently—"maybe you'd still be together."

"I don't think so," she said. She'd told him about the professor. Had kept quiet about the other two, even on the form that asked for personal history. She didn't think of it as deception, just a margin of privacy a human being was entitled to.

But convert? Still, it was kind of him to have pondered her past and plotted the route to a happy ending.

"How about another round?" he asked.

"Sit still, I'll go." She was sure he was watching her as she threaded her way among the tables and up to the counter. On the way, a breeze lifted her skirt, and she smiled.

"You have beautiful hair." She was unloading the tray, placing his coffee in front of him. Suddenly bashful, she busied herself dealing out packets of sugar and plastic stirrers, then tossed her hair back as she slipped into her seat. It felt good to be with this person.

"What?" she asked, sensing that he was holding something back. "Go ahead, what?"

"Nothing. Just . . . well, let's put it this way. Did you ever think of wearing a scarf?"

It took her a minute to catch on that he meant a *hijab*.

"A rag on my head? No, thank you."

When she got home, she kicked off her shoes and paced from one small room to another. What a fool she'd been, and just when she thought she was growing smart. He was using her, like the others had, except for her sweet Jamaican boy, the only one who'd ever loved her, loved home more, though. Her mind was racing. The other two, why had they wanted her? Not for herself, she decided, but smitten by some one thing about her, just as she might love the shimmer of silk in a certain light or the texture of a ripe avocado. She came to a halt in front of her bedroom mirror. No wonder those marriages had left so much of her beside the point. No wonder in the balance she'd been feather-light. But, oh—she started pacing again—Mr. Sheik-of-Araby was the worst. Trying to wrest her into something she wasn't.

"I was going to show up in a chador," she told him the next time they met. "I was going to walk straight into this café, like a black shadow out of the desert. If I could've found a camel, I'd have walked him right in with me."

"I don't think they'd let you do that."

A waitress in a striped jumper came by, and she asked please for iced coffee with milk.

He smiled at the waitress. "I'll have the same."

"Look," she said, "I think we're a mismatch. That's all I came to tell you. We look good on paper." She ran her forefinger across an imaginary page on the table. "But I'm not the woman you want."

"I think you are."

At an impasse, they waited until the waitress had set down their order. "Enjoy," she said and pulled out a pencil and pad, her eye already on another table.

"What can I do to change your mind?"

"Nothing," she was about to say but thought better of it.

"Tell me you'd hate me in a scarf."

"I'd hate you in a scarf."

She'd meant to stay calm, not get angry, but exasperation was moving her close to tears.

"Don't say it like that"—she rapped the table in irritation—"say it like you mean it."

"I do mean it," he said slowly. "Scarf, no scarf, it's up to you."

For a minute, she watched him watching her. "You don't care if I've been married more than once," she said, then thought, *Oh, what the hell.* "Three times, in fact." She glanced away to give him time to take it in.

"What counts is now," she heard him say. Well, of course, anyone could say that.

"You won't expect me to roll grape leaves or pickle turnips?

"Did I ever say I did?" That sounded almost testy, she thought. Good. It wasn't natural—the way he was always brimming with goodwill. She remembered husband number three. Never a harsh word, but that hadn't stopped him from abandoning her.

"Listen," she said, though his eyes were still on her. "Don't think I'm going to recite the Koran five times a day. Or whisper Arabic in your ear at night." She tried to think of something else. "Or join the Ladies' Aid."

"I think the Ladies' may be kaput by now."

She looked at him sharply, but his face was sober. "Of course, I want children," she said, her tone softening. "But"—edgy again—"it doesn't follow that I have to tell them the folk tales my father told me about Jeha the fool, or teach them how to dance three kinds of *dabki,* or how to roll out Arabic bread." She paused for breath. "Or to kiss the loaf if it drops to the floor, like my grandmother used to."

"I can live with that." His tone was level.

"Because"—she was still agitated—"if there's one thing I'm not, it's pious. Or sentimental. I'm not going to fill the house with the music of Fayrouz and Im Kaltoum."

"I like a quiet home," he said, but she was hardly listening.

"And you might as well know right now"—she rested her hand on her purse—"I don't carry pictures around of our stone house in the village. And you won't hear me carrying on over the terraced garden that got blown up in the fighting or the olive trees uprooted, or the mulberry and quince." She felt tears rising and tried to blink them away. "Or my gorgeous cousin." She opened her purse and pulled out a tissue. "My cousin Fawzi. He got himself killed trying to cross the green line. And do you know why he was crossing?"

He shook his head.

"It was love. He had a girlfriend on the other side."

He drew in his breath, but she hadn't finished.

"If only I'd been in the city and not in the mountains that day." She swiped at her tears. "I'd have grabbed him by the arm and held on tight. I'd have said, *Listen to me.*"

He reached out his hand, but she shook her head. Then dabbed at her eyes with tissue, taking her time.

"Another thing." Her voice was almost steady.

He folded his arms. "Go ahead."

"This. I will not teach you Arabic."

"No?" He sounded not peeved but curious.

"Can't," she said. "It's a sophisticated language, it says more than the words." She paused for a second. "Do you see what I mean?"

"You know best." His tone was reassuring. "If you can't, you can't."

The sun through the picture window was warm on her cheek. At the next table, two middle-aged women were giggling like girls. A young man with ruddy cheeks toting a bike wheel walked through the door. She played with the straw in her glass, bending and unbending it, plunging it up and down, creating a sea of foam. Then looked up shyly.

"Your lies show you have a good heart," she said.

His face was serious. "You, too."

She looked around at the café curtains, the vintage pottery on display, the fancy breads on the counter. "This is a nice place."

He waited.

"Tell you what," she said with a smile. "No promises, but let's give this thing another chance."

He took a deep breath. *"Shookran,"* he said in an absurd American accent.

She ran her hand through her hair. "You're most welcome, *habibi.*"

"Now what's that again?"

"And you call yourself Arab! Don't you know anything? *Habibi,* my dear."

"Habibi," he echoed.

"No. If you mean me, it's *habibTi* with a *T.* Because I'm a girl. Do you see?"

"I think so."

"Let me show you." She pulled a ballpoint pen out of her purse and began making squiggles on her paper napkin. Then shifted her chair closer to his and lifted his drink out of the way. "Now pay attention," she said, tapping his wrist. "Gender is easy."

Fire and Sand

Laila Halaby

Khadija. In Islam, Khadija was the Prophet Muhammad's wife. She was much older than he was and had a lot of money. He was said to have loved her very much.

In America my name sounds like someone throwing up or falling off a bicycle. If they can get the first part of it right, the "Kha" part, it comes out like clearing your throat after eating ice cream. Usually they say Kadeeja, though, which sounds clattering clumsy. It never comes out my mother's soft way; *she* makes it sound almost pretty.

It's not like I'm dying to have an American name. I'd just like a different Arabic one. There are so many pretty names: Amani, Hala, Rawda, Mawal, and they all mean such pretty things—wishes, halo, garden, melody—not just the name of a rich old woman. My father would slap me if he heard me say that. I'm sure the original Khadija was very nice and that's why the Prophet Muhammad married her and why my father gave me her name, but I'm also sure that if the original Khadija went to school in America, she would hate her name just as much as I do.

I think Princess Diana is beautiful, and even though Diana is a pretty Western name, I thought I'd like to have it, so I told my friends at school that I was going to change my name to Diana and they should call me that from now on.

"But you don't look like a Diana," Roberta told me.

"What do I look like then?"

"I don't know. Like a Kadeeja I guess."

My father is a mechanic. He is very clever with fixing things and our house is always filled with tools and engine parts. He works as a third mechanic in a nearby repair shop. The "third" means that he is the extra, *yaani,* if they have a lot of business, then he has a good job. "Which is not often enough," my mother says to explain the foreign-looking shame money we are sent every month to buy our groceries with.

My father has many dreams that have been filled with sand. That's what he tells me: "This country has taken my dreams that used to float like those giant balloons, and filled them with sand. Now they don't float and you can't even see what they are anymore."

I try to be understanding, but I wish my father wouldn't tell me these things. I feel empty and scary and I get that stomach feeling like something awful will happen.

My mother seems too busy to have lost any dreams, and she never talks to me about things like that, only about house things and taking care of your brother things, and sometimes don't-do-that-or-you'll-never-marry things.

Sometimes my father loves my mother—and the rest of us—so much that he becomes a kissing and hugging machine. Sometimes, though, he is an angry machine that sees suspicious moves in every breath. But most of the time he is sad, his thoughts somewhere I cannot visit.

I'll tell you what the scariest thing is: when he drinks. He doesn't do it that often and he doesn't have to drink that much before his eyes become bullets, his fists the curled hands of a boxer, and our living room the ring of Monday Night Wrestling.

"It's fire from hell," my mother says about the liquor.

I believe it. One time I went into the yard to look for a ball I had lost in the bushes the day before, and I found my father drinking. He grabbed my arm and held his bottle in front of me. "Drink," he said.

I didn't say anything.

"Drink, girl. What's wrong with you?"

"You said we should never drink from that."

"Well, you should always do as I say, and I want you to try it this time so you know what not to drink."

It sort of made sense, but I had a feeling I should not do it.

"Drink," he insisted and stuck the bottle under my nose. It had a horrible smell and I turned my face away.

"Drink, girl, and you'll never have to drink again."

I took the bottle, held my nose, and put it to my lips. As I lifted it in the air I felt fire catch on my lips and in my mouth and I spat it back out. My father glared at me. I got the stomach feeling.

"Drink."

I lifted the bottle again and I felt the burn on my tongue, on my throat, and down the inside of my neck. I swallowed fire. My father just sat and stared. He took the bottle from me, closed the top, put it back in the box, locked it and stood up. I remained where I was, but the fire went from my belly to his eyes and he pulled me by the arm and then by the ear and dragged me into the kitchen where my mother was cutting vegetables.

"Oh Mother of Shit," he called to her. "Your little dog of a daughter has been drinking. Smell her mouth."

My mother leaned over and sniffed my mouth and I closed my eyes. She slapped my face and the fire came back to me.

"He made me drink it," I screamed and saw my father's eyes enlarge.

"A drinker and a liar!" he shouted and started hitting me everywhere. I screamed and screamed and finally got free and ran to my room. I opened the closet and closed the door behind me and prayed to God the fire would burn elsewhere.

Auntie Maysoun made a party for my twelfth birthday. She cooked a lot of food and my cousins danced all night. We don't usually give each other presents, but my American Auntie Fay sent me a diary. It's pale green and has a shell on the cover. She wrote my name on the inside with a skinny black pen: KHADIJA MUNEER.

"Why would anyone want a book with blank pages?" Ma asked me.

"So I can write my own book," I told her in English.

Ma doesn't like Auntie Fay.

In the card she sent with the diary, Auntie Fay wrote, "The book is so you can write your secrets and no one will have to know them."

Ma, who doesn't read English, asked me what it said. Instead of saying "secrets," I said "stories and things," but I don't think she believed me and will probably have someone else read the card and translate it for her.

Mr. Napolitano, my social studies teacher, makes fun of everyone's name. He calls me DJ. It makes me laugh. He expects me to know more than the other kids because my parents are not American, though there are lots of other kids in the class who aren't American themselves. I want to scream at him that I am just as American as anyone here.

Ma and I have the same argument, only she gets really mad: "You are Palestinian," she says in Arabic.

"*You* are Palestinian," I tell her in English. "I am American."

"You are Palestinian and you should be proud of that."

"Ma, I can't speak Arabic right, I've never even been there, and I don't like all of those dancing parties. I like stories and movies. I can be American and still be your daughter."

"No! No daughter of mine is American."

We have this fight all the time. She is always telling Baba how shameful it is that I don't speak my language, that I don't mind her, and that I walk like a boy. I sort of like the boy part of what she says, because those girls are so silly—always brushing their hair and listening to music. I hate dancing in front of all those people. My boy cousins are more fun, but I'm not supposed to play with them anymore because I am getting too old.

Baba sometimes especially likes me because I'm his only daughter. (Mina and Monia are from Ma's first husband.) He used to let me sit with him and his friends, even when Ma wanted me to help her in the kitchen. I liked to listen to their stories and when they yell at each other about politics though they are all on the same side. But now I'm older and I have to cut vegetables.

I have a friend at school, but I don't tell my parents about him. His name is Michael and he's Jewish, but the real problem is that he's a boy and I'm not supposed to be friends with boys. He's very funny. When I first met him I forgot his name and called him David. I was so embarrassed, but then he called me Fatima and we were even.

"My grandmother died," he told me like he was telling me he saw such and such movie.

"I'm sorry," I told him.

"Thank you, but that is not the point of my story. We went to my uncle's house to pray for her. Did you know Jews face Jerusalem when they pray?"

I didn't know that. Michael likes to bring up the similarities between Muslims and Jews, I think to show that we can be friends. I just try to forget all those things and listen to his stories.

"I didn't either. It's funny, because if you were in Jerusalem, a Muslim and a Jew would face different directions, but by the time they come to America, it's all just east. So there we were at my uncle's house and we were supposed to face east, so we all faced the television and prayed, and I thought to myself, are we praying to the television god for my grandmother's soul? I mean, she never missed her soap opera, but really!"

See what I mean about him being funny?

Baba yells so much, mostly at the boys. He only gets mad at me if he's been drinking or when I do something really bad—like the time he caught me with my brother and my cousin and we were in the closet lighting matches. It wasn't even one of those big closets, but I guess we were so small we all fit nice and cozy. We were pretending that we were in the woods having a campfire.

When Baba found us, he yelled, "You are the shame of this family, trying to burn the house around you. Your mothers would have been better off if they had goats instead of you children!"

He got my brother first and hit him all over with his belt, and then my cousin. Both of them were screaming. Then he hit me with the belt and I screamed and cried for hours. He yells at Ma a lot too. Ma just stands there and mutters words I don't understand. I feel sorry for her.

It's been the longest time since I've written anything in my diary.

I have a new friend. Her name is Patricia, but she likes to be called Patsy.

I told Ma about her and she keeps saying, "Batzy, Batzy."

She is in my social studies class. Sometimes we would say hi to each other, but she seemed snobby. She has thick whitish-blond hair. It's always smooth and fluffy and she is constantly playing with it. Sometimes she lifts it up and when it falls it's like water cascading down her back.

I sit behind her if she takes the front-row seat that I like, and when she plays with her hair, some falls on my desk. Her hairs are so shiny, like plastic, and if you make a double knot, you can tie pencils together with them.

The first time I really talked to her was today. Mr. Napolitano was reviewing for our test on world capitals.

"Jordan, DJ?"

"Amman, Mr. Napolitano."

"Good. Of course that was an easy one for you."

"Burkina Faso, Pat-a-cake?"

Patricia didn't move and I knew she didn't know the answer because she doesn't ever know the European capitals.

"Patricia?"

I leaned forward and whispered, "Ouagadougou."

"Wagdoogoo."

"Very good, Patsy. I can see you have been studying."

When class was over, Patsy turned around and thanked me. "Do you want to eat together?"

"Sure," I said.

We talked a while and she's nice. Her eyes are so blue.

It's raining so hard now that it sounds like big men running back and forth on our roof. I hate the rain.

Baba's mother died twenty years ago today.

"Maybe that's why it's raining so hard," I said.

"Maybe." He seems sad today, quiet and gloomy.

Ma got mad because I have had a new school friend for three weeks now and I haven't had her over for dinner.

"You shamed?" she asked me in English, which made me feel pretty bad because it's sort of true. It's not that I'm ashamed, but there are things that an American wouldn't understand, like my mother's language or my father's yelling.

I invited Patsy over for dinner anyway, but I hope Ma cooks American food because I don't think Patsy and her blond hair will like our food too much.

We were at Auntie Maysoun's new house in Glendale. Everyone else, including my mother, was outside eating. I came in to bring some more soda and I heard Maysoun telling her sister-in-law, Dahlia, about my mother, her own sister.

"She lets them speak English at home," she hissed. "She treats them like American children. She cooks American food for them. The worst thing she does, though, is she lets them talk back to her. If my Tariq or Soraya did that, they would get a beating, and that would be the last of it. And talk about beatings . . ."

Then Auntie Maysoun went on and on about how Baba hits us too much and then again how Ma gives in to him and to us and is a softy which will make us very difficult and ultimately disloyal.

Ma says Maysoun is fake and talks big but has nothing inside her. Maysoun smokes a lot and wears gold jewelry and fancy sandals like a young bride. Ma also says Maysoun criticizes others so much because she can't accept that her own daughter is practically a whore.

That's another reason why it's better to be a boy, because then you don't have to spend all your time noticing what everyone does wrong.

Patsy came for dinner yesterday. Ma cooked *musakhan,* which is my very favorite so I couldn't get mad. She made French fries too, which Patsy couldn't believe.

"You actually *made* these French fries? They're not frozen? You cut them up and everything?"

Ma smiled and nodded, though I didn't think she understood what Patsy said. I started to explain in Arabic, but she interrupted me.

"I understand," she said in English.

Patsy even liked the *musakhan,* though she didn't eat that much, which is probably good because all of the olive oil and onions would have given her a stomachache and then she'd hate me.

Patsy asked me to a slumber party, and when I asked Ma she refused.

"You are not going to sleep anywhere outside this family until the day you are married."

I didn't argue. I knew that was what she was going to say. And even if she had said yes, Baba would probably have hit me just for asking.

When I told Patsy, she laughed. "How are you ever going to have sex with a boy if you always have to sleep at home?"

I felt funny, like she was laughing at me. I had never thought about sex with a boy before I got married. I know that American girls do that, and probably even my cousin Soraya, but that's different.

Scary is the rumor started by my brother Muhammad, whose two dollars I took to buy a barrette, that he saw me at school kissing Michael behind the gym at lunch and having Baba not believe me because he doesn't have any reason to.

Scary is when the yelling doesn't stop and when everyone has bruises "from the devil," as my mother says. I know better. I know they come because the sand sends him inside that small bottle of liquor he keeps locked in his toolbox and turns his insides into fire.

I went to Patsy's house for dinner. It was like going to a TV show.

They have a room where there's a huge television and her father sat in front of it the whole time I was there. He barely said hi or anything, just sat in front of the huge screen and stared.

Her mom came home after we had been there for an hour and she had a huge bucket of fried chicken. I was excited because we never get to eat food from outside.

Patsy has a little brother who is six, like Hamdan. He took one look at his mother and screamed, "Again? We have to eat fried rats again?"

"Shut up, Mickey."

He's named after the singer Mick Jagger.

I told Ma that Patsy had a little brother who was named after a rock musician and she gasped.

"Swear to God," I told her.

"*This* is the problem with America! Instead of naming their children after family or saints or heroes, they name them after rock stars. Who would believe such a thing?"

I laughed, but she didn't find it funny.

"Do they drink beer in front of you?"

"Who?"

"Batzy's parents."

"No."

My mother was silent. I knew what she was thinking. I knew she was remembering Jennifer, the other American friend I had.

Jennifer lived down the street and went to the same school. Everything in her house was hippie style, including her tiny bedroom that didn't have a door, just dangling pink beads. She was very nice, but she had an older brother who drank beer at all hours of the day, and looked at nasty magazines. The first time I went over there to play, she showed me a stack of them. All of them had naked ladies with huge breasts and I knew that I shouldn't be looking at them.

Jennifer and I played normal games too, but her feet smelled a lot and Ma encouraged us to play outside whenever we were at our house. One day Jennifer wore boots and the stink was so bad that Ma made her leave the shoes outside.

"Deadly. Doesn't she bathe?" Ma said in Arabic while Jennifer was sitting next to me. I pretended not to hear.

When Ma left the room, Jennifer showed me two of her brother's magazines that she had brought over.

I was looking through one of them, and on one page, there were nine small pictures of a blond woman with large lips. In the first picture she wore a white, man's shirt and black pants. In the next picture she wore the same shirt, no pants, and high-heeled black shoes. In the third picture she wore the black pants from the first picture, suspenders, and nothing else. The combinations continued until she was naked, except for her high heels and a bow tie, and was resting one foot on a black chair.

For some reason this picture fascinated me, which is why I didn't notice when Ma came in the room. Suddenly she was in front of me.

"What is that?"

Before I could answer, she grabbed it, and after a couple of seconds she screamed like I have never heard, and half of which I could not understand.

She looked at Jennifer and screamed in Arabic for her to leave. Jennifer ran, grabbing her shoes, but not stopping to put them on.

Ma slapped my face, cursed me, cursed America, cursed my father, and cursed God.

She burned the magazines and then dinner, which made Baba angry. But Ma decided not to tell him what I had done. I was not allowed to play with Jennifer after that.

I know this is what Ma was thinking when I told her about Mick and Patsy.

Ma was sick with something no one will explain to me and that they only talk about in whispers. I had to stay home from school to babysit Hamdan and Hamouda when Baba took her to the doctor's and then to the hospital. She had been very tired and grumpy and we didn't know what was wrong, especially since she didn't complain, just accepted her pain. I was scared for a while because she looked so scared, but she is much better now. She's better than when she was sick, and she's better than before that too. She is almost happy.

She invited Patsy's whole family to dinner—I think she's trying to make up for making me do everything when she was sick. She even said she'd make American food, for the sake of their blue eyes.

I finally have a secret, but it's an ugly secret and I'm not sure what to do with it.

Ma always used to tell my two half sisters about boys, especially American boys, and how they will take that secret thing between your legs for nothing. "No committer." That's why Mina and Monia were married so young. I think it's also because their father, my mother's first husband, was dead, and Baba wanted to get rid of the problem of unmarried girls in his house.

"Your husband has to be the one to take it from you," Ma told me once. "Otherwise you are a disgrace to us and we are stuck with you forever." Then she said in English, "You shameful."

One day I went over to Patsy's house after school. Her parents weren't there and the house felt quiet with no television on. I was surprised when the doorbell rang and Michael was there. At first I was happy to see him, but then I got a funny feeling and went back to the dining room table to do my studies. He was looking at Patsy funny and it seemed like he was someone else.

"We're going to go study in the back, OK, Kadeeja?" Patsy said, without even looking at me.

My ugly-sounding name sounded uglier than usual, and it seemed strange to me that she had me over but then was going to study in another room, but I said OK. I don't know how much time passed, but I started to feel panicky when I didn't hear any noise. I went toward her mother's bedroom, which is all pink and purple. I had been in there a couple of times before when we jumped up and down on the water bed. The door was closed. I knocked on the door. At first there was no answer, but then I knocked again, and Michael said, "Come in, Khadija." (One of the reasons I like him is because he says my name how it's supposed to be said.)

I don't know what I was expecting to see, but it wasn't Michael and Patsy under the covers in the water bed.

"Is everything OK?"

"Yeah, Kadeeja," Patsy said. "Just leave us alone, OK?"

I turned away and shut the door behind me. I felt horrible like can't see and can't think kind of horrible. My books were all over the place and I couldn't stuff them in my bag fast enough. I ran from her front door to our apartment building. Thinking about what I saw made me feel dirty, like when you go by a car accident and look by accident and on purpose at the same time, but then you feel sick because of what you saw.

When I got home, my mother was playing with little Hamouda, who is two and a half years old. When I saw them I started to cry.

"What's wrong, little cucumber? Are you sick?"

"Sick, sick," said Hamouda.

My mother hugged me and felt my forehead.

"I think I'm getting sick," I told her. "Lots of the kids at school are sick," I lied.

"You stay home with us and we'll make you better, won't we, Hamouda."

Hamouda looked at me and shouted, "Yes!"

My father is a traditional man, my mother says. That's why he is so strict and why I'm not allowed to talk to boys and why he wants to have more children, even though we are already four—six if you include Mina and Monia—and my mother can barely manage us as is.

"Like wild dogs," she screams, when we are driving her more crazy than usual. "Like wild dogs with ticks in your asses."

She doesn't say this around my father though, because he doesn't think women should swear and he'll slap her if she does.

Siddi (my father's father), who is staying with us for a while, is very old and sometimes smells of going to the bathroom, but he tells us stories and pats our heads and sometimes gives us candies. He even says nice things to Baba for us, but it takes him some time to get the words out and by then, my father loses his patience.

Once I heard my mother tell Monia that she thought Baba might be crazy because of all the things he did, but especially because he didn't respect his father properly.

That evening my father started talking about the sand that filled his dreams again. "How could you not be a little crazy when you have watched your dreams be buried the way I have?" he asked as if he had heard my mother's conversation.

Scary is the day Baba drinks the whole bottle—I know because I saw it empty outside by his car—and he goes inside and Hamouda is figuring out how talking works and he looks at Daddy and says "wild dog with a tick ass" plain as day, like he's been saying those words since time began.

Daddy sets on fire and I'm in the kitchen trying to be invisible and slap slap slap and the baby cries so I go to see and Hamouda's arm is in my father's teeth and blood and then Siddi comes up to hold my father or to take the baby from him, and my father hits him hard, his own father, and knocks him to the floor and then goes back to the baby who's just crying and crying and crying.

I do what I have never done. I pick up the phone and dial 911 like they say to do in school.

"You are at 755 Marengo Street?" the voice asks.

"Yes."

"What's your emergency?"

"My grandfather is on the ground. My baby brother too."

"Did they fall?"

"My father is hitting everybody!"

I come back. My father stops for a minute and stares and Hamouda stops crying for just a second and stares back, like he knows what my father could do. My father looks at his father lying on the floor, looks through me, and then he's down on the floor, right on top of Hamouda. At first Hamouda holds out his arm, thinking he's going to have hugs or get picked up, but then he feels the weight of my father's body and starts screaming even louder than before.

That's how the police find him when they come. My father's fire just goes away like it started raining inside him and he lets them take him, pull him off Hamouda who I pick up from the ground as soon as the police pick up my father.

Scary is whether my mother is going to get back from the store with Muhammad and Hamdan before the police take me and Hamouda away.

I close my eyes tight and imagine she's here. "It's OK, little cucumber," I whisper in English in Hamouda's ear. "We'll be OK. We'll be OK. God willing."

News from Phoenix

Joseph Geha

After three years in America, Isaac's mother was still afraid of Jews. Damascus remained fresh in her, the dark evenings huddled with her sisters, fearful and giggling around the brazier while her uncle told stories. He was an archimandrite in the Maronite church, and even now Sofia trembled at the thought of him. His cassock reeked of sweat and incense, and she remembered, too, the thick bitter smell of the Turkish anise drink he favored, how his beard glistened with oil as he sipped—and such stories! No! She put both hands to her ears and shouted at her husband: "Amos!"

Who paid no attention. It was closing time, and Isaac's father stood at the cash register counting money. His lips made the quick, breathy sounds of numbers.

"Amos, they are Jews!" she shouted. "Jews!" as if that word said it all, and anyone who had an ounce of sense would understand.

Isaac was almost six years old and he had heard her stories, her uncle the archimandrite's stories, of what Jews did to little Christian children, of throats slit and blood taken for secret ceremonies, the children found white and limp in the morning, thrown into some alley behind the weavers' market or the gold *souq*. Even so, he did not understand. (What had Charlotte and Erwin Klein to do with all that?) But he became frightened anyway. Somehow there had been danger in the ride downtown for ice cream and the little gifts Charlotte had bought. He and his brother had just had a narrow escape, that much he understood, and he began to cry. Then Demitri, younger than Isaac by three years, took his thumb from his mouth and gave out that slow, toneless wail of his that understood nothing except that Isaac was crying.

"Hoost!" The sound came from their father, and immediately the boys fell silent. "Izraiyeen take you!" Amos cursed his wife with the angel of death. He slapped the money into the cash drawer. "Look how you're scaring them—why?" His voice was big, although he was not yet shouting. That would come. "Give them back the toys." He wiped his hands across the belly of his apron and waited.

Sofia lowered her eyes. Then, whispering a prayer against the Evil Eye, she handed the package of crayons to Isaac and the balsa-wood airplane to Demitri.

"Hoost!" Amos said again. She turned away, but her lips continued to move, silently, as little as the syllables of the prayer would allow.

Demitri tossed the airplane, and the four of them watched it float up in a gentle arc. It banked just shy of the flypaper that hung in coils above the butcher block, hesitated, then dropped abruptly into a banana crate.

"G'wan now," Amos said in English. "G'wan, take da ara-blane downstairs."

They obeyed, Demitri following Isaac into the cellar. Beneath the stairs was the toilet stool. Isaac nudged the lid down with his toe, then sat listening to the voices above while his brother threw and chased the airplane among the racks of empty soda pop bottles. His father's shouting, when it came, would be full of curses, but it would be brief. Afterward a silence would fall between them, stiff with exaggerated politeness; and in the silence his curses—of blood, of lineage and the womb that gives issue—would hover above the tiny store and the flat upstairs until finally, through small familiar signals of regret, Amos would take them back one by one.

And the two of them would have something warm to drink then, they always did. Sofia lit the gas burner and stirred the base of the Turkish samovar around and around in the flame, adding anise seed in pinched doses until its strong licorice smell filled the kitchen, and still Amos would say, "More . . . more," and she would add another pinch, and yet another. The yellow brew, called *yensoun*, remained syrupy even after it settled. Amos drank it that way. Into her own cup Sofia first spooned plenty of sugar, and when she poured for herself she poured *yensoun* and cream at the same time, two-handed, lest the cream curdle in the strong brew.

Sometimes Isaac asked for a taste, but always they told him no, that it was too strong for children, and they would send him out of the kitchen. So he would sit in the front room and listen to the silence dissolve between them, Sofia gazing into the dregs of Amos's cup and finding journeys there, money, business for the store, news from a friend. Her voice would grow high, childlike with foretelling, and soon Amos would be laughing.

Because, after all, his wife wasn't a mean woman. He told people that. More like a child, he told them, she believed everything. Blood and secret ceremonies—an uncle's bogeyman stories! And would an archimandrite, in the Latin rite equal to a monsignor, tell such horrors to a child? Probably not. Probably she simply remembered the stories that way, adding his authority to them later, as children sometimes do; and who would curse a child? Especially one so often ignored, left to herself here in a tiny flat above a tiny store, surrounded by taverns and pawnshops and the blue-eyed bums asking for wine. America was hardly what a child must have expected it to be. A child, he told people, given to petulance when things were boring, when the weather was hot and there was nothing to do.

Isaac pressed his nose to the door screen and stared at the way the air wiggled between buses and trucks and automobiles when there was a red light. Too hot for business, his father had said. Amos was sitting behind the counter with his cousin Milad, playing a hand of *baserah*. There had been no customers for hours. Sofia stood at the display window with a piece of newspaper, fanning herself and Demitri, who stood close by her despite the heat. It was quiet in the store, only flies and the rustle of paper. Now and then Uncle Milad would mutter something at his cards—Arabic or English, it was hard to tell with the cigar in his mouth.

"But there is nothing to do in this country!" Sofia shouted as if in the middle of an argument. Isaac started at the suddenness of her voice. The men looked up. Amos kinked an eyebrow but said nothing, and after a moment Milad gathered the cards and began shuffling them.

"The children! Poor things, look how they have nothing to do."

"Take them to the park," Amos said. He nodded for Milad to deal.

"I do not know the buses." Milad dealt, and the men studied their cards.

"I do not know the buses," she said again. "You must come with us."

Amos glared up at her. Even Isaac understood: customers or no, business is still business.

"Have they been to the *arta muzeem?*" Milad asked.

"Truly," Amos said, "take them to the *ara muzeema.*"

"What is that?"

"It is free. They have pictures on the walls. You can go look at the pictures."

"And sometimes music, too," Milad said. "Violins, pianos."

Sofia thought a moment.

"And in the summer," Milad added, *"aira condition."*

"Still, I do not know the buses."

"You do not have to change buses," Amos said. "It is right here on Monroe Street. That way, not even four kilometers."

"The driver will not understand me."

Milad put down the cards. "I will take them in my *machina.*"

"Sit down," Amos said. "It is your play."

Sofia knew only the Adams bus that went downtown and the Jefferson bus that brought her back. Her English was still terribly broken, even after three years; some said she wasn't even trying to learn. Charlotte Klein had offered to drive her to a high school where English was taught at night, but Sofia refused to go. She wouldn't leave the children alone, she said. Also, Charlotte Klein was a Jew.

"Take the bus on the corner and say to the driver: *De ara muzeema,*" Amos said. "Sit behind him, and he will tell you when he reaches it."

"*D'Aram muzeema,*" Sofia sighed; then she put down the news-paper. "*D'arama amuzeema.*"

Amos gave her money from the cash drawer. "And dress up the boys," he said.

She washed Isaac and Demitri and had them put on the blue trousers with suspenders and the white shirts they wore for church. Then she packed a shopping bag with lunch.

When the bus arrived, Sofia told the driver several times but he still couldn't understand her. Finally, Isaac tried, speaking slowly and carefully, and the man appeared to understand. They sat behind the driver, Demitri moaning a little because he was still afraid of buses and the noise of traffic. While Isaac wasn't afraid, he could never seem to get used to the diesel smell that buses had, nor the whine of gears building, but not enough, not quite enough, before the releasing lurch and hiss of the air brakes. It went on that way for blocks until at last the driver turned to them. "This is it," he said.

Sofia looked at him.

"Your stop, ma'am."

Sofia smiled.

"The art museum," the driver said. "Ar-rt mew-see-uhm."

Isaac understood first and took his mother's hand. But after the bus had moved away, leaving them on the sidewalk, they saw no art museum, no pictures on walls; only a hot summer confusion of streets and buildings and changing traffic lights. Although there were signs set low in the power-trimmed lawns, the words were meaningless to them. After a moment Sofia took a few steps in one direction, turned —the boys wheeling beside her in wide arcs—and started in another; then she stopped. She began to curse the art museum and the bus driver and Amos, too, using not the exact pronunciation of the profanity but changing a letter or a syllable, therefore cursing but not the words of cursing, not the words of anything, and so not a sin.

They crossed the street and waited for the homeward bus. But no sooner had they sat on the bench than they began to hear music from, it seemed, just around the corner. They listened to it a while. Finally, the return bus nowhere in sight, they picked up the shopping bag and turned the corner.

The music was coming from loudspeakers atop the roof of a small white building. There were pictures painted on the walls and windows, bright cartoon shapes of blue and yellow and orange. Little plastic pennants flapped from wires. Above it all, high on a white post, was a painting of a red horse with wings.

Sofia and Isaac and Demitri sat down on the tiny lawn in front of the place, took out their lunch—lamb meat patties, turnips pickled in beet juice, rolled grape leaves, olives, and cheese and fruit—and began to eat.

"*Aira condition,*" Sofia snorted. She fanned herself with a piece of wax paper.

Automobiles drove onto the lot, and the attendants in spotless new uniforms immediately began polishing the windshields. Children pointed and laughed from backseat windows. Someone in a green car, a woman or a young man, yelled, "Hey, Gypsies!" as the car pulled into traffic. Sofia understood that word. She stood and cast a sign after the car—thumb and two fingers clenched, the fig—and shouted as she did so, forgetting to change the letters or the syllables. Sitting down again, she said a blessing to erase the curse.

A horn honked from the street behind them. The boys turned together; it was Charlotte and Erwin Klein. "Mama, Mama!" Demitri shouted in the only English he knew. Sofia would not turn to look. "Hoost," she said. When Demitri began to move, she grasped him by the suspenders and pulled him down. Charlotte got out of her car, smiling as she always smiled whenever she saw Demitri. She bent over and spoke to Sofia in careful, distinct English. Isaac understood. She was offering them a ride home. Sofia also understood (that much Isaac could tell) but she opened her hands and shook her head no. "*Yahood,*" she said to Isaac and Demitri, *Jews,* so they would understand.

Charlotte was a small, very thin woman. She had straight hair, and Isaac thought it pretty just now how outdoor light changed it from blond to almost red. Her eyes, however, weren't pretty at all. Magnified by glasses, they seemed too large for her face, and the harlequin slant of the frames made them look squinty. But Isaac never paid much attention to eyes; he would always remember hers as blue, maybe. It was mouths that he looked to. Tears or laughter or anger, for him it was the turn of the mouth that each time signaled first, and not the eyes. (Once, when Amos had removed his belt and stamped after the boys as they cowered together in a corner, Isaac pulled loose of Demitri and said, "Papa, your pants are gonna fall down!" and he remembered how his father had stopped short, and, although his eyes never blinked even, one side of his mouth began working against the laughter. Twisting and clenching against it, before he dropped the belt and shuffled into the kitchen where Mama was already laughing.) Charlotte had a wide, full-lipped mouth, with that little bleb of flesh in the center of the upper lip that Isaac would forever like in a woman, associating it somehow with generosity and kindness.

Charlotte looked back at the car. She exaggerated a shrug, and Erwin waved her the come-on sign with his arm. Sofia continued to smile at all this as if she understood none of it. Charlotte talked a moment with Erwin at the car; then Erwin went inside the white building and stood at the pay phone in the window. When they drove away, Sofia was still smiling, looking straight ahead.

Only minutes passed before Milad pulled up in his ancient creaking automobile and told them to get in quickly, quickly. When they got home, Amos was furious.

The building where the Kleins lived and where Erwin Klein had his law office was within walking distance of the store, but toward downtown and away from the bums; an area where the streets began to be lined with trees and shrubs set in white half barrels. Doormen wearing gold braid stood beneath scalloped marquees fringed with gold. The buildings they served housed expensive shops on the lower floors, as well as the offices of doctors, brokers, attorneys like Erwin Klein. From the paneled lobbies elevators carried residents to their apartments. One rainy afternoon Charlotte took the boys up there with her, to the elegant quiet of her living room, where Demitri was fascinated by his blue image in the blue-tinted mirror top of the coffee table.

She had no children. Married in her mid-thirties and resigned, it seemed, to never having them, she made Demitri her favorite. It was only natural; Demitri had the deep brown eyes that women liked, and his mile-a-minute Arabic must have sounded cute to an American. Demitri took to her as well, and soon she was driving him to the dime store or the Saturday movies. Of course, Isaac went, too, so there would be no jealousy.

Sofia raised her voice against all this, "In their temple they learn the Evil Eye!" and Amos would blow up at her, "Think of it, a woman childless at her age, just think of it!" Then he would add, "You are no neighbor."

Two years ago, when Milad Yakoub first sold the butcher shop to Amos, it was Erwin Klein who had taken care of the legal matters—the loan, the transfer of deed, licenses for beer and wine to carry out. "He understands business," Milad had told Amos in Arabic. "Trust him and keep your mouth shut." And so when Erwin advised that the name, "Yakoub Market," was worth something to the business, Amos kept his mouth shut and did not change the name of the store to his own. Later, when Erwin suggested a line of party products—soft drinks and packaged snack foods—Amos trusted the advice. He ordered from the wholesaler according to a list Erwin drew up for him, and he realized a profit and an increase in business.

"This one," Amos told the boys in English, "he is schooled," and he would raise one hand toward Erwin, indicating a respectful silence.

Erwin did look like a smart man; he had a high wide forehead, glasses, and a straight, even line of a mouth that could answer squarely to anything, or so it seemed to Isaac. He was very tall, too, and very, very skinny. "He was sick probably all his life," was how Sofia saw it. "Probably his mother had thin milk." And indeed there was a kind of sickliness about him, even his laugh; you expected it to be bigger than it was. Nevertheless, he did laugh, breaking the respectful silence as he lifted Demitri up almost to the ceiling of the store. Then he would pick up Isaac, too, so there would be no jealousy.

In June of their third year in America, Amos received a letter from St. Patrick's School informing him that Isaac would not be admitted into the first grade. That same morning he took both boys and walked them hand in hand to the school. Two nuns who were standing in the foyer with their black book bags made a fuss over Demitri, and Amos let them. Then he asked to see the nun whose signature appeared at the bottom of the letter.

She was an old woman with a quick, friendly smile, and yes, she remembered Isaac well. Several weeks before, she had observed him during a series of tests, how he'd fretted in tight-lipped defeat over nursery rhymes and geometric puzzles and even her own simple directions. So, when Amos began to explain that his son was bright and his only problem was that he didn't know English well enough yet since they almost never spoke it at home, her smile vanished. She interrupted him with a stiff shake of her head, no. Amos tried again—"Maybe, Mum, wit' the extra help," and "Maybe wit' special books"—but the more he tried the more she seemed to grow impatient. Isaac could see it all in the set of her mouth. Finally, when his father asked to speak with the principal, her lips formed a rigid curve: *These people,* she was thinking. But she didn't want trouble, Isaac could see that too, and after a moment she signaled them to follow her down the polished halls to the office.

The principal must have been expecting them; she was adamant from the start. "This boy," she said, busily moving a sheaf of papers from one corner of her desk to the other, "is simply not ready for first grade, at least not at St. Patrick's." And that was all. An uneasy silence followed; then the principal stood up as if to dismiss them. But Amos remained seated, smiling; he was trying everything.

"Listen, Mum," he said, "I have a joke . . ."

He usually tried this with customers when they complained about prices or the freshness of the meat. The joke was one of his funny ones, about the rabbi and the priest. Even so, the principal kept a stone face all through it; when it ended, she was actually frowning.

Outside, Amos cursed both nuns by name, a short vicious curse concerning, as Isaac would always remember, nipples and squirting blood.

Then he brightened. He hitched his trousers and told the boys to wait for him here on the school steps while he went across the street.

Beyond the traffic Isaac saw a row of small shops. "What for, Papa?"

"What for? Telephone. Never mind what for!"

Isaac watched him go. He looked silly, hurrying off toward a phone booth in those large gray trousers, the butt-fold wagging left-right-left like a tail. But Isaac could not turn away from it; his eyes fixed themselves on that rear as it worked anxiously through the indifferent roar of Monroe Street for his sake alone. Poor butt; his father was trying everything.

When Amos returned, he gathered the boys to him and sat down on the steps beneath the principal's window. He began to sob loudly, all the time muttering curses and wiping his eyes with a red handkerchief, although Isaac could see that there was nothing to wipe. Now and then Amos would look up at the window, pause, then bury his face in Isaac's neck or Demitri's curls. At last the door opened, and soon Isaac was again sitting with his brother in a corner of the principal's office.

She was still firm, but this time she spoke slowly, in little words, the way some people talk to bums. But this time it was Amos who interrupted. "I called up a friend onna telephone," he said. "Him he's gonna talk for me."

The principal sighed. "All right," she said, "all right."

Finally, Erwin Klein arrived. He had on sneakers and tennis shorts and a white V-neck sweater, but when he began talking everything changed. He spoke such perfect English—so rapidly Isaac could barely make it out—and with such confidence that he looked the principal directly in the eye. He didn't look sick at all that day. He was handsome without his glasses, sunburned on the cheeks and forehead, and skinny, yes, but so much taller than Amos. When he was finished, the principal's stone face had relaxed into a smile. "Well, yes," she agreed, "I suppose it's worth a try."

At that, Amos made an exaggerated, grateful bow. *"Kes umeek,"* he said in Arabic, *Your mother's vulva*. She smiled. Demitri began to giggle, and she reached out and touched his curls the way a mother would. Isaac could see then that she wasn't a mean person, not really. She just didn't want trouble.

And so Isaac was admitted into the first grade. With the help of a novice nun who tutored him after school, his English improved greatly, and by the following June he would become one of the five gold-star readers in his class.

Amos showed his gratitude to the Kleins: the groceries he had delivered to their door were always wholesale. And even Sofia's protests began to diminish; eventually, she said nothing at all. It was in October of Isaac's first year of school that she told her husband about the slowness she'd been noticing in Charlotte, a slight change in her walk, and the way her mind seemed to be on other things. Then one night Sofia dreamed of a death, and she awoke laughing.

"Good news!" she said at breakfast. "Soon they will have their own."

"How?" Amos was still in his nightshirt.

"In dreams, death always means a birth."

"Who died?"

"Missus Charlotte—so it will be a boy. Think of it, they will have their own now."

"Inshallah," Amos said. *God willing.*

But even in the happiness of that moment, while his mother stirred the samovar of *yensoun,* clucking on like a nested pigeon, Isaac saw his father's eyebrow go up in doubt.

The doubt vanished one Saturday afternoon, only a week or so later, when Erwin stopped by the store. It seemed one of his usual after-lunch visits except that when he spoke his voice had a forced casualness to it. Finally, unable to mask his feelings any longer, he told Amos that Charlotte had seen the doctor and that, yes, it was certain.

Amos laughed. "Good news!" he said in Arabic, echoing Sofia's words. Then he leaned over the butcher block and muttered something that Isaac didn't catch, and both men began to laugh. Leaving Sofia to watch the store, Amos led Erwin into the back room and opened a bottle of Jewish wine with the star on it.

Less than a month later, the baby was born dead. When the phone rang with the news, Isaac was doing his after-school chores, carrying empty soda pop bottles down the basement stairs to sort them.

"Missus Charlotte!" Amos smiled. And forever in Isaac's memory of that day his father would be standing at the pay phone, smiling and listening, and his smile fading. "No, Mum, he is not here. He was here after the lunch, but not now. Downtown, he tell me."

Sofia, too, had sensed something wrong. She put Demitri down from her lap and stood up.

"He don' say no more"—his voice was shaking now—"only downtown. No, Mum, I don' know where." He listened a moment more, then nodded his head quickly and hung up. Rushing, searching his pockets, talking to himself and to Sofia, he scooped some dimes from the cash drawer and ran back to the phone.

"Where?" Sofia asked.

"He's downtown! Where? Shut up! Downtown!"

Amos inserted a dime and dialed. "Quickly!" he said over his shoulder, but Sofia was already out the door. Isaac saw her pass the display window, pulling on her coat as she hurried down the sidewalk in the direction of Charlotte's street.

A woman's voice came on the line. Amos was polite to her, but he could not keep his voice from shouting. Then there was Doctor Binatti's voice, big even over the phone.

Amos began in Arabic, caught himself, and started again in English. Then he noticed the boys, Isaac with pop bottles hanging from both hands, and he turned a little away and said the rest quietly into the receiver.

Hanging up, he said, "Close your mouth," and Isaac closed his mouth.

A customer came into the store, then another. Demitri began to fuss, and Isaac took his hand and led him upstairs for a nap. When he returned, his father was slicing liver for the first customer's order. After a while, Isaac went down into the basement and used the toilet, remembering later to jiggle the handle. Then he continued sorting —Coke, Hires, Whistle, and Crush. He came up again at the sound of the back door, but it was not his mother, only one of the bums looking to earn wine money. His father sent the man away; there wasn't any work. Later, Amos made liverwurst sandwiches. Demitri awoke from his nap, and they ate. Amos drank a beer after his sandwich. Sofia still was not back.

"G'wan, get out-a-side," Amos told the boys in English, but Isaac lingered in the back of the store. Demitri, eyes liquid and calm and understanding nothing, stayed by his brother.

When Sofia came in, her face was white. She sat on a stool behind the counter while Amos finished with a customer. She had been crying, and when she spoke she used Arabic so the customer would not understand. "Little, little," she began, so quietly that Isaac could barely make out the rest. "Small as my hand," she said, "but perfect." The customer left. Isaac crept toward the front so he could hear. "Perfect," Sofia said again. "Everything. It even had a little pee-pee."

Amos looked down and made a noise with his tongue, *tch*.

"And Mister Erwin?" he asked.

"He was downtown."

"Woman, I know that. Has he been told?"

She nodded. "He is there now. He is going with her to the hospital."

Amos made the sound again, *tch*.

"Even so, it is all as God would have it," Sofia said, and Amos looked at her. She smiled. "It did not die a Jew. While Doctor Binatti he was busy, I took water from the kitchen"—she was not looking at his face—"and gave it baptism."

Amos turned away from her. "Watch the store," he said. He came to the back of the store and stood there a moment, looking down at the spattered sawdust beneath the butcher block. Then he noticed Isaac. Nudging the boy aside, he lifted a soda pop crate and carried it down into the cellar.

Isaac listened at the doorway. He could hear the roar and suck of the toilet, its float frozen with rust. He heard his father lift the tank lid and adjust the valve. Then Isaac, too, picked up a soda pop crate.

Amos was standing before a row of bottle racks, head down, his arms loaded with bottles. He was sorting them. "Tch," he said when he heard Isaac behind him, but he did not send the boy away. After a minute, Sofia followed, carrying Demitri.

"What is it, Amos?" she asked, but he kept his back to her. "I shouldn't have?"

Amos turned around. Isaac could see that he was ready to blow up. Then it went out of his face. He sat down on a soda pop crate and put the bottles at his feet. "Is this how you watch the store? No matter." He spoke quietly. "No difference." Then he looked up, blinking into the lightbulb behind Sofia's head. "Go upstairs. Make *yensoun*," he said, his fingers dangling helpless among the bottles. "I want something warm to drink."

In December Amos phoned to invite the Kleins for Christmas Eve dinner. Although it was practically a last-minute idea ("So what if they are Jews," he told Sofia as he dialed, perhaps forgetting that the idea had been hers in the first place, "how can Christmas offend them?"), the Kleins not only accepted; they arrived, like a bachelor uncle, two hours early. "Before the stores close," they explained, and they took the boys to a shopping center—Isaac unsure about seeing Santa, Demitri breathless with excitement—and brought them back loaded with gifts. They brought red wine with them, too, with the star on it, and after dinner sat drinking and talking, asking Sofia about the customs of Christmas in the old country. Then they told of a vacation they were planning to begin in January, an extended tour of the Southwest and Mexico.

"To get away from Ohio's winter," Charlotte said. Isaac glanced briefly at Erwin. His face was pale, the corners of his mouth pinched in. There was a brief silence, and then Amos turned the talk to houses; he was seriously considering a place across town from the store. As he began to describe its two stories, its yard, and its real neighborhood, far from the bums and broken glass, Sofia's face glowed.

Then Charlotte confessed that they, too, were looking to move, and that this was another reason for their trip. Phoenix had wonderful sunshine, she said, year-round, and the—she paused—the facilities there had been highly recommended.

And it was then that Isaac began to sense that things were changing. Soon everything would be different, and somehow he would have to accustom himself.

Later, when the others were busy—Erwin putting together a toy Ferris wheel for Demitri, Sofia busy with dessert—Charlotte and Amos sat down together on the couch and began to talk very quietly. Isaac didn't think it was right to listen on purpose.

"And if anything happens to him," Charlotte removed her glasses and put them back on again, "well, I don't know what I'll do." But she said it as if she did know what.

After dessert there was, of course, *yensoun.* Charlotte and Erwin exchanged glances, then laughed in disbelief at the third or fourth time Amos called out "More!" and Sofia added yet another pinch.

They laughed again, afterward, when Sofia began reading the cups—journeys and money and love. The drink must have heartened her; she told how her uncle the archimandrite had taught her to read cups, and when she began to describe the man himself ("Hees beard, it come down to here, an' my father he said you can comb a pounda grease outta it!"), there was another peal of laughter.

But what if anything did happen? The thought came to Isaac amid the laughter, himself laughing. Erwin looked so thin, sitting back from the table now, balancing the tiny cup and saucer on the bone of his knee. And if anything did happen, then the news, when it came, would come from Phoenix.

Turning to the stove, Isaac took the samovar in one hand, the creamer in the other, and poured himself a cup as he'd seen his mother do it, two-handed. If she noticed, she said nothing; and his father, looking his way now, also said nothing. So Isaac took a sip. It was bitter despite the sugar and milk, and terribly strong, as he'd always imagined it would be. But somehow the adults had liked it. They were laughing harder than ever now, probably at the face he was making. Charlotte and Erwin had drunk theirs without even wincing. Maybe they were used to it, maybe he wasn't. He took another sip to accustom himself.

That night Erwin showed Isaac how to load his Christmas camera with color film, but when it was done and Isaac put his eye to the viewfinder, Erwin turned his face away. Isaac understood; there was no need for his father's warning, the raised eyebrow. Charlotte wore a blue dress that night.

AND WHAT ELSE?

JOSEPH GEHA

Only an hour or so after sunrise it begins getting hot on the street. But it is still quiet, and the faint honk and roar of the traffic farther downtown only adds to the silence and the sense of hush. A boy, who will one day marry an American girl and open his own supermarket with her family's money, begins sweeping with wide, playful strokes in front of the grocery store. Slanted morning light fills Monroe Street with yellow, pushing the shadows of lampposts and fire hydrants and boy down the long concrete. Scattered by the broom, wine bottles and beer bottles glisten as they roll along the curb to the gutter. The red brick of the buildings warms in the sun, the old, silent buildings that will be torn down twenty years from now, in the summer of 1958, and the holes they leave paved over.

Across the street a man turns the corner, a fishing rod and canvas sack in his hands. He is staring up as he turns, his eyes on the rooftops, and because of the silence of the morning, the slap-slap of his large shoes (he wears no stockings) carries all the way to where the boy has stopped sweeping to watch, shielding the sun from his eyes with what looks like a half-hearted salute. A woman, curled asleep in a doorway, stretches out her legs. The boy shouts a warning, but the man does not look down. He walks directly into the feet and stumbles forward on his hands and knees. He falls slowly, and it seems to the boy that with a little more balancing, a little more waving of the arms back and forth and trembling of the knees, he might not have fallen at all.

The man picks up the rod and sack and, saying nothing, nudges the woman several times in the legs with his toe. She stirs and rolls over, still asleep. The man moves on. When he has crossed the street, the boy puts a finger to his lips and points to the roof of the apartment above the store. A pair of pigeons flutter timid on the spine of a gabled window. The man sees. He smiles his thanks to the boy, then clicks the safety of his reel, and the heavy lead sinker, followed by a dozen hooks, falls and dangles about a foot from the tip of the rod. The boy salutes with both hands as he looks up again. One of the pigeons looks down from its perch, and the man casts. The heavy lead strikes, the hooks catch and dig. Blue-gray feathers fall in a small, thick cloud and the man and boy shout, filling the street with their noise.

"Got three of 'em for ya," the man says, and he dumps the sack on the thick wooden block in back of the store. "One of 'em's still alive."

The butcher, whose English is not so good, puts down his knife and takes the living pigeon out of the sack. "Habeeb," he says to the boy, his son, "get for this bum three bottlesa beer." The man smiles, grateful, and the butcher returns the smile as he twists the neck of the living pigeon. "An' I make you san'wich, too," he says.

Since there is a bar on either side of the grocery store, and three more across the street, and since, moreover, the store itself sells beer and wine to carry out, the word "bum" is the first English the boy and his father have learned. They use it as Uncle E, the owner of the store, uses it, brother to the boy's grandfather, who refers to neighborhood adults (those neither Syrian nor Lebanese) as bums, and who, on this summer morning, lies silent in his bed in the apartment upstairs, awake and thinking about—only God knows, for Uncle E has spoken to no one for nearly a year.

But when Uncle E ran the store, when his wife Maheeba was still living and the boy and his father were new to this country, he would stand behind his butcher block and shout to the boy's father, "Ya Milad! This bum, he's gonna sweep out the backa the store!" And Milad, the boy's father, would show the man the back room and a broom. Then the boy, a preschooler in those days, would be told to sit in the back (with a bottle of soda pop) and yell like hell if the man tried to run off with anything. But the bums never tried to run off with anything, not once in the boy's memory. When the job was finished Uncle E would cut the man a thick slice of liverwurst and open him a bottle of beer. And even if the man had not only done a good job (getting the sawdust out of the cracks in the floor) but was stone sober as well, Uncle E still called him a bum. He checked the back room and looked at the boy's father. "This bum, he did a good job." He had no other word. "You come back," he told the man, if the job was well done. The man would nod. Bums hardly said anything, and when they did their voices were high-pitched, asking for one more of something, a sandwich or a beer. But they never got it. Once Aunt Maheeba gave the boy a candy bar and sent him running after a bum, a very lean man, who had asked for another sandwich. He took it from the boy without a word, unwrapped it, and ate it as he walked away.

The next English the boy had picked up was "enwaddyelse." Uncle E said this when he completed an order for a customer. After weighing and wrapping a cut of meat, he placed the package on the counter, smiled at the customer, and asked in a pleasant voice, "Enwaddyelse?" And what else? Aunt Maheeba, too, said this after ringing an order through on the cash register. A regular customer said, "Nothing, thank you," or "That's all for now, thanks," but new customers did not understand at first. "Huh?" they said, or "Whazzat again?" So Aunt Maheeba would say it again, slowly and distinctly, just as she had learned it from Uncle E, "En-waddy-else?" If they still did not understand, she smiled her terribly charming smile that Uncle E talked so much about before his silence and handed over the change. "Tank-you verry much," she said, and this they understood.

But "enwaddyelse" was not used only with customers. Uncle E used it when his patience with Maheeba ran out. This usually happened when a customer came in with a large order. At such times the boy and his father roamed the small area of the store, finding the articles the customer asked for and bringing them to the counter. There, Uncle E would wipe his hands across the large stomach of his apron and begin wrapping with brown paper and string. As he did so, he read the price, which was marked in English, translated, and called it out in Arabic to his wife, who translated the Arabic to French and found the numbers on the cash register. At times, usually when she was suffering from one of her headaches, Aunt Maheeba would begin to cry as she muttered the numbers in French. After a little while she would sit on the small stool behind the counter and press an apron to her face. When this happened Uncle E knew that the last three or four prices he had called were not rung correctly. "Enwaddyelse!" he would shout, and take over the cash register. Then Aunt Maheeba would move to the end of the counter and wrap, reading the numbers in French, calling them out in Arabic. The work went slowly, then, for Aunt Maheeba was not quick at wrapping, and Uncle E, who found it difficult translating Arabic numbers to English, took his time.

With the boy, too, he often lost his patience. When the boy begged his uncle for a nickel (he was a softer touch than Milad, and Aunt Maheeba never had any money) the old man would at first refuse with a click of his tongue. Then as the boy insisted, anxious to buy a roll of caps for his toy pistol, Uncle E would say in Arabic, "Stop! Enough!" So the boy would sit at the bottom of the stairs that led up to the apartment, curl his lips, and sulk. After a few minutes of silence Uncle E would look up from the leg of lamb he was slic-ing. The boy, too, would look up, and their eyes would meet, look away, meet again, and Uncle E would wipe his hands, reach into his pocket, and slap a nickel on the butcher block. "Enwaddyelse?" And what else? The boy would grab the nickel and kiss his uncle's hand. "Truly," he answered in Arabic, "there is nothing else."

Milad soaks the pigeons in the sink behind the butcher block. Behind him, sitting on a wooden fold-out chair, the man who had caught the pigeons is finishing his second beer.

"This is a fine boy ya got here," he says to Milad, putting his hand on the boy's head and pressing down lightly.

Milad does not turn around. "Leave da kid alone," he says. He looks at the Coca-Cola clock above the sink. "G'wan, get Uncle E his oatmeal."

The boy ducks away from under the man's hand and runs upstairs to the kitchen. As he lights the stove with a match, he can hear Uncle E moving around in the bathroom on the other side of the wall. The oatmeal cooks, and the boy, who can only wait, stands on a chair and looks out the window at the flat tar roof and the pigeons that walk on it. The sun is higher now, and its heat rises from the black surface of the roof, making everything shimmer before the boy's eyes. He steps down and gets a bowl and spoon ready. Uncle E still has not come out. This makes the boy uneasy for he once found his uncle passed out and bloody on the toilet. Turning the fire off under the oatmeal, he knocks on the bathroom door. Uncle E opens almost immediately, smiles quickly, and shuts the door again. The boy cups his hands to the keyhole and says that the oatmeal is ready. Uncle E says nothing. He has said nothing for nearly a year.

"Doctor Binatti says it is goddamn stubbornness," Milad tells the different guests who visit after Mass every Sunday. "He even called specialists and they could find nothing wrong with his voice."

"The poor man is past seventy," one of the guests would always say.

"And strong as a mule," Milad says to this.

"He has had an operation, and still his stomach pains him."

"And still he sneaks his whiskey."

"It is for the pain," the guest would say. "He has lived to see the death of his children, and now his wife too, God give her rest."

"God give her rest, she has been dead more than a year. Grief should not last this long."

"She was young."

"Doctor Binatti was right."

"Not even fifty."

"Goddamn stubbornness."

Aunt Maheeba, though never really a robust person, had seemed healthy enough just the same. Yet she died one night in the middle of her sleep. Uncle E had called up the stairwell to her, yelling for his breakfast, shouting that customers were coming in already. Finally he sent Milad upstairs to find out why she did not answer. And when Milad came back down his face was yellow. "Get Doctor Binatti, quickly, quickly," he told his son in Arabic. So the boy ran up Monroe Street to the doctor's office above the barbershop, and Doctor Binatti took his black bag from a shelf behind the desk, shouted at the nurse who had just taken her coat off, and hurried after the boy. (In later years the boy would go to Doctor Binatti's office on the twelfth story of the downtown medical building. The doctor would hug the boy and in his huge and booming voice he would say, so that all the waiting room could hear, "Habeeb, Habeeb, when you came to this country you were fulla worms and I had to clean you out!" Then he would kiss the boy on his forehead and ask what was the matter. The boy would say, very quietly, "The flu," or "My nose is plugged up again." Doctor Binatti died in 1954 of a heart attack. At the time he was chief surgeon for Mercy Hospital, and he died at the hospital, in an elevator.)

Aunt Maheeba was in bed. She had died there in the night, and Uncle E thought she was still sleeping when he got up to open the store. Doctor Binatti said he wasn't sure, but he thought it was a blood clot. Then Uncle E, who had been quiet and shaking all this time, spat on the floor and at the top of his voice goddamned blood clots; he goddamned Doctor Binatti; he goddamned the boy and his father and himself; and he went downstairs to close the store, goddamning the customers as he chased them out.

The Maronite priest from Cleveland came and said a Syrian funeral. Afterward, at the cemetery, Uncle E picked a white carnation from a wreath that was placed near him and dropped it into the open grave. Then he opened his mouth (he wept like a child, with his mouth open) and began the wail, "Ya Maheeba, ya Maheeba," and his voice broke the hearts of all the mourners. So they joined him in the lament until the tears choked off their own voices and they stood dumb, dropping flowers into the hole. The boy, too, picked a carnation and, stepping up close to the lip of the grave, threw the flower in. He swung his whole arm into it, and the flower shot down and struck the casket lid with a hollow knock. The sound was loud, seemed to come from within the box, and the boy ran to find his father's knees.

"It is a hard thing," Uncle E used to say after that. He would be standing over the butcher block, slicing a thick liver with smooth strokes or flipping a carcass to where he could cut the meat from the bone. The customer would stand on the other side of the scale and answer him in Arabic.

"It is God's will, bless His name."

"Bless His name," Uncle E would say, using the standard response. But after a pause he'd add, "She should not have been the first."

"Elias," the customer would say to this, "there is nothing to be done. God give her rest, she is with the saints."

"I am past seventy," he'd say. "I should be with the saints," and he'd wipe his hands on the already bloody apron. "Not Maheeba."

"Elias, if you talk too much about her, God give her rest, you will make yourself sick." And Milad, standing behind the cash register, would agree. "There is nothing more to say, Uncle."

Then Uncle E would wrap the customer's order and ask if there was anything else. "That's all," the customer would say. "Just don't make yourself sick."

But Uncle E had made himself sick. His stomach hurt him, and he refused to eat Milad's cooking. Instead he fixed his own meals, sandwiches of raw lamb meat ground with onions and cracked wheat. In the evenings he sat in the alley in back of the store with two or three bums. The boy joined them sometimes, hidden in the darkness, until a glance from his uncle sent him back into the store. The old man, older in the light of the small bulb above the back door, drank whiskey then, for the pain, and he talked about the store, Roosevelt, the old country, but never about Maheeba, not to the bums. They sat or squatted over the stones of the alley, listening to him, drinking from the bottle as it came around. When the bottle returned to Uncle E, he wiped its mouth with the palm of his hand.

Finally, because the raw meat did not heal his stomach, and the whiskey did less and less for the pain, Uncle E saw Doctor Binatti.

"Elias, what's the trouble?" The doctor's giant voice echoed into the waiting room where the boy sat between two women, paging through a comic book he could not read.

"The pain, Doctor. I got pain."

"Elias, you were born with pain, you live with pain, you're gonna die with pain! Take off your shirt."

"Enwaddyelse?" This was angry, and the boy looked up toward the closed door. But a moment later one of them mumbled something, and the laughter of both their big voices shook the office. A woman in a corner chair smiled at the boy. He turned sideways on the couch and stared straight at the comic, his face in a pretended scowl. He knew he was cute and that American ladies were not used to seeing such curls. With a little twist of his head he made a face in her direction. She chuckled and looked away, smiling at the far wall.

For several weeks Uncle E took the milky-white medicine that Doctor Binatti had prescribed, ate only the foods listed on a paper the nurse had given him, and, for a while, even stopped drinking whiskey. But still he talked.

"It is a hard thing," he would say to the boy's father, and to customers in the store, and to relatives when they came to visit on Sundays. "It is a hard thing," and he would nod his head; and the listeners would nod their heads and say nothing.

"Why is it you say nothing?"

"Elias, is there anything else to say? God give her rest, she is with the saints."

"The saints!" He spat on the floor. "Goddamn every one of them! Listen to this . . ." And Uncle E would tell another of his stories about Aunt Maheeba, about how she was a child when he met her in the old country and she could already read and write French, or about the courage she showed at the funerals of both their sons, how she got him to go to Mass several times, even how it was to go upstairs after opening the store and find her sitting at the kitchen table with her black hair undone, brushed down her back, and breakfast smelling just ready.

The boy sat with the others and listened. When the story was finished, he, too, was silent.

In September, before he started school, the boy had found Uncle E on the floor of the bathroom. The toilet was full of blood, and he began to scream down the stairwell to his father. His father ran up the stairs, and one of the customers called an ambulance.

At Mercy Hospital, Doctor Binatti came out of the emergency room and told Milad to send after a priest. The boy began to cry when he heard this, and the doctor picked him up and carried him into the elevator. He tickled the boy on the way up and left him in the lobby with a comic book from the gift shop.

The boy waited and, as time passed, grew hungry. The clock on the wall was no help, for the movement of its hands meant nothing to him in those days. He was beginning to doze when the elevator door opened and the doctor walked out, followed by the boy's father. They were laughing. This made the boy cry again and he rushed up to hug the two men.

"Bullshit? Is that what he said?" Doctor Binatti asked, and laughed even harder, leaning on the elevator door.

"Boolsheet," Milad said. "He open up his eyes and seen the priest putting oil on his head, and he said 'Boolsheet' and went right back asleep." Laughing, he picked his son up and hugged him. "You kiss Doctor Binatti's hand," he said, "because himself he stop the bleeding." The boy tried, but the doctor stuck his hands in his coat pockets and said, "Boolsheet." Then the boy said "Enwaddyelse?" in a tone of mock impatience, and the three of them stood laughing in front of the open elevator.

With administration of the Last Sacrament, Uncle E's long silence had begun. The next day there was an operation, and Doctor Binatti removed part of the stomach. During the whole of his hospital recovery Uncle E spoke to no one, answering questions with a tired nod of his head for yes or a click of his tongue for no. At home he did not go back to work, but stayed in his room, in his bed. Guests who came all the way from Cleveland or Detroit to see him sat in his bedroom talking among themselves, or simply staring at the bed. And propped up by pillows, he would stare back at them. Soon they would stand up and go into the living room, saying to Milad, "That is not like Elias at all. He has lost weight. His face is all eyes."

Doctor Binatti had specialists come over, but they could find nothing wrong with the throat or the tongue. They wheeled him back to the hospital for X-rays, and the X-rays showed nothing, and they brought him home again. And still he was silent. So Milad and the doctor tried trickery. They surprised the old man by sending for people he had not seen in years, Aunt Anissa from New York, Danny the butcher from the old store on Congress Street in Detroit. But he merely wept and hugged the visitors and kissed them on the neck. They tried funny stories, and he smiled at them, silently. Milad even woke him in the middle of a deep sleep. But this, too, failed, for the old man opened his eyes and calmly waited for Milad to say something. And realizing that Milad had nothing to say, he closed his eyes and went back to sleep. "It is not depression," Doctor Binatti had finally said, "it is goddamn stubbornness."

The boy ladles the oatmeal into a bowl and pours milk over it. Through the kitchen doorway he can hear the grind and ring of the cash register. Customers, he thinks. His father will want him to come down soon and help out. Beyond the wall the toilet flushes, roaring and sucking. The boy sticks a spoon in the oatmeal.

Uncle E is sitting up in bed when the boy nudges the door open and enters, the bowl in both hands. The old man smiles his thanks and begins to eat, but the boy does not leave. He stands at a corner of the bed, his dark eyes scheming as they scan the photographs and holy pictures on the wall. A few moments pass, and Uncle E smiles again, this time a brief, impatient smile that means his nephew should leave now. The boy knows that smile well, but he waits still a moment more before leaving. Closing the door behind him, he hurries to the kitchen and runs downstairs to the store. His father is making change for a customer. When he finishes, he turns to his son.

"Put the soup up."

"Feel my forehead, Baba," the boy asks in Arabic.

"You sick?"

"I don't know."

Milad puts his lips to the boy's forehead. He feels that it is, perhaps, just a little warm. "Go upstairs, get in bed," he says in Arabic.

The boy trudges to the stairs and climbs slowly until he reaches the top. Then he rushes to his uncle's room, enters, and sits in a chair at the foot of the bed. The old man, napping after his breakfast, is startled and sits up. But the boy says nothing. He stares at his uncle, looks him full in the eyes from his place at the end of the long bed. The old man waits, then lays his head back against the pillows and gazes at the ceiling. The boy looks up there too. There is a small crack and, in a corner, a water stain. There is nothing else.

Uncle E pats the bed with the flat of his hand, another signal that he would like to be alone. But the boy does not leave. He puts his feet on the rung of the chair and traces with his eyes the flowered pattern of the pillowcases. The old man releases a great breath of air and seems to fall asleep. Outside the curtained window pigeons mutter in high, throaty voices on the flat roof of the bar next door. That and his uncle's soft snores lull the boy, and the sound of his own deep breathing soon falls into the rhythm of the room's quiet murmur. He sleeps uneasily in the chair, dreams he is falling, and wakes with a shudder to catch himself, safe, still seated. Uncle E raises his head and, with one eye open, sees that the boy is still there. He makes a terrible face, but it seems to plead more than threaten, and the boy turns to the wall. Time passes quickly, for soon the boy is hungry. He has been studying the face on the pillows, the large nose with its deep black nostrils, white hair in the ears; but now he is hungry, and he goes into the kitchen.

When he returns, with a poached egg on toast for his uncle and a liverwurst sandwich for himself, the old man is sitting up and seems, by his half smile, in a better mood. As they eat, the uncle watches his nephew, waiting for him to say something. But he says nothing. The boy clears his throat once while swallowing, but nothing follows. There is only the chewing and the silence and the pigeons outside. The man cannot eat, and the boy finishes only part of his sandwich.

It is beginning to get dark in the apartment. The boy puts the plates and the oatmeal bowl in the kitchen sink, goes into the bathroom, and turns on the light. There are a few drops of blood on the lip of the toilet bowl. He feels a pain, sharp and tight in his stomach, and he runs into the bedroom and finds the light switch. As the overhead light snaps on, the old man sits up and throws a pillow at the boy. "Uncle E!" the boy shouts, and the flowered pillow strikes him in the chest and knocks him backward against the door. He tosses the pillow aside and stands glaring into his uncle's eyes. Then slowly, deliberately, he turns to one side and spits. Nothing comes from his mouth, only the sound.

The old man leans forward. "Enwaddyelse?" he asks sharply, and his voice is high-pitched and full of breath.

They continue to stare at each other, uncle and nephew, and the boy trembles as though with fever, but he says nothing. He nears the bed, takes his uncle's hand and kisses it. "We will eat pigeons tonight," he says, and his uncle nods.

Less than a month later the boy will stand in the sunshine of the cemetery, weeping with the other men, wailing his uncle's name. But he does not join the others in the throwing of flowers, when that time comes, not at this funeral nor at any of the other many funerals he will attend: his father's when cancer takes him, that of a teacher he loved in high school, the sad and painful funeral for Doctor Binatti, the military funeral for his own first son. Instead he will weep by the grave, as each is opened with time, and then return home. The next day he opens his supermarket, business as usual, working behind the butcher counter, marking prices on white wrapping paper. And when he has added everything up he asks the customer, "And what else?" And the customer thanks him, saying that there is nothing else.

THE SALAD LADY

In memory of Eva Elias

RAWI HAGE

I met Sarah at a restaurant. I was the waiter; she, the quiet customer with the soft voice and long gaze that passed through her puffed cigarette smoke, crossed the glass window and always landed on the same spot on the paved sidewalk. She came every Wednesday and ordered the same Greek salad. Whenever she came in, Stavros, the owner, would call me in his thick Crete accent, "Your lady-salad is here." I would rush with a glass of water and greet her calmly with a soft nod, careful not to shatter her deep meditative mood. I never asked her if she wanted "the usual," though I was tempted every time. To say it, I felt, might acknowledge her existence, expose her routine, and make her visible to the world. She was the kind of customer who wanted to be left alone. You know, the kind who erects barriers and turns tables into refuges of contemplation and solitude.

I made sure her coffee cup was always filled and warm; the little glass bottles of olive oil and vinegar, which she poured slowly and always after the first bite of her salad, were also always filled. I would leave her the check, usually after the third coffee and right after her ashtray was filled with crushed cigarettes—a kind of subtle acknowledgment on my part of her routine, and my timing skills. She would walk to Stavros, pay him, walk back, give me the tip, and leave. Stavros, with his thick droopy mustache, would wish her a good day from behind his mechanical cash register that opened with a loud ancient voice. The machine was covered with Orthodox icons and Greek flags; on the wall behind him, a series of postcards from Crete showed a deep blue sea and white clay houses; and at his side were two signed photos of seventies Hollywood celebrities.

Stavros was a pain in the ass.

In the kitchen worked Ahmad, the Egyptian, whose conversation and obsession with cars bored the hell out of me; at the end of the kitchen, there was François, the Haitian dishwasher, whose overzealous Jehovah's Witness preaching was a joke among all of us. Outside the kitchen there was Claire, the waitress, who served the left-side tables and the bar. Claire had worked in the restaurant for fifteen years. She never stopped reminding everyone about it. She talked about horoscopes, the weather, and her trip on the morning train to work. We all knew she lived in the Bronx and took the R-train every day. She had a very peculiar relationship with Stavros; and when she talked to him, she always reminded him of what a gorgeous broad she once was, and what a fat and stingy pig he turned out to be. She had met Stavros on a Greek island in the eighties, during a trip that she won on a radio show. There Stavros, young and handsome, seduced her that same night in a Greek bar that had no ceiling to keep the stars from shining on the bouzouki band that played loud and happy music, and no walls to keep the Mediterranean Sea breeze from mingling with the tourists' sunburned thighs. Claire and Stavros spent two weeks together. He showed her the rough beaches outside the city, and they danced and drank every night. He took her to his birth village up in the hills and, in a cold flowing river, bathed her naked in his arms. He made her feel what no northern man was ever able to. And when she left the island, she wept and he kept her address. A few months later he showed up at her door with a suitcase. She took care of him. Then, slick Mediterranean that he was, he took care of himself, and in a few years had made enough money to open a small Greek diner with Claire as his manager. No one knew how Claire became the waitress and Stavros her boss, nor how he managed to hold her for such a long time under his command, nor why he, all these years, tolerated her contempt and verbal abuse.

Her relationship with me was also a paradox. In private she often told me that I was doing the right thing by going to school; she told me to study well and not to waste my life. But in public she would call me "college boy," and once in a while she would say that people never learn at school.

Though she had gone to the Mediterranean once, Claire had no clue about geography nor where I came from. She often confused Lebanon with Libya; and the few times Qaddafi was on the news, she tried to talk about him with me with some dismay and confusion.

When I spoke to Ahmad in Arabic, she would often shout, "English, English here. It is America—English!" Ahmad would laugh and ask her for a kiss and a date, insinuating one sexual favor or another. Claire knew that he did it to embarrass François, the pious dishwasher. François would shake his head and splash water at Ahmad and go back to tossing dishes and humming to God.

One bright Wednesday, the sun poured its light on the city from a bucket filled with rays and warmth. Some of it splashed on Stavros's place and fell on the Wednesday table. The table was warm, the cigarette was lit, and the Greek salad flew from the kitchen to her mouth. And then just when that world of her dreams had started to form and to veil the salad lady from the universe, I walked to her with a coffee cup in my hand, in silence. Somehow, I tripped and spilled the coffee in her lap, slashed through her dreams, and stained her morning and day. Frantically, with my sleeves, I tried to stop the brown liquid from dripping more on her black skirt; Claire and Stavros ran, and we all held white cloths, wiping away my shame and the horror that penetrated her thighs.

Claire, who acted like a chambermaid, helped her. Stavros was apologizing to her like a troubadour who had lost his tongue. I stood dumbfounded with nothing to say. I waited at the counter, and as soon as she walked out from the ladies room, Stavros started pushing me and asked me to apologize to her again. All along she was quiet and silent. When I approached her, she waved her hand to me and mumbled something that I interpreted as a gesture of forgiveness, but Stavros kept on pushing me toward her.

I approached her and said I was sorry again.

She went back to her seat and lit a cigarette.

She left earlier than usual that day. And Stavros waved her bill and wondered if she would ever come back again.

The next Wednesday, the clouds poured their water on the gloomy city from a bucket filled with water and mist. Stavros's place looked dim and empty. Claire stood there in silence, smoking at the bar, tapping the dead ashes of her long cigarette into a plastic white tray that said "Greece" on it. Stavros stood like a bronze statue, gazing at the rain outside. And I wondered if the salad lady would come that day. The door opened and with the pouring rain, she showed up. Stavros ran with a towel and gave it to the salad lady. He smiled when her head was hidden under the towel. I ran and poured water in a glass, feeling triumphant and relieved. She sat and I approached her with caution and uneasiness. Her cigarette lit the place with assurance; she gazed outside and her quiet dreams came with the water of the outside rain. She finished, paid and stood at the door, waiting for the rain to stop. Stavros called to me, handed me an umbrella and asked me to walk her to her destination.

Under the black umbrella, the salad lady and I hid from the rain and walked. Her hair was still wet, and our shoulders touched. I looked at her closely for the first time. She had high cheekbones, black eyes, and a hooked nose that stopped short of being narrow at its end. She was in her forties, and her gentle quiet manner gave assurance and comfort to me.

"What is your name?" she asked me.

"Khaled," I said.

"What language is that?" she asked.

"Arabic," I said.

"What does it mean?"

"Eternal."

"Eternal?" she repeated. "Eternal?" she said and smiled.

I shrugged my shoulders.

"I am sorry about dropping the coffee the other day," I said. "We all thought that you would never come back again."

"And I thought the man with the mustache would fire you."

"You come every Wednesday," I said.

"Yes. You noticed."

"Why every Wednesday? And you eat that same thing."

"You notice that too, eh?"

"Well, yes, you have been doing it for a while."

"It is the only routine I have in my life. We all need a ritual, don't we?"

"What do you do?" I asked her.

"Nothing now. I have money and I am waiting to die," she said.

"Are you sick?"

"Yes . . . I am home now. Do you want to come up for some tea? You must be cold now," she said.

"I do not know how Stavros would feel about it."

"The place is empty anyway. Come. I will make you some tea."

We entered and the doorman greeted her. I folded the umbrella and watched the water drip on the marble floor through the elevator all the way to her door.

"You can leave it outside," she said.

I did and entered her place. There was a mirror at the entrance, with a vase that held dried dead flowers.

"Come in, take off your shoes and come in. I will put the water on the stove."

I took off my shoes and entered.

Her house was filled with books. She had a large painting of a wolf under a dead tree and an orange sky. The floor was brown shiny wood. Her desk held piles of paper and newspaper clippings, and a red phone. There were no family photographs anywhere to be seen.

She asked me to sit and she brought tea.

She asked few questions. And I answered. I told her that I was going to school at night and that I shared an apartment with a friend. And that I had come alone to America.

She told me that she would be starting her chemotherapy the next week. And that she would be smoking pot.

I finished my tea and went down the stairs.

The next Wednesday, the sun came and shed a graceful, tasteful light on the city. The taxis that passed seemed more yellow than before. The vendors on the streets sold more liquid than the day before. And the salad lady entered the restaurant and we called each other by name.

The Wednesday after, there was a murder on the train, and the tabloid showed pictures of a dead man. And the salad lady came with a hat on her head, and that day Claire had a big fight with Stavros.

The Wednesday after, somewhere next to a bench, pigeons were fed crumbs by an old lady. And the salad lady came with the same hat on her head, and François told Ahmad that he forgave his sins.

The Wednesday after the churches in the city were empty. Businesspeople walked, it seemed, a little faster, and talked on their phones louder. And the salad lady came with the same hat on her head, and Stavros was on vacation in Greece.

The Wednesday after that same light came back and shone again; the trees absorbed every little ray and drove it to the ground, mixed it with water and earth and turned it to bigger leaves. And Claire quit her job, the salad lady did not come, and I never saw her again.

With special thanks to the
Conseil des arts et des letters due Québec.

The Coal Bin

D. H. MELHEM

An old man tended the furnace of a tenement house. Each morning and evening he stoked the coal. In exchange for this labor, the Superintendent gave him a tiny stipend and allowed him to live in the cellar bin where the fuel was stored. Since the Super was expected to do all the maintenance and repairs, the arrangement remained private between them.

Although the Super disliked the tenants and occupied the least desirable apartment, times were hard and he had a wife and child to support. He ignored the old man as much as possible, except occasionally to shout instructions or to glare as if at a trespasser. The Super never addressed his assistant as anything but "You," which he uttered with a kind of sneer. "You," on his part, was relieved to have a place to sleep. He dreaded returning to the homeless shelter, a farrago of soggy beds, vermin, and predators. The Super kept the building relatively free of mice and cockroaches. He was proud of the absence of rats and kept a steady eye on the garbage gathered for collection at the curb.

Despite this amenity, the old man never deluded himself into thinking that the coal bin was a good place to live or that the Super was kindly disposed toward him. "You" had once experienced what he considered "real" life—being a night watchman, having a wife. But his bride soon left him and disappeared. Afterward, he drifted from one miserable job to another. He preferred to leave rather than to complain uselessly. Even if he did find a sympathetic ear, he believed his ineffectual manner would betray him.

Everything above and outside the cellar You called the "Upper World." He was convinced it was run by thieves and criminals who trashed it with war and cruelty. From time to time he gleaned from discarded newspapers that the country was at war, with someplace near or far. "Good" people here fought "evil" people abroad. Enemies. You noted that the evil people were mostly swarthy. Enemies were hostile but no one questioned why. Their grievances were dismissed as envy. You wondered why anyone on earth would envy him.

His signal misfortune was his appearance. Even with hair thin and gray, even with gray-flecked beard neatly trimmed (it was expensive to keep shaving), You looked like an Enemy. He made sure his face was clean of the coal dust that made him appear surly, as well as dark. As hard as he scrubbed, however, there was only so much that soap could do.

Privacy was one of You's meager possessions, and he held on to it. He shied away from talking to strangers. He stayed away from policemen, who eyed him suspiciously. He dressed in a kind of camouflage. His black pants and threadbare pea jacket didn't show dirt, and in winter he wore a simple, navy woolen cap. The pea jacket associated him with maritime servicemen. He found a pin of his country's flag, and wore it like a charm, the way some people wore blue beads to ward off the Evil Eye. But the flag was different. It gave him an appearance of legitimacy. He thought more frequently of shaving his beard and trying to "blend in." Most of the time he stayed off the street, out of sight. He felt safe in the park.

You owned two pieces of furniture: a discarded folding chair and a metal pail, which he filled with water when he bathed. He had a dingy toilet and rust-stained sink, over which he draped two towels. A bar of laundry soap and a cup rested between the faucets. The man was grateful for hot water, proud that his efforts kept it in good supply. Each morning he would wake up coughing, bringing up a dark phlegm. As he leaned over the sink toward the cracked oval mirror, he groaned at the sight of his body covered with coal dust, which his blanket seemed to absorb. He scrubbed himself with the laundry soap and one towel, then dried himself with the other.

Mornings, when his work was done, he would go to the park with his coffee and day-old donuts from the bakery. He would watch people feeding the pigeons. He tossed a few paltry crumbs of his own, so that he, too, could be kind to the birds. Once in a while someone left a bag with crumbs or peanut shells on a bench. Sometimes You would find a whole peanut or two, and savor them as a delicacy. He liked tossing food to the birds. It gave him a sense of benevolence, a kind of power. A feeling of belonging. He was like the other bird feeders. Pigeons and sparrows were his kin of sorts, sharing the starkness of life. He stayed away from bums on the benches. He was not like them. They had no jobs, no dignity.

The cellar was dismal, with little light entering from the street. Near the toilet, suspended from a wire, was a bare electric bulb. Sometimes the old man burned candles. It was like attending church, but better, because it wasn't. Although the clergy were forbidding, churches were welcoming. Empty ones. You would occasionally enter a church, amazed that any place kept its doors open. He enjoyed the serenity. Once, while seated in a pew, he picked up a Bible from the open rack before him. Although he had never stolen anything in his life, he took the book home as a kind of souvenir. He placed it in a cardboard box outside the toilet where it lay, unobtrusive, seldom opened, yet available.

What he liked best to do in the evening after stoking the furnace was to sit by candlelight and draw. He drew on the wall with a piece of coal. Sometimes he plotted a calendar; at others he sketched the ocean and a rectangular ship with large, empty portholes. Before going to sleep, he wiped off the marks he had made. Once the Super had seen the scribblings and accused him of defacing the property with graffiti. You's new interest was unanticipated, like a crack in the ceiling or a leak in a pipe. Something forcing itself to the surface, strangely comforting. It was frustrating to have to erase everything. You enjoyed making the shapes and even imagined creating a large fresco, like those in ancient and even prehistoric times he had heard about.

As You felt more thwarted, his anger intensified. He began to caricature the Super. Super saying You do this and You do that. Though he erased the drawings before going to bed, his mental images became fierce and he would daydream about violent encounters. Throwing the shovel at the Super. Shoving his beefy face into the furnace and watching it roast and crackle. Sometimes You raged against himself.

Wasn't he the most humiliated of creatures, passive, timid, never rebelling except in his head, never killing anyone the way things were done in the Upper World? Suppose he climbed into the furnace himself? Burned HIMSELF to a crisp, becoming a martyr to hopelessness and rage? He conjured a newspaper headline: "ILLEGALLY UNDERPAID WORKER COMMITS SUICIDE TO PROTEST TOTALLY HOPELESS LIFE." The Super would be arrested, handcuffed, taken away by the police. You pictured the Super in tight handcuffs that chafed his fat wrists. Piggy-blue eyes squinting. Fat red face contorted. Beer-bloated stomach, shaking. Super afraid! Super in jail! But he would hire a lawyer and go free. People would think You a jerk for killing himself instead of the Super. They would not like You's looks and find him guilty of something. Even worse, nobody would care.

The Upper World cared only for itself and its comforts. The Upper World had no patience with losers. And a man who slept in a coal bin—he was the Prince of Losers. Not a King, mind you. The world had no respect for anyone who came in second at anything. A Prince was Number Two. Only Number One mattered. And he was Number Zilch. Minus zilch, even.

Several times You had tried to find another job. He would start out with enthusiasm toward a place where a messenger or a caretaker might be needed. Then his pace would slacken as he began to think of his humble station, his good fortune in finding any job at his age, and the possibility that he might be fired from the new job and left with no work at all. He returned home and fantasized about life as a hobo, living on the road, on freight trains. But he was too old for a vagrant life. Years passed as he tried to submerge his misery.

The seasons rolled over him. Sometimes he thought his unvarying routine excluded him from the flow of time, as if he were forever bending and shoveling coal into a furnace of days with his back to the cellar door. Sometimes it seemed like death, an eternity in which he was damned to repeat his task, with his back to life. He spent more time in the building. It began to tire him to walk to the park. There was no one to visit—he had a couple of cousins who lived far away. Maybe they were dead. And who would want to visit him in a coal bin? Except perhaps a wayward mouse or water beetle?

He began to hate the coal bin. At night he would lie on the floor, open-eyed, furious. He looked up at the ceiling where he saw all the comfortable, neatly made beds that were stacked on the floors above his head. He had nightmares about parties upstairs at which people discussed their wonderful bedrooms and soft mattresses. Someone asked him where he slept and he said, "In a coal bin." And everyone looked very ashamed of him.

You could not fall asleep. Sometimes he doubled his thin blanket and threw it over the coal. Still the lumps pressed implacably against every point of contact with his bony frame. It was as if the coals, barbed and alive, felt his dislike and were retaliating. They were pressing him to acknowledge it was *their* room. Mornings were more painful. His joints creaked and he thought he heard the coal chuckling. He grew weaker with lack of sleep. He threw the coal angrily into the furnace. He was too weak to draw on the wall in the evening. He sat hunched over beside the candle, wanting to cry, to sleep, to strike at something, at the Super, but all he could do was stare ahead into the darkness, a mass of quiet misery, like a large lump of coal. At last he addressed his tormentors.

Why should I have to lie on your black rocks, feel you jabbing my head and my back, coating my arms and sleeves—even my lungs—with black dust? You cannot evict me! With that cry he rose, pushed open the top half of the door, and climbed out. He stood panting, staring inside. Then he grabbed the handle and pulled open the bottom half. Some of the coal poured out at his feet. He took the shovel from its hook near the door. Steadily, perspiring, he began shoveling the coal out of the bin.

You continued shoveling until all the coal lay outside. By candlelight he found a few chunks scattered in the corners and hurled them out. For the first time, he spread his sooty gray blanket on a level floor in his new room. After extinguishing the light, he stretched out flat on the empty floor and went to sleep.

And dreamed. In his dream the coal assumed the shape of a huge mattress suspended above him. A few coils of coal popped out and struck his arms. Soon the whole mass began to crumble, pelting his body with stinging chunks, covering him till he was nearly buried alive. He awoke, choking, coughing, and in pain. He made himself stand up.

His arms ached. The muscles of his back pulled in all directions. He felt the cement floor around him. The bin was still empty, but it was filling up with his fear. Some disaster was at hand.

Soon it would be time to stoke the furnace. He had hardly slept. The aches in his body drew him toward the ground, but he remained upright.

Was the coal really coming to life? Like the Super and other humans, it would surely be vindictive. Vengeful coal! Not meekly waiting to inherit the earth. No, it had already been dug out, cut out, cast out of the earth by the mighty! The mighty inherited the earth. Super—and his boss—landlord—Lord of the Land—they inherited the earth. Upper World inherited the earth. The meek inherited lumps of coal. Earth inherited the meek, their ashes and bones. And ashes of the coal.

You looked almost sympathetically at the heaps flung out of the bin. The Super would come downstairs and fire him on the spot. Since he'd hidden You's existence from the owner, the Super probably would not call the police. The old man decided with a sigh that he couldn't blame the Super, either. Some things had to stay in place.

And so You began to shovel the coal back into the bin. Steadily, arms aching, he shoveled it all back, reserving a small pile with which to feed the furnace in an hour or two. He hung the shovel back on the hook, took up his blanket, and climbed back into the bin. The bumpy surface recalled all his former anguish, intensified now by aching muscles.

Maybe if You thought hard, shaped his ideas like lumps of coal, and threw them into a furnace of some greater plan, maybe he could fire up his hope again and revive his life. Difficult as it was for him to accept, there were others nearby even worse off than himself. He remembered the shelter, the bewildered homeless people in it. He thought of the street bums and park bums to whom he felt so superior. They had had jobs once, perhaps good jobs. And families. Maybe a bunch of people could get together. March together down the street. Chant something. Carry a banner. What should it read? A simple slogan. WE NEED HOPE! Something like that.

You had to write those words down. With effort he got up. He took a piece of coal and printed on the side of the bin: "WE NEED HOPE." The letters were not large. He paused, erased them reflexively, but they were still visible. He raised his hand to erase them further, and stopped. Maybe he'd leave the words there. Yes. They were barely visible, but clear to him.

You got into the bin and pulled up the blanket over him. He thought of going to the park tomorrow. He had a plan and the weather was promising. With a flicker of satisfaction, he went to sleep.

MANAR OF HAMA

MOHJA KAHF

The food here is terrible. The meat smells disgusting. There is no real bread, or coffee, or olives, or cheese. They have a nasty yellow kind of cheese and even the milk—Khalid says make cheese yourself if there is no cheese, but even the milk is tasteless. Even the eggs are pale-yolked. I don't know what they eat in America. I have lost five kilos already in the months since we left Syria.

Khalid keeps saying you will get used to it, Manar, things will get better. But I don't see how. Back home I was a smart, capable woman who could make her way around in the world. I am Manar Abdalqader Sharbakly of Hama. Whether I was in my hometown of Hama or in Khalid's city, Damascus, it didn't matter. The ground knew my feet. Here I get lost if Khalid isn't with me on every little errand; the streets all look the same in this horrible little town. Back home I was top of my class. Here I am queen of the dunces. I have not been able to learn more than ten words of their miserable chaotic language. I think these people invented English as a sort of mind-torture for foreigners and newcomers.

My children can babble away in English by now and they look at their mother who cannot speak two words to the school secretary and I know they are embarrassed. They are already in another world, one I don't understand. They do things that make the hair go white as if these were normal things to do. Boys talking to girls, girls talking to boys in school and sitting next to them. Even Khalid is shocked sometimes. I said what do you expect, putting them in American schools that mix up girls and boys. What do Americans care about modesty, they are the world leaders in immorality, this everyone knows. But we have no choice—there is a private Catholic school for girls only but we can't afford it.

I have no one to talk to. There is one other Arab family in town, the engineer who invited Khalid to work in his company. This is how we got permission to enter the country. His wife is Palestinian but she was born in America and has forgotten her roots. She wears pants and knows only a choppy little Arabic and speaks to me out of her nostrils. Treats me as if I were an ignoramus. I look backward to her because I wear the kind of dress that, in our social circle back home and among people who have taste, is the dignified thing for a woman to wear. There, she and her pants would be seen for what they are: tasteless, ill-bred, and unbecoming.

When we left Syria months ago, my family had just been killed in the Hama massacre. Massacre, massacre, massacre, the Hama massacre, there I said it. It is real. It happened. Even if I am surrounded by people who have never heard of it. Hama: blank stares. Asad: blank stares. Syria: blank stares. A government that would gun down twenty thousand of its own citizens: blank stares and nervous shifting of eyes.

They have no idea that anyone in the world outside Sonora Falls, Illinois, exists. Except maybe the next town over, where the rival school team lives against whom they compete in that savage sport Americans play instead of soccer. The one where the object is for the players to ram each other like mad beasts. I do not want my son to start liking that game.

The most imaginative intellect in town is capable perhaps—on a good day when his mind is working remarkably—now I am laughing at myself, Manar girl, look at where you've ended up! it's a wonder I haven't lost my sanity—yes, an intelligent specimen on a clear day is capable of imagining Chicago. This is where we landed in America, the airport of Chicago. That is the farthest afield their minds will take them. I, Manar Abdalqader Sharbakly of Hama, am a ghost from a nonexistent place.

The week before I left this nonexistent place, we in Damascus waited, tense and starving for scraps of news from Hama—word from my parents, from friends, neighbors, anyone at all. No one was allowed in or out of the city. All month they had been committing murder in my beautiful Hama, Asad's troops, shooting and killing, while the government denied everything, the newspapers printed nothing, the world said nothing. When it was over and we could finally get clear news, it was this: My mother, Fatima Rizkalla, my father, Abdalqader Sharbakly, my brothers Omar and Muhammad, my sister Omaima and her three children—all of them dead, the house rubble. My brother Adli, they say he escaped massacre but not prison. We have no news of him. No one knows and everyone is afraid to ask, for fear of drawing the attention of the authorities.

All that week I felt I was in a horrible dream. Surely someone was about to wake me, tell me it was all untrue. I would go to Hama, taking Khalid and the children to visit my family as usual, and we would find everyone there as usual, in the house where I grew up, the house of the Sharbaklys in the Nouri Mosque neighborhood. Even now, months later, sometimes the feeling comes to me that none of this is really real: us here, in this foreign place, this life without the taste of life.

After the massacre there were soldiers everywhere and *mukhabarat* spying on people even more closely than usual, and sweeps and arrests. We were told to get out of Syria fast. Who told us: Khalid's sister Lamees. She and Khalid haven't spoken since the day she joined the Party. But she did come through this time; Lamees went to Khalid's mother with the tip. In time for us to make the Jordan border station an hour or two ahead of the warrant with our travel ban.

So we left home. We could only take a few things in small bags because we couldn't afford to draw the Syrian border officials' attention with a lot of luggage. We left it all behind. We left behind the people and the landscape and all the things we knew, all that had ever given our life its taste.

In this country there is no squash, no eggplant. What they call squash is long and skinny. What they call eggplant is gigantic and seedy. They have skimpy orange carrots, not the fat purple kind you can hollow out and stuff. Most repulsive of all is the enormous slimy thing they call cucumber. Waxy outside, watery and seedy and taste-less inside, it simply cannot be eaten. I can't find fresh mint. Mint! Let alone coriander. I looked up the English name for it in the *Mawrid,* but when I asked the girl at the grocery store she looked at me as if I had asked for something from the Land of Waq-Waq. There is no allspice, no sumac, no cardamom. So I cannot even make the food smell like food.

Wait! Yesterday I smelled allspice. I confess, I followed the girl. She smelled like incense from the mosque where the Mawlawi order holds their Circle of Remembrance. I was entranced, I was like a lunatic. I only recently dared go to the grocery store by myself, so scared am I of getting lost away from home and not being under-stood, yet when I smelled the allspice I dropped everything and fol-lowed. Here was a scent from home!

She got into a Volkswagen buggy painted in bizarre gypsy col-ors and drove right out of town, leaving the highway and cutting through farmland on dirt roads. I followed, not even knowing how I was going to get home. She stopped the car in the meadow and dis-appeared behind a camper.

I got out of my car and heard chanting. *La ilaha illa allah, illa allah.* It sounded funny, not correctly pronounced, but I recognized the words. It was not the birds and it was not the wind rustling the trees. I cried out madly in love and pain. Someone here in Sonora Falls, Illinois, speaks my language! Like a crazy woman, I scrambled through tall grass toward that chanting, my long dress skimming up burrs and startling small furry animals.

There were nine or ten people standing in a circle, eyes closed. They were swinging their heads side to side like the Sufis back home and chanting *"la ilaha illa allah"* or something that sounded like it. But they could not be Sufis. Sufis would not have men and women circling each other's waists. Sufis would not be wearing cut-off jeans. Never. Bare midriffs—long wild hair—beads and bandanas—these people must be gypsies. I, Manar Abdalqader Sharbakly of Hama, had walked into a den of gypsies! I backed away in terror, but someone came up behind me and touched my shoulder. A man—touching me!

"Hey, traveler, you're like, welcome to join us," he said, in such a sleepy voice I wondered if he was on drugs. He was wearing a headband across his forehead and no shirt. Like a ruffian. He must have noticed the expression on my face. "Hey, don't be afraid," he said. "We are all groovy beings in the divine wonderland." Something like that; half his words I didn't understand and the other half he mumbled.

By this time one or two others noticed me. A tall blond girl in a long willowy skirt—which I at first thought was the only modest garment in the lot until I saw that it was slit up to the thigh in three places—put her arm on mine. "Hello! You are welcome here," she said. "Wel-come," she repeated, separating the syllables.

"Hey, she's not retarded, Suzy, just foreign."

"Hey, I know that, Baron. I was just trying to go slow, OK?"

"Thank you." I finally achieved speech. "I want to go home. Home."

"You don't want to eat?" Suzy brought her fingertips together and to her mouth. "Eat? We have plenty of food." A table was covered with plastic-lidded containers and covered pots.

God Almighty knows what kind of food these people have, I thought. Look at the way they are dressed—or undressed—and the dirt under their fingernails. But remembering the scent that made me follow the girl from the grocery, allspice in this barren land, I craned my head toward the table.

"We have three-bean salad, yogurt, apple crisp, some hummus—"

"Hummus?" Did she say hummus?

"Yes, hummus." Suzy pointed. Yes indeed, there in a small chipped bowl was something grainier and thicker, but still reasonably close to hummus.

"Chapatti?" Suzy asked. I looked blank. She held out a round flat loaf, my first sighting of anything shaped like real bread since I came here. It's Indian, she told me. It looked like *tanoori* bread to me, flaky and textured. I was almost delirious with hunger at the sight of it.

This was unreal. I had never done anything like this in my life. Come running across a meadow to total strangers. Sat down to eat with people whose families and faiths I do not know. I was very careful, taking only some hummus and yogurt with bread, not wanting to eat any impure food. And a little bit of some roughly cut tomatoes and lettuce. I guess there is no danger in salad. We sat on the grass.

Theirs was the kind of bread I know how to break and I became completely unselfconscious for the next few minutes as I used it to scoop up hummus. The tomatoes actually had flavor.

It was my first filling meal in this country.

"Very good taste," I said, pointing to the tomatoes.

"Organic," Suzy replied. I asked what that meant. She said it meant they were grown naturally. How else can tomatoes be grown?

"You are Indian?" I asked. Because of the headband on the man with no shirt. I have never met American Indians before. We were taught in high school that the racist American government had nearly wiped out the original inhabitants of the land with campaigns of disease, war, and mass murder.

"Nah, we're hippies," Suzy said. "Although Baron here is one-quarter Lakota."

"Where you from?" Baron asked.

When I said Syria, they didn't look blank. "That borders on Turkey, doesn't it?" said a black man with an Afro the size of my mother's village. I had never seen a black man before, except on television. I was alarmed. He was called Frank.

"Next to Israel, right?" Baron said. I blanched at the mention of Israel.

"Oh yes, and Egypt," a dark-haired girl with a delicate silver nose-ring said. I recognized her as Allspice—the girl from the grocery.

"Ah, Egypt," everyone said, nodding.

"I learned to dance in Egypt," Allspice added, raising her bare arms in a supple motion. Great. I, Manar daughter of Shaykh Abdal Qader Sharbakly of the Hama Society of Learned Ulema, and his wife Fatima Rizkalla of the sparkling reputation, was sharing a meal with dancing girls and ruffians and, who knows, maybe even Jews from Israel.

Frank put his arm around Suzy and she leaned her head against his bare black chest. I shuddered and remembered: the children would be home from school any minute. And I was in the Land of Waq-Waq, sitting in mixed company, with men and women touching each other's bodies. Sitting here eating hummus with orgiastic pseudo-Sufi hippies, which must be what people call gypsies in this country.

"I must go home now." I stood up, putting my hand to my chest in a gesture of acknowledgment. "Thank you, thank you."

"You're welcome, you're welcome," they said.

"You come one day to my—" Before I knew what I was doing, I was inviting them to my house. It is the way you behave as a guest, drummed into me for too long for me to do anything about it. I prayed they didn't take me seriously.

Suzy got up. "Do you know how to get home?"

I shrugged. Actually, I didn't.

"Janice!" she called to the allspice girl. "Hey, give me the keys to the bug. I'm gonna make sure she gets to town." Janice tossed a key ring.

Suzy walked me to my car. Before I got in, I turned to her. I was dying to know. "You said: *la ilaha illa allah,*" I said. "This, from my faith."

Suzy brightened. "Yeah! *La ilaha illa allah.*" She mangled it with her heavy accent.

"Then you are—are you—" I was incredulous, but I uttered it. "Are you—Muslim? Are you Sufi?"

She laughed. "Yeah, Sufi," she said.

A Sufi! Here, in Sonora Falls, Illinois!

"Also Buddhist. You know, Buddhism?"

I nodded. But how could she be that idol-worshiping religion and Muslim too?

"We're everything. Sufi, Buddhist, Hindu, Christian, Jewish—" Here I bristled and mistrusted again the moment. "Tao, Native, Pagan. All is good. All is love."

No, it isn't. All is not good. All is not love. I know this. My family would not all be dead if all was love, my hometown would not be rubble. But Suzy drove to town in the wildly painted bug and I followed her until I spotted the grocery where I had found Allspice. "All is love! Good-bye!" Suzy cried, waving, at the intersection where I recognized my way home.

The Hama massacre occurred in February 1982.

THE SPICED CHICKEN QUEEN OF MICKAWEAQUAH, IOWA

MOHJA KAHF

"He was choking me. His arm was locked around my neck and he was saying, 'I'll kill you, I'll kill you!'" Mzayyan's face was bruised along the left jawline and her right hand was bandaged. "So I bit him. Here—" She pulled up her heavily embroidered caftan sleeve and showed Dr. Rana Rashid the place in question on her own arm, covered with old bruises.

The woman's sentences came in a thick, smoky colloquial unfamiliar to Dr. Rashid and she had to work hard to understand. Dr. Rashid, a physicist who worked at the local nuclear energy plant, never expected when she'd signed the volunteer form and put "Arabic translation" under "other services she could render" to the women's shelter that she would actually be called on to provide that service. There were scarcely any Arabs in Mickaweaquah, Iowa. The nuclear energy plant ("Safely Empowering Your Tomorrow Today!") was the only thing going on in town except a small iced-tea bottling operation, and Dr. Rashid and her husband were the only Arabs, and they weren't Arab. They were Arab-American. The hyphen said that they had been here a while. They were not the huddled masses of the Greater Jersey City Mosque, reeking of incense and henna and wearing their *jubbas* everywhere, and jabbing their fingers at the waiter and asking, "Is there pig in this dish? Is there pig in that dish?"

Still, when they'd called her to the shelter to meet Mzayyan, Dr. Rashid had taken the woman's hand and without thinking had leaned forward and kissed both her cheeks, first the right then the left then the right, three times. A greeting she hadn't given or received in years. The caseworker had asked if they knew each other from before, glancing from Dr. Rana Rashid with her well-cut hair and tailored Talbot's skirt-suit ensemble in navy and taupe to the darker, squat woman in a voluminous embroidered caftan, sweaty black curls escaping from under her black head kerchief, this woman with her hands folded across her chest like the third millennium B.C. icon of a priestess at Cayal Hayak. Maybe they had known each other in an ancient, chthonic before, too long ago to leave any memory.

"Hold on, please, while I convey that bit to the caseworker," Dr. Rashid said to Mzayyan in languid, Syrian-accented Arabic. Dr. Rashid turned to the caseworker sitting across the table and said in English, "He was trying to choke her. She bit his arm to get away."

"It helps if you translate in the first person, if you don't mind," the caseworker said.

"Pardon?"

"Translate as if you were her. Say, 'He was trying to choke *me*.' Makes it easier for me to record the facts."

"Did you tell them to look at his arm?" Mzayyan tugged at Rana's sleeve. "Because it proves my story. Can they check his arm and take a picture before it fades? Tell them."

"She wants the police to photograph his arm."

Hector, the caseworker, blinked. "Sure, when they arrest him. The important thing now is to get this form filled out so we can admit her here at the shelter. So," he continued, "on August 3, the battery began with him trying to choke her. What then?"

"Oh wait!" Dr. Rashid said suddenly to Hector. "I forgot something important. She says he threatened to kill her. Wait—you want me to say 'he threatened to kill me'?"

Hector nodded and scribbled on his notepad.

"OK—so—he threatened to kill me—" Rana said hesitantly. The rims of her eyes reddened inexplicably. Allergies, she thought, and blinked.

"Then what?" Hector prompted.

"What else happened on August 3? After the choking?" Dr.

Rashid asked her. In the silky tones of Rana's Arabic, the choking sounded like an entreé on an elegant dinner menu. In Mzayyan's Omani Arabic, it sounded like choking.

"Not on August 3," Mzayyan said. "Choking didn't happen last night."

Dr. Rashid was taken aback. "But—you just said—"

"That was last week. Yesterday he didn't try to choke me. Yesterday he just burned my hand on the stove-top. Last week was when he tried to choke me. He wanted the pictures of the woman. I hid them away and he wanted them back." She twisted and untwisted a corner of her long black veil.

Her sentences fell in thick unwieldy coils and Rana had to grab hold of the tail end while sorting them out in her mind. "The woman?"

"Yes, the second wife he took last summer behind my back. I know that's illegal. For Immigration. So he is afraid I will tell Immigration. He wants the documents back. He starts choking me, he goes, 'Take those papers out or I'll take out your soul.'"

"But not on August 3? Not last night?"

Hector looked inquisitively from Rana to Mzayyan.

"No. A week ago." Mzayyan frayed the hemmed edge of her veil. "Because—can I confide something in you? As an Arab sister, not to translate?"

"Oh—well—OK—"

Now Mzayyan folded and unfolded the cuff of her caftan sleeve. "Because I fought back yesterday. I did. That's why I don't want to tell them about yesterday, I'm ashamed. I kneed him in the eggs. Twice. It was his hollering the neighbors heard."

Eggs were balls in Arabic. Thank goodness that at least was the same in Omani dialect, Rana thought. "You said he's been abusing you for three years. You defended yourself. Don't be ashamed," she said, patting Mzayyan's hand. "Hector," she said in English, "the choking business happened a week ago. In another beating."

Hector stopped mid-scribble. "Tell her we'll get to the earlier beatings. That comes later on the form: 'Other dates abuse occurred.' We need what happened last night."

"Because—can I tell you something, Dr. Rashid?" Mzayyan went on, her voice quavering.

"Please, call me Rana."

"Rana. The neighbors heard him holler, but they never heard me. All those times! Because I don't want disgrace. I do not holler, no. I hold my pain inside, see." She put her hand to her belly.

"But Mzayyan, this man needs to write what happened last night," Rana said patiently. "Not some other night. What made you call 911 last night?"

"No, I didn't phone the police, no!" Mzayyan cried. "I didn't turn him in, I swear. The neighbors in the apartment downstairs did it. My uncle phoned me this morning from Philadelphia saying all the Omanis are scandalized that I turned my husband in." She plucked at a thread in her veil and stifled a sob.

Mzayyan's veil was beginning to unravel at the edge and Rana was beginning to lose patience.

"The whole mosque is talking about it," Mzayyan went on tearfully. "But I didn't even—I—" She sobbed once and wiped at her eyes with the edge of her veil. Then she commenced sobbing wholeheartedly.

Rana sighed and pushed a box of tissues across the table. Mzayyan needed several. At first Rana held her hand sympathetically, but then Mzayyan needed both hands to blow her nose, so she let go. Hector told Rana to tell her that every woman at the shelter felt that same pressure, that it was a typical part of the battered woman's situation. This didn't help much.

After more tears and nose-blowing, and fits and false starts, and much sighing on Rana's part because she wished Mzayyan would not play with her veil so much, the form was filled out.

"So why didn't she call the cops?" Emad wanted to know, at home with Rana later that evening.

"The last time she called the police was in Alabama and he sweet-talked his way out of it," Rana said. "The policeman claps the husband on the back and says, 'She's mad 'cause you got another woman on the side? So do I, man!'"

The garage door was already up when Dr. Rana Rashid had pulled in earlier that evening. Dr. Emad Rashid was getting out of his coupe. Emad was handsome and knew it. He was cleanshaven, with a complexion that was white for an Arab but sun-bronzed.

"Picked up your apricots at the farmers' market," Emad said, holding up a paper sack and beaming at Rana. "Organically ripened to perfection."

"Ooh." Rana reached through her window. "Give me my darlings."

Emad, tall and broad-shouldered, lifted the bag up high like the trees of Tantalus. "Give me a kiss first."

So she gave, and he gave.

"And these Omani relatives of hers in Philly," Rana said to Emad as they showered together in their custom-made dual-head shower, "they sound positively tribal. Where do these people come from?" Not the Arab world Rana used to visit during summer vacations, when Mother would get out her best jewels, the ones that were too gaudy to wear in dressed-down suburban Connecticut, and go to glittering soirées and dance with Father in his smartest suits.

"Oman, huh?" Emad said. "And the prize for 'most remote and backward part of the Arab world' goes to . . . I don't even know where Oman is."

"Neither do I," Rana said. She pronounced it "nye-ther." "I guess it's the Mickaweaquah, Iowa, of the Arab world."

Dr. Emad Rashid was the real sort of doctor, not a Ph.D. He was a cardiologist in a flourishing practice with several partners and privileges at the regional hospital. He and Rana had met at a testing center when she was taking her GRE's and he was taking his MCAT's, and thus doubly fulfilled the fondest dreams of Rana's mother for her daughter and of Emad's mother for her son. That Rana, while pursuing the noble but impractical idea of a scientific career and refusing to return to the grandparental home in Syria to be available for a suitable match, should have found a man, an eligible Arab man right in suburban Connecticut, and on his way to being a doctor, no less, proved to Rana's mother that the Compassionate One provided with a liberal hand even in these days of estrangement from the homeland.

That the boy's family was from Aleppo and not Damascus was but a small failing.

Emad's mother would have preferred to return to Syria to hand-pick a bride for Emad. As handsome and accomplished as he was, she was confident that it would be easy to find him an exquisite girl in Aleppo, and had been startled that Emad did not want to go that route. Emad's father, although he had been educated in one of Aleppo's French lycées and had recited Kabbani poems in college and was very modern—Emad's father understood that really there was such a thing as being too tolerant and progressive. The flooding of Aleppo by uncouth peasants and dark minorities who had once been content to live on the fringes of the Syrian mainstream was partly what sent Emad's parents to America, the opportunity for Emad's father to make money in a free market far more readily than Syria's socialist economy allowed in the 1970s being the other part. But America had its own dangers. The prospect of their son bringing home an American girl, especially one of unknown parentage, had caused Emad's mother and father no small number of insomniac Connecticut nights. The parents were relieved, then, when Emad had chosen a nice Syrian girl from one of the old Damascene families, after all. And this girl of his choice was fair-skinned, to her credit. Although her hair was now very dark brown, almost black, the girl's mother had shown pictures of the girl as a child, and her hair had been lighter once, chestnut-colored. This boded well for the coloring of the future Rashid grandchildren, in Emad's mother's discerning eyes.

There were not that many plum nuclear physics jobs, especially for a woman who wanted to work not in academe but in the industry, where the money was better, as Rana did. When the Iowa job was advertised she and Emad had to look it up on a map. They were lucky that one of Emad's buddies from residency days had a colleague who was relocating his practice to Iowa and was looking for a partner. Iowa was the sticks, true, but the money was good and the living easy, and they could take frequent trips back East to visit family.

Rana's husband got on the Internet and looked up Oman, then checked stock quotes. "My brother says hello," he called to Rana while instant messaging. "He's sent more pictures of the baby." Rana looked over Emad's shoulder as he clicked open three JPEG attachments.

Osama's first smile 1 Aug 2001.jpg—"Look at the little fellow, he's practically blond," Rana said admiringly.

"Yes, he has Mother's ivory coloring and light hair," Emad said.

Osama da Champ 2 Aug 2001.jpg featured three-month-old Osama in a tiny soccer uniform complete with cleats. "Where did he ever find it!" Rana exclaimed. In *Osama takes a bow 3 Aug 2001.jpg,* the fat baby boy, who was indeed fair-skinned by Arab standards, was lying in his bassinet in a tiny tuxedo with bow tie and cummerbund.

"My cousin Shukry wants us to sign another e-petition," Emad said, reading an e-mail.

"But of course he does." Rana slipped a Marcel Khalifeh CD into the sound system.

"This one's about 'secret evidence.' Senate hearing sometime in September. ACLU to protest, as well as the Arab-American Youth Rally Against Bias . . . yes, AYRAB is on board."

Rana pulled a New Orleans étouffée from the labeled and dated stacks in the freezer—she cooked on weekends when she and Emad took turns trying out gourmet recipes from *Global Sautéeing* and *The Bliss of Baking*—and set the microwave to "defrost." From the speakers, Marcel and Omaema began to croon the sad melodies of the politically aware.

Joseph and Jocelyn Altonjay came by later for crumb cake and pistachios. So actually there were other Arab-Americans in Mickaweaquah, if you counted the Altonjays. But the Altonjays were so Republican, so American Legion (Joseph) and so Daughters of the American Revolution (Jocelyn), so many generations removed from the slightest hint of Arabic accent or whiff of cardamom, that no one would notice if you dropped the "Arab." They were close to the age of Rana's and Emad's parents. Joseph had been decorated in the Korean War. Rana had met Jocelyn while shopping for a suit with padded shoulders at Talbot's.

Joseph was a military history buff with a fascination for ancient Greek and Roman warfare. Tonight he brought a book about Zenobia, Arab queen of Palmyra.

"She defied the Roman Empire, you know," Joseph said, lighting a cigarillo. "Decided she'd rather her city be independent of Roman rule."

"And got her city and herself destroyed because of it," Jocelyn retorted. The Altonjays had done the Holy Land tour years ago, and had put the Rashids through the slide shows of Palmyra and Petra and the rest of it. Rana and Emad had visited these places, not as tourists, but as children sent to summer with relatives in Syria so as to keep their Arabic. They'd sat patiently through the Altonjays' vacation slides as they had before through the Arabic tutoring.

"Look here. Paraded in golden chains through the streets of Rome." Emad shook his head, examining the glossy images in Joseph's book.

"But after years of successful rule," Rana said. "She had herself a good time."

"She killed her husband to be queen," Jocelyn pointed out. "I don't think she was such a savory character."

"We don't know that for sure," Joseph said. "It was said to be a hunting accident."

"Listen to this one, defending her," his wife said.

"How did she die?" Emad asked.

Joseph drew on his cigarillo. "In blazes, like she lived. She went down with her city when Rome gutted Palmyra as punishment."

"You like that, do you," Jocelyn said.

"In blazes. For her country," Joseph murmured. "Why not?"

"Hey, you're forgetting the other version," Rana said. "In which she lives out her days hale and hearty in the Italian countryside."

At the shelter, Mzayyan set a platter of spiced chicken, its juices dripping over heaps of steaming rice, on the common table as if setting out a banquet. She wiped the thick black curls matted to her sweaty forehead in a gesture of triumph. Fragrances heretofore unknown in that corner of Mickaweaquah, Iowa, suffused the shelter. From the lonely rooms of the house, other residents gathered, ate, and praised her. Mzayyan did not need a translator to understand this.

"Tell her they've got him." It was Hector phoning from the shelter the following week. "But only for a short time," he said. "Unfortunately, according to the state, beating your wife is not that big a deal, in legal terms."

Mzayyan came on the line. Rana relayed the message.

Hector again. "But she's got to press charges, Dr. Rashid. She wants to drop them. Talk to her."

"I can't do that to him, I can't," Mzayyan said. "My uncle—all the people at the mosque are saying—the disgrace—" She dissolved into heaving sobs.

Rana held the phone receiver away from her ear while Mzayyan blew her nose.

"Mzayyan!" she said. "Listen to me. Who's the disgrace? His beating you is the disgrace, Mzayyan. It's un-Islamic. This is what you tell them at the mosque: it's contrary to the teaching of the Prophet. Tell your uncle." Rana fingered the embossed spines of Arabic classics on the living room bookshelf, gifts from Emad's great-aunt, a professor at the University of Kuwait.

Mzayyan blew her nose some more.

"Want me to quote chapter and verse?" Rana said. "'I entrust you with the kind treatment of your women kin'—the Prophet's Farewell Address. 'Women—only the lowly man acts lowly to them, the noble man is noble to them'—the Caliph Mu'awia." Rana rattled off Arabic citations. She half remembered some moderately useful things from a few college afternoons spent at Muslim Students Association meetings.

Mzayyan whimpered, "I can't put him in jail." Rana wanted to shake her.

"He's put himself in jail, Mzayyan!" she shouted. She took a deep breath. More calmly, she went on, "But he'll be out tomorrow—"

"He'll kill me!" Mzayyan interjected.

"He doesn't know where you are."

"He'll find out. You don't know. He can talk his way into anything."

"Then get a protective order from the court."

"I can't go to court against him, I can't . . ." Mzayyan started to cry again.

Rana wanted to smack her. Snap out of it! Stop that blubbering. Dr. Rana Rashid was good at nuclear physics. Not Arab hysterics.

Hector got back on. "That was Shelby at the county sheriff's," he said. "They found a gun out at the apartment. It's licensed, but the name on the license is spelled differently. It may just be a technicality, but they're going to hold him until he satisfies them it's his license."

Rana had a feeling the name discrepancy wouldn't pan out, but she wasn't going to say anything. Let the sheriff find out from someone else that an Arab name can be spelled a number of ways in English.

"He's in violation of his Immigration status," Mzayyan said suddenly. "They can hold him for that, can't they?"

Rana repeated this to Hector.

"I can call INS," Hector said. He didn't sound hopeful.

The nearest INS office was four hours away, in Fort Dodge. Hector left four messages over the following days. The agent who phoned back a week later opened with a speech on how overworked and understaffed INS was. He took down the address of Mzayyan's husband's convenience store and said they would get to it when they could.

The day after next, Rana got a call from the shelter. It was after midnight. "I'm sorry to call so late," Hector said. "Can you come right away? She got a phone call from the uncle in Philly and she's having some kind of crisis. I think she wants to drop the charges again."

When Rana got there, Mzayyan's face was tear-stained, her eyes swollen. She sat on the edge of her cot, twisting and untwisting her filmy black veil.

"He—he was in jail for a night and it was awful, Rana, just awful. Everyone is saying how shameful that his own wife is putting him through this," Mzayyan whimpered. "The toilet was in the middle of the cell. Americans have no shame, Rana. He couldn't do his business in front of everybody the way they do so he held it in. The next day he had to be taken to the hospital in an ambulance! They had to give him enemas, he was constipated!"

"His shit?" Rana exploded. "You're worrying about his *shit*?" Her silky Syrian dialect seemed suited more to light sarcasm than anger, even when she was worked up.

Mzayyan looked very small on the edge of the cot, hiccupping from her crying.

"Who phoned you?" Rana demanded. "Who phoned you about your husband's shit?"

"M-my uncle," Mzayyan stammered. "From Philadelphia."

Hector knocked on the door and came in. He looked from one woman to the other in bewilderment as their conversation went on in two very different kinds of Arabic that were both Greek to him.

"Mzayyan, I would like to talk to your uncle. Can you get him on the phone for me?" Rana said tersely.

Mzayyan was silent.

"Shame on him," Rana fumed. "Shame on him."

"Rana?" Mzayyan said in a small voice.

"What?" Rana said impatiently.

"It wasn't really my uncle who called."

Rana looked quizzically at her.

"It was him."

"But—how did he get the number? They keep it very secret—"

"I phoned him." Mzayyan hung her head.

Appalled, Rana did not translate. "She's not dropping charges," she said to Hector, a little curtly. Then she went home and climbed into the dual-control, fully adjustable king-sized bed with Emad, who was long since sound asleep.

Mzayyan asked Rana to try INS again. "These might help," she said shyly. She took out a large pouch stuffed with papers. "I took these from the apartment before the police brought me to the shelter. I did not want to show all this to Hector, only to you. Here are tax returns for the last two years. He's a great con artist. There isn't a tax cheat he hasn't done, I know all about them because I—oh, see! This here is the title to his store. The title to his car. His bank account statements. Insurance papers. Do you think," Mzayyan said in her jagged Omani dialect, "that I could have the title to his property transferred to my name? Or—well, if I just make a little change on this little bit of paper here, the title, would anyone notice, do you suppose?" Rana looked at Mzayyan, flummoxed. Was she thinking of forgery?

"She's a lot sharper than she lets on, Emad," Rana said that evening at dinner. "Think about the presence of mind it took for her to collect all those documents."

"This is great food!" Emad exclaimed.

Mzayyan had sent Rana home with a generous helping of her spiced chicken and fragrant yellow rice. "I managed to find some of our spices—you know, the spices we Arabs like. When they helped me slip back into the apartment to gather some of my things," Mzayyan had said, holding out the foil-wrapped platter.

Rana protested; Mzayyan insisted. "Now, now, we are not Americans," Mzayyan reproached. "Take, eat."

"And she's had this packet all along," Rana said to Emad at dinner.

"Really great food!" Emad said again, diving into the rice with his fork.

"You want me to give up nuclear physics and cook for you?" Rana snapped.

Emad looked bewildered. "I—I just meant, thank you. For bringing it home. That's all."

"She's sharper than she lets on, Sharon," Rana confided to a friend over coffee at Sister Bertrille's Hole-in-the-Wall. The waitresses wore nuns' habits with aerodynamic wings. All the tables were decoupaged with stills from *The Flying Nun* and *Gidget*. The walls were papered with publicity posters from *Smoky and the Bandit I, II* and *III*, and *Not Without My Daughter*. "I just wish she'd stop the frightened rabbit deal. I wish she'd be angry."

Sharon smoothed back her unsmoothable frizzy hair, fried from too much home perming and Miss Clairol experimentation. "Maybe she's getting the results she wants."

Rana was nonplussed.

"About two years into my marriage with Evan," Sharon said, "we had a huge fight. I yelled and screamed my head off. You know me. I'm a screamer."

"I know it."

"Thank you. So we were calling it quits. I drew a bath, lit a candle, and decided to have me a good long cry. Evan overhears me crying. Suddenly he's on his knees by the tub, saying he didn't realize how much I cared. I said through my sobs—and I am hiccupping huge, hacking, *Days of Our Lives*–quality sobs here—what do you MEAN you didn't realize? What the fuck do you—sob—think all that fucking—sob—screaming and shouting was about? Of course I care, I fucking CARE."

Frankie Pollack and Joe Zimmer swiveled around on their stools to see what the ruckus was about and swiveled back when they saw it was just Sharon Glebb, hair all afrizz, being her loud self.

"Our marriage lasted another year off that cry."

"Act strong and you're a bitch and not believed, but cry and be soft and feminine—"

"—and men listen."

"Well, I do declare. Scarlett O'Hara, behind your feminist facade."

"Scarlett yourself. My tears were real. Call me Miss Melanie," Sharon said in Southern falsetto, signaling for the bill.

It was September 10, 2001. The charge against Mzayyan's husband had come to trial. Rana drove to the county courthouse. Billy Joel was singing "We Didn't Start the Fire" on her car radio. Hector and Mzayyan were waiting for her in the parking lot.

Mzayyan was talking on Hector's cell phone. "No, *he's* the disgrace. No, *he's* the disgrace," she said hotly.

"Who is she talking to?" Rana mouthed to Hector.

"The uncle in Philly," he said.

"The Prophet never beat his wife," Mzayyan said stormily. Then she turned aside and jabbered sotto voice in that heavy Omani colloquial Rana found difficult to follow.

"Your honor, my client was savagely attacked by this woman. He was only defending himself when he hit her." The judge glanced over at the husband, a dark-skinned bearded man with a powerful physique.

The lawyer followed the judge's gaze. "She kneed him, your honor."

When Rana translated, a whimpery gasp escaped Mzayyan's lips. The judge looked sharply in her direction. Rana had seen the judge reprimand other people that morning for emotional displays. One woman had jumped up during her ex-boyfriend's testimony and screamed, "You lying son of a bitch! You lying son of a bitch!" and was cited for contempt of court and hauled out by the bailiff, kicking and scratching.

As the lawyer continued to narrate Mzayyan's husband's version of the matter, Mzayyan began to sob quietly. Rana shot her a look of warning.

"She bit me," the husband said up in the witness stand. He was glib. "I don't know if you've ever experienced a biting woman," he said with a sly look at the judge.

. . . .

"She threatened me with a gun, your honor." His beard was thick, black.

. . . .

"She threatened to have her uncle in Philadelphia kill my kinfolk in his city." His eyes glowered. "She said he'd burn down my cousin's Wah-Wah Mart in Philly, your honor."

Mzayyan sobbed a huge sob. She put her hand to her mouth to muffle the sound, which only made it more pathetic. Once, in the Jersey City backyard of Egyptian friends of her late father, Rana had watched rabbits being slaughtered. They made a sound like Mzayyan's muffled sobs. Later they were cooked with *mulokhia* and garlic and Rana enjoyed them very much. Tasted like chicken.

The judge kept an eye on Mzayyan, watching her reactions to the testimony. Rana gave up trying to get Mzayyan to quit crying and just handed her tissue after tissue. Mzayyan blew her nose, balled up the tissue, and laid it next to her. She dabbed her tears with the frayed edges of her black veil and looked up at the judge with big, brimming eyes. The pile of snot-filled tissues on the bench beside her grew bigger.

It was time for the judge's ruling. Rana squeezed Mzayyan's hand.

"In most domestic violence cases, it is simply the wife's word against the husband's," the judge began. "Because of this typical lack of evidence, there is usually very little the court can do.

"In this case, however, it is clear to me that the complainant's version of events is more credible than the defendant's."

Rana's face lit up.

The judge went on. "I base my finding on two factors. The first is, it is generally known that Arab women are submissive."

Rana's face fell.

"If the complainant had been some American wildcat bitch from Madison Trailer Park on the south end of town, I may have given credence to the defendant's story that she was the one who attacked him," this product of Iowa's finest legal education said.

Rana remembered to close her mouth, which had dropped open in shock.

"However. She is not. She is an Arab woman. The alleged aggressive behavior is not believable of an Arab woman. Now, the second factor is the complainant's demeanor. Throughout the proceedings, she has not shown the least bit of vitriol or hostility."

Or backbone, Rana groaned inwardly.

"All her behavior has expressed is fear and sorrow," the judge continued. "In my judgment of human nature, I thus find the complainant to be the more credible of the two."

Mzayyan approached the judge. Holding the edge of her black veil in her hands, eyes brimming with thanks, Mzayyan needed no translator. The judge, like any knight in shining armor, understood.

The husband, scowling, was led out by police. Rana was not at all sorry to see him hauled off. He hissed something through his beard that was too Omani for Rana to understand. Mzayyan stiffened.

"What do you mean," Mzayyan said, horror-stricken, at the shelter the next day. "Free? He is free to go?"

"He paid the five-hundred-dollar fine and signed up for community service and that's it," Rana said, crestfallen. "I'm as baffled as you." In English: "Hector, how can this be?"

Hector shook his head resignedly. "That's how the law is. There's very little we can do. She still has the protective order. She should call the police immediately if he approaches her."

"If he approaches her—you mean she's not going to be here at the shelter?" Rana asked.

Hector looked apologetic. "We can get them to the point of the court hearing, but then we have to ask them to move on. To make room for others."

"You have the protective order—use it. Call 911 if you see him," Rana cautioned Mzayyan.

"But he'll kill me," Mzayyan said tersely. "He looked straight at me while the cops were taking him out of court and said so. By the time they come it will be too late."

The next day, September 11, 2001, Rana at the Mickaweaquah Nuclear Power Plant and Emad at the regional hospital watched with their coworkers the morning's horrific news. Over and over they watched it. Then they left work stunned and ashen-faced to watch it over and over at home together, and to call everyone they knew in Connecticut, and then everyone they knew off the Beltway in D.C., and then everyone they knew who flew in airplanes, just to make sure they were OK.

"Oh God," Emad said. "I just remembered—Kennedy and Rajiv—" Emad's old high school buddies were stockbrokers who did the daily commute from Connecticut to Wall Street. He picked up the phone again.

Rana thought about her father's friends from his Jersey City days. Didn't Abu Ali, the old mosque janitor, work near the Bowery?

Mzayyan phoned Rana. "What do you think will happen now?" She had to move out of the shelter in a matter of days and had not yet found a place to live or means to pay for it. Rana had put in a call to Jocelyn, hoping her Junior League connections could help. Jocelyn had not yet returned her call, which was not like Jocelyn. Rana left messages for Jocelyn at her work, cell, and home numbers, but no response came.

"I don't know, Mzayyan," Rana said, in low spirits. The FBI was questioning Emad's brother about why he had named his baby Osama. As if it hadn't been a perfectly respectable Arab name for two thousand years. Shukry had called, shaken; he had been roughed up and held nine hours for questioning in Virginia after being stopped for a traffic ticket. "They're rounding up Arab men. There's backlash violence everywhere."

Rana and Emad had come home to phone messages from Frankie Pollack and Joe Zimmer saying, "If anybody bothers you guys, just call us, we'll slug 'em," and Sharon calling to see if they were all right.

Rana choked back tears. "I don't know what's going to happen next, Mzayyan."

"Remember the Oklahoma City bombing, Rana?" Mzayyan asked.

"Yes."

"Maybe this one will turn out to be white American guys too."

"God. I hope so," Rana said.

"White guys on a rampage. You wait and see." After a pause, Mzayyan said, "Rana? Are they really rounding up Arab men?"

On September 13, 2001, Mzayyan went to her husband's Wah-Wah Mart, took his gun, locked him in the stockroom, and closed up the store. She drove his Chevy truck four hours to the Immigration and Naturalization office in Fort Dodge and told the INS agents exactly where he could be found—a dark and threatening-looking Arab male, prone to violence, with Immigration violations. She handed them a packet of papers, slightly thinner than the one she had shown to Rana. This time the understaffed, overworked tribe of agents careened into action against this threat to the security of the nation, right there in a convenience store in an Iowa locale. They even turned on their sirens, which they rarely got to use, not nearly as much as other sorts of law enforcement agents did.

They sent Mzayyan's husband to one of the FBI's new detention camps, where he was held for seven months along with five or six thousand others without evidence or trial. He was deported the following February.

Mzayyan quietly took over her ex's Chevy truck and his Wah-Wah Mart, the title documents being already in her possession, although there was a slight discrepancy about the spelling of her name on them. She started serving spiced chicken and saffron-colored rice in foil-covered Styrofoam dishes along with the floppy corn dogs and sad potatoes under the hot glass at the front of the store. Frankie and Joe, who became her regular lunch customers, report that she expanded the spiced chicken deal into a franchise, with branches as far out as Darlington County. To the best of anyone's knowledge, she remains hale and healthy as its sole proprietor, although every once in a while shadowy reports surface about a tall, powerfully built, foreign-looking man supposedly skulking in the doorways of eateries in Mickaweaquah and the surrounding countryside.

STAGE DIRECTIONS FOR AN EXTENDED CONVERSATION

YUSSEF EL GUINDI

The television special shows a scene of female circumcision in an Egyptian village. The voice-over informs viewers of the risks the woman took in bringing in a camera, hiding the camera in the folds of her dress. Time is spent explaining where the small video camera is located in her *gallabiyah*. The young girl is brought in. The other women are present. The knife.

Joeline brings her hand to her mouth in response to the visuals of the girl, the women, and the knife. She turns to Karim. Karim is slouched on the couch beside her. He turns to look at Joeline. She turns back to the TV, as does Karim. Then there's a commercial.

Later in the bedroom, Joeline is awake. She turns to Karim, who was beginning to drift into an uncomfortable series of dream images: bare feet traversing an extended valley of sharp rocks. He was able to say, "Why here?" before he lost control to the forces that were taking him deeper into sleep; and then Joeline pulls him out.

"Why do they do that?"

"What?"

"Did you know they do that?"

"What are you talking about?" Karim tries to make out her face in the dark.

"Never mind," she says.

Karim lies back down and is unable to sleep for the next two hours.

"Can I ask you a personal question?" They are eating breakfast. Karim skips a beat in the rhythmic spooning of cereal into his mouth. After four months together, he thinks they should be past putting in formal requests for inquiries into private matters. Her question relates to the program they saw last night. She asks him if any members of his family, female members, have undergone the procedure. Have they . . . at this she takes a breath and leaves it hanging.

Karim at that moment thinks he has a sense of what keeps a healthy relationship from going stale. Those times, well into a relationship, when both parties realize neither of them really has a clue about the other person. True, the revelations that come after a couple has settled into a routine usually tend to be negative, as opposed to the more positive revelations that occur in the beginning, and which tend to be flirtatious in nature.

Karim is startled, both by the question and by the sudden if brief shift Joeline undergoes from someone he thought he knew to someone he doesn't and back again to someone he thinks he knows, but who's just asking an odd question.

"Have they what?" he says.

"Have they had their clitorises removed?" There is a stiffening in her body posture—as if she were wearing an overly starched uniform that restricted relaxed, flowing movements. He also notes the strange, bureaucratic glaze in her face, the kind one associates with seasoned officials used to hearing lies from applicants.

Karim doesn't know which end of the question to grab hold of and so he doesn't. He lets it boomerang around in his mind a couple of times as he observes Joeline and recalls the time she carefully instructed him on how to stimulate her and bring her to orgasm.

"You're asking about my mother and sisters' . . . ?" But he is unable to muster the necessary irony he thinks the occasion requires in order to defuse the accusatory nature of her question and side-step a mounting irritation on his part. He leaves the question hanging. To finish it would have taken him closer to that irritation than he wanted. But leaving it hanging unintentionally gives it that irony anyway, which Joeline interprets as his being dismissive of her question, the issue, and the suffering of thousands. Karim senses this and says, "I don't know. We could phone them up."

Joeline, in turn, also comes to the conclusion that she doesn't know anything about Karim. And that the characteristics she ascribes to the kind of man she'd never go out with may make up aspects of his personality that she will yet discover in the coming months; and—the second realization—those characteristics may be exactly what she's looking for, and were she not to find them, she'd be disappointed. It may be that Joeline unconsciously looks for those personality quirks in a man that will enable her to end the relationship when she chooses.

"I don't mean to pry," she says.

"It's a legitimate question," he says.

"You don't think it is?"

"Inquiring about my family's genitalia?"

"I was wondering how widespread it is. Is it a class thing? A religious thing?" Then, as if to emphasize that this wasn't some open-ended academic inquiry with room for ambiguity and cultural relativism: "It's hideous."

Following this comment, Karim says nothing and hopes his silence will speak for itself, but soon realizes that in the battle of silences, hers was doing a better job. She had a righteous argument biding its time in her pause, whereas all he could offer, after all was said and not said, was a confirmation of her opinion. Yes, it's hideous. Of course it's hideous. And no, none of his female relatives have had that done to them. They'd be the first to howl at the practice and he'd howl right beside them. But it wasn't about that. He understood the argument would not have ended had he agreed with her. This was about staking a moral claim as their relationship naturally entered its next, post-glow phase. The ground was being set for future arguments. In terms of moral high ground, she was making a land grab—from which subsequent disagreements, whether they were about taking out the garbage or presidential politics, would be waged.

It isn't said, for how can you admit to yourself that in the midst of loving someone, or at the very minimum, comfortably living with them, there may also exist a need to put them in their place. Because you never know. Because it's a good idea to have a fall-back position when you're made to feel most vulnerable by the person you love. For those times when you fall short in their eyes and the mea culpas you're obliged to swallow to keep the peace begin to feel like chicken bones stuck in your throat. And the only way to dislodge them is to have a sense of your own unimpeachable values.

The discussion proceeds less tentatively now, with Karim questioning why they would show such a program in the first place, and saying that no, it wasn't a widespread practice as far as he knew, and then segueing into a broader discussion about female sexuality, about how the East differed in acknowledging—in its concern with honor and its fear of not being able to satisfy—female desire, and sometimes viewing it as rapacious, in contrast to the West's chastity-belted (keep the clitoris, but keep it locked up), perched-on-a-pedestal-and-don't-get-off-it view of women (the Madonna/whore thing), and Joeline switching gears to tell Karim that he needn't be so defensive, at which point he knows he's lost, because when you have to spend most of your time explaining yourself, you have.

The argument occasions the first cooling-off period in their relationship. Efforts are made to get over it. The matter is taken over by other issues. Two days pass before they make love again, and when they do, it becomes a reaffirmation of their desire to be together. But a strange thing occurs. A disorientating series of interlocked thoughts occupy Karim as he kisses his way down past her belly button. Though experiencing genuine and personal sexual pleasure, following their discussion, and with the subject of their heated talk in full view, he feels, oddly, that what he was doing was only serving to confirm her argument. He makes an attempt to quiet the mind and focus on the present pleasure, but the specter of Joeline's face twitching as she drove home her points rears itself up before him. And where he had refused to cede completely to her sense of indignation, what he was doing now only further underlined her criticisms and showed how wrong he was for not being more forthright in his condemnation. His nuzzles and licks were adding the final touches to her moral victory, and as he continued, he frowned, which is hard to do while sincerely attempting to make love. He was surprised to find himself feeling oppressed, put in his place, in this position, by this act—perhaps in the same way women have for a very long time when forced to occupy a similar position, and engage in a similar act. Only he wasn't feeling put-upon as a man, but as a man from that part of the world where such acts take place. And the oppression he felt was taking on a colonial bent. As if he were being educated in the proper conduct of a civilized Westerner. That this was how civilized people behave. These were the right and true erotic expressions of a civilized man. And didn't he now feel awful about that show, that practice, and all the other unspeakable things that happen in that part of the world.

Joeline was not unaware of what Karim might be thinking. That night, Joeline rightly claimed her right to pleasure, and climaxed with some pride, loudly and on behalf of many other women.

IT'S NOT ABOUT THAT

SAMIA SERAGELDIN

It's not about that. It was never about that, between us, so when did it become about that? It was never about my being from Egypt and your being American, about our coming from opposite ends of the spectrum on almost every issue. A few months after we met, I wrote to you: "It's a miracle that we come from worlds so far apart, and met the way we did, and connect the way we do." I saw the distance between us better than you could, because I could see your starting point as well as mine. Your world has always been part of mine, long before I became part of it. I grew up watching *Bonanza* and *Hitchcock Presents* in Cairo; you didn't grow up reading *Les Malheurs de Sophie* or El-Mutanabi's poetry in Connecticut.

You remember where you were when you heard that President Kennedy had been shot; it was your freshman year at Harvard. You didn't enjoy college: you weren't athletic, you didn't get into the right fraternity. Maybe that's where you learned to make your credo: If you can't join them, beat them.

I remember where I was in 1967, when the Six-Day War broke out. I was a student in middle school. It was June, and unusually hot, even for Cairo; I was sitting in the bathtub, studying for finals, holding up my book to prevent it from slipping into the water. I had my own system of mnemonics to memorize international treaties: Bismarck, Balfour Treaty, Pax Britannica.

Then the air raids over Cairo began. In the living room my father was listening to the radio. "Ten Israeli war planes downed!" the announcer exulted. A few minutes later: "Five more planes shot down!" My father was looking grim.

"But that's good, isn't it, Papa?" I asked. "I mean, that we're shooting them down so fast?"

He looked at me impatiently, something he almost never did. "Use your head. If we're shooting down ten planes in ten minutes, how many must be coming at us at once?"

Then he saw the expression on my face and added: "Don't worry, the announcer is exaggerating, they always do. Let's try to get the BBC on the shortwave radio."

In those days, in Egypt, there was zero confidence in any announcement made by government officials—even about something as innocuous as the weather. Even the temperatures in summer seemed to be consistently underreported by several degrees, as though people could be manipulated into feeling the heat less, or as if they would blame the government for the weather.

You could be arrested for listening to shortwave radio, but we did it anyway. The Israelis were attacking with overwhelming force, and the Egyptian air force had been obliterated before it ever got off the ground.

We followed the black-out instructions, papering over our windowpanes with the navy wax paper with which we covered our copy books at school. I had stopped studying for finals completely, and so had all of my school friends. We were in a state of feverish excitement, waiting to be called upon to do something, we had no idea what. Only one girl in the class went right on studying for finals. "Whether we win, or whether they do, there will be exams anyway. Even under Israeli occupation, there will be exams eventually. And I'm going to be the only one who's prepared."

We looked at her the way you do when someone utters blasphemy or unspeakable obscenity.

The war was over almost as soon as it began. Israeli forces swallowed up the Sinai and stopped short just the other side of the Suez. When President Nasser announced the total defeat of our much-vaunted armies, we were disbelieving. We were so used to the "spin," as you would call it today, that it was devastating to realize that this defeat was beyond even Nasser's ability to spin or obfuscate.

Later that year the song that was top of the pop charts all over the world went:

> Those were the days my friend
> We thought they'd never end
> We'd sing and dance forever and a day
> We'd live the life we choose
> We'd fight and never lose
> For we were young and sure to have our way.
> Lalala lah lala, lalala lah lala
> Those were the days, oh yes, those were the days.

We sang it over and over, stressing "we'd fight and never lose," defiantly; it could be construed as subversive. In those days, in Egypt, you had to watch what you said and did.

And you? Where were you in 1967? The Six-Day War was merely a blip on your radar. You were staying out of the Vietnam War. Vietnam was your war, of course, a real war, the one that shaped your generation of Americans. You were on the right side of the great moral divide of your country: you demonstrated for civil rights, you had black friends; you're still a card-carrying member of the ACLU.

I remember where I was when I heard that President Nasser had died in 1970. It was in the evening, and the maid came up to tell us she had heard on the street that the "Rais" was dead. We warned her that she could get into trouble spreading rumors. I had been born under the Nasser regime, as had the overwhelming majority of Egyptians. No one could believe in his death. Television footage of his funeral showed scenes of mass hysteria. Even my father, who had suffered so much at Nasser's hands, was subdued. In Arab culture, you owe respect to death, not to the man; you walk in your enemy's funeral cortege.

In 1973, there was the October War, the Ramadan War, we called it, while the other side called it Yom Kippur. I was in London at the time, studying at the university. At every church corner people were handing out flyers advertising: "Come celebrate with the music of Handel's Israel in Egypt." At Hyde Park Speaker's Corner on Sunday the Arab students demonstrated at one end and the Israeli supporters at the other.

You had married and moved to Connecticut. Your first son was born, and you started to grow a beard. When I knew you, you had a full, reddish beard. I asked you once if that was a Jewish tradition, to start growing a beard when your first son was born, and you said that's not why you did it, you were very secular.

I remember where I was when I heard that President Sadat had been assassinated. It was 1981 and I was living in faculty housing on a Michigan campus, with my husband and child. I was nursing the baby as I watched the funeral on television. Carter was there, and many other heads of state, paying their homage to Sadat, the martyr for peace. The Egyptian crowd was strangely subdued, the commentators noted, so unlike the scene at Nasser's funeral.

Did you watch the same coverage? Maybe not, you were busy building up your business then, with that single-mindedness I know so well. It must have taken its toll on your marriage. You didn't see as much of your children as you would have liked while they were growing up.

And me? The years passed and I blended into my new environment like a perfect chameleon. My sons grew up engrossed in Ninja Turtles cartoons and Transformer car-robots; they played hockey in Michigan and Connecticut. There was no room in this brave new world for memories of Egypt.

By the time I met you, your days of itching ambition were behind you and success had mellowed you. You attended your college reunion and realized that you had been more popular than you remembered. The bar mitzvah you held for your son eclipsed those of all your friends' children; you were very secular, but it wasn't about that.

When we met, it wasn't about what we were to the outside world. It wasn't about that, whatever it was. You said to me later: "I was like a man who carries a picture around in his pocket all his life, and one day he looks up, and there's the woman in the picture. There you were." And months later I wrote to you: "You are my portion of passion in this world."

I remember where we were when the market crashed on Black Monday, 1987. We were in your car, driving along some New England country road; you had the radio on, and you were following the free fall of the market. You took your hand off mine long enough to adjust the volume, and then you found my hand again, palm against palm.

The first time we argued about international affairs was in a pub in a random small town along the route of one of our aimless drives in the country. When we pulled off the highway into the village, you said: "I wonder where the local watering hole is." Then you caught sight of a man shuffling along the sidewalk. *"He* looks like he'd know." You stuck your head out of the car window. "Sir? I say, where's the pub? The bar?"

I have a confession to make: I liked your sense of humor at times like that when you weren't trying to be funny; I didn't care as much for your jokes.

In the pub you had your beer and ham sandwich, and I had a glass of wine and picked at your chips. I liked to watch you eat; you ate recklessly for a man with a full beard. I liked to watch your eyes: intensely blue, deep-set, quizzical. You kept trying to make me have some fried clams. I was never hungry when we were together, I was either too happy or too miserable.

I don't remember what brought the conversation around to the Middle East, what set us off on that argument. It doesn't matter. That issue was like a nightmare merry-go-round; you could hop on at a y juncture, but as soon as you tried to look behind you to see the starting point, or look ahead of you to the resolution, it all became a blur, and in the meantime the merry-go-round never stopped still, the cycle of grievances went on and on, and all you could do was go round and round until you bailed out, dizzy and battered.

You liked the idea of me as your Arab pasionaria, one of the new roles I somehow found myself playing for you. You found conflict stimulating; I had no stomach for it, especially with you. I gave up without ceding, or you ceded under the unfair pretext of "make love, not war." But we agreed that we were two of the most open-minded, well-intentioned people we knew, and if we couldn't discuss this issue sanely, no one could.

That was our year of living dangerously. When we broke up, it wasn't about that, whatever it was.

In 1990, when the Gulf War started, we were very far apart, in every sense. I don't know if you watched Saddam Hussein's televised speech promising "the mother of all battles." Isn't it amazing how quickly that expression—"mother of all something"—was adopted in American everyday idiom? I hear and read it all the time now, used by people who don't even remember the context.

During Desert Storm, I thought, for the first time, of leaving the States. My children, all of a sudden, became "Arabs" at school. It didn't matter that the Egyptians were fighting on the same side as the Allies. But the war ended almost as soon as it had begun, and we stayed.

I don't know what you were doing then. But I know you must have thought of me at the time. You always did, whenever there were reports of a hurricane devastating the Carolinas, or some other threat. The telephone would ring, the morning after some tornado or hurricane, as I was clearing out the defrosted fridge or estimating the damage to the roof from fallen trees. I would pick up the receiver, and there would be silence at the other end. Then, after you heard my voice—it was you, wasn't it?—you'd click once, slowly, softly, like a kiss, and hang up.

Years later, we became friends, at a distance. Whatever brought us back together, it wasn't about that.

From a distance, we shared what we could: opinions on books and music and current events. Those were the heady days when peace seemed at hand in the Middle East. You were more optimistic than I was; you believed human beings would ultimately act out of rational self-interest. One day you called me, elated: the orchestra at your son's college was planning a "peace tour" of Egypt and Israel during spring break. I was just as thrilled. Then there was the massacre of tourists by Islamists in Luxor, followed by the massacre of Palestinians in a mosque by an American-Israeli settler, and the peace tour was canceled.

At some point we decided to risk a meeting, in the lounge of an airport in a city neither of us knew. I was looking around for you, but I didn't see you, or didn't recognize you, until you were standing right in front of me. It's your eyes I recognized first; your eyes were the same. You said I hadn't changed.

Before we parted, you said that you hadn't changed, about me, about us. If we were to stay no more than friends, it would have to be at a distance, it was too painful to try to do it a breath's length apart. It was your decision to make.

When the millennium came around, we were as weary as the rest of the world with the eternal and insoluble problems of the Middle East. One day we were arguing over the phone about the new intifada when we came close to a meltdown. I was the one who saw the danger first and pulled back. This time there was no point in getting back on the merry-go-round. I'm not sure why it was different this time: whether we had changed, or whether the situation had become too hopeless and too volatile.

Afterward you wrote to me: "If two open-minded people like us can't discuss this issue sanely, no one can. You're mistaken if you think lack of communication brings us closer, in matters personal or political. That's not what intimacy or friendship is about."

I wrote back: "I want us to be friends. But there's so much space between us right now. Don't let's fill it with the crackle of brittle cerebral volleys. I don't want to argue with you. It makes me feel sad and hurt."

And you wrote: "Funny, I don't feel any space between us. Can there be one-sided space? Doesn't sound real. But I guess emotions and geometry are different."

But I stopped discussing Middle Eastern affairs with you. The problem, you thought, was that there were too many facts to choose from. But I knew it went deeper than that; we had no memories in common. If we lost our friendship again, I didn't want it to be about that, whatever it was.

Like everyone else, we both know exactly where we were when we heard the World Trade Center towers were attacked. I was checking my e-mail that Monday morning when the small box popped up on the screen, the box that typically features a picture of a teenage pop idol and the caption: "Britney Spears or Christina Aguilera: which is hotter? Click here." This time the box showed an image of the World Trade towers in flames and the caption: "America Under Attack." I thought it was a commercial for the latest apocalyptic movie until someone called and told me to turn on the television set.

My first thought was to pray that my son was not one of the victims—he worked in one of the World Trade Center buildings. He called to say he was all right. My second thought was to pray that the perpetrators would turn out to have no connection to the Middle East. That prayer went unanswered. My third thought was for you; your son worked in New York too. I called you; he was all right.

I reached out to you at that moment, with everything I thought we had in common. You responded with a reductionist diatribe against all Muslims everywhere. I don't remember exactly what you said; after the first few words all I registered was my own pain. It's not that I didn't understand your reaction. If I had read your opinion in a newspaper as a letter to the editor from a stranger, I could have riposted, point for point, with equanimity. But coming from you, it undid me. I cried for a long time afterward, mourning someone I knew—or thought I knew—that I lost that awful day.

In the days that followed, kindness made me cry more often than unkindness. Everyone I knew tried to be concerned and supportive, considerate in their choice of words around me. Still, I left gatherings early.

Almost immediately, you called. The best of us try to be better than their first instinct. You said you never meant for me to take what you said personally; that you were willing to put aside our differences for the sake of our friendship. I know that. I know you wouldn't hurt me for the world, not in cold blood. I will always wish you well. But try to understand. We have nothing left to talk about. This time, it is about that.

AIRPORT

PAULINE KALDAS

He paced the airport waiting room, his steps marking a path in the carpet between the rows of seats. At first those sitting down looked up at this man who could not hold his feet still like the rest of them and curb his agitation. After a while, some returned to their own thoughts or families. A few kept their gaze on his coming and going, perhaps to ease their own turmoil. Even after he left, a few repeated his path with their eyes as if permanently held by the ghost of his movement.

Samir was about five feet seven, with black hair cut short because otherwise it would frizz and wave. His nose was rather large, but his eyes compensated, their brown glimmer and long lashes giving his face an unexpected beauty. He was slender, his physique almost that of a young boy. But around the middle a slight roundness was beginning, probably because for the past year he had been going to a Chinese restaurant and ordering pupu platters for dinner. Once, his coworkers had talked him into going out after work. He was frightened at the prospect of having to understand the menu and perhaps not having enough money. When they ordered something to be shared, he was relieved. The assortment of fried foods soothed him. Although some of the tastes were unfamiliar, he had grown up with the smell of food frying. His mother fried fish, potatoes, cauliflower, so now he could eat with a certain security. He asked a couple of times what this was called, his tongue moving silently in his mouth to repeat the words *pupu platter*. After that, occasionally, he would go to the restaurant alone and order the same thing. He didn't catch the odd twist of the waiter's face, and he ate confidently.

It was eleven o'clock Sunday morning. He had woken early, a little before six, despite having stayed up late cleaning his small apartment thoroughly. Glancing at his watch, he noted there was still another hour before the plane was due. He stretched his pacing out of the waiting area to look at one of the arrival terminals. Flight 822 from Egypt via Switzerland. Yes, the arrival time was still twelve o'clock P.M. He turned his gaze around the airport until his eyes fell on some tables and chairs that he hoped were part of a coffee shop. He headed over, lengthening his stride a little. Ordering the coffee, he was tempted to get something to eat but was afraid his stomach would turn, so he settled at a small table with the Styrofoam cup awkwardly balanced in his hand. It was too hot to drink so he could only sit, the sounds of the airport mingling together till they became a steady hum in his head.

She stared at the empty suitcase on her bed. How do you pack for moving to another country? she thought. She circled the room, stopping to sift through open dresser drawers, to flip through clothes hung in the closet, to slightly rearrange items on top of dressers, only to find herself back in front of an empty suitcase.

Her mother appeared at the door. "Hoda, you haven't done anything! The suitcase is empty."

Hoda shifted her eyes to the suitcase as if seeing its open cavity for the first time. "I will. I'm just organizing," Hoda replied to appease her mother.

"You leave early in the morning," her mother said as if ringing a bell.

As her mother stepped out of the room, Hoda sat on the bed, giving her back to the suitcase. She was an attractive woman, but not in the traditional Egyptian sense. Her body was slim without the usual roundness around the hips and legs, probably because she insisted on walking everywhere. Taxis are too expensive and buses are too crowded, she argued. Her black hair was cut straight just above her shoulders. She never put anything in it, didn't use henna, and wore it simply as it was. Her mother had tried to coax her a little, to style it in some way, but after all these years, she knew it was a useless effort. Her face held the energy of youth, and people often found themselves looking at her. It was her mouth that was her most prominent feature. Although it was considered slightly large, there was still something captivating about it, the way her smile pulled you in and made you listen to whatever she was saying.

It was eleven o'clock Saturday morning. She had woken early, a little before six, despite having stayed up late saying good-bye to friends and relatives. The first thing she did was call the airport to check the departure time. Flight 822 to Boston via Switzerland. Yes, it was leaving at two o'clock A.M. in the morning and due to arrive at twelve o'clock P.M. American Eastern time. After she hung up, she made herself a cup of coffee although she rarely drank it. The traffic outside began its erratic rhythm of fitful stops and starts accentuated by the loud honks of impatient drivers. She sat in the kitchen almost in a trance until her ears tuned the noise outside to a steady hum in her head.

Would she be on the plane? It was his brother who had written with the flight information. He had received one letter from her parents, accepting his proposal and giving their blessing. Everything else, signing the church marriage papers, processing the immigration documents, had been done through his brother. And it had taken longer than expected, almost two years of filling out forms, presenting proof of this and that, till he felt his life had transformed into a sheaf of papers. He sometimes forgot the purpose behind all this, that it would eventually lead to marrying someone whom he didn't know. At times, fear chimed through Samir's body. Perhaps he should've listened when his brother had urged him to return to Egypt, to choose for himself. But Samir was reluctant to leave his new job.

In the meantime, all he could do was wait and work. He had arrived in this country with little money and little education. The only school that would accept him in Egypt was the agricultural college. For two years, he sat and listened to professors lecturing about crops, soil, irrigation till his mind blurred and he knew if he didn't leave, he would end up another man with a college degree selling cigarettes in a kiosk. He was not a lucky person, but he entered the green card lottery anyway. It was free and they only asked for your name and address. The rumor said fifty thousand each year would be chosen to come to America. And he had heard of people who won and actually went. What a strange country, he thought, to make its immigration decisions through a lottery. He curbed his joy when he received notification that he had been selected. It was clear that the process would be long. Now came the applications to be filled, the requests for documents, the interview which, in halting English, he felt sure would eliminate him, but the end was indeed permission to immigrate, to chance his life in another country.

Would he be there? What was she doing going to another country to marry a man she didn't even know? Her parents had helped convince her that this would be best for her. "He's from a good family and after all he's in America and not many people can get there." "Besides," her father added, "this America is more suited to your independent nature." "Yes," her mother added, in a resigned tone, "and they like educated people there." It was true that in Egypt Hoda often felt like a piece of rough wood that needed to be sanded down. No one understood her desire to continue for a master's degree in chemistry. "You have a college degree," her parents argued, "and you're twenty-one now. Look for a husband. It's time to settle down." When a young man approached her parents to propose marriage, she accepted, thinking this would keep people quiet. But she had been naive. The young man was insistent that she quit school and devote her time to setting up their new home. Finally their heated arguments led to a breakup of the engagement, and not surprisingly this only worsened her reputation. She knew her parents feared that now she would never marry.

When the proposal from America came, she hesitated. She had one more year until she completed her degree. But everyone assured her the paperwork would allow her enough time to finish. And they were right. Things dragged out for so long that at times she forgot she was engaged or that she was going to America. So when Samir's brother appeared at their door two weeks ago with the plane tickets and the approved visa, her head spun like a top.

He had arrived with some hope and trepidation. The process had been difficult, but each time he pictured himself standing inside the kiosk, his body trapped and his arms reaching for cigarettes, he was able to push himself and do what was requested. Surely in America there would be more possibilities. But that first year, America kept him dog-paddling and gasping for air. The language confounded him, quick mutterings with hardly any gestures or even a direct look. He took an English class, but the rules of grammar and the purposely slow pronunciation of the teacher did little to improve his understanding. He found a job washing dishes in a restaurant where contact was limited to *Good morning, How are you* and *See you later.* When the radio in the kitchen broke one day, followed by the mumbled swearing of the cook, he offered to fix it. The cook gave him a perplexed look and tossed the radio to him with a *Go ahead.* The dishes piled up a bit as he fiddled with the switches, found a knife to use as a screwdriver, and then managed to make the music reemerge. After that, other radios and sometimes clocks, telephones, or calculators were handed to him. Most of the time he could fix them, and the added conversations made him more confident.

Fixing things was the one thing he could do. It was like a sixth sense to him. When he was a child, if something broke at home, they couldn't afford to buy another one. Since it was already not working, his family figured there was no harm in letting him fiddle with it, and so he learned how everything was put together, how to take it apart, and how to reconnect the parts so it worked. He was most comfortable staring at the inside of a machine with its intricate weaving of wires and knobs. But he had never perceived his ability as a skill; it was simply an instinct.

When the restaurant manager caught wind of his reputation, he approached him with a request to fix his stereo, adding, *I took it to the shop but they couldn't do anything.*

He spent a day at the manager's house, surrounded by components with wires stretching like a web of animal tails. Every time the manager walked by, Samir saw him shaking his head with a look of doubt clouding his face. By the end of the day, the tails had been untangled, and when Samir pressed the power button, the music spread through the house. *Thank you, thank you,* the manager repeated, and Samir stood puzzled by how a boss could lower himself to thank an employee. The manager sent Samir to the same shop that couldn't fix his stereo. He was hired on a trial basis, but he proved himself quickly. He had found his niche in this country that could make many things, but didn't know how to fix what it broke.

It wasn't that she didn't want to get married. She had always hoped her life would be with a partner, and at some point she expected to have children. But she knew she didn't want the life she saw around her. Women dragging their chores like chains, cleaning house, washing clothes, cooking food, all for others. She had watched friends marry at eighteen and nineteen, sometimes even men of their own choosing whom they loved. Within the first year, their spirits dissipated like sugar crystals in water. It frightened her to envision her life in this way, her days filled with the care of home and family, her body growing heavy with the idleness of her brain.

That is why, against everyone's understanding, she enrolled in the master's program in chemistry. She was one of two women, but the other was there only to pass the time until she found a husband. Her family had determined that it would be more respectable for her to continue her studies than to remain at home waiting. But for Hoda, it was a different matter. Chemistry had caught her fancy and it was the only thing she wanted to do. As a child her mother had to pull her out of the kitchen, where she would find her sitting cross-legged on the floor with a bowl in front of her, mixing starch and water, baking soda and vinegar, or some new combination. "Just to see what would happen," she answered her mother's shouting inquiries. Finally, her mother banished her from the kitchen. The result, aside from Hoda never learning how to cook, was that she began borrowing chemistry books from her friend's older brother who was studying at the university and moved the experiments to more secluded parts of the house. She struggled through the master's program, where the male students laughed directly at her and the professors didn't take her seriously. Still she persisted and gained high marks. It was an act of faith since she knew the only job Egypt would give her would be in a lab analyzing blood and urine samples.

Perhaps that's why she accepted the roll of dice that would lead her to America. There might be a chance there of having a real job, of doing research, of working with someone who would take her seriously, not turn everything back around to her femininity. Her English was strong since all the sciences were taught in English, and she had occasionally had American or British professors with whom she had no trouble communicating. What concerned her was this man who had extended his proposal across the ocean. What kind of man would marry a woman without even seeing her, would choose as if picking a number out of a hat?

After two years in America and turning thirty, Samir knew he had to get married. And he also knew he needed a certain kind of woman, not one who would lean on him, who would expect to be at home while he worked. He needed someone who could stand in this world next to him, perhaps even lead him a little. He sent his request to his brother: a woman who was educated, who knew English well, who wanted to work; a woman who could swim in deep water, he added. His brother argued with him that he was asking for trouble, that such women should remain unmarried. But Samir was insistent and said he would accept nothing else.

Hoda was twenty-five years old. If she didn't marry soon, she would be looked on with either pity or suspicion. And if she remained in Egypt and married the next man who proposed, her life would inevitably fall into the repeated pattern of other women. She couldn't articulate what she wanted, only that it was not here. Hoda caught her breath like the reins of a horse and began to fill the suitcases. She counted the number of dresses, skirts, and pants she had, then divided by half: that's how many she would take. Then she proceeded to do the same with all other items. Within a few hours the two permitted suitcases were filled.

BLUEBIRD

PAULINE KALDAS

That morning she glimpsed a bluebird as it flew by the window. She chased it to the next window to see if it had settled on a tree branch so she could catch full view of it. She suspected a nest nearby but had not been able to find it. Sonya's Saturday-morning ritual was to sit on the couch for several hours by the front window, drinking coffee as her hair dried. It didn't need that long now that she had cut it to her shoulders, an attempt to minimize the gray streaks that were rapidly taking over the black. It hadn't bothered her initially, the few gray hairs like accent marks, but when they multiplied in the front, it became disconcerting to look in the mirror, each time surprised by the indication of aging. Finally, she cut it short, letting it fall in the front to minimize the appearance of white. It framed her face on both sides, making it look elongated, and highlighted her nose to an even sharper angle. The result was that her brown eyes and long lashes, once her most pronounced feature, now seemed sunken. Her body, still slender except for her full hips, kept her youth intact for the time being. At thirty-eight, she mostly felt younger, except when the realization of thirty-nine and then forty approaching held her illusion in check. There was no sign of the bluebird. She gave up on her quest and began the household chores, occasionally turning her head to the window.

Later, when her husband returned from the hardware store, his arms packed with piles of wood and another sharp-edged tool that looked menacing and unbending, she tried to explain how the bluebird had returned. He nodded and responded with an agitated explanation of his plans for renovating the space in the basement to turn it into a media room, moving the TV there and buying a new state-of-the-art stereo system with surround sound. Sonya smiled approvingly and helped him carry the new purchases downstairs. But she had grown accustomed to these new projects and their end results. Rick would spend the next few weeks continuously downstairs. Each weekend's plans would be canceled due to his project. She'd hear hammering and the occasional yell after some crashing sound. It'll be a surprise, he'd answer when she offered to help. Finally, he'd emerge, sawdust covering him like powdered sugar, and invite her to view the final project. She had learned to fabricate her initial response, to express the excitement he anticipated. But it was difficult to identify the change. Often it seemed like he had done nothing more than paint or perhaps put up a shelf on the wall. The house looked endlessly the same to her and the renovations he claimed to have made eluded her eye. The first time, when she said she couldn't see the change, he had proceeded to give her a tour of the project, this first being one of the upstairs rooms. Look, he said, I put new baseboards and new caulking around the windows, and look, I shaved the closet door so it would close all the way. She tried but felt like one of the advisors in *The Emperor's New Clothes,* with too little wisdom to see the riches described.

He fixed up that upstairs room a month after the abortion, claiming that one day they would have children and the house needed to be ready. But after a year of trying and the first test results, he limited himself to renovating various parts of the basement. The pregnancy had come too quickly, just after they had signed the lease on the house.

"You're pregnant," he said, emphasizing each syllable of the word.

"Yes," she answered, keeping her eyes focused on a dirt spot on the rug.

"Well, what are we going to do?" he announced, bouncing his long body on the couch and reaching his arm out as if to embrace one of the back pillows.

Sonya shifted her gaze to another spot. "I don't know," she mumbled. She had expected a warmer response.

"We have to pay a mortgage now, I've got to work overtime, and you said you'd do extra work at home." His lower lip pouted slightly as he spoke and his blue eyes, normally narrow, widened. She knew the look, one that had initially attracted her to him.

"I guess we just can't," she finally answered.

He ran his fingers through his blond hair and that ended the conversation.

She went alone since he had to work. In the waiting room, there were mostly girls, much younger. She could only notice details: one had a nose-ring, another a purple streak in her hair. One held tight hands with the boy sitting next to her. When the girl was called in, the boy left the waiting room and returned later with a bag of donuts that he proceeded to eat.

Sonya laid down, knees up, legs apart, only the doctor's head visible, his hair black and curly, a glimpse of brown skin. The nurse said she could squeeze her hand. The pain was sharp, scratching her body, chalk against board. She pushed her tongue flat to the roof of her mouth, swallowed back the scream. She took the thirty minutes allowed on the cot, body turned into a semicircle, the cramps snapping against her stomach like a racquetball hitting a wall.

Rick came home late that night, after she was already in bed, almost asleep. "How was it?" he asked, slipping into the covers. "Fine," and she turned back into sleep. That night, again and again, she dreamed of a young boy. His hair was blond and smooth like Rick's, but his eyes were round and brown, staring like hers. The boy was maybe four or five. He stood still or turned his head slightly so she could better see him, but he did nothing else. She shook the dream off when she woke up the next morning. But a few days later, on her way home, she walked by a school as kids were being dismissed. They were gathered in front of the building, eager to be given the signal to run. As she looked at them, one boy turned his head to direct his gaze right at her. His hair was blond and his eyes round like her dream. She almost turned to walk to him, to take him, as if he were something she had dropped and needed to retrieve. But the school bell rang, and she continued home quickly.

Over the next two years, both she and Rick were promoted and the mortgage was easier to pay. When they started trying, they expected it would happen right away. With each month, Sonya assumed they had just missed it by a day or two and it would work the next time. After six months, both their energies were depleted and they avoided discussions of what they would name their child.

It was Sonya who finally gathered the courage to make an appointment with a fertility specialist. Each month, as her period arrived, she would become almost immobile, spending days in bed, eating. She had always assumed she would have children, had wanted to have several although now she realized her age would make that impossible. In the corner of her top dresser drawer, she kept a small black and white photograph of her great-grandmother. When she was a child, Sonya's mother would bring out her secret box of various odds and ends, take out the picture and begin to tell Sonya what she knew between her own memory and the stories she had been told. Sonya's great-grandmother was the last one to live her entire life in Egypt. She was married at sixteen, had raised eight children but had given birth to more, perhaps twelve. Some died at childbirth and some as young children. Sonya wondered how you could learn to survive the death of a child as a repeated pattern of your life. She knew little else except that her great-grandmother had been married to a stingy man who watched over the household expenses. But stories had come down about how her great-grandmother had succeeded in outwitting her husband. Each year, as she was the eldest, the women in the family would gather at her house to make the Christmas or Easter cookies, one by one, by hand, the *kahek, ghoriaba, petit fours*. They sat around the table in the kitchen, gathering the dough they had kneaded in their hands, shaping it in the groove of their palms to a circle they could open, stuff with nuts or dates, then pat flat, decorate with the *monash*, sharp like tweezers. The women talked, laughed their secrets, while in the living room the men debated the current regime. Every once in a while, her husband would come in, demand an account of how much flour, how much butter she had used. Only one kilo, she would reply, thumb and two fingers held together in a plea for forgiveness. And he believed her, despite the abundance that would appear on his table each year. No one knew how she manipulated her budget, how she fed them all with the illusion of so little.

The doctor did test after test, always assuring her the process would yield results. Sonya's days revolved around doctor's appointments, keeping track of her cycle, measuring, recording. Rick kept himself aloof, his only contribution being, "I hope it works." Each test yielded nothing significant: some minor hormone imbalances, a slight blockage. She followed every lead like a detective, taking the appropriate medication, doing the recommended procedure. Rick was asked to go through a series of tests. Sullenly, he complied, but everything appeared normal and he retreated back to fixing the storage room in the basement. Finally they were faced with the option of doing in vitro.

"Do you think we should do it?" asked Sonya. She had gone down to the basement and was sitting precariously on a stool while Rick hammered at an old bookcase.

"I don't know. Is it going to work?" he replied through a nail held in his teeth.

"The doctor said the chances were excellent since there isn't actually anything wrong with either of us." She shifted her weight to keep her balance on the stool.

"That's what he said about the inseminations and those didn't work." Rick started hammering the nails in.

"I know, but we have to keep trying."

"Is the insurance going to cover it?"

"I don't think so."

"We can't afford it."

The house grew large after that. There were too many rooms that sat still, unused, except for the kitchen and the bedroom and, for Rick, the media room he had fixed up in the basement which contained simply a couch and a TV with headphones. It was a large colonial house, somewhat typical for New England, white with slender columns in the front, giving it a kind of miniature mansion appearance. But the pillars were too thin for its large structure, making it seem like the house would tip over if they were removed. The inside was room after room painted in clean white strokes with straight angled walls. Sharp lines, no nooks or crannies; nothing distracted the eye.

Sonya began buying bird feeders in the hope of catching sight of the bluebird, which she hadn't seen for some time. She hung one by the kitchen window. A few birds came, mostly sparrows and doves. She bought another feeder, this time putting it in the front, and she took extra care in choosing the birdseed to make sure it would attract bluebirds. As she stood by the living room window, she saw a few cardinals, one bird with yellow feathers, but still no bluebird. The bird feeders multiplied and were joined by several birdhouses. Sonya kept watch, filled the bird feeders and peeked into the birdhouses. A variety of birds flocked to the yard, but still no bluebirds.

Sonya began to grow uneasy, agitated. She jumped when a bit of wind blew against the window, her shoulder twitched at every creak in the house, and her left eye began fluttering so much that she had to place two fingers on it to keep it still. She tried to remember. Her mother had said something about eyes fluttering and bad omens, but it could also be good, depending on which eye, but each person had to figure it out for themselves. Sonya had paid little attention.

Rick suggested a vacation, but she was reluctant to leave in the summer when there was a good chance of catching sight of the bluebird. She continued watching until one morning when she finally glimpsed it through the window. When she lost sight of it, she stepped out to pursue it. Her search took her through the yard from one tree to the next. She even crawled under the Christmas tree, the one they had planted seven years ago when they first moved into this house, now almost ten feet tall. Branches snapped at her sides as she tried to make her way. The pine needles prickled her knees, and she kept picking up her palms, licking them to cool the sharp sting.

EDGE OF ROCK

MAY MANSOOR MUNN

This is the last breath of summer, its heat suffocating, weighing her down. Laila is on her knees in her front yard, scraping at earth, when she sees the boy once more loop around in the street on his bicycle. Not more than eleven, she thinks, a small figure of a boy in an odd-looking hat. He reminds her of her son, Omar, when he was that age: a grapevine, resting on air, its tendrils reaching toward the sun.

Her dog, Charlemagne—a gift from her Texas son-in-law—tugs at the chain secured to the porch railing as the boy, welded to his bicycle, weaves past moving cars in the street. Just then, brakes screech and a car comes to a sudden stop in front of Mrs. Rhodes's house. A man leans out the car window, shakes his fist at the boy who has barely escaped with his life—who now races toward the sidewalk, hits the curb, and lands, splayed, near Laila's driveway. His hat, taking off on its own, lands in Mrs. Rhodes's rosebushes.

"Damn!" he says, loud enough for Laila to hear.

He gets up grumpily, crosses over to the roses and retrieves his hat.

"Guys like him," the boy says, scowling, "should be put away."

Laila glances covertly at the house with the rusted car where, she knows, the boy lives. She says, "Your folks might worry . . . riding your bike in the street like that. Taking risks."

"Ma expects me to be a *sissy*, like some girl. But Dad don't worry none." He taps the crown of his hat. "He got me the hat two years back—just before he skipped town." He flashes a grin. "It's been around, that hat. Fell in a creek near Livingston a year ago. And once, it blew out my ma's car window . . ." A small pause. "Dad's a Louisiana man. Last time he wrote, Ma tore up his letter . . ." A sly look touches the corners of his eyes. "But I got them pieces when she weren't looking. Made out his address in New Orleans."

Laila marvels at his straw hat, with pheasant feathers forming its headband. Frayed and drooping, it rests lightly on the crown of his head.

He points to the patch of brown earth in the midst of green, and the clumps of wilted grasses at her knees.

"It's against the law, Ma says!"

Momentary fear stings her throat. "To dig in my front yard? To make a garden?"

She understands harassment in a land under occupation. *Her* land. But not here, in America, from this scarecrow of a boy.

She looks into the restless gray eyes of the boy, their color reminding her of a Wadallah winter sky.

"To build in your front yard. It's the law, Ma says."

"It'll be a fall garden," she explains. "The backyard is too shady for growing vegetables."

But here in the front yard, away from the shade of the mimosa tree, she has chosen a few meters to receive full benefit of the sun. Barely a stone to dig, and no edge of rock to scrape or cut into flesh: only rich, loamy earth to weed and till.

Crouching, the boy begins to stroke the amber-splashed fur of Charlemagne. He asks, looking up, "Does he have a name?"

"My son-in-law, the history teacher, named him Charlemagne."

"Funny name for a dog." A reflective pause. "Think I'll call him Charlie, for short." The boy's gray eyes glint in the sun. "My name's Billy. What's yours?"

"Laila el-Fihmi." She says it slowly, carefully, the way her Detroit teacher pronounced it in English class.

Billy scratches the back of his head. "Never heard *that* name before . . ."

"It's an old country name." Laila smiles. "Mrs. Rhodes next door calls me Miz El—for short. You can, too."

Billy stands up, looks back at the dog. "Ma don't allow no dogs at our house." A matter-of-fact statement brooking no sympathy.

Tenderness, like a breeze, filters through Laila's defenses. "Come by tomorrow at one and have dinner with us," she says. "You'll get to meet my daughter, Salwa, and her family. You can play with . . . Charlie."

Billy shrugs. "Don't promise nothing."

He gives the dog a quick pat, leaps on his bike, and like a young horseman, gallops across the lawn and back into the street. He turns and waves his hat at her—a small city boy, playing at cowboy.

Work in the garden for now must wait. Coring and stuffing the squash for tomorrow's dinner will have to come first. A few weeks before, when Salwa finally persuaded her mother to leave Detroit for Houston, Salwa and her family started to come to dinner every Sunday—the children spilling over Laila's small house, filling its corners with a vortex of motion and noise. Ramzi, five, his brown eyes questioning the hidden meanings of the adult world, often came to her for comfort. Katy, two years older and more self-sufficient, and Jesse, eight, played noisier games outside, with Charlemagne.

Laila brings out the mound of squash, corer and pan, sets them all on the patio table, and settles down in the porch swing.

As her hands begin to deftly hollow out each squash, she considers the shape and color of the houses on her street. Except for Mrs. Rhodes's brick house, all the houses in her neighborhood are made of wood, with wooden doors and no bars to secure windows.

Their Wadallah house is built of stone, with iron bars across windows and heavy steel doors. Her grandfather built the house to last the centuries.

But here, in this rented house, a thief could easily break glass, or pry open windows and crawl in—unhampered by steel or stone. For the first few days of her arrival here from Detroit, the thought had kept her awake—until Bob, her son-in-law, gave her the dog, to allay her fears. A dog named Charlemagne.

"He's a half-Sheltie," Bob said and expected her to understand.

In Wadallah she learned her English from a children's book with colored pictures and a dog named Spot—not Charlemagne. And in

Detroit, she took "intensive" English classes after work, but could not quite master American slang.

Her husband, Bakri, remained behind in Wadallah—refusing to abandon the house, the vineyard, and the olive tree to strangers.

"Your brother in Detroit is right," Bakri had said. "Go now, for the children's sake. You can always return when our world is safe again."

A promise and a hope.

Laila's brother, who owned an import store in Detroit, even sent them tickets. But her daughter, Salwa, seventeen, and her son, Omar, fourteen, left Wadallah reluctantly.

Laila worked long hours in her brother's store, and practiced her spoken English every chance she got.

"Is your husband well, Mrs. Brown?" she asked a regular customer once.

"Well enough to nag the daylights out of me," Mrs. Brown replied. "Between you and me, I think he's got bats in his belfry . . ."

"And how are the bats in your poor husband's belfry?" Laila asked the next day. Mrs. Brown shook her head, and hurried out with her jar of marmalade, her black olives—perhaps too worried about her husband's condition to answer.

Independence—Laila's children gloried in the word. She raised them to explore their talents, to test their strength. But in the end, each chose a separate path. Her daughter, Salwa, fit into American life like old-fashioned bread around pebbles in a *taboon* oven. In college she met Bob, with Texas roots, and brought him home to meet her mother. When Laila inadvertently called him "Boob," his laughter exploded in her face. Later, in private, Salwa gave her mother a lesson in accents and American slang.

Her son, Omar, missed his father, worried about political events in their country. Two years ago, at age seventeen, he decided to return to Wadallah to live.

As a small boy, Omar had rebelled against authority and the wisdom Laila offered—probing and testing for himself. Once at age six, defying warnings, he climbed their olive tree to the highest branch, and promptly fell, breaking his leg. Her scoldings only served to spur him on toward a second and even third try.

If Laila had her way, he would study medicine. He had the brains for it. My son, the physician, she would say to anyone who asked.

As Mrs. Rhodes hobbles across the yard toward Laila, Charlemagne strains at his leash, the beginning of a growl forming in his throat.

"I've lived in this neighborhood for thirty years," Mrs. Rhodes says, leaning against the porch railing. "But, my dear, this place is fast going to the dogs."

"I usually keep the dog in my backyard," Laila says apologetically. "But today, I thought the change . . ."

Mrs. Rhodes's laughter crackles across the yard. "I'm not talking about *real* dogs. Just houses and people." She sniffs, drawing up the muscles of her sagging face. "Like that family with six kids down the street. And the dump where Billy lives."

Laila's hands pause momentarily in their task. "How old is Billy, anyway?"

"Not a day under fourteen!" Mrs. Rhodes plunges her cane into the grass at her feet. "But he's small for his age. And not too bright. This is his third year in the sixth grade, you know." She waves her hand in the air above her head. "And that sloppy hat he wears. I bet a dog's ear he sleeps in it."

She focuses pale green eyes on Laila's face. "By the way, what's your son up to these days?"

What can Laila say? Mrs. Rhodes would understand little, if anything. Since *she*, his own mother, fails to understand.

In his last letter, Omar wrote, "I've joined the Resistance. I've pledged to fight this unjust military occupation till the end . . ."

Concerned, she wrote back that same day, to dissuade him, to ask: "But how will you earn a living? What does your father think?"

She was still waiting for answers.

Laila meets Mrs. Rhodes's glance, allows herself a careful smile. "Omar has been accepted in medical school." She speaks clearly, without flinching, waits for words to find their mark.

Mrs. Rhodes curls her lower lip. "When he becomes a *real* doctor, maybe he can find a cure for my arthritis . . ." With a flourish of her cane, Mrs. Rhodes turns and heads back to her own yard.

Midway into their Sunday dinner, Billy walks in, his hat pushed back, his face pink with scrubbing. Hesitantly, he slides into the empty seat between Bob and Ramzi.

Laila serves him the stuffed squash with the sterling silver spoon her children gave her for her fortieth birthday. Billy runs his finger over the raised indentations on the handle. "Never seen real silver before," he says, wide-eyed.

"The rest of my 'silverware' is stainless steel," Laila admits.

Later, over coffee, Salwa looks uncertainly into her mother's eyes. She and Bob are contemplating a possible trip to Mexico—without the children. A chance for the honeymoon they've never had.

Laila feels a surge of compassion for the small girl Salwa once was. At eight, seated cross-legged on the floor, she had tried to fit together pieces of a broken doll. An hour passed before she brought its shattered skull—bisque oozing with glue—and set the pieces before her mother. "Help me this time, please," she said. "I won't ask again. I promise."

Until the next time. And only if absolutely necessary.

Of course, she'd be glad to stay with the children for a week. What were grandmothers for?

Monday morning, when Billy stops by Laila's house on his way to school, she says, "I won't be here next week, Billy. I need someone to take care of Charlie. And to water my new garden."

He stands in the doorway, his hat light and airy on his head. "How much?"

"Five days. Five dollars."

"In advance?"

Laila nods. "If you like . . ."

He flicks his fingers at the inner rim of his hat. "Will do."

"I've planted cabbages and carrots," she says. "Water mornings if you will."

"Plant corn," he says. "I like corn."

"I'll plant corn in the spring."

Before he leaves, Billy asks suddenly, "You got more kids of your own?"

"One son, almost nineteen, who lives with his dad in a place further, even, than New Orleans."

She shows him the photograph of a grinning Omar in blue-striped shorts, a soccer ball balanced precariously on his head.

Billy shrugs. "He's big. Not like me."

Laila glances at Billy's hat that adds inches to his height. "You're a good size, Billy. Just right for you."

"Wouldn't hurt to grow two, three inches more," he says skeptically.

Later that day, as Laila rakes the garden soil smooth, the postman brings Laila the hoped-for letter from Wadallah.

Her husband, Bakri, writes of pruning their old olive tree. He plans to graft it with a cultivated olive sprig, a plumper type. Then, as if speaking about the weather, he tells Laila of the arrest of the cobbler's only son, age seventeen. He'd been interrogated and forced to sign a confession. "Their house or business may be in jeopardy because of it. One is never quite sure what else the military will do in collective retaliation . . ."

"But don't worry about us here," Bakri adds. "Omar has finally found a job he likes. He comes by my coffeehouse nearly every day to eat a falafel or kabab sandwich, to ask about my day. He promises to write you soon . . ."

Omar's promised letter arrives on Friday. Laila glances at the crisp, rounded handwriting, the alien stamp. She pictures Omar seated across from her, his eyes—a smoky brown rimmed with a fringe of dark lashes—intent on her face. A poet's eyes to cause a girl's heart to melt, a mother's heart to weep.

"We watch over each other, my father and I," he writes. "But we do miss you and your home-cooked meals. God willing, we'll see each other soon." He adds, almost as an afterthought, "Did my father tell you of my job at the furniture factory? I enjoy working with wood. I like the feel and smell of it . . ."

This is his answer then—to alleviate a mother's worries. My son, the carpenter, Laila thinks. It will have to do for now.

At her request, Laila's grandchildren call her Sitti.

"*Bahib-kum!*" she says and gives each a hug. "That means I love you."

" . . . *hib-kum!*" comes back in a Southern drawl, the guttural sounds turned to mush.

They listen to her memories of her own childhood, of a grandfather who, seated cross-legged under a canopy, had chiseled each stone of their Wadallah house; had even carved his name, the date, and a horse on the lintel, above the front door.

Together they make the dough for the thick pita bread that she will bake in Salwa's modern, self-cleaning oven. And in the backyard, away from prying eyes, she teaches them *takka wigri*, the "pop and run" game—a baseball-like game with sticks.

A day before their parents are due back home from Mexico, they all take a walk to the nearby park. The children climb the wooden pyramid with its rounded holes and slide down—laughing as they bounce onto matted grass. At their urging, Laila allows herself a sudden, dizzying glide, and lands in a rumpled heap on the ground below.

On their way home, as they watch a mockingbird chase away an orange cat, Jesse observes, "Billy has bird-feathers in his hat."

"Bird-hat," Ramzi says with a giggle.

Katy tugs at Laila's sleeve. "Do birds cry when you pull their feathers off?"

But what can she tell them of pain and tears? How could she explain it?

During the drive back to Laila's house, Bob describes with awe the wonders of the Aztec temples and ancient Mexican pyramids.

"Please come to dinner Sunday," Bob says. "I'm cooking barbecue on our outdoor grill. Not as complicated as your stuffed squash . . . but just as good."

She wonders now whether Salwa ever spoke to Bob about

Wadallah. Did she ever describe the rock-strewn hills, the lingering sunsets, the anemones growing wild in the spring? Did he follow the politics of her tortured country?

Did he care?

Laila turns the small brass key in the lock and opens her front door. In their house in Wadallah, their key was made of iron and required muscle power to turn. Inside, she finds the mail pushed through the slot in the door and scattered on the rug. Junk mail, a magazine or two, a letter from Detroit, and the anticipated letter from Wadallah.

She walks outside to check on Charlemagne. Dry dog-food nuggets still remain in his bowl, and his water bucket is almost full. She sighs with relief. Billy has kept his word.

Laila settles down in the living room with a cup of hot minted tea, props her legs on a stool, and carefully opens the letter from her husband, Bakri.

For a long time, she sits with the open letter in her lap and stares at beige walls, leaning. She is sliding down a dark and narrow tunnel, deep into rocky earth. Empty, airless space covers her like a blanket, takes her breath away.

And no one knows her name.

She hears a loud knocking at her door. When she opens the door, Mrs. Rhodes walks into the living room, a hat dangling between thumb and forefinger. Billy's hat! She sits across from Laila, and drops the hat on the rug at her feet. From a small coin purse, Mrs. Rhodes takes out a folded piece of paper sealed with tape, hands it over to Laila.

"Gone to New Orleans to look in on my old man," begins the scribbled, misspelled note. "The fiver wasn't enough for bus fair. So had to hock your silver. Pried your window open to get in but didn't take nuthin else. Fed Charlie. And watered the garden. Keep that hat til I make good on your silver spoon. Billy."

Mrs. Rhodes's glance moves in an arc, settles on the air letter in Laila's lap.

"So—how long will it take before that son of yours hangs up his doctor's shingle?"

Laila's answer is crisp, filled with a mother's pride.

"Several years, I'm sure. Besides, he's planning to specialize . . ." Laila's mind skims over options, settles on one. "Eyes, he says."

"Tell him to hurry up—before my cataracts get any worse . . ."

"My husband," Laila adds softly, "is planning to come here for a visit."

"I suppose it'll be good to have a man around the house." Mrs. Rhodes draws in her breath. "Mine's been gone these twenty-odd years."

"Dead?" inquires Laila solicitously.

"Nope, just run off." A glazed look settles on Mrs. Rhodes's face. "Left me just before Thanksgiving. Told me he couldn't stand my sweet potato pie." Mrs. Rhodes heaves an involuntary sigh. "And all these years, I thought it was his favorite."

She adds, after a pause, "But I've learned to cope—with or without him. Learned to stand on my own two feet—even if they *are* old and crippled."

After Mrs. Rhodes leaves, Laila reaches for Billy's hat, studies its nicks and crevices, runs a finger across its feathered hatband. She thinks of Billy, small and vulnerable without his hat. She missed him already.

The face of her son, Omar, suddenly imposes itself under Billy's hat. She can see Omar's slow-spreading smile, the flickers of light in his dark eyes.

What "terrible" crime had he been accused of?

"Someone, under interrogation in the *zinzanah* prison, claimed Omar 'conspired against the military,'" Bakri wrote. "When the soldiers came to arrest him, he . . ."

She draws in her breath as words shift, go under—like ducks drowning. She waits for words to reappear, unscrambled, on the page. She rereads the letter twice. Three times.

Finally understands.

Laila remains alone in her living room until the sun melts into the rooftops outside her window. She feels light-headed, like a child on a swing pushed to the furthest corner of space. She will have to hold on tight, lest the rush of wind in her face make her dizzy and cause her to lose her grip and fall.

Later, at dusk, when the earth has begun to cool, Laila goes outside to look at the garden. She gets down on her knees and discovers tiny sprigs of cabbage and carrot leaves breaking through rock-free earth. She remains on her knees for a time, her husband's letter still tucked into her bodice.

He'd tell her the details later, when he saw her face to face, he wrote. Then, as if to reassure her, he tells her of their olive tree.

The blast the soldiers had used to dynamite their house had not even scorched the olive tree. The tree remained standing, rooted in rocky soil, towering over the strewn and blackened stones that had once been their home.

SHAKESPEARE IN THE GAZA STRIP

SAHAR KAYYAL

When Muna stumbled toward the teacher's desk, Miss James could barely contain her annoyance at this late time in the school day. She peered into the little girl's face, whose cheeks were as red as plums, her wide eyes brown like their pits. The girl wore a traditional blue and white striped uniform wrapped around her body like a chef's apron. Underneath the uniform dingy jeans with worn kneecaps bashfully peeked at the teacher. Miss James sighed as she sized up Muna, mentally counting the times she had summoned the girl to her desk in the last four months.

"Muna," Miss James said, drawing out the girl's name so that it sounded like *moona*. "This is the third time you have not brought your supplies. How will you even begin a project that the other girls have almost completed?" Miss James spoke slowly and deliberately. The other girls looked up with alertness from their desks, recognizing that tone which teachers often used to express their discontent when a child fails to follow instructions, throwing the small scheme of classroom life out of whack. Miss James continued to watch the girl's face for any movement of expression or beginning of speech. But the girl only silently looked back, gazing into her teacher's blue eyes, then above to the black mascara and the hints of yellow shadow on Miss James's lids. Miss James blinked with stern purpose for a few more seconds, waiting for a suitable answer.

Muna did not respond and the spot between her soft eyebrows crinkled and she seemed to be pondering the weight of this dilemma as though it were not hers at all but the burden of the teacher. When Muna looked up into Miss James's eyes, the teacher could see that this girl had detached herself from the problem, rerouting its head in the direction of Miss James to head off. Miss James gave her a wide frown and sent her back to her desk.

The young girl slowly moved away, her eyes darting around the class of fourteen-year-old girls busily assembling their shoe box dioramas. Fallen debris from the slicing of construction paper and colorful yarn lay scattered in the aisles. The girls had been careful to dispose of their waste as soon as it was produced, but as class time passed, the girls absorbed themselves in their work, allowing scissors to fly without bustling to pick up the deposits. In spite of her aversion to disorder, Miss James did not interrupt the steady buzz of activity, priding herself on her efforts to engage her students.

The project was a culmination of their unit on Shakespeare, complete with readings from *A Midsummer Night's Dream* and student-made replicas of the Globe Theatre. Although the intifada shut down the market place without warning and for erratic lengths of time, some students had managed to secure old shoe boxes, or some other rectangular cartons. If they were industrious, the girls brought extras to share with their classmates.

For her part, Miss James managed to find Styrofoam chunks from discarded office supply boxes that the girls could pierce with decorative pieces, producing a frieze of the heavens, or perhaps carve a column for either side of the stage. When she had planned the unit weeks earlier, she had been fiercely confident about her objectives. She was oblivious to the fact that most of her students did not purchase shoes that came in boxes with crisp tissue paper, but trod to school and back in secondhand, thrice-retongued shoes. The original pairs did not come from carpeted mall shops where Israelis milled on their side, but from Jerusalem alleyways where street vendors with dirty fingernails sold three for the price of two. Sometimes, chagrined mothers found they had purchased a pair with two right feet. But they stored them away, as though they might chance upon finding the other half of the odd pair. With barely enough to get by under curfews, these mothers had not the heart to throw them away.

Any lack of supplies never dampened Miss James's enthusiasm, however, and she continued to straighten her back with the stiff support of a mission statement that she had been forced to make up herself. The administration's goals at Al-Zuheir School for Girls were less progressive and limited to short-term aspirations. Locating an adequate number of books that were only missing their cover page or which required just a quick rebinding of their broken spines was a tremendous achievement. This year the school had managed to recycle broken legs of wooden desks to create bookends. She was endowed with positive thinking, and its wings allowed her to continually float above wretched frustration when projects disintegrated because the majority of her students could not follow through on materials or activities required outside of her realm. As the days passed she was not always able to hold back a sense of weariness that seeped into some of her mornings. Brown paper bags, Popsicle sticks, and rubber bands were elusive items. Instead of serving as tools for creative products, they became tiny pellets that shot down her ideas, before escaping into the indifferent eyes of her students. Miss James had trouble believing that the students of Al-Zuheir School did not own much beyond the unattractive uniforms and their own limbs.

When she vented to her colleagues, they offered sympathetic smiles and nods that only further embittered her. She could not comprehend their lack of initiative, and saw their apathy as "the very root of regression that perpetuates ignorance and illiteracy in the student body of Al-Zuheir School," as she wrote to her family. She did not understand why they failed to try harder. It was not as though they were unlike her; the majority of the staff that worked for the school had been recruited from the United States. She had enlisted through a charitable organization called Tomorrow's Youth in central Nebraska. Ignited with empowerment, she accepted her position to teach in the heart of the Gaza Strip. She gave up the full-time benefits of a sales manager in a local department store. The aftermath of the 1980s corporate boom had left many like her "wanting something more." After minor certification procedures and with an inherent love of literature, she was ready.

She had to consult a map to find the school's exact location in the

Middle East, not altogether familiar with the region; she had only heard tidbits in the news about "escalating violence as 1987 draws to an end." At any rate, she told herself, she was not foreign to feeling compassion for others. She knew the experience would offer a once-in-a-lifetime opportunity to help and understand "a third-world under-class of disenfranchised men and women," as she told her parents.

"Particularly, those poor women," she added, "who already have one count against them because of their religion, as you know."

She felt exalted as she packed her bags, filling an overnight with a dozen sticks of deodorant (she had heard that the hygienic habits of Middle Eastern people were different than those of Westerners) and professional salon conditioner. She stocked up so as not to find herself in an indelicate situation.

Al-Zuheir School was a mass of small buildings that catered to the primary through secondary grades. Its grounds were quite beau-tiful and lacked any of the uniformity that Miss James was accus-tomed to in the well-manicured landscapes of American suburbia. She nodded at the thick-trunked fig trees and a few random willows, carefully breathing in a whole new nature. Although Muslim girls were generally non-athletic, the school had a small basketball court where daily physical education classes participated in track drills and volleyball spiking techniques.

The first semester had been quite an adjustment for Miss James. In the month before the new school session, she spent time sight-seeing around Gaza's dusty and heavily populated city and acquaint-ing herself with local flavors at the *hisba,* a common marketplace. In the beginning, she reveled in the natives' awe of her long, blond hair that softly swayed in the dry breeze as she moved from stall to stall, picking up persimmons or guava and sniffing them. Girls gravitated toward her, their own hair coarse and hanging heavily down their shoulders, the color of the cool licorice drink vendors coaxed her to try. Others wore the *hijab,* betraying nothing of the texture that was hidden beneath. When they made quick chatter that she guessed was an affirmation of her beauty, she felt quite special until those times when she stopped at a particular stall, to purchase cactus fruit, which she had no idea how to eat, and people began to actually touch her head. Women and men, without her permission, gently grabbed strands of her hair, blessing and envying it at the same time. Soon, it became quite an intrusion to her, but she shrugged it off as yet another eccentricity of culture. After each vigorous tug, she smiled politely, her white teeth slightly grating.

By October, Miss James had settled into Arab life as smoothly as can be expected during rough political times, and not without glowing enthusiasm and staunch idealism that she would be making a contribution greater than any that had come before her. She never feared for her own safety, and was more impassioned by the risks she took in educating these unfortunate children. Teaching a race of girls who were quite anti-Western did not discourage her. On the surface, she saw them as merely another cluster of stars that shone dimly in humanity's universe—she ignored the fact that actual light years existed between her and them.

Settling into a new culture was made a bit easier by the demographics of the student body. It included a sliver of American-born children whose families had turned their urban grocery store profits into an extended living income and one-way plane tickets to their native homeland for a more traditional lifestyle for their children. Of particular concern were their daughters, whose chastity would be better preserved in a place where roller rinks and arcades would not tempt them to date American boys. But these girls had sipped a modern way of life and they were boldly outspoken, unlike their Palestine-born counterparts, whose tongues were tempered by the fierce gaze of their mothers. This new breed of Arab girls was quite petulant, but enormously compelling to the greater population. They responded to Miss James's quick questions on themes and settings in almost perfect English, and behaved with more audacious mannerisms than their native Palestinian sisters. As much as she enjoyed their presence in her class, these American Arabs barely sprinkled the rundown desks that were jointly occupied by the natives.

The second group that attended Al-Zuheir did not resemble the former set of students in the least. The natives could not fathom the luxury of eating Hershey bars from their fathers' store shelves whenever they wished, or turning on a television set that aired *The Brady*

Bunch instead of Islamic sermons. Their upbringing was bleak and uneventful, as nightly raids and rock-throwing demonstrations had become no more startling to them as young women than when they were infants in their mothers' arms. They were quiet and listened intently when Miss James asked questions and turned solemnly toward their American-born sisters, who often answered. They seemed to enjoy being near those Western-clad bodies, with faux-fur-trimmed boots—although it never snowed in Gaza—and thick wool sweaters during November and December when winter gusts were severe. Their own coats had too many holes in the pockets and were frayed at the cuffs, as Miss James came to learn, from two or more siblings sharing each coat's sparse warmth. These students came from the dregs of refugee camps that formed clusters around the Strip, a generation of children "whose futures had been marred by displacement," she wrote to a friend, "who grieved the loss of brothers to bullets." At the beginning, Miss James stared at their coats when they read silently, quickly looking away when students felt her eyes upon them. She tried hard not to let their poverty deter her from her goals. Miss James was of the opinion that any child, no matter what her socioeconomic status, could be educated.

For the rest of the first marking period, Miss James spent most of her energy concentrating on guided paths. She was quite optimistic about her presence and glided around the room in regal complacency and sniffed at her students with superiority as they sat uncomfortably in mismatched desks, some etched with pro-Palestine graffiti. She consulted her literature files. Poe, Whitman, Dickinson and Twain—she had planned to unleash as many gems from Western humanity as possible. She pointedly ignored the majority of vacant stares from her students at the close of each masterpiece. With time, she also learned to ignore their physical appearance, itchy heads and jaundice-color faces, until they melted away and the only thing left of their existence for her to confront were their eyes. Sometimes, she wished those would disappear, too.

Shielding herself from the negative responses of her colleagues about a Shakespeare unit, Miss James forged ahead, determined to prove an unimaginative faculty wrong. Only minor setbacks occurred, the first having to do with selecting a piece. Although her favorite was *Romeo and Juliet,* she was dissuaded from using that play because of its themes, inappropriate to a Muslim population. Some of its content, a few colleagues insisted, such as its premarital encounters and suicides, might be too sensitive for the girls. To avoid any heated confrontations by fathers and elder brothers, Miss James, inwardly disappointed, chose a comedy instead, *A Midsummer Night's Dream.* She quickly self-inflated again with excitement at the prospect of puns and misconceptions. She set about casting the class for readings from their shared scripts from a copy of her Riverside edition of Shakespeare's complete works, as there was a restriction on paper copies, generated from the only Xerox machine the school owned. When a few of the native girls were assigned their roles as fairies, their faces screwed up in confusion at names such as "Cobweb" and "Peaseblossom." Miss James chuckled with good humor and asked one of the fluent speakers of English to explain what a fairy was. Panic replaced the looks on their confused faces and the girls began to shout.

"What?! Jinn! Jinn!" They refused to participate and a few began to sob.

A colleague of Miss James later explained that the girls had associated the fairies with mischievous, demonic figures in the Koran that harassed and led good-doers away from Allah. For approximately eight minutes, she could do nothing to alleviate their anxiety or stop the quick, biting Arabic that the girls switched to during those excited moments. Her spirits sank within a body that ached with exhaustion, and she had not realized until that day how tired she actually was. Her mind had always coaxed and placated her physical self, but it failed to submit the next morning. For the first time in half a year of school, she called in sick. When she returned the girls had made a banner from her supplies box welcoming her back. She was quite touched by their affection and resumed her struggle to elevate them.

For the remainder of the month, Miss James continued to work toward her students' enlightenment, while makeshift homes were raided nightly in the refugee camps, tin roofs pounded by rifles, producing an awful clanging of metal that she sometimes heard as she lay in her relatively safe bed in a room shared with a colleague on the school's grounds. The death toll rose over the months, but the intifada drew its strength from spilled blood and breathed even more vehemently in the face of oppression. Her family worried and continually begged her to return to Nebraska where she could easily find a teaching position. She did not doubt that prospect, as her experience abroad would embellish any resume. However, she would not give in and woke every morning with consistent objectives and creative projects. After all, her students needed her.

Muna, her most disorganized and disheveled student, was gone for approximately two weeks. Miss James asked her class if the girl was ill. There were a few minutes of timid silence, as though she had demanded if someone had used her markers without permission. A native student with glasses that were held together on the left with masking tape finally spoke up.

"Miss, Muna's brother . . . he die."

"He died? How?" Miss James asked as she shuffled a stack of papers into a neat stack on her desk. "Was he sick?"

The girl gave a quick, puzzled look to her neighbor, while an exchange of raised eyebrows ensued among the rest of the pairs of eyes now on Miss James like the dirty pigeons of the *hisba* targeting decaying fruit on the street.

"Oh, of course not!" Miss James hastily said. Although Miss James rarely exhibited a variety of emotions in front of her students, her thoughtlessness could not be checked quickly enough. Blood saturated the inside of her cheeks as the heat of embarrassment raised the temperature under her armpits.

"He was the oldest, Miss. He was caught in a *muzahara*. A demonstration after prayers on Friday," the girl with the glasses said. She removed her battered lenses to wipe away a few quiet tears. Other girls began to sniffle, and Miss James immediately regained composure in order to stop a contagion of weeping. She loudly instructed them to open their spelling workbooks and concentrate silently for the remainder of the period. Time passed slowly until they collected their notebooks and pencils for their next class. Miss James did not look up, busying herself with a set of papers she had pretended to be grading. No one said anything to her as each left, single file out the door. After the last girl had departed, Miss James began sobbing uncontrollably. She could not stop, but struggled against a new tide of tears every few minutes. In exhausted submission, she allowed her sobs to ease into silent streams until she could gather herself to find rough brown tissue in a nearby washroom stall.

A colleague consoled her later on and offered to accompany her if she wished to pay respects to Muna's family. Her colleague was familiar with the inner streets of the refugee camp where Muna lived, having habitually escorted young girls who remained after school until dusk and who were afraid to enter their homes without a chaperone. Miss James declined the offer, telling her colleague that an American face would be the least welcome thing to the grieving family. Inwardly, she cringed at the thought of entering the home of a family that had lost a son to senseless violence. She felt somewhat of an enemy, trespassing across their lives. Although her colleague pressed her, Miss James angrily refused.

The following week, she resumed her lesson plans with slower movement, and was reluctant to begin a contemporary poetry unit. Her students continued to diligently work like little chicks vying for the attention of the mother hen. However, Miss James no longer looked in their faces, but secured her watchful eyes above their heads and spoke to someone invisible and sympathetic. Her voice, once authoritative and loud, was now level and soft. She did not recognize her own writing on the board—handsome penmanship that was as out of place as her blond hair.

A few days before spring break commenced, a week of relaxation and reflection for Miss James, Muna returned to school. Before the first-period bell sounded, Miss James caught sight of her speaking with another teacher, the colleague who had offered to escort her through the refugee camp. Muna smiled fondly into this teacher's face and did not pull away when she was gathered into her arms for a quick embrace. Miss James quickly walked in the opposite direction toward her classroom.

The other girls greeted her with an equally warm reception. The

American-born group overwhelmed her with hugs and gave her candy bars that their relatives had brought with them from the States. Her native sisters spoke soft words of bereavement and she nodded at their kind tones. She shyly accepted all of their condolences, in the different, yet sincere shapes they took, and found her seat. Her once soft and expressionless face was slightly harder now, and her eyes that had roamed over Miss James's face with obstinacy had filled with a sorrow that belonged to someone else. She held the look of a woman who had given birth to a stillborn child, confined to a corner of the house where her groans might be discreetly suppressed within the cracked walls.

Miss James did not immediately address her, feeling awkward and suddenly clumsy as she dropped her eraser and knocked her knee against the back of her desk chair. When she finally locked eyes with Muna, she was overwhelmed by a feeling of alienation, of being lost and without the language to call out to someone for help. Muna's dark mooneyes did not blink at her, but reflected a dim light from somewhere that Miss James could not tap.

She watched the girls settle into a steady chatter about their weekend affairs in pleasant tones, some retrieving crumpled homework assignments from their book bags, while others dug at cakes of dirt under their fingernails from plucking and mincing *mulkhiyah* leaves. She turned her eyes to the walls that held motivational posters and several that highlighted the basics of composition. Before the first day of school, she had carefully tacked up a cluster to hide the peeling and chipped walls. She noticed, now, she had not gotten every crack.

Arabic Lessons

David Williams

In America, Nour never mentioned she had once been a nun. Out of respect for her suffering, we kept our questions to ourselves, but didn't know what to think. Not only had her vocation been a mark of family honor ("Your mother's cousin in Lebanon took Holy Orders!"), but she had nearly been martyred for the Faith. Her kidnappers had been about to do God knows what to her when Arafat himself intervened by phone. "Wasting a nun would have been bad PR," my Uncle Joe explained with authority. "We don't owe that dog a thing."

When the war in the old country started, Uncle Joe rediscovered his Maronite roots. We didn't know what to think. Since high school, he'd pushed away his parents' immigrant ways and modeled himself on Sinatra. His attitude had sparked endless family dramas, and guaranteed a yelling match each Christmas. We kids couldn't guess when it might explode, or understand why the adults fought so hard. Uncle Joe, my mother said, could charm anyone until they got to know him. My sister and cousins and I still thought he was more fun than anyone, at least until a fight broke out.

But starting in 1975, he made a point of driving forty miles to attend the Maronite Mass while we continued to worship down the street at Our Lady of Vilna. My mother said politely, "I'm glad he's going to church again." But my sister Paula and I knew it was weird. This was the same Uncle Joe who had never done what was expected of him. Who'd refused to either go to college or take his place at the mill, and instead sang and played piano in a lounge. Who could have made records and left town for the Big Time if he'd only gotten a break. Who told me, "Everyone knows Sinatra's Italian, but he's so great it doesn't matter." Who got into trouble at the track, and needed the family to rescue him from a loan shark. Who refused to settle down with a good Lebanese girl, stayed out all hours, and married some beatnik Unitarian agnostic he met in a jazz club.

Well, not some beatnik, exactly. Libby Blake, whose grandparents had owned the mills our grandparents, and most of the rest of the family, worked in. The snapshots from their courtship show a pale ballerina whose image seems to have been pasted into the dark crowd that was us. She wore a black sweater, black skirt, black pumps. "Who died?" my aunts joked behind her back. And being too young to get it, I asked Libby, with great concern, "Who died?"

"No one, honey," she answered. "Why do you ask?" And I sensed I shouldn't explain.

About a year after she married Joe, we started finding him some mornings asleep on our couch. "He worked late and didn't want to wake up Aunt Libby," my mother whispered.

"He didn't wake *us* up," I whispered back, unconvinced. "Doesn't he have a couch at home?"

"Your father is his brother," she replied, and I nodded as if that explained everything.

After my father died, Uncle Joe spent even more time at our house. To help us out, he told everyone. My mother rolled her eyes. Mostly he ate, smoked, watched TV, and complained about Libby, who wanted him to quit gambling and gigging and get a steady job. "Since the goddamn Beatles killed real music, the only gigs I can get are weddings. I do a wedding almost every weekend, sometimes two. She says any more weddings and she wants a divorce. Where did I find her? A real piece of work. If I come in late, she thinks I'm fooling around. Sure I connect with the crowd. Is that a crime? I ask you. Is it? Absolutely not. It's part of the job. Anyway, Shirley says her father has a spot for me selling furniture. Strictly commission at first, but it's a foot in the door. She says I'm a natural. She says I could sell ice to Eskimos. She's sold on me. So guess who's jealous? Hell, I've known Shirley since high school."

Our questions about homework received unreliable if entertaining answers. Especially in social studies, he'd bend the topic to a theme he favored, and hold forth at length. His unlikeliest tales turned out to be true. Every symphonic instrument, for instance, really did have an Arabic prototype. This information came second-hand from Aunt Libby, who not only had a music degree, but liked reading about Middle Eastern culture. Other matters, including Islamic conspiracy theories, came from more obscure sources, and were harder to grasp. We often went to bed with our assignments incomplete, our minds uneasy with the strangeness of the world he had described.

"Every family gets a quota of wildness," my mother once told me. "Your Uncle Joe hogged it all for himself. No wonder Daddy was so quiet." Loving Father, Devoted Husband, who said his flu was just a cold, and died from a ferocious asthma attack. How the hell could that have happened? I still don't get it. I was ten, and my father was dead. Paula was eight, and her father was dead. My mother was thirty, and her husband was dead. I can still feel him near, shy in the doorway, delighted with any little thing that Paula and I did. And the way he looked at my mother—it was something from a mushy movie.

After Joe got religion, he grew concerned about our moral upbringing, though we'd never been in trouble. By now we were adolescents. Disco beat at even the strongest door. We were in danger.

Once he had us all watch *The Sound of Music* on TV while he provided commentary. "The Countess has money and outer beauty. But Maria, who has nothing, has inner beauty."

"I should have been a nun," my mother sighed, her knitting needles clicking.

"Hey! Then how would we be born?" Paula said.

"I didn't mean it that way."

"I know, Ma. I'd become a novice if I could end up with Christopher Plummer."

Joe leaped out of my father's recliner—no mean feat. "What did you say, young lady?"

We froze.

"Joe, sit down," my mother said quietly. She kept her eyes on her knitting, but the needles were still.

"You have no idea! No idea! Think of your mother's cousin, Nour, a nun in Lebanon. She was ready to be a martyr for the Faith! *That's* what being a nun means to *her*."

"Paula's not deaf," I muttered. "Anyway, Arabs invented romantic love." I was willing to draw fire from my sister.

"What's that supposed to mean?"

"Aunt Libby's got this book."

"She's got a book on everything. Anyway, we're not Arabs."

"Arabs are people who speak Arabic." OK, I'd drawn fire.

"We're direct descendents of the Phoenicians. Green eyes, fair hair . . ."

Why quit now? I'd go down in a blaze of glory. "And they said no one would marry my mother because she was too dark. The exact quote was 'too black.'"

My mother sat upright. "Who told you that?"

"Like it's a secret," I said. This was getting way too complicated.

Joe lowered his voice and tried another tack. "Never forget we're Maronites. Never forget what that means."

"What does that mean?" I replied. "Left-wing Maronites? Right-wing Maronites? Extreme . . ."

"*True* Maronites!" he cut in. "You should know what that means. In Lebanon in the twenties, the Muslims martyred the Christians. And not for the first time. That's a fact."

"That's true," my mother said.

"So Sittu and Jiddu could have seen that," Paula said. "Why didn't they tell us about it?"

"That's not necessarily the kind of thing you'd be in a hurry to discuss with your grandchildren," my mother said. "Before that, during World War I, they were in a man-made famine. The Turks controlled Lebanon and took the harvest for their troops. The French blockaded our harbors so nothing could get in. The Lebanese starved."

"Sittu always wanted to feed everyone," Paula said.

"Caught between Christians and Muslims," I said quietly. "When the Moors were in Spain, Muslims and Jews and Christians sat around the fountains having intellectual conversations about science and philosophy and everything."

"And what did they come up with?" Joe snapped. "Romantic love?"

Direct hit. I was fourteen, and wanted to believe Joe and Libby's love had—at least once upon a time—been great enough to blow away all limits. I wanted to believe my mother had once looked at my father the way he looked at her, that their marriage was more than a sensible arrangement, more than the best deal available for two outsiders. I wanted to believe whatever it was the great singer Fairuz released in the dark translucent honey of her voice that made the world suddenly still and deep, even if I couldn't get the words. Even here in the land of the free, where everything was for sale.

Before she came to America, Nour spent a year in France, but couldn't make a go of it. Her relatives here said they'd help her start a restaurant in town. Uncle Tony the bone surgeon and Cousin Charles the computer engineer would take on the bulk of the expenses, as everyone else was waiting for the bounty of Reaganomics to trickle down to us.

"But she doesn't speak English," Paula said.

"She's been studying it," my mother explained.

"She learns French in Lebanon and English in France. What's she going to learn here?"

"American," I said.

We put on our Sunday best to meet Nour at the airport. Our sacred mission of mercy was invisible to the world of strip malls and exit signs we passed on the way. To perky, professional flight attendants, impatient vacationers, preoccupied business travelers, all casually confident in flight, Nour's sorrow was no doubt unrecognizable. But we would understand with one look.

Aunt Libby stayed home so there'd be room in the car for Nour. Joe drove one-handed, weaving cavalierly through traffic while my mother gritted her teeth. He made a parking space appear in the hopelessly packed lot, and slid into it with a single fluid move. We used to think this stuff was cool.

In the terminal, we checked the arrival and departure board. So many places, names I'd only seen in books. Her flight was on time.

We'd always pictured her in her habit, serving poor children with big dark eyes, praying in a mountain convent fragrant with incense and pine. Suddenly there she was, looking small by the airport's huge windows and endless halls.

A family resemblance. Short, thin. Short curly hair. Big, dark, soulful eyes. Navy blue cardigan, plain white blouse, gray skirt, sneakers.

She and my mother embraced and exchanged three kisses on the cheek. My mother's eyes were wet, but not Nour's. I felt the presence of mysteries beyond my experience, a sorrow deeper than my father's death. And all beyond words.

Nour exchanged three kisses on the cheek with the rest of us. Paula beamed and made her smile, the way they almost bumped heads. Nour kissed me delicately, and I responded in kind, as if she had just taught me how. She said my name the Arabic way—"Eh-lee"—and I felt she was addressing someone I'd never known was there.

Joe bent over, scooped her in his arms, and gave her three audible smacks; she barely touched her cheek to his.

Then he stood stiffly at attention and clicked his heels.

Nour froze. Being sixteen, I assumed she thought what I did—that Joe was nuts. In retrospect, I wonder if she wasn't afraid she'd lose her mind.

"Q'taib," he said, naming a far-right Christian militia group, and saluted.

Nour blinked and looked at my mother, who said something gentle in Arabic. Her cousin nodded and remembered to breathe.

While Joe was claiming her suitcase—only one!—I asked my mother what she'd said. "I told her it was just a word from a guy he met at church. He doesn't know one group from another. Typical Joe. He never lets ignorance hold him back. I hope he doesn't scare the hell out of her."

"Wouldn't a militiaman make her feel protected?"

"Guys with guns just get innocent people killed. She's had enough of that crap."

"Is that what she said?"

"You know I was the one who made all the phone calls and wrote all the letters to set this thing up. Tony and Charles are paying for it, and everyone else is all talk. So by now Nour and I understand each other. So here she is feeling in our debt with nowhere else to go. Let's try not to drive her crazy."

On the way home, my mother and Nour spoke Arabic, exchanging news about family members. All I caught were the names. I'd always been amazed at my mother's ability to keep up on all these people she'd never met—four generations, cousins upon cousins— and now Nour was asking about every blood tie we had in America, including folks in Ohio and California I didn't know and could never get straight. From my mother's repeated response of *"Haraam,"* I figured a lot of the news from Lebanon was bad.

Paula was actually following parts of the conversation, having picked up some Arabic during holiday baking sessions with my mother and aunts over the years. The older generation clucked their disapproval that we "didn't speak," but how were we supposed to learn if no one would teach us? Besides, the adults switched to Arabic when they didn't want us to follow what they were saying. Arabic meant sin as much as liturgy, and we Amr'cani were shut out of both. Though Paula, my amazing sister, rode the shifts from one language to another and started filling in the blanks. Sometimes the older women would forget she was even there until my mother cleared her throat and said, "Little pitchers have big ears."

"Let her listen," said my Aunt Yola. "She needs to learn how men are before they start giving her their lines."

I was excluded from the kitchen. My interest in being there put my manhood in question. I hung out with the guys in the living room, watching the game, eating snacks Paula delivered to the men, and now and then standing in the doorway to overhear and interpret what I could from the language of sin, liturgy, kitchen, and soul.

The plan was that Nour would have Paula's bed, and my sister would sleep on the couch. But Nour negotiated in Arabic with my mother, and then went to take a shower.

"You can have your bed back," my mother told Paula.

"Why?"

"She's going to sleep on the floor."

"Why?"

"Sometimes people in the old country promise God to do things like that, and then they have to do them."

"Why?"

"They promised God."

"She promised God to be a bride of Christ," Joe muttered behind the sports section.

"Your wife is expecting you home," my mother said.

"I'm reading something."

"Take it with you. No one here cares about sports."

"I just drove back and forth to Boston. Can't I even have a lousy cup of coffee?"

She sighed. Lebanese hospitality—he had her there. "My coffee isn't lousy."

While Nour was in the shower, Paula and I looked at the things she had unpacked on my sister's night table. Two small black Arabic books—a Bible, probably, and a prayer book, judging by the crosses and the red and black ink. A French book with the words *Nag Hammadi* in the title—that sounded Arabic. A rosary. And a small shortwave radio, much heavier than the transistor Uncle Joe used to carry to check results at the track.

"Leave her stuff alone," my mother told us from the kitchen. Then we heard her tell Joe, "Drink up. Your wife is waiting."

With Nour under our roof, I felt an unexpected peace. We were finally doing something, however small, about the war. Something real, something connected. Over the years, Paula and I had sat up late while my mother had tried to get a phone line through to Lebanon to find out who was dead, who was hurt, who was missing, who was on the road. Kahlil, Amineh, Jamal, Bernadette, Souheil, Samira.

In the early days: "He was a sick old man. He refused to leave his house. Everyone knew him. He dealt with Muslims his whole life on nothing but a word of honor. He couldn't believe his neighbors would kill him. His wife would not leave him. Michel told them they were out of time, but my great-uncle was stubborn. Michel said he'd evacuate his family and be back. But then it was too late. No, it wasn't their neighbors who killed them."

Seven years later: "Now the Southern Lebanese Army has moved in and commandeered Lodi's house. It has a good view of the valley."

"What do you mean, 'commandeered'?"

"They took it."

"Won't they protect the town?"

"Not really. They draw fire. And they expect the local men to join up with them and patrol. Or else they think they're traitors. A lot of the Muslims that the Israelis drove out ended up in the cities, in the poor neighborhoods. The young men are joining Hezbollah. It never ends."

"So why'd the Israelis invade?"

"The PLO was hitting them from southern Lebanon. Now Hezbollah is hitting them in southern Lebanon."

"Lodi's family wasn't hitting anyone. Where are they now?"

"Squashed in with Antoun's. She says the people in the south are caught between the hammer and the anvil."

We decided early that it wasn't much use to discuss all this with our classmates. It was hard enough ducking jokes about terrorists, hostage takers, and Arab Nazis. Our membership in the human race was under investigation. Guilty until proven innocent. My history teacher, Mr. Stiles, made a point of directing questions about the Holocaust to me.

"Why don't we just carpet bomb Lebanon?" Chris Whitlock asked him once.

And Mr. Stiles, who had proudly supported the Vietnam War by joining the National Guard, blamed "Vietnam syndrome."

I had enough nightmares about Lebanon to dread bedtime. I couldn't get the smoke of war out of my nostrils. I started to tell my Uncle Tony, but my mother walked in and interrupted. "Eli, think about someone besides yourself. He doesn't need you reminding him of all that." All that was Vietnam, where he'd served as a medic, and his fellow soldiers called him Tony Bones.

"It's OK, Mary," Tony said.

But I shrugged and escaped. The whole thing was too weird. If I closed my eyes, I'd be on the other side of the world, where the dry wind was barren and everything burned. I was afraid of going crazy. I told no one.

But with Nour under our roof, I went to bed peaceful. And woke from a dream filled with smoke.

The house was still. No explosions, no screaming. The view from the window was intact, familiar. I went to get a drink of water.

Nour was sitting in the living room where she slept, intently listening with earphones to the shortwave. A streetlight reached her from the window. Caught in a net of tenderness, I watched from the dark outside her door. All day long she was the indebted alien. Now she was just herself.

I coughed. She pulled her bathrobe closed and turned on the light. Slipped the headphones off, smiled at me, looked concerned.

"Hi." I blushed. "I just wanted some water."

She patted the couch beside her. I sat down. The delicate warmth from her body was welcome. The dream had left me feeling empty, blown out, cold.

"What are you listening to?" I whispered.

"The news. From Europe and the Middle East. The news here confuse—confuses—me. Wait. I get you BBC." She put on the earphones, searched the dial, then placed them gently on my ears, still warm from hers. A guy with a British accent was talking about cricket in India. I smiled.

"They are awake while we sleep. We sleep while they are awake," she said. This sounded like poetry. Like all the people on earth were dreaming each other. "Eli, are you fine?"

"Yuh. Fine. I'm fine."

"You look like . . . afraid."

"I had a dream . . . about Lebanon."

She nodded. She understood. The warmth returned to my body. My eyes were wet.

"Eli . . ."

"Sometimes I can sense it, feel it, the war, even when I'm not dreaming." Tears escaped. "I'm going crazy."

She touched my hand. "Not crazy," she said. "Eli, no." She thought a moment. "You know the body mystic?"

"The Mystical Body of Christ." I never knew what that meant. "They talk about it in church."

"Eli, you know the mystical body crucified. Not crazy, Eli. True."

Shouldn't I be protecting her from my nightmares? But she seemed so calm. So *present*. More there than I'd ever been in my life.

"I don't want to go crazy," I said.

"The mystical body raise . . . rise."

Nour started making us breakfast before we woke up, and dinner before my mother got home. "She wanted to," Paula, whose chore it was, explained sheepishly. As soon as we finished, Nour leaped up to clear the table and wash the dishes. Flushed with anger, barely keeping her voice neutral, my mother spoke in Arabic to Nour, who protested, but dutifully sat down. My mother put on the kettle and returned to the table.

"After dinner," she said in English so everyone understood, "you and I have a cup of tea. Paula and Eli take care of the dishes. And we don't need eggs every morning." Nour stared at her cup.

My mother was a nurse. She organized things, solved problems, assigned tasks. She liked to say, "Next on the agenda."

Next on the agenda: Uncle Tony, Nour's official sponsor for Immigration, would have a dinner at his house in her honor. Everyone remotely involved with bringing her over, and anyone remotely related to them, was invited. My mother said we would make pastries. Lots of pastries. Since there weren't any old people around to worry that my presence in the kitchen would undermine natural law, I got to help.

"He's good at this," my mother said. "He could bake for your restaurant."

"No, no. You help me too much."

"Help him with French while you're working."

"I'm practically flunking French," I beamed.

My mother explained flunking to Nour.

"And what can I do for Paula?"

"Paula gets A's in French. She's a whiz at languages," I said.

"Teach me Arabic," Paula said.

"Me too," I said.

The restaurant was a small storefront. That weekend the four of us swept it out, washed it down, and painted the walls. Joe arrived to demonstrate the skilled use of a roller, but mostly supervised. Any time Paula or I overlapped a freshly painted area by a quarter inch, he'd snap, "Flashing! That's going to show." After an hour, he had to go somewhere.

Paula and my mother left to do errands. It was just Nour and me. The doors were open to vent paint fumes. Spring air stirred the newspapers on the floor. Sunlight poured in through the storefront window. Nour and I folded the drop cloths—a little dance like folding bedsheets—and brought in the five small tables. She unwrapped a picture of the cedars, and asked where I thought it should be hung when the paint was dry. She called me to the kitchen and made tea.

In that little room, the world felt wide and calm. I could have stayed there with her a good long time.

"My grandmother used to say this thing in Arabic," I ventured. "Like 'Your soul and my soul are two souls as one soul.'"

Nour looked puzzled.

"Like '*Ruhe ruhi* something.'"

Nour smiled. "I know it. 'Soul,' maybe 'spirit.' *Ruhe*. But you can say 'soul.'"

"What's the difference?"

"Hard to explain. *Ruhe* is the breath, the spirit that gives the life.

> *Ruhe ou ruhik, ya ruhi,*
> *Ruhain b' ruh . . .*"

"That's it!"

"That's one half. There's more:

> *'N rahit ruhik ya ruhi,*
> *Ruhi bitruh.*"

"I don't remember her saying the second part."

"It rhymes with the first half. You can hear the rhyme?

Otherwise, it is not complete. *Ruhe ou ruhik* . . . the Lebanese say *ou*. In Arabic, really, you say *wa*."

"But what's the meaning of the whole thing?"

Line by line, she repeated the Arabic, then thought through a translation, using the word "soul," it seemed, out of respect for me.

"Your soul and my soul—Oh my soul!"

"*Ya ruhi!*"

"Yes, 'Oh my soul!'

> Your soul and my soul—Oh my soul!—
> Are two souls in one."

"That's what my *sittu* said. What's the rest?"

She had to repeat the first two lines before continuing the translation.

> "If your soul goes—Oh my soul!—
> My soul will go."

"'Go' . . . like 'follow'?"

"No, 'go' like 'pass away.'"

At Tony's party, Nour kept slipping into the kitchen, and the guests were soon busy talking among themselves. None of us really knew her, I thought, but everybody had a strong opinion about what her presence here meant. My grandparents, newly arrived in the twenties, were labeled "Black Turks"; last week Chris Whitlock called me a diaperhead. Hadn't we learned anything on the receiving end of all that?

In the black-and-white of my sixteen-year-old mind, I tried to work it out. Everything was at stake. As beings with souls, we had the capacity to know each other deeply. Otherwise we just lived trapped in someone else's dream.

Joe had brought someone he'd met at the Maronite church, a dapper young immigrant named Fuad who Paula said had a terminal case of Travolta. He may even have been a militiaman—a rumor he would neither confirm nor deny. He'd gotten some laughs early in the evening by demonstrating how Americans slouched around with long faces, while he, a refugee with nothing but the shirt on his back (nice shirt), was bursting with vigor.

"He knows us better than we know ourselves!" Joe declared. "Our people have spirit!"

Fuad and Joe were drinking *arak* in a corner with my Uncle Richard, a mild man inclined to nod pleasantly while his wife held forth. A nice guy who liked to garden just to give away zucchini and tomatoes. He'd taught me, his fatherless nephew, how to play with the carburetor to start an old car on a frozen morning. I went over to say hello. "Who kidnapped her, exactly?" Richard was asking.

"Communists maybe, Muslims probably, Palestinians definitely," Joe replied.

"Did Arafat really save her life?"

"That's what they say."

"Lucky woman," said Fuad Travolta. "Fly to Paris. Fly to Boston. Nice life."

And who flew you to Boston? I wondered. They hadn't noticed me. I'd say hello another time.

Aunt Libby, who'd brought homemade apple pies (having learned long ago that her attempts at Lebanese cooking would always be judged not quite right), was struggling to remember enough French to talk with Nour. My mother proudly introduced Libby as a college professor and professional musician, while Libby tried futilely to explain that she was just an adjunct instructor who also gave piano lessons at home. She retreated to the living room to set up the big coffeemaker.

Fuad strode in, trailed by Joe and Richard, who had both picked up some of his swagger. Fuad said something to Nour in Arabic. "English, English," Joe insisted. "Mary will translate." My mother glared at him.

"We were just trying to get your story straight," Joe said while Fuad poured the three of them another round of *arak*. Richard looked for cookies. Nour opened a Tupperware container and arranged some for him on a plate.

"Before the war, you spoke for Palestinian rights. You said they needed a homeland. And you said the poor needed justice—

Christians, Muslims, everybody. Those Palestinians and those Muslims killed fourteen members of your family. But you still say they need their rights."

"I don't understand too much English," she said quietly, avoiding his eyes.

"What I don't understand is even after those people did that to your family, your people, your country, you continued to feed their children. Why?" Joe spoke in the confident tone of a prosecuting attorney.

"The children were hungry."

"The Pope said if you want peace, work for justice," my mother said, hoping that would be the end of it. No point arguing with the Pope.

Tony approached through the living room crowd, a doctor sensing an emergency.

"I think we're entitled to an explanation," Joe said.

Nour looked him in the eye, strangely calm. "Our Lord said to give the other cheek."

"We go beyond Jesus!" Fuad roared. "We give no cheek!"

Tony appeared. "Why don't we get some coffee in the other room?"

Fuad headed for the buffet.

"What about Damour?" Joe demanded.

"Damour pays for the Qarentina, Tel Zataar pays for Damour. And so on and so on and so on," Nour said quietly, "to Sabra and Shatila."

"It's a war, for Chrissakes!" Richard exploded, surprised as anyone by his outburst.

"The war is pointless," Tony said. "Maybe if the Syrians and the Iranians and the Israelis and Palestinians and the Soviets and the Americans would stop using Lebanon for a playing field, the Lebanese could put their house in order." For years, this had been his litany for the dead.

"When's that going to happen?" Joe demanded triumphantly, backed by the force of despair.

My mother looked at Richard and Joe. "You two are guests in his house. Now since you were both too young for Korea and too old for Vietnam, I suggest you go have a cup of coffee. Out on the lawn. In the fresh air. Here, take this." She held out a plate of cookies.

"American boys died in Lebanon," Joe pressed on. "They showed the flag."

"And shelled the Chouf," Tony said. "Reagan set up the Marines like sitting ducks. For what? Semper fi." He lifted his empty cup to the commander in chief.

"This isn't Vietnam, Tony Bones," Joe said, and then fixed on Nour. "American boys died for Lebanon. America let you in. We're entitled . . ."

"*Leave her alone!*" I screamed in his face.

Silence flashed through the house. Someone in the living room said, "What happened?"

My mother grabbed my arm and whispered, "What are you, crazy? In front of all these people? You never yell. And now you yell in front of everyone?"

I couldn't meet their eyes. I ran out the back door. Who was following me. "Eli?" Paula's voice. "Eli!" Nour's. But I was too confused and ashamed to face them. I started running down the street, amazed at the energy pouring out of me. I would run until it was all used up. Till I was all used up.

I didn't notice the police cruiser till it blurted its siren beside me. I stopped, hung my head.

"What's your hurry?" One cop blinded me with a flashlight. His partner was on the radio, describing a "Hispanic youth" who was wearing my clothes.

"Nothing . . . sir."

"Just getting some exercise in your Sunday best?"

Anything I said would be wrong.

"Got some ID?"

Nothing they'd recognize.

"Look at me when I talk to you." The other cop came up behind me, shoved me against the cruiser and patted me down.

"Now what's someone like you doing in a nice neighborhood like this running so hard in the dark?"

"My uncle lives over there."

"Well, let's go check that out."

When we arrived, Joe was sitting on the front steps, smoking. He talked to the cops and went to get Tony.

I shrunk in the backseat while Tony cleared things up. They looked suspicious and asked him for ID.

When they let me out, he put his arm around me. Guests watched from the porch.

Joe was on the stairs. "Eli, I was waiting for you. To talk. We're family. No hard feelings, bud."

I kept my eyes down.

"If you don't all go in and have coffee," Tony told the guests, "you'll have my wife to deal with." He held the door for them as they shuffled by.

That left only Paula and Nour. They sat down on the glider. "There's room," my sister said. I sat down between them. Still could not lift my head.

"Eli," Nour said very softly.

"What'd they nail you for?" Paula asked.

"Looking Hispanic," I muttered. "I don't belong in this neighborhood."

"Good for you," Paula joked.

"I can't believe I did that," I whispered.

"Did what?"

"Lost it in there."

"It's a dirty job, but somebody's gotta do it."

"Come on, Paula. Tony was cool. Ma was cool. Nour . . . Nour was *totally* cool."

"Cool?" Nour asked.

"He respects you very much," Paula explained.

"After all she's been through, Nour is totally together, and I can't handle anything. I wouldn't last five minutes . . . I'm useless . . ." I burst into tears. "The world is falling apart and I'm totally useless!"

Paula put her arm around my shoulder. Nour took my hand and looked at my sister, who couldn't translate, couldn't explain.

Instead, with a little kick, she set the glider going. Nour kicked from her side for balance.

My mother came to the door. "Everyone's having dessert." Her presence cut short my sobbing. Her tone said, "Come in and act normal."

"OK," Paula answered. Her tone said, "Go away." My mother retreated.

We could hear the crowd inside, and the creak of the glider, and a car now and then. A plane descended toward the airport and I felt Nour tense. That sound must remind her of the war.

"*Ya ruhi*," I whispered.

"'*N rahit ruhik, ya ruhi*," she said. Then to Paula, "If your soul goes, oh my soul . . ."

And I made it complete: "*Ruhi bitruh.*"

THE TEMPTATION OF
LUQMAN ABDALLAH

NABEEL ABRAHAM

Luqman Abdallah dropped his *Detroit News* paperbag on the sidewalk and climbed three short steps to the door of the York residence, where he pressed the buzzer. Weary under an overcast winter sky, he resisted thinking about the drudgery of being a paperboy at fourteen, and how much he hated spending his Saturdays coaxing $1.75 from each of his customers.

Take any newspaper route in Luqman's Detroit neighborhood and you would encounter three types of customers: The Tippers: those who gladly paid up weekly, throwing in a handsome tip to boot. They were the minority. The Begrudgers: those who ponied up regularly although it obviously pained them to do so. They were the majority. And, finally, the Deadbeats: those who artfully dodged paying their bill with excuses that invariably ended with "come back later." Fortunately, the Deadbeats were only a tiny fraction of Luqman's forty or so regulars. Still in his first year of delivering newspapers, Luqman sensed there was little else he could learn about his customers because they rarely let him past the door of the cash nexus. True, he could spy a tidy or disheveled life here, sniff a foul odor there, but he never got beyond the front door. Well, almost never. On this day, the door of the York residence door would open for him.

I

After waiting several minutes, Luqman decided no one was home and started heading down the stairs. That's when he heard the door crack open behind him. He turned to find Ann York coming slightly into view.

"Sorry, I was asleep and didn't hear the bell till now," she said, placing a hand over a plum-shaped yawn. Stepping out from behind the door, Ann rubbed her eyes slowly.

It was then that Lugman noticed she was wearing a negligee. Embarrassed that he had caught her this way, he apologized, offering to come back. He made a point of keeping his gaze from veering toward the opaque nightgown.

"It's OK. Come up and I'll see if Mother left some money for you," she said nonchalantly.

Lugman stood motionless as Ann made her way up the steep flight of stairs. Free to look without being noticed, he made out the thin outline of her panties. He traced her bare white legs up and down and up again, noting their slender shape, and how their color offset her brunette hair.

"Did she say to come up?" Lugman asked himself. Everything was confusing—the negligee, the panties, the legs, the hair, the invitation upstairs. His head swirled like water running down a drain. "What if I didn't hear her right? Better to stay here than make a fool of myself," he thought.

Lugman had never seen a girl his age in panties. Except for his mother, who'd occasionally raced from her bedroom to the single bathroom in their house clad only in her underwear, an arm covering her breasts, he'd never seen a partially dressed woman except in the girlie magazines that he and his brothers smuggled into their overcrowded house.

"She did say to come up," he reassured himself. "I'd be a fool not to go upstairs. She's going to think I'm some kind of sissy. But what if one of the neighbors across the street saw her? He'd think I was up to no good. I've got to do the honorable thing and stay put," he told himself. Just as he grew comfortable with his decision, Ann called down, "Aren't you coming up?"

Lugman detected a slight irritation in her voice. His indecision weighed on him as he counted the steps on the way up.

"I found the money," Ann said, handing him an envelope, her

sleepiness no longer evident. "Would you like to have some tea?" she asked, smiling.

"OK," he said, trying not to appear eager.

The row of windows overlooking the street below combined with the yellow shag carpet gave the room a light, airy feel. He went for the upholstered orange chair not far from the door. The room held a matching sofa and two armchairs, the one he occupied and another across the room with an ottoman. A TV sat silently in a corner. Nearby, a large sombrero and two maracas occupied a place of honor on the credenza.

Instead of leaning back into its softness, Lugman sat at the edge of the chair. He felt hot under his coat, but refrained from unbuttoning it. His back was to Central Avenue and all the burdens it represented: home, work, and school, the triangular boundaries of his adolescent life.

Still feeling guilty about having disturbed her sleep, Lugman took comfort in Ann's offer of tea. He took this as a sign of her sense of duty to be hospitable, something he had learned growing up in an Arab household. Ann was merely upholding the custom of honoring a guest, he convinced himself, nodding to the sombrero. Traditions like hospitality, Lugman believed, distinguished his family and other ethnics from the rootless Americans, or *Amrekan,* who dominated his working-class neighborhood. He was beginning to feel a bond with Ann.

She disappeared for what seemed like a long time. He figured she was changing out of the negligee into something more proper. The thought of no longer seeing her half-naked left him feeling disappointed. When she reemerged still dressed the same way, he hid his satisfaction, but kept his gaze fixed above her chin.

"I brought some cookies that I know you'll just love," Ann said, as she maneuvered a large tray near the end table beside him. "They're chocolate chip, Mother's specialty."

"Did your mother bake them?" Lugman asked as he readied a compliment, the image of his father talking to a customer in his dry goods store flashing in his head.

"Yeah," Ann responded, grinning.

"That's rare nowadays," Lugman intoned like a young sage in training. "Fewer and fewer women bake anymore."

Ann hesitated, grinned again, and added softly, "She used a ready-mix."

Not wishing to acknowledge Ann's tactical victory, Lugman deployed another compliment, a strategy he had picked up from watching his father. "Still, she had to put it in the oven; you gotta give her credit for that."

Ann ignored the comment as she leaned close to Lugman, the way a cocktail waitress might. "Would you like some milk and sugar?" she said in a voice that sent a pleasant feeling surging through him.

"Yeah," he mumbled, his seriousness disarmed. As Ann drew closer fussing over the tea, he looked off into the room as he was wont to do when a nurse was about to draw blood from him. She brushed his arm; the room became a blur.

She then sauntered across the room, disappearing through the archway again. Lugman was thrilled to be fussed over by a girl partially draped in gossamer. But he was also anxious over what might happen.

In her absence, his mind's eye ran over the silhouette of her slender body. Every time he grew excited about the prospect of sex between them, he heard his mother's voice uttering in Arabic the word "pregnant." No other negative cognate—guilt, shame, sin, syphilis—crossed his mind in that infernal moment. Like a bottle floating in water, "pregnant"—that life-altering word—continued to bob between the waves of excitement rushing over him.

Ann returned from the kitchen and slid into the armchair across the room, plopping her feet on the ottoman. Lugman wondered if there was any meaning or signal in Ann's decision to remain dressed the way she was.

"How's the tea?" she asked, looking straight at him.

"It's good," Lugman said as he pressed the porcelain cup to his lips, tipping it to the point where a few drops ran down the side of his mouth.

"Say," Lugman wondered aloud after a quick wipe of the chin, "how is it that you guys drink tea with milk?"

"What do you mean?"

"Well, most people put milk in their coffee, not their tea," Lugman said as he shifted again into a sage-like mode. "In my house we drink tea with milk, but that is because my parents once lived under British rule, and that's something the British do. Americans tend to put milk in their coffee, not in their tea." Caught between two worlds, Lugman tended to notice cultural nuances the way, say, felons might compare conditions in different prisons.

Ann appeared nonplussed by Lugman's discourse on tea drinking. "I don't know. We've always put milk in our tea," she volunteered.

"I was just wondering because your parents are from Mexico, right?" said Lugman, feeling on top again.

"My mother is from there," Ann responded. "I mean my mother's people are from Mexico, but she's American. So is my dad." Ann crossed one leg over the other and rocked it slowly, revealing her annoyance at where the conversation was going.

Lugman fumbled with his cup and saucer as he struggled to keep his gaze from landing on her legs. Still hoping to find a common bond in their ethnic backgrounds, he persisted.

"What you're saying is that your mother's people are from Mexico, but your dad's aren't."

"Aa-ha."

"Do you speak Spanish?"

"A few words," Ann said with a blank stare, as if she were concealing a buried skeleton in the closet of her heart.

"Does your mother?"

"Yeah, but only to my grandmother."

"It's too bad she didn't teach you some Spanish," Lugman said as he leaned back in the chair, satisfied the conversation was going his way.

"Why? I'm American. Why do I need to know Spanish?" she retorted, growing feisty.

Lugman now sensed that the conversation was taking the wrong tack. Under the guise of feeling he had to make himself understood, he unconsciously struggled to regain command of the situation.

"Well . . . what I meant to say is that knowing a second language has some advantages."

"Like what?" Ann asked, rocking her leg faster.

Lugman paused momentarily before asking her point-blank: "Don't you think you might visit Mexico someday?"

"No," Ann responded as she reached for a cookie.

Lugman started feeling his position was slipping yet again. He decided to offer a rationalization for his line of query—a verbal olive branch.

"My parents are both immigrants, you see. My dad is from Yemen, my mom from Palestine. Have you heard of those countries?"

Ann shook her head.

Lugman took her answer to be a green light to elaborate.

"Yemen is in South Arabia—the land of the Queen of Sheba. Palestine is the Holy Land; you know, Jerusalem, Bethlehem, Nazareth —the land of Jesus."

Ann slouched in her chair.

Before he could make his point, Ann switched the subject. "So is that how you got your name?" she asked.

Her question delighted Lugman. It suggested she just might be interested in him.

"Yeah. My father insisted on naming me. He named me after an ancient Arabian sage. I think he had something to do with fables. My name should be spelled L-o-k-m-a-n, but my dad preferred L-u-g-m-a-n. My mom wasn't too happy with the spelling, but she had to give way to my father. My dad's been here a long time. But he's still an immigrant. Once a boater, always a boater," Lugman said with a laugh.

"Do you have a nickname?"

The question caught Lugman off guard.

"Kinda." He paused and stared up at the ceiling as if he were preparing to say something momentous. Inhaling deeply, he volunteered, "My brothers have a name for me, but we never use it outside the house."

"What is it?" Ann asked softly, her slouched body barely visible behind her slender legs which were still perched on the ottoman.

"They call me . . . they call me 'Lucky.' Sometimes they say 'Lucky Strike' like the cigarette, but I don't like it."

Ann giggled. "Lucky is the name of a *dog*."

"I know. That's why my parents don't like it. Anyway, I don't feel lucky. My parents think it brings bad luck to call someone by that name."

Ann giggled again. Luqman was torn. He had Ann's attention, but at great expense to his self-esteem. He wanted to get back on track, on the highway leading back to her, him, and the negligee, but he was lost on some back road.

"Sometimes the kids at school try to change my name to 'lug nut.' They've even called me 'Legman,'" he added with a devilish smile as he took in Ann's bare legs. "But I don't let them play around with my name," he affirmed.

Luqman caught Ann staring intently at him. He suddenly felt nakedly self-conscious of his body bundled up and perched on the edge of the chair.

"I'm overheating in this stupid coat. If you don't mind, I'm going to take it off." Luqman worked the buttons of his coat before removing it without getting up from the chair. He laid it across his lap.

Luqman used the opportunity to shift the conversation to more familiar ground. He discovered that Ann attended the local parochial school, St. Gabriel's; that she was a year older than him; and that she had no friends in common with him. Curiously, these revelations made Ann even more appealing to him. She had magically morphed into terra incognita, a far-off island where he could explore his romantic sensibilities free from his family's prying eyes.

Luqman's older brother, Ahmed, had been ushered into an arranged marriage to a girl from his father's village when he was seventeen years old. Ahmed was the child of his father's first marriage to a Yemeni woman. Now in his early twenties, with children of his own, he was rapidly turning into his father. He was high-strung, overweight, and unstylish. A virtual boater. His wife, unlike Ahmed, who had grown up in Detroit, was an actual boater. She was hobbled by the three tasks that defined her existence: birthing, cooking, and cleaning. Saddest of all, Luqman thought, was that once upon a time Ahmed had evinced a romantic side. Not many months before he was packed off to Yemen, he had brought home a girlfriend, an *Amrekya*. His father would not speak to her, telling Ahmed in Arabic to "take her back to where you got her." Lugman's mother spoke to her politely, but later told Ahmed not to marry her.

Several years later, Lugman asked Ahmed why he had brought the girl home knowing how their father felt about such things. Ahmed told him that he had reached a point in his life where he had to make his own decisions. He reasoned that he was not going back to the old country, which was foreign to him anyway, and that it was time to start adopting the positive things from America. He admitted that the idea of introducing Joan, his secret girlfriend, to the family was hers. After giving her proposal some thought, he concurred that there was something abnormal about the secrecy cloaking their relationship. He decided to bring it out into the open. He reminded Lugman of the day he brought Joan home; about how he and the other brothers quietly buried their heads in the TV set, leaving him to fend for himself with their parents.

Most everyone in the Abdallah household suspected that Ahmed had been secretly dating anyway. But no one spoke about it openly. It was alluded to in roundabout ways, like "don't marry whomever you are seeing." Or it was couched in an abstract rule, "We don't marry *Amrekan.*" Their father's turning a blind eye to Ahmed's secret dating life ended that fateful day. His previous avowals that he had no intention of marrying a non-Arab no longer worked. Not long after, Ahmed and his father were on a plane to Yemen. When he returned a month later, he was married to his first cousin.

His older brother's capitulation to boater habits frightened Lugman in ways he was not entirely conscious of. He knew his parents expected him to marry an Arab Muslim girl. She didn't have to be a relative, just a good Arab girl. His mother wasn't fond of the Abdallah clan and so could be counted on to block attempts on Lugman and his younger siblings to marry from the clan. Lugman, too, fully expected to marry an Arab girl. Yet he was inexplicably drawn to the non-Arab girls who populated his school and neighborhood. Just why—biological instinct, burgeoning manhood, romantic impulse—he never stopped to ponder. Doing so would have caused the Arab and the American halves of his self to clash.

There was another side to Lugman. He was secretly embarrassed, even repelled, by the Arab girls in his circumscribed world—the girls at Arabic school and the *jamaa* (mosque), his female relatives, who were not yet donning head scarves, but might as well have been. Arab girls, for Lugman, had dark complexions, skin blemishes on their legs from cuts and bruises, ratty hair, ornate but cheap dresses, girlishness minus the femininity. They came off as boaters even when they were born in the U.S.A. Their houses smelled funny. The places and the people seemed permanently wrapped in a melange of cooking odors—fried onions, garlic, curry, and the pungent odor of mutton. Worse, the older women, especially the mothers, aunts, grandmothers, even the older married sisters, were an embarrassment. On the streets and in the local parks they stood as reminders of an ungainly world: babushka-wearing, herb-foraging, public-breastfeeding, sexually unappealing old world mamas.

Lugman was only faintly aware of this, but he was aware of it just the same. He had never forgiven the people from his father's village who married off Yasmine, a smart girl his age. Her family and his had teasingly pitted Yasmine and him as rivals for the dubious title "Best in School." On a visit to her house the previous summer, he asked about her whereabouts, only to learn that she was back in Yemen.

Lugman's brief life in urban America, negotiating school and neighborhood, coupled with heavy doses of TV, taught him in ways he had not yet comprehended that love and romance are escapes into an earthly paradise. The choice of a girl determined whether a guy was old-fashioned or cool, a boater or a local. For all their ignorance about bread, lamb, lentils, chickpeas, fava beans, cumin, saffron, olives, and goat cheese, the *Amrekan* had it over the Arabs in the love and romance department. For all their obliviousness about hospitality, parental respect, self-sacrifice, and the importance of family ties, the *Amrekan* evinced a more appealing lifestyle than the one Lugman knew.

The same was true of religion. Lugman knew the *Amrekan* had it all wrong about Jesus. He wasn't God, only a prophet. This business about crucifixion and resurrection was pathetically wrong. He wanted to feel sorry for the poor *Amrekan* who believed these things. During the great newspaper strike he sold newspapers on Sunday mornings outside St. Gabriel's Church, but stood as far as he could from the open church doors, driven away by the incense and liturgy of the Mass. But just as there were aspects of their cuisine he secretly longed for—smooth, whipped mashed potatoes, meat loaf, hamburgers and fries—he also envied the kids in his neighborhood for their ability to express their religious affiliation in an unselfconscious way. They could talk openly about going to church and feel part of something greater than themselves, whereas he had to do lots of explaining about his religion, so much so that he sometimes chose to remain silent rather than talk about his "house of worship," the place at the end of the Baker bus line with the onion-shaped dome on top.

Ann shook her brunette hair and asked whether Lugman would like more tea.

"Sure," he responded. He watched her leave the room again. Taking a deep breath, he thought about the incredible situation he found himself in. He was becoming attracted to Ann, and wondered if she liked him.

He also wondered what she had in mind. Did she have a plan? He had never kissed a girl, let alone run any of the bases. Thoughts of seeing her naked, of touching her body, excited him. He did his best to conceal this. He was helped along by the voice reverberating in his head, "If you get a girl pregnant you will *ruin* your life."

Ann returned carrying a tray. This time Lugman looked directly at her as she walked toward him, keeping his gaze fixed on her face. She knelt beside him with an offer of more tea and cookies. Lugman helped himself without making eye contact. His eyes followed her back across the room. The word "pregnant" jabbed him in the back.

Ann reclined in her chair. She appeared older than her age.

The conversation turned to Frats and Greasers, the opposing music and fashion styles contending for the minds and wallets of Detroit's public school kids at the time.

"What are Greasers?" Ann asked, blowing softly over her cup of tea.

Lugman sat up in his chair, striking a know-it-all pose. "It goes like this: Greasers dress in sharkskin pants and have slick hair and listen to Motown. Frats wear plaid and don't grease their hair and listen to the Rolling Stones and the Beach Boys."

Uncertain of Ann's preference, Luqman cloaked his own identification with the Frats.

"I know for a fact there aren't any Frats at St. Gabe's," Ann retorted. "My friends and I must be Greasers, because we love the Four Tops, the Supremes, Gladys Knight and the Pips. How can you not like Smokey Robinson and the Miracles? They're *sooo* hip." This nearly drove Luqman back into the Greaser fold.

"Hey, don't get me wrong," he protested. "I used to love Smokey Robinson, the Temptations, and the Supremes. I still have dozens of Motown 45's, but there's new stuff to listen to like the Stones."

"Me and my friends, that's all we listen to."

"I've got an idea," Luqman said. "I'll sell you and your friends my old singles."

Ann hesitated. "How would we do it?"

"I'll give you the records and you can sell them at school and we'll split the profits."

"I guess that would be OK," Ann said.

A long pause ensued as Luqman and Ann pondered what had just transpired.

Luqman leaned back in the chair, stretched his arms over his head, and looked out the window. He asked Ann for the time.

"It's two thirty."

"It's late. I've gotta get going or else my customers will think I quit."

Ann walked Luqman to the top of the stairs leading down to the front door. Luqman took his time buttoning his coat. He mumbled something about the weather, and the need for Ann to give Frat music a chance. She smiled. He thanked her for the tea and cookies, trying not to gaze at her breasts under the negligee. He stuck out his hand. She took it. They shook hands like business partners.

Back on the street, Luqman could barely contain his happiness. Safely out of sight of her apartment, he juggled one, then two folded newspapers in the air. He tried to kick one like a football only to have it scatter. He forgot about the weariness of being a paperboy. He smiled at his customers, even the Begrudgers and the Deadbeats. Nothing seemed to bother him. But it didn't take long for the euphoria to wear off. A tide of unease rolled over him. He worried his dallying with Ann might be exposed. He feared his parents might find out. They had drilled into his youthful head their dictum that girls are trouble. They distract boys from completing their education and launching their careers. That was the least of it. Messing around with girls led to unwanted pregnancies, which spelled certain ruination of a boy's life. What the pregnancy might mean for the girl, her reaction and future, or for any offspring, was of little concern. Everything was viewed through a simple black and white lens: girls were B-A-D.

II

It was almost closing time when Lugman arrived back at the *Detroit News* station. His brothers Fouzy and Salih ("Sal") were on their way out.

"Where have you been, Lucky?" asked Fouzy, nicknamed "Fuzzy Wuzzy" by the girls at school because of his teddy-bear-like charm.

"Wait up till I finish," Lugman said as he rushed past them to the front counter to settle his weekly account.

Fuzzy and Sal waited outside, keeping a distance from the other paperboys. The Abdallah brothers were viewed as interlopers by the mostly German and Irish Catholic schoolboys, whose near monopoly of newspaper routes in the neighborhood had been breached by the brothers during the previous year's newspaper strike.

When Lugman joined his brothers outside, Fuzzy asked why he was so late getting back to the station.

"You won't believe what happened!" responded Lugman. "I spent a couple hours talking to a girl who was wearing nothing but a see-through."

"Come on," Sal said.

"It's the God's truth, Wallah! She was only wearing a see-through."

"That means she wanted to screw," Fuzzy volunteered.

"*Noooo*, I woke her up when I went to collect," Lugman explained.

Fuzzy and Sal laughed.

"Idiot, no girl comes out in her negligee unless she wants to screw," Sal said, seconding Fuzzy.

Lugman was embarrassed. He saw his naivete reflected in their laughter, but was not willing to admit it.

"You're both crazy. If I had screwed her, she might have gotten pregnant."

"Not if you had used a rubber," Sal retorted.

"A *rubber*? Where in the hell am I going to get one of *those*? You make it sound so easy."

"Jerry Luna has some," Fuzzy offered.

"He does?" Lugman said, glancing at Sal.

He wanted to ask how his younger brothers came to know such things, but he refrained. Instead, he regaled them on the walk home with descriptions of Ann's legs, ass, breasts, hair. He kept coming back to the negligee—the unmatched thrill of seeing Ann's panties and the shape of her body through it. The thrill of seeing a barely naked girl had eluded the brothers Abdallah, for there was not a single sister among them.

He wanted to confess the feelings of love stirring within him for Ann, but kept this to himself. To admit such feelings, to reveal a soft side, seemed unnatural, perversely odd even. There was no hugging or fraternal kissing in the Abdallah family, and none was displayed in the ranks of the extended family either. The only emotion that was safe to display outwardly was the least desirable, anger.

The idea of using a condom struck Lugman like a thunderbolt. The next day he paid a visit to Jerry Luna, the fourteen-year-old condom salesman. He found him watching television in his basement. After some idle chatter, Lugman worked up enough courage to ask him if he had a rubber to spare. Jerry appeared startled by the request, as if airing the question in broad daylight would expose his secret trade. But Jerry had forgotten that he had divulged the source of his supply—a shopping bag full of condoms hidden in his parents' bedroom. In the first flush of excitement he had shared his discovery with

Fuzzy and Sal, and even parted with a few freebies. They in turn had carefully tucked them in their wallets, talismans to their adolescent libidos.

Seeing that Jerry appeared reluctant to allow him into his Secret Order of the Condom, Lugman presented his brief.

"Look, Jerry, I really need one. There's a girl on my paper route who talked to me in her negligee."

Jerry's face lit up. "Really? Where?"

"Up Central," Lugman said nervously.

"What's her name? I might know her."

Realizing his mistake, Lugman pulled back.

"She doesn't know you, I already asked her."

"Come on, what's her name?"

Lugman felt vulnerable. Jerry's insistence suggested he might go after Ann. Yet he didn't want to tick Jerry off and lose his chance at getting his hands on the prize.

"Her name is . . . Lisa."

"Lisa what?"

"I'm not sure . . . I think it's Halbrook."

Lugman's lie seemed to have worked.

"What's she look like?"

Lugman gave Jerry a brief description of Ann's legs, breasts, hair color.

"Is she pretty?"

"Kinda. The negligee makes her hot."

"Yeah, I know what you mean," intoned Jerry. "Like the chick I made out with in Patton Park a couple weeks ago. She wasn't hot at first, but when I felt her boobs, man, she was *gooood*."

The two laughed together.

Feeling Jerry was sufficiently predisposed toward him, Lugman popped the question again: "So, have you got an extra rubber?" His heart beat so loudly he was sure Jerry could hear it.

"It'll be a buck, man," Jerry retorted.

Lugman reached for his money.

With the condom tucked safely in his wallet, Lugman grew taller, older, sexier. The wavy hair over his ears felt slick-cool like the tailfins of a '57 Chevy.

Back home Luqman cloistered himself in the bedroom which he shared with Sal and Fuzzy. Still dressed in his street clothes, he lay down on the bed, where he examined the small crinkly packet of contraband, heeding the warning "Do not open until ready to use." On one side in bold letters was the word "S-h-e-i-k." He was slightly disappointed that it wasn't a "Trojan," as the talk at school had it that they were the best. He'd never heard of Sheik Condoms and worried about their quality.

He wondered what the manufacturer was thinking when he named his product. The connection between Arabs and sexual prowess hadn't crossed Luqman's mind. He found it amusing that someone would think of Arabs in a sexual sense, for nothing in his own limited experience had suggested anything of the sort. Still, seeing an Arabic word on an American product inflated his ethnic pride. Luqman's thoughts drifted to Saladin and the Crusades and the day he opened a world history book in school and saw drawings of the Saracens doing battle with the Crusaders. Oh, how he wallowed in the greatness of the Arabs that day! As Luqman tried to reconcile the disparate images, Saracens and sex, Crusades and condoms, he suddenly glimpsed in his peripheral vision a peeking head pulling away behind the doorjamb. The door to his room had been left open so as not to arouse suspicion. Closed doors in the Abdallah household suggested someone was trying to hide something. Luqman froze as he waited for the Peeping Tom to reappear. God, it was his father!

"Hey!" Luqman screamed. "What's going on?"

Just then his father dashed into the room, demanding to see what he was hiding.

"I'm not hiding anything," he said, sliding the condom under the bunched-up sheets.

"*Yallah,* let me see what you've got there, boy," his father commanded.

Luqman's heart pounded.

"I haven't got anything!" he squealed.

With a swift jerk of his right arm, Luqman's father pulled up the sheets, revealing Luqman's ticket to sexual ecstasy.

"What's this?"

Before Lugman could say anything coherent, his father was out the door shouting, "Zarifa, come and see what your boy has!"

Lugman jumped out of the bed in terror and followed his father into the dining room. Girls were a forbidden subject in the Abdallah household. There was hell to pay when a girl called the house or when Lugman or any of his brothers were even seen talking to one. Possession of a condom was ten times worse as it implied the ultimate contact with a girl, sexual congress!

When Lugman reached the dining room his mother screamed at him.

His mother's scolding was a foretaste of Judgment Day—a litany of prosecutorial questions riddled with insinuations delivered in a shrill tone, occasionally accompanied by slapping and hitting.

"Who gave you this?"

"Ah . . ."

"Who is the bitch who is playing with your mind?"

"There is no . . ."

"Do you want to ruin your life?"

"No! Let me explain . . ."

"Who gave you this thing?"

Within minutes Fuzzy, Sal, and several of the other brothers had formed a spectator's gallery nearby. In the middle of her tirade, Lugman's mother ordered Sal to shut all the windows so that the family would not be further scandalized in the neighborhood.

After what seemed an eternity, his mother's voice started to fail. This was the signal for Lugman's father to speak.

"Boy, where did you get this?"

"A kid at school gave it to me."

Lugman's mother interrupted, "Don't lie, who gave it to you? Jerry, Alberto, or one of those other *zut* you hang out with?" *Zut* was one of her favorite words, a general purpose catchall for riffraff, hoodlums, and other lowlife scum.

"Mom!"

Nothing hurt like the aspersions Lugman's mother cast on her sons' buddies.

"Why can't you hang around with good people . . ." she asked, before his father cut her off.

"Where did you get this?"

"Look, I got it from a kid in school . . ."

"Who, who is this son of a bitch?" the mother interrupted again.

"*Bess, ya hurmah!*" (Enough, woman!) the father snapped. "We want to understand."

"A kid at school gave it to me," Luqman responded. "He said it was a *lu'ba*. Let me show you."

As the words rolled off his tongue, Luqman snatched the tiny packet from his father's hand. Holding it up to the light like a magician, he began tearing it open. All eyes watched as Luqman struggled with the wrapper.

"See, it's a party balloon!" exclaimed Luqman as he withdrew the latex artifact from its protective sheath.

Without introduction, Luqman placed the condom over his mouth and began inflating it. Stunned amazement soon gave way to grins popping up around the room like fireflies on a summer night. Even the mother got caught up in the hilarity of the moment. As the grins turned into muffled laughter, the father ended Luqman's ordeal by ordering him to hand over "the balloon" and leave the room.

Luqman survived the scandal and the attendant humiliation, for the incident was never mentioned again. But the loss of his precious prophylactic meant his next rendezvous with Ann would have to be tamer than he had originally wanted. Fear of embarrassment and ridicule stopped him from going back to Jerry for another condom. He knew Jerry would check his story out with Fuzzy and Sal. They could not be counted on to keep Luqman's Houdini-like escape to themselves.

He thought of checking with his younger brothers to see if they had a condom, but feared rejection and disapproval. Even if they possessed the contraband, he suspected they thought him incapable of deploying it properly. He himself wasn't sure, although he would never have admitted this to them.

Luqman wanted to project a tough-guy image: the guy with a heart of stone whose only ambition was to score with a girl. This was the way of the neighborhood. But it was also a way of concealing his growing feelings for Ann. To share such feelings with a guy like Jerry was out of the question. Luqman's reticence, however, extended to Sal and Fuzzy. The Abdallah brothers were secretive about their intimacies. They kept their love interests and sentiments largely to themselves, masturbated in secret (unlike some of the neighborhood boys, who were rumored to engage in group sessions), and raided each other's private stashes of girlie magazines, appropriating the most provocative ones for themselves. This subterranean world of libidinal fantasies was rife with intrigues and vulnerabilities. In the end, Lugman decided that to encounter Ann alone without the aid of a condom would be less risky than venturing any farther onto the minefield of male adolescent sexual appetites. He would at least take the Motown records to Ann.

III

Saturday took forever to come around. Lugman got up earlier than usual to ensure no one would be awake. He sat down cross-legged before the RCA hi-fi, which stood in the dining room. Combing through the 45's arrayed haphazardly in the metal rack below, Lugman selected twenty-five singles, all Motown hits, passing over hits by Abdel-Halim Hafez, Farid al-Atrash, Perry Como, and Frank Sinatra, his mother's favorite crooners. He carefully rearranged the rack to fill the empty spaces, figuring no one would notice amid the disarray that was the Abdallah record collection. Only Lugman's mother listened to records regularly anymore.

Lugman faced the problem of transporting the fragile vinyl records. He retreated to the basement, where he always went to find solitude and think in peace. He searched for a suitable container, a cardboard or tin box, one that was big enough to hold the records and yet small enough to fit in his paperbag. Nothing.

The floorboards above began to creak; someone was in the kitchen. Soon everyone in the Abdallah household would be up wondering where he was, or, worse, find him in the basement and ask what he was up to. In a moment of desperation, Lugman hit on the brilliant idea of encasing the singles in two pieces of cardboard taped together. It worked! He tucked the package in his paperbag and went upstairs, slipping into the kitchen just before his mother got there.

The household was divided into two camps—those waiting to get into the family's only bathroom and those no longer needing to get in. Timing was everything. Often two, sometimes three, brothers would jump the queue and stand around the toilet like drag cars around the start pole. On one occasion, Lugman's dad had inched his way into the fraternal circle. Lugman couldn't help comparing his father's manhood, which stretched like the hood of a '59 Lincoln Continental, to his own small hood ornament, a Pontiac Indian or British Jaguar. He contemplated the difficulties of maneuvering his father's four-door luxury sedan into its parking place. When his father joked about Lugman's harmless *hamama* (dove), it went over Lugman's head, for he was unfamiliar with this Arab joking idiom.

That Saturday morning, the family matron was ill-humored, snapping at anyone in her line of sight. Lugman sat quietly at the kitchen table, trying not to draw her ire. She stood over the stove brewing a pot of Turkish coffee, her back to him. As usual, she was wearing her bedtime attire—a knee-length see-through negligee. Lugman averted his gaze when he reached the faint lines of her underwear. Mercifully, when she turned around there was sufficient material to conceal her breasts. He avoided looking directly at her because the sight of his mother in such revealing dress repulsed him. He wondered why she never bothered to wear a robe; why she never felt vulnerable. He suspected mere laziness on her part, the same laziness that led her to leave the bathroom door open when she thought no one else was around.

There was a time, not many years before, when Lugman thought his mother beautiful. He was about seven at the time. He could dimly recall the day he passed by the bathroom and saw her combing her hair in the mirror. She was fully dressed. He watched for a few minutes through the open doorway, his mother conscious of his presence. She appeared happy. He broke the silence by volunteering that when he grew up he wanted to marry a woman just like her. It was one of those spontaneous utterances, unplanned and unwilled, that bubble up straight from the heart. His utterance delighted each of them. She smiled and said in tender Arabic, "May God be pleased with you."

Lugman and his mother hadn't experienced a similar moment of tenderness in the intervening years, at least any he could recall.

Neither stopped to wonder why. The filial bond had devolved into the emotionally drained social roles of housemother and resident-son, a relationship possessing all the emotional tenderness of the tie between a bus driver and her passenger.

As Lugman shoved a piece of bread into his mouth, his mother stepped into the adjacent room and yelled down the short hallway in Arabic, "What are you doing in there, I have to pee!" Then, lamenting to Lugman's father, who was somewhere in the back of the house, she shouted, "Each of your sons holes up in the bathroom. Allah only knows what they are doing in there. It's gotten so I'm afraid to sit on the toilet seat for fear of getting pregnant." An embarrassed silence met her comment.

Lugman's brothers turned down the volume on the living room TV. Lugman bowed his head as he dipped another piece of Arabic bread in olive oil and *zaatar*. He thought of Ann and how lucky she was to be an only child. He imagined living in her upstairs flat, alone, away from the yelling; away from the fighting *over* the bathroom, *over* the TV, *over* a window seat in the car, *over* another piece of dessert.

Before he could slip away, his mother turned her wrath on him. "And *you*," she said, looking directly at him, "stop imitating the *Amrekan* before they get you in trouble."

"I'm not taking after anyone," Lugman responded in English to her oft-repeated warning.

"Your friends are no good! Jerry and Alberto and your other *ashaab* are teaching you lewd things. You are going to ruin your life. Do you hear? Ruin your life . . ."

"They are not teaching me anything," came Lugman's stock response to his mother's stock accusation.

"If you impregnate a girl, don't come back here for help. I'm not going to help you."

This time his mother's skewering hit bone. Normally, the warnings skirted the core issues of girls, sex, and pregnancy. Their mere mention triggered embarrassment for everyone. Girls only existed as remote abstractions in the Abdallah household. The few times girls called the house looking for one of the Abdallah boys, the abstract suddenly became real and the household shook.

His stomach in knots, his head swirling, Lugman left the house clutching the strap of his paperbag.

The short walk to the newspaper station wasn't enough for Lugman to shake off the morning's gloom. He continued to feel the sting of his mother's scorn as he folded his consignment of newspapers. The gloom began to lift as he fussed with the records, trying to find a safe place for them amid the crushing weight of the newspapers.

Back on the street his attention shifted to Ann. As he tossed newspapers on front porches, tucked them behind storm doors and under the doormats of his persnickety customers, Lugman tried to imagine how the encounter with Ann might move from dull conversation to something spicier. How would it start? Would she rise from her chair and saunter across the room, take his hand and lead him into the bedroom? Or might she set the tray of tea and cookies down beside him and gently caress his hair before sliding into his lap? Either way, any way, he would cede complete control to her.

He drew a blank every time he tried to visualize taking the initiative. He tried picturing himself rising from the orange chair, walking across the room and pressing his mouth against hers or even just holding her hand, but was paralyzed by the fear of overstepping some invisible boundary. Perhaps it was just the terror of being rejected. His knowledge about love, romance, and sex consisted mostly of what he had seen on television. Schoolboy talk—tales of making out on park benches, peeping and groping, and busted condoms—offered little guidance. Had his heart and penis come with an owner's manual, he would have scored an A, as he did in his schoolwork.

On the approach to Ann's block, a more familiar fear overtook him. "What if," Lugman thought, "things get out of control and I get Ann pregnant? What will I do?" He didn't have an answer other than seeing his life in ruins. He lamented his lousy luck with the condom. As he approached Ann's two-story duplex, the fears gave way to eddies of excitement. The steps leading to Ann's door appeared fluid and dreamlike. Nothing, absolutely nothing—Father, Mother, and God Himself—could stop Lugman's rendezvous with destiny. He was on the open highway.

Lugman pulled a folded newspaper from his bag and slipped it under his left arm. He pressed the doorbell, made a gallant turn sideways, and struck a nonchalant pose.

The door buzzed, startling Lugman. He turned quickly, dropping the paper. He missed his chance to open the door. He felt clumsy and stupid. The buzzer buzzed again; this time he turned the doorknob on cue.

"Hi," Ann said from the landing. "Come on up."

Lugman noticed immediately that she wasn't wearing the negligee. Instead she was attired in a blouse and skirt. He concealed his disappointment.

"Here's the envelope from Mother. I think she put a little extra in it for you."

"Gee, that was nice of her."

"Would you like to come in for some tea? It seems so cold outside."

"Sure." Ann disappeared into the back as Lugman took his coat off and laid it beside the orange chair. While waiting for Ann to return, he systematically examined the room as if he were seeing it for the first time. His eyes stopped at the chair across the room, Ann's chair. He imagined her in the negligee.

When she returned bearing a tray, Lugman asked if she had brought some of her mother's cookies. He examined Ann closely as she knelt beside the end table next to him. He admired the shape of her small nose, her long eyelashes, and her thin lips. He noticed her upper lip was so thin as to be nearly invisible. He wanted to reach out and feel her creamy white skin and stroke her wavy hair. He felt the tug of attraction; he was in love.

"You look like you've been up for a while," Lugman said with a grin as Ann rose to her feet, still holding the tray.

"Yeah, the nuns are taking a group of students to help feed the hungry at St. Anne's Church. I volunteered," Ann said, raising her head.

"Where's St. Anne's?"

"It's down by the Ambassador Bridge."

Lugman watched Ann as she made her way to the other side of

the room. He felt out of step. He was unsure how much time he had, and, more importantly, where he stood with Ann.

"Hey, I almost forgot!" Lugman piped up as Ann sat down. "I brought the records." With that, he stood up and hurried out to the landing to his paperbag. Running his hand through the half-empty bag, he retrieved the cache of records.

Ann appeared surprised. "Records?" she said softly.

"The Motown singles. Remember I said last week I've got a bunch of 45's I no longer need?" Lugman's eyes searched her face for recognition.

"Oh, those records!" Ann said.

He sat at the edge of the chair, where he struggled to open the makeshift package. He declined an offer of scissors.

"I had to come up with a way to transport the records in my bag without damaging them," he said, holding up the package as if it were an exhibit in a courtroom.

"Well, here they are," he said with the air of a proud collector. "'You Can't Hurry Love,' The Supremes; 'Baby, Baby, Baby,' Smokey Robinson and the Miracles; 'My Girl,' The Temptations. I almost hate to let this last one go," he added wistfully.

Lugman went through more records, reading off the labels, waiting for a reaction from Ann. She seemed unmoved. With nearly a dozen labels spread out before him, Lugman grew weary.

"You can go through these later if you like. Even if you don't instantly recognize them, your friends who love Motown will know their value."

"How much should I ask?" Ann said, her voice barely audible.

"Oh, I don't know. I'd say about seventy-five cents for each," Lugman suggested. "Heck, you could ask fifty cents for each, that would be all right."

"How much do you want for each record that I sell?"

Lugman was thrown for a loop. He hadn't thought this through. "Well . . . if you sell them for seventy-five cents each, then I'll take fifty cents; if you only get fifty cents, then I'll take a quarter. Either way, it's a good deal for you." An uneasy smile came over his face.

Lugman was like a drug addict wanting to get past business

matters to his anticipated high. But a sinking feeling was coming over him.

Looking away momentarily, Lugman turned back to his interlocutor, proclaiming in a tone laced with a plea, "Yeah, keep it at seventy-five cents, that will be better for both of us. I still have to pay off my brothers."

"OK," Ann responded in a tone which Lugman took to mean she understood his dilemma and that he could count on her. He was relieved.

Ann looked at the clock on the wall in the adjacent room and jumped out of her now familiar slouch.

"Hey, I'm going to be late," she said, rising from the chair.

Feeling immediate sympathy with her, Lugman also rose. He collected the singles spread around his feet, placed them in their protective sheath, and handed them to Ann. She set them down on the end table next to his unfinished cup of tea, nearly spilling it. Lugman watched with alarm. He wanted to rearrange the table so as to lessen the possibility of an accidental spill, but stopped himself. He could see that Ann was anxious to leave.

"I hope to see you again next week," he said, stretching his hand out like a salesman, but equally moved by sentiment and desire.

"Yeah, that would be nice," Ann said, shaking his hand awkwardly.

Lugman grabbed his bag and quickly made his way down the stairwell. He listened to see if Ann closed the upstairs door before he left. He took the fact that she hadn't to be a good sign.

He spent the rest of the day brooding over his handling of the record deal with Ann. He chastised himself for not having worked out a better pricing structure, for not having kept a record of each label, for not having set a timetable for when Ann and he would settle up.

In the end, he looked on the positive side of his relationship with Ann. Wasn't he spending time with her alone in the flat? Hadn't a bond developed between them? Lugman convinced himself that even if he had awakened her that fateful day, she'd had the option of changing out of the negligee. But she hadn't. He took that and her regular offers of tea and cookies to mean that she liked him, nay, *desired* him. Only one question remained—was she as desirous of him as he was of her? And, if their mutual attraction for one another were true, where might it lead? In the back of his mind, however, there lurked a faint unease about Ann.

Back at the station, Luqman met up with Sal and Fuzzy, who he knew would be anxious to hear about his latest encounter with Ann. For reasons Luqman ill understood, he felt compelled to cut short any probe into the details.

"What's up, Lucky?" asked Sal.

"Oh, not much."

"What's new with the chick?" inquired Fuzzy.

"Not much. I saw her again, spent some time up in her place."

"Was she wearing the negligee?" inquired one of the brothers.

"No. She was on her way out," Luqman said, staring off in the distance.

"So you didn't do anything with her?" asked Sal.

"What was there to do? She had to go, and anyway, I didn't have a rubber," Luqman fired back.

Sal and Fuzzy laughed.

"Yeah, blame it on the rubber!" said Fuzzy.

"I've got a relationship with her," Luqman asserted.

"Is she your *girlfriend*?" Sal asked mockingly.

"Not yet," retorted Luqman.

"So, what's your relationship with her?" asked Fuzzy.

"We've got a business deal together," said Luqman.

"A business *deeeal*?" the brothers squealed.

"Yeah, a business deal. She's going to sell the old Motown records to the kids at St. Gabriel's."

"Our records?" asked one brother. "Those are our records!" said the other.

Luqman was rapidly losing ground. He needed to mollify his brothers, who were visibly upset. He felt guilt about what he had done. He also felt vulnerable to the charge of being exploited by Ann. In the Abdallah family, there were few curses more humiliating than being called a "sucker." It was doubly humiliating if a male was allowing himself to be taken for a sap by an outsider, especially a romantic interest. More than anything else, Lugman wanted to preempt his brothers from leveling this charge against him.

"Look! They're *my* records, too. She's going to get seventy-five cents for each."

"Seventy-five cents!" screamed Fuzzy. "They're worth two bucks today!"

"No they're not. They cost a buck or a buck and a quarter at most," retorted Lugman.

"They were a buck-fifty new!" shouted Fuzzy, ever the business-minded brother.

"Yeah, Fuzzy's right, they cost us a buck-fifty. And now they're collector's items, you fool!" Sal intoned.

Lugman started feeling sheepish, for he wasn't good at keeping track of such things. For all he knew they were probably right. The bit about them being collector's items made him squirm.

"Well, no one was listening to them," Lugman reasoned.

"You should have asked our permission," said Fuzzy.

Lugman conceded the point even as he reiterated his partial ownership of the records.

"OK, so what do you want me to do?"

"Tell her that we want a buck a record for them," Fuzzy said, sounding a bit like their father.

"A buck a record? That means she's got to ask a buck and a quarter in order to get her profit; no one will buy 'em for that price!"

"That's your problem," Fuzzy said, as he motioned Sal to move on ahead.

"OK, how about a buck a record with us getting seventy-five cents for each?" Lugman offered.

"We want a buck, or bring 'em back," shouted Sal as he and Fuzzy walked away. Lugman felt sick to his stomach. No matter how he turned, he faced humiliation before his brothers and embarrassment before Ann. He was caught in a vice of his own making.

The following week Lugman approached Ann's house with a mixture of excitement and anxiety. He debated whether he should tell her that his brothers were demanding a dollar for each record.

Doing so might lead her to pull out of the arrangement, removing his excuse to continue seeing her.

He approached the door, dropped his bag, and pressed the buzzer one short ring. He turned to face Central Avenue, repressing the image of Ann in her negligee, lest he set himself up for another disappointment. Instead, he laid his hopes on building a friendship with her that might lead to romance and sexual exploration. He saw her as a special friend, though he knew she was nowhere near being a "girlfriend." That term triggered another round of anxiety, for he immediately thought of the many complications should Ann ever call his house or, heaven forbid, drop by in person!

The sound of the door cracking open sent Lugman into an about-face. Standing behind the door, wearing a big smile, was Ann's mother, Mrs. York.

"Hello," she said in a businesslike tone which he recognized from collection days past. Handing her a newspaper, Lugman acknowledged her greeting, reminding her it was collection day. She returned upstairs to get some money.

Her smile appeared friendly, but it unnerved him just the same. It occurred to Lugman that a neighbor might have said something to Mrs. York about his long stays in the apartment. Someone may have even noticed Ann the day she came down in the negligee. Mrs. York's smile suddenly took on an inauspicious appearance. The thought even crossed his mind that Ann herself might have confessed to having him in the apartment.

His yardstick in matters involving the sexes was what he had learned at home. He knew that his own mother would never have approved of having a girl and a boy sitting alone in a room. Moreover, the idea of a girl entertaining a boy clad only in a negligee would be a scene fit for a brothel. No decent, self-respecting parent would allow such scandalous behavior. Lugman projected these standards onto Mrs. York.

By Arab standards, even asking about the whereabouts of Ann was taboo. But he needed to know if her sudden disappearance was related to their encounters or if this was all a mere coincidence.

When Mrs. York returned, she handed Lugman a white envelope, thanking him. Detecting no sign of anger or displeasure, Luqman chanced a question.

"Mrs. York," he began, "tell Ann I said 'hi.'"

"Oh, do you know Ann?" she asked.

Seeing her puzzled look as a good thing, Luqman pressed on. "Well, you know, she paid me for the past two weeks and we chatted a bit."

"Oh, how nice."

It was becoming painfully obvious that Ann's mother wasn't going to divulge more information unless he dared a follow-up question. "Is she around?"

The pause that met his question embarrassed Luqman.

"She's visiting her father," she said with downcast eyes. A polite smile signaled an end to the conversation.

Luqman knew that Ann's father was not living at the house, and suspected the parents were separated or divorced. But Ann had never said anything about it. His heart went out to her. He pictured her as the victim of feuding parents. His own parents regularly hurled the threat of divorce at each other when they quarreled. This always frightened him, almost as much as the thought of one of them dying. He felt vulnerable and insecure at such moments. He knew his mother would use the fact that Ann came from a "broken home" against her; that his own father had divorced his first wife would carry no weight in Ann's defense.

Each collection day his heart beat with anticipation as he approached Ann's house, only to be met with disappointment. He hesitated asking about Ann or inquiring about his records, lest Mrs. York suspect his motives. In late spring, Ann's mother canceled her subscription, claiming the paper went unread. All summer Luqman scanned the streets hoping for a chance encounter with Ann. By summer's end sadness turned to resignation that he would never see her again.

For weeks Luqman turned the brief exchange with Ann's mother over and over in his head the way his own mother turned her demitasse cup round and round trying to catch a glimpse of the future in the swirls of dried coffee grounds. He couldn't help wondering whether there was more to Ann's sudden disappearance. Had Ann's mother conspired with her estranged husband to pull her out of a potentially damaging relationship with Luqman?

The mere thought that her parents might view him as a sexual predator bringing dishonor to their daughter made Luqman squirm. For he thought of himself as an honorable person, a good Muslim, even as he harbored sexual fantasies about her.

One autumn day, Luqman chanced upon three girls heading in his direction on a busy street. He was wedged in between Fuzzy and Sal as they were walking. The brothers fell silent as the girls approached. They were dressed in the trademark Catholic school uniforms—white blouses, navy blue pleated skirts, matching knee-high stockings, black shoes. Whatever the moral intentions of the nuns who designed the ensemble, it never failed to fire the imagination of the neighborhood boys.

Luqman had focused his sight on the girl in the middle, who resembled Ann, but he couldn't be sure until he got a closer look. Just as the two groups were about to cross paths Luqman recognized Ann. She, too, startled into sudden recognition of him. After hesitating for a second, she flashed him a quick smile, followed by an abrupt "hi," without falling out of step with her companions.

Luqman watched helplessly as the two groups went around each other like ballroom dancers. He attempted to stop, expecting Ann to do the same. But she kept her pace, and so did his brothers, who pushed him along. He looked back in time to see Ann whispering something to the other girls. A ripple of giggles erupted. The girl on Ann's left darted a look back and quickly turned away. They hurried down the street.

Luqman stopped his brothers.

"That was the girl; that was the girl in the negligee," he said, his mind still reeling. "The tall one in the middle."

"What girl?"

Luqman pointed down the street at the three receding figures.

"Do you see the one in the middle? That's the girl in the negligee."

"The one in the middle?" asked Fuzzy, somewhat incredulous. "I noticed her coming up the street. What's so hot about her?"

Luqman turned away, mumbling, "You had to have been there."

FIRST SNOW

KHALED MATTAWA

He reached for the pack of Marlboro Lights that sat among a crowd of magazines. There were empty soda cans and dirty mugs crammed on the coffee table, with a gulf between them where he rested his feet sometimes. He lit a cigarette, his last one, and rolled the pack into a ball; its edges stung his palm as he aimed it at the wastebasket next to the small bookcase across the room. The ball hit the rim and rolled next to other three-point attempts that were waiting to be dunked into the trash. Instead, he adjusted the cushion under his head, raising himself a little, and puffed his cigarette. The amber glass ashtray was full of butts and looked like a mound of bent plastic tubes in a junkyard. Their hideousness reminded him of the stretch in which he'd quit smoking. That was a cease-fire that ended soon after he left Knoxville.

He sat up and reached for the *TV Guide* he had bought along with the cigarettes earlier that day. It smelled like fresh plastic, or like the packaging of new LP's. Some of the pages were stuck together. They made a hissing sound when he ran his hand through them, and he enjoyed their cool softness. The *TV Guide* turned out to be next week's, starting tomorrow, a Sunday. He turned the TV on anyway, thanking God for the miracle of remote control.

The folks on *Hee Haw* were having a go at it, whatever it was. They danced as if they wanted to kick off their shoes by flinging their feet as far and as fast as possible while circling and holding hands. The music played at an increasingly faster pace, creating suspense, as if one of the dancers was about to leap into the air and somersault, bringing the number to a resounding end, or, all of a sudden, the dancers' shoes would all go up simultaneously like caps at a graduation ceremony. OK then, he thought, you just have to let your mind wander and even *Hee Haw* can be fun. But his facial muscles could not break their day-long glumness. The last *Hee Haw* seemed like yesterday.

That last thought bothered him. But what could you do in a place like Athens, Tennessee? It was a mercy that time passed quickly here. That did not exactly cheer him, but it was no longer his fault and his sense of guilt loosened its grip a bit. And, really, he was in America getting an education; that couldn't be too bad. The winter quarter would start before he knew it and life would be back to normal.

He got up from the sofa to make tea and remembered that he had used the last of the dried mint leaves earlier that day. No cardamom pods either. You couldn't get any of this stuff at the local Piggly Wiggly. He had to settle for another Taster's Choice.

He washed the dishes as the water boiled in the kettle. One of the mugs had a murky gray-green layer in the bottom. He tossed it away, then dunked all the three-point attempts and the soda cans in the trash bin, wiped the coffee table with a wet cloth and brought the dirty cups to be washed. A last glance at the kitchen after he was done. Sort of decent, he thought. He brought his fresh cup of coffee to the table and sat again. Suddenly, Tina Turner began complaining about the typical male.

The noise was coming from Donna's "end of the semester party." Of course, Donna had been out of school for three years. It might be her, or some friend's, birthday party. She'd come by earlier that day with Mike, her boyfriend. Ali knew it was Donna by the way she knocked on the door. Four quick loud knocks with her fleshy right hand, for as many times as it took to get someone to open the door.

"Hey, Ali," she said, sidestepping him and getting into the living room. "What you been doing?" She didn't wait for an answer.

"Listen, you got to come to my party this time. You never came to any of them. I know you were here all the time watching TV," she said with a pout.

Then a smile flashed on her face as she moved closer to him. "Listen buddy, I fixed you up with a nice girl. She doesn't drink either. I know you'll like her," Donna whispered.

She turned to Mike. "Where is Nima from? Iran? No, she's from Ecuador," she said before Mike could answer. "I know that's not near where you come from, but I know you'll like her."

"I don't think so, Donna," Ali said with a smile.

"Are you blushing, Ali? Look at him, Mike, he's blushing."

Ali never knew why Donna was so insistent with him. Sure, he'd helped start her car once. It was a fuse, and he searched his toolbox and found one that matched it. Then she asked if he'd be willing to change her oil for money, and he did it for free. And once when he was looking at her engine, she said, "What's your friend been up to these days?" with a slight emphasis on "friend" and a nod toward their apartment.

"Amjad!" said Ali, as he paused from wiping her dipstick on a rag.

"Yeah, your roommate, I mean."

"He's fine. I don't see him much. Between work and school, you know."

"You guys are so private, cooped up in there all the time."

"What do you mean?" He paused to wipe the dipstick on a rag.

"I'm sorry. I just thought . . . Well, it doesn't matter. It's OK with me."

"You're running a little low on oil. Otherwise, it's OK," he said after another pause, avoiding looking at her.

Then he went to his trunk and brought a bottle of oil and poured some in. He twisted the lid shut and wiped a few drops. Donna was silent now, with an apologetic look on her face. He closed the trunk slowly and pressed down on it to shut it.

"We're religious. We're Muslims so we don't go out and we don't drink and all of that. We're not like what you think."

A few days after that she stopped by, knocking in a slightly timid version of her usual knock, and apologized for suspecting they were gay. He offered her some tea he'd just made. They talked for a little bit. Then she said, "Don't you all get lonely?"

"No," he said, knowing better. "We have friends to see in Knoxville and Atlanta. We keep busy with school. And we pray so we don't get lonely."

"You must get a little lonely even when you pray."

"A little, yes," he smiled.

"All right then," she said, smiling back. "What you put in that tea, Ali? It's really good."

And since then she'd been trying to set him up with "nice girls." And so far he'd been cordial but not the least cooperative.

Mike was looking at a poster of Jerusalem on the wall while Donna was still trying to convince Ali to come to her party. It was the only thing decorating the apartment.

Ali turned to Donna and said, "They say there's going to be a big storm tonight. Maybe snow. You think your friends will come to the party?"

"Sure, Mike'll pick them up. Won't you, Mike? In his four-wheel drive."

Mike shrugged and continued to look at the poster. Ali offered to make some tea and Mike started to sit down.

"No, Ali, we don't have time. We got to go pick up stuff for the party and get ready," said Donna. Mike got up and shrugged again. "I'll drag you out this time if you don't stop by," she added, waving good-bye and leading Mike out before her.

Now the party was getting on in earnest. The thudding of the bass line was making the dishes vibrate in the drying rack. *Hee Haw*'s credits rolled as some guy sang a tune with lots of yodeling and with whoops that followed each of his solos. Ali thought of praying; he'd not done any of his daily prayers except for the morning one. Sunset was more than two hours ago and he always liked to pray Isha before he went to bed. But who could pray with all this noise? This was a half-hearted question. He'd prayed before during Donna's parties and found that he could concentrate if he put his mind to it. A cheer went up through the wall, and the door was slammed shut. Ali wondered if it was the girl Donna had talked about. He imagined what she looked like. Dark-haired for sure.

The phone rang for the first time that day. It was Vickie. She wanted to know if he'd like to come to her house for Christmas dinner.

Vickie called all the time. The first time she'd called him, Amjad picked up and shook his eyebrows, teasing Ali. Ali didn't take a long time to ask her how she got his number. "It's listed in the directory," she said.

Then he said, "How can I help?" and it felt very strange to say such a thing.

She just wanted to chat. He told her they had guests and he'd talk to her on campus. For a few weeks after that Amjad teased him, saying, "Can I help you?" at the most unexpected times, and they both laughed. Other times when she called, Amjad would mouth out, "Can I help you?" or hand him a folded note with "SOS" written inside.

Vickie called whenever something happened. When there was a heat wave last summer, she'd asked if he had an extra fan. He told her they had central AC and she said, "Oh, yeah, of course." And when he had the flu a few months ago and missed some classes, she'd offered to come and fix him chicken soup. "No, no, don't bother," he said in an alarmed note she recognized.

So he apologized for not being able to make it to the dinner. "I'll be in Knoxville then," he said.

"Well, if you don't go, you know you're always welcome. My parents really liked you."

He had had Thanksgiving dinner with them a few weeks ago and he had spent a lot of time speaking with her father and uncles about the Middle East.

"I'll see about it. And do say hello to them for me."

He wanted to end the conversation with that.

They always talked for much longer than he wished. He didn't feel he was wasting time or that he disliked her. But their conversations felt like a long detour to him, a kind of prolonged period of hazy focus. He told her a lot about his life and family back home in Jordan, about his faith, and even his childhood. But whenever he finished talking with her, even though she did most of the talking, he felt like he'd told her too much. And that she was not the right person for such intimacy.

It was almost strictly a telephone friendship. Being around her made him frigid. The first few times they met, and when she offered her hand to be shaken, he'd held it lightly and briefly. She stopped wanting to shake his hand altogether. And while they were talking in class or at the student union, he apologized every time he accidentally touched her. She started apologizing too whenever her hand brushed against him.

He'd met Vickie when he first came to Wesleyan, more than a year ago. He had just moved from Knoxville then. He had many friends there and they were surprised at his decision to leave the university. They did not want to embarrass him by asking why, as they knew he'd not been studying. There were many things to be done at the mosque and he was always willing. In Jordan, he'd kept to his school and whatever family obligations he was asked to do. But at the Knoxville mosque, a rented wood-frame house surrounded by rowdy apartment complexes, you did not just pray, you sat down and had tea and friends to drink it with and talked and talked about religion and politics and school and so on. There were books banned at home. Ali invited guest speakers, organized a day conference, and relief drives for the famine in Somalia. And when he was at the mosque all he had to do on a weekend night was look out at all the coming and going in the adjacent apartment building. The screaming women, the young men sometimes puking behind the mosque, the loud music, and the cheapness and frivolity of human contact there all seemed repugnant. There was nothing he wanted from that world, and it was not hard to come to the mosque.

His first quarter at the university was a disaster. The following quarters were worse. So he followed the advice of a friend who said, "Find an easier school, and do your work." Wesleyan was the first four-year college down the interstate that would admit him. And he decided he could not hack engineering, though he could not bear the thought of telling his family that news. He switched to business administration, and began working at the campus cafeteria—and, on the sly, as a bus boy, at the steakhouse near his apartment—and though studying accounting was like sleeping on a bed of nails, he did his work and even felt cheered by his improved grades.

Vickie wanted to keep talking. Tina Turner's complaints had long since surrendered to Madonna and A Flock of Seagulls. The thumping continued with another song he didn't recognize. Another cheer went up, another slamming of Donna's door. He switched ears.

"Do you guys still have your prayer service on campus?" said Vickie.

"I don't know; we may not have it at all with school closed."

"Well, I can call my church. We have a nice minister there. They might let you have it over there."

"We could, but most people leave town. I'm getting out of town too."

Then there was the usual unease. Why did she keep calling him and why could he never quite shrug her off? Now he regretted accepting her invitation to Thanksgiving.

"How did you do in finance?" she asked.

Then she talked about how much she hated the finance professor and the cheerleader, Mitsy, who sat in the front row. Vickie's descriptions were so vivid that if you walked into her classroom you could easily pick out the cheerleader and start treating her the way Vickie would have wanted you to. Then there was the story about the uncle who hunted possums and who kept wanting her to try them. And the time she went hunting with her father a few weeks ago.

He enjoyed her stories, he admitted to himself. He thought that was what his life had been missing. Sure, he had some Arab friends at the college. And he'd gotten to know some of the people who worked with him in the cafeteria. But you never knew who would stand next to you the following work shift on the service line or at the dishwashing machine. George, the cook, the only one who had been working there for years, liked him and liked to chant out "Ali, Ali" when he gave him a pan of macaroni and cheese or meat loaf. George invited him to his church, and Ali brought him a pamphlet about Islam. And that became the subject of all their conversations.

He was sure he did not want to stay in the U.S. Here you didn't have to worry about hosting a guest or attending and helping with the chores of a cousin's wedding, a nephew's circumcision, or an old relative's funeral. Vickie's long telephone calls reminded him of tł t kind of life. And his nostalgia after talking to her drove him to write a letter to his family or a friend. Or he'd pick up the phone and call home, a call that cost him his pay for a whole afternoon shift. "Where's my mother?" he'd ask the first person who answered. His mother would tell him about the meal she was about to cook. Or about the brother who forgot to bring her what she asked for from the grocer. Or the nephew who was going for his junior high exams. "Is he old enough for that?" he'd ask. "Of course. He's taller than your father now."

Yes, he enjoyed Vickie's stories, how grounded she was. But why did it seem sometimes like her whole life was unreal to him, a kind of story that might as well be set on another planet? She knew (he'd told her that much) that he would only pursue a relationship if it was marriage-bound, and that he'd only marry a girl from his country. And she agreed. Much as she was bored with East Tennessee, she'd never really want to leave.

He remembered all of this now, looked at his watch, and sat up. It was a few minutes past nine. "Listen, I've got to go. I've got to meet someone."

"Well, just let me know if you're coming over on Christmas day."

"I will. Thanks. Bye!"

"Bye," she said, still pausing.

"Bye," he said once again and hung up, feeling relieved they didn't get to talk about the impending storm.

He slouched back down into the sofa again, closed his eyes, and listened to the thudding, and occasional cheers and whoops from behind the wall. He tried to imagine what was happening at the party—what did she look like, this Nima?—and whether someone had convinced her to take a little drink, or a whiff of a joint Mike was passing around. He thought again about doing the four prayers he'd missed. His body felt heavy to him, his mind weighed, darkened and lacking the flash that seemed to beam inside of it when the mood for prayer overcame him.

He remembered one night last summer when he'd met Mike at the railing in front or the apartment and Mike came up and gave him a hug, something he'd never done before or since. Donna said, "I guess you've never seen him stoned, have you?" and giggled.

Ali had backed away from Mike and looked at him.

"He's at his best when he's stoned, Ali. That's why I stayed with him all this time. Isn't that right, honey?" said Donna, nuzzling Mike. Then they began to slow dance up and down the walkway and forgot about him.

He remembered the storm again and thought he should go to the supermarket and stock up on some groceries just in case. In the bathroom, he looked in the mirror and decided to shave and then went on to clip his mustache. He grabbed his coat and went to the closet to look for his hat.

Outside, the sky was a solid mass of russet, colored by the pinkish lights in the parking area below. He stood by the railing and looked about and saw that a few drifts were swirling about, but no snow yet. Milk, tea, bread, cheese, eggs, tomato paste, and chicken. That's what he needed to get.

Donna's window was rattling from the loud music. "One look," he thought. "I just want to see what she looks like." He looked up at the sky once again.

No one opened after his first hesitant knocks. He knocked again, louder. The door opened and he had to shield his eyes from the strobe lights flashing. As he stepped in, cheers and whoops rose to greet him. Then quickly someone slammed the door shut behind him.

THE HIKE TO HEART ROCK

FRANCES KHIRALLAH NOBLE

The idea of a vacation in the mountains evolved over a period of months into a full-fledged rental, sight unseen, of a cabin in Crestline that, we hoped, could house us all. It was natural that we should go together—one grandmother, three aunts (married to three brothers) and seven cousins. It went without saying that our fathers, the uncles, would not stay, would only drive us up and bring us down, possibly visit us on the middle weekend; three dark men in their short-sleeved white shirts in a used sedan, curving up the mountain road.

We took the second-cheapest cabin advertised in the paper. I say "we," but I mean that my mother, Olga, decided as she usually did when it came to family matters, flinging aside dissenting opinions with the sureness of a juggler, until the only voices that remained were the ones that agreed with her. Her intensity amused my father.

"Olga," he'd caution her quietly if she got carried away.

In response to which she'd raise her elegant black eyebrows and, for the next few minutes, move through my grandmother's tiny house making amends—a cup of coffee, a shoulder rub, a joke about how she forgot herself sometimes when she started talking.

Every Friday night, we congregated at Situe's: perched on the back steps regardless of weather because there was so little room inside; or sitting solidly on the front porch, which, generously, surprisingly, extended the width of her house. Everyone arrived at Situe's after dinner, although why we ate at home when we ate just as much at her house again later was never discussed. At any time of night or day, Situe could feed an army: always Syrian bread and cheese and olives, kibbe, stuffed grape leaves; sometimes spinach pies, meat pies, her version of spaghetti. Candy in the glass jar in the living room. Duke cigarettes in a cup on the coffee table. A case of Budweiser claiming a full shelf in her refrigerator.

My family always arrived first. My father drove us fifteen miles from our new house in the new subdivision. Situe, usually stoic, looked relieved each week to see that my mother and my father (Philip) and I and my younger brother and sister had once again successfully escaped from our suburban neighborhood (a place where there were no other Syrians, no sidewalks down which your neighbors strolled—the Shaheens, the Courys, the Thomases—so that you could wave from your porch) and returned safely to hers. Situe thanked God under her breath that my family as a whole had not been punished by way of accident or flat tire for my mother's impudent ambition of wanting a house of her own. Far enough away to make visiting a more formal event.

Aunt Eva and Uncle Assad arrived next. They lived around the corner from Situe. Each week they came late and left early. They had three young children, who seemed to me less interesting than they once were, consumed as I was with the delicious melancholy of being fifteen. Aunt Eva was the only one of my parents' generation to have been born in the old country and had lived in the United States for fifteen years, most of them in Los Angeles like us. Uncle Assad and my father ran a shoe repair business on the side, in addition to their regular jobs.

Last to appear were Aunt Helen and Uncle George. And, of course, my cousin Georgie.

Everyone thought Georgie was a Mama's boy, but I knew better. He was the same age as I. We were the two oldest cousins, and we escaped from the presence of the others as much as we could. Anytime my grandmother or one of the uncles wanted cigarettes, Georgie and I offered to go to Frank's Market down on Main Street, where Frank would hand them over, grumbling at being asked to sell cigarettes to children. Or we walked around Situe's block again and again, lingering before anything that could reasonably command our attention. Or sat on the bench behind the little shed in back.

I say he was not a Mama's boy (although he looked so much like his mother that it was startling—both soft and plump and dark, with a small separation between their two front teeth) because, since we were twelve, he had not acted like one with me.

One warm evening Georgie and I sat in our shorts, alone, on Situe's front porch under the light. We were talking about something when he said, "You have a mole on your inner thigh a few inches above your knee." He pressed my mole with his index finger. "Do you have any more?" I shrugged my shoulders. Another time he said, "Meet me in back of the shed. I want to try something."

What he wanted to try was a kiss. I said I wasn't interested. But I did it anyway, and made a mental note to try it again soon with someone who wasn't soft and damp.

"Don't you open your mouth?" Georgie asked.

"Do you?" I said.

"Sure."

I want to be fair. My mother wasn't the only reason I couldn't launch myself into sexual adventure. I should be honest, too. I'd have blushed and cringed if someone had even said the phrase "sexual adventure" in front of me, much less with reference to me. Yet it hovered beneath my surface like those little white triangles that float to the top of the fortune-telling black ball urging, "Try it," or "You'll see," or "Why not?" I suffered from a lack of opportunity in the broadest sense, distorted through the prism of adolescent uncertainty: too tall, too odd, too foreign looking, too awkward, too eager. So, even though I hated being with my family, hated being seen with them in public, they constituted my entire social life. If I hadn't gone to Situe's on Friday nights, I'd have gone no place at all.

We met at Situe's one Saturday morning in July and, within two hours, our slow-moving caravan was driving in the mountains. Ear-popping ascents; waves of motion sickness. Spearmint gum and Saltine crackers. I watched as the terrain changed from scrub tree to pine forest.

After we'd spiraled upward through lush deposits of trees and ferns and dogwood and wildflowers, with our windows rolled down at my mother's insistence so we could inhale the fragrances ("You too, Michelle," she said to me, and I was so furious at being grouped with my younger brother and sister that from then on I hardly noticed anything more outside); after we'd stopped for directions at a small market at the edge of the road which sold fruit and auto parts, beer and every kind of candy; after my father, the driver of the lead car, signaled out his window with his tanned, muscular arm for the others to pull over, we finally rounded one last curve and arrived at our cabin.

It looked authentic. Real logs. A round-stoned chimney. A low wall of the same stones protecting the front. Several seasons of pine needles and leaves covering every inch of its roof and adjoining tennis court.

Yes! A tennis court! Can you imagine our surprise? For sixty-five dollars a week, paid in advance, a tennis court! Why hadn't the newspaper mentioned this? Probably because the cracks were as wide as canyons and filled with pine tree saplings. We didn't care. Nobody played tennis. It was the mere fact of the court that pleased us. My mother's sturdy arguments in favor of this particular cabin vindicated by an unknown and unusable tennis court.

Even Aunt Helen was moved to agree. And I simply loved imagining how I'd weave it into renditions of my summer vacation.

Aunt Eva said, "Olga, looks like you hit a home run." She could just as easily have said, "You were on the money," or "Bull's eye." I should explain Aunt Eva's speech patterns.

When she first arrived here, she was eager to learn English as fast as possible and she enrolled in an English class at the local adult school. There was a section on American idioms and it stuck; she took a great fancy to the catchy phrases. When she spoke, she wove together standard English, out-of-fashion American expressions, and Arabic; consequently, few people fully understood her, although I thought I did.

I liked Aunt Eva's confident way of plunging into the unfamiliar. She had, however, incurably alienated my mother—my mother, who fairly prided herself on her fine features and delicate figure, the sleek way she put herself together—when she said to her one day, "Olga, you look like something the cat dragged in."

That Aunt Eva said these kinds of things all the time and that my mother was recovering from the flu and did appear rather drawn did not blunt my mother's rage.

There was, of course, no appeal, no recourse, no tribunal for either of them. They were family and they had to get along. Their husbands were in business together; Assad was my father's favorite brother. Nevertheless, my mother tried to get even.

"Look, Philip." She waved Aunt Eva's records of receipts and disbursements before my father's face.

"What? What?" he said.

"Here." She touched one spot on the papers; then another.

"I don't see anything worth fighting about," my father said.

"They're cheating us, a little at a time," my mother insisted.

My father's response was to breathe deeply. Eventually my mother gave up. Nothing was more important to her than getting along with my father. Not even us. My mother's primary regret about our mountain vacation was, I thought, that he was leaving and we weren't.

My father and my wordless uncles had carried in the suitcases, the food, the supplies. "We won't have a car until the weekend, when the men come up to visit," Aunt Helen offered, as if in apology. One uncle said for all of them, "We'll see. We'll have to see about that."

I didn't care, though. I was fascinated by the cabin. In the living room a bobcat and an eagle on a branch stared silently down, flea-bitten and worn, nibbled by mice around the edges. I rearranged the lamps so light shone on them, hunting and defending. There was a huge stone fireplace. There were spiders and spiderwebs. Dust. Not enough dishes. "No iron," said Situe.

In a matter of moments, Situe began scrubbing the kitchen while Georgie and I, in the exquisite self-centeredness of adolescence, unannounced, left for a walk.

The men had already gone since they wanted to get down the hill before dark. I was sorry to see my father go, although I never could predict whether he would respond to me with affection or with a special new brand of anger that seemed to have developed as

I did. Even so, my father kept my mother happy. When he was around, she laughed more. When he left, the beam of attention she shone on him she redirected toward me. But, in changing her receptor, she changed her tone, her approach—from musky and mellow to taskmaster, without a beat in between.

"Michelle."

"Yes."

"Unpack your clothes."

"I did."

"Did you put them away?"

"Yes." (With as much edge to my voice as I dared.)

Then, what was I reading, watch your sister and brother, button up that blouse, what did I think I was doing . . .

I couldn't resist. I brushed my dark hair so it hung over my shoulder, I tossed the bottom curls with my hand. I showed her how I could look if I wanted to. "I don't know why you get so mad," I said.

And so there we were that first evening, a cabin of women alone in bedrooms, and children sleeping in sleeping bags on the floor: Situe, my mother, quiet Aunt Helen, Aunt Eva, Georgie and I and the younger cousins. With two weeks ahead of us in Crestline, California.

"Let's get the lay of the land," Aunt Eva said first thing next morning. Stout-calved in Bermuda shorts and sheer stockings up to her knees, Aunt Eva stomped her solid shoes on the front porch, as if preparing for a race. Which we who accompanied her on this first hike of the vacation learned was her standard outdoor pace. Anyone who tried to pass her encountered her accelerating gallop and a hearty "Hold your horses!" I wouldn't have gone, but my mother decided I needed to relieve some of this dangerous new energy I was accumulating. She, of course, never went. She said she'd stay with the younger children and called it a fair tradeoff.

I have a vision of my mother—her thick, dark hair held back by a peach chiffon scarf, her silk kimono (a birthday present from my father) tied with a floppy bow—as she watched our hiking menagerie move out of sight of the cabin. I imagined her sitting next to a window whose panes Situe had recently rendered clear as crystal, sipping hot coffee and reading a book. My imaginings, however, were short-lived: concentrated attention was required to survive the routes Aunt Eva devised. Over rocks, down hills slick with pine needles. "You stopped yourself just in the nick of time," she told me one morning as I went sliding down a small mountain, out of control, kicking up pinecones.

Georgie lurched behind me (with Aunt Helen trailing preposterously, protectively behind him). That first morning of monarch butterflies and blue jays staring with black sequin eyes, of ferns covered with shards of dew—and of us, racing behind her—inspired Aunt Eva to lead daily hikes. She hummed Arabic songs and exhorted us in Arabic, the tone of her voice sufficient to convey her meaning. It was she who decided we'd undertake what has become for me, at least, a shorthand reference for our trip: the hike to Heart Rock.

There really was a Heart Rock, the clerk at the local post office explained. It was about four miles off the road. A rugged climb for part of the way. It was in a stand of rocks twenty feet high over which trickled a summer waterfall. In late winter and spring, the water cascaded, uninterrupted and noisy. Years of water dropping onto the flat middle rock below had worn a hole, three and a half feet wide, in the shape of a heart. An act of God, the postal clerk said. An act of love, you mean.

Aunt Eva decided we'd make the hike to Heart Rock near the end of our trip, when we'd be in our peak condition; when we, led by her, could "put our best foot forward." We would make the hike toward the end of our second week, Aunt Eva and I (Georgie had silently withdrawn after two outings).

Of course, we didn't hike every waking minute. Most afternoons, we hopped the ten-cent shuttle to the town and the lake: climbing onto the back of the old truck, getting a good grip on one of the wooden slats on the sides, and planting our feet to withstand the bumps and turns in the mountain roads, as the air whipped across our faces and lashed at our hair. By the middle of the first week, we'd been to the lake three times. By the beginning of the second week, we were going every day, including the Saturday and

Sunday after Aunt Helen had called home on Friday, using the pay phone at the market, and returned to tell us that the uncles would not be coming that weekend.

"George said they'll all be working around the house. Or in the yard."

Aunt Eva snorted. My mother said, "Since when?" And later, in the same tone of voice, "Doing what?" We cousins didn't care. We loved the lake.

Lake Gregory. I surveyed it from the terrycloth platform I'd spread evenly over the rocky sand. Lake Gregory. Where for the first time I clearly saw the point of my streamlined body, my perfumed hair. I'd already become bored with my cousin Georgie. Because in every direction around that windy shore, in front of the food stands, on top of the floats, were boys. Greased and grander than I'd dreamed. Smelling like pineapples. Tanned and salty from sweat.

I'd bake in the sun until I could tolerate it no more; then I'd stand, carefully pulling down the bottom of my suit in back, reverently pulling my straps up, and preen my way to the water. One quick dip and I was out. I smiled at the same boy I'd been watching for three afternoons. Back on my towel, which I'd managed to locate a good distance from the rest of my family thanks to Aunt Eva ("Let her go, Olga; don't sweat the small stuff"), I stretched out, face down. I was two minutes into conversation with a deep, teasing voice before I turned over and sat up.

"Old enough," I answered.

"How old is old enough?" he said.

"Seventeen."

"Are you coming to the dance?"

"There's a dance?"

Situe never came to the lake with us. She never left the cabin. "Because of her heart," said my mother. "She shouldn't move around too much at this altitude," added my Aunt Helen. Nevertheless, Situe swept the tennis court every day with a push broom she'd found somewhere. She hauled buckets of water to wash the front walk.

"Situe. Stop. Rest."

One afternoon when all of us trudged up the hill, tired and hot from a day at the lake and in town, we found her sitting in back of the cabin on a splintery lawn chair smoking a cigarette. Her stockings knotted below her knees. A squirrel swirled around the trunk of a nearby tree. "He's my friend," Situe said, always matter-of-fact. "Not possible," we children thought.

Situe said, "Here, Squeaky." She looked up at us. "I named him Squeaky." She clicked her tongue and held a piece of cracker in her open palm. With a little effort, she lowered her hand to the ground. Squeaky raced forward and took the food. My mother said, "You children. Don't touch the squirrels. They can have rabies."

Later that evening, my aunts and my mother talked out of Situe's earshot.

"She looks green."

"It's the altitude."

"Her heart."

"One of the boys should come get her."

"I'll call Assad. Where's the nearest phone?"

"You'll have to take the shuttle."

My mother said, "I'll go. I'll call Philip. He'll come tomorrow."

And so it was decided that my father would come up the mountain the next day on the pretext of missing his family and take his mother home.

The next day was also the day of the dance. Wednesday night. There were signs posted all over town and I didn't see how my mother could ignore them, but she did.

"Where is it?" asked Aunt Eva.

"At the lake," I answered, as my mother pointedly did not look up.

I'd told the boy from the lake—who said he was eighteen and was as golden as a palomino—that I'd be there. The shuttle didn't run past seven o'clock and that's when the dance started. In the morning, I said, "What time is Daddy coming?"

"After work. He'll sleep over and take Situe down tomorrow."

"Does she know?"

"No."

"The dance is tonight, Mother."

"How can you ask me to think of a dance when your grandmother is ill?"

Each day our hikes had become more daring, more physical. I had a skinned knee, which I displayed like a battle scar, although Aunt Eva remained unscathed. She led me down inclines so steep that footing seemed impossible, made descents standing straight up that sent me to the seat of my pants, struggling and slipping. Nothing was too rugged for her if there was someplace she wanted to reach.

"How can you hike like you do?" I asked.

"I grew up in a village in the mountains."

"As pretty as this?"

"Prettier. Overlooking the sea." Then she said, "We're going like clockwork now. We're ready for the hike to Heart Rock. We'll do it tomorrow."

Later, in front of my mother, Aunt Eva said, "Are you and Georgie going to the dance tonight?"

"It's easy to see you don't have a daughter her age," my mother responded.

I turned to Georgie, giving him my most appealing look because I had ignored him at the lake, and everywhere else for that matter, for the past week and a half. I said, "Georgie really wants to go, don't you?" And Georgie, to my great relief, said, "Yes."

At six o'clock my father arrived. I'd taken my shower early. Just in case. I'd told Georgie to stand by. That maybe we'd be lucky. The unerring sensors of a teenage girl had—back home in Los Angeles, before I'd seen the pine trees or the boy at the lake—directed me to pack my most revealing summer dress. It had spaghetti straps and a tight waist. When my mother saw me in it for the first time, she quickly stitched a bolero jacket from the scraps. Why, I wondered, had she chosen this material for me, gotten the pattern, sewn it together, if she didn't want me to wear it? It was lovely and foamy, in lavender and green.

When I came into the living room of the cabin, my father's face lighted up. Then he said, "Why are you wearing that?" I told him about the dance, distracting him momentarily from holding Situe's hand, from asking her in Arabic, how did she feel, telling her she didn't look good and come on, I'll take you home tomorrow. I went over to my grandmother, too. "Situe, bitue." Just a word game I'd played with her since I was small. "Situe, bitue, are you sick?"

"Maybe," she conceded. She sat so still. Behind her thick glasses, her darkest brown eyes were frozen onyx.

"Why don't you go to bed, Situe?" I asked.

"Yes. Everyone be quiet so Situe can sleep. Let's put you to bed, Ma," my father coaxed.

Then Aunt Eva said, "I don't mind driving Georgie and Michelle to the dance. I'll take your car, Philip." She nodded to my father— her friend, she knew.

"Well," my father began and he looked at my mother. Situe gave a little cough, not deep, just a warning, and I could see I'd been dropped from my father's thoughts. "Olga," he said anxiously and there was no energy reserved for counterpoint about whether Georgie and I would be allowed to go to the dance. Aunt Eva said, "There's nothing for Georgie and Michelle to do here tonight. I'll drive them."

She was to drive, she was to pick up. Georgie and I climbed into the backseat, leaving her in front alone like a chauffeur. Almost immediately, we drove into pockets of fog, which we'd been told descended without warning like evil spirits this time of year, and we slowed to half the already cautious speed limit.

I thought I would scream with impatience. I could never forgive Aunt Eva, the fog, the distance, anything, if I was too late. If he'd arrived early and gone because he thought I wasn't coming. If he found someone else before I got there. I hadn't thought of Situe since we walked out the cabin door.

"You two stay together," Aunt Eva said when she dropped us off. "There's safety in numbers."

"Thank you, Aunt Eva. Thank you. Thank you."

The first thing I did was remove the bolero jacket. I tucked it behind one of the benches that lined the huge, cement patio, where the dance was to be held. A four-piece band—with amplifying equipment piled up like children's blocks—was beginning to play. Georgie said, "I don't suppose you want to dance with me, do you?"

"No."

We stood against the wall of the concession stand. The band played four more songs, so loud the concrete vibrated beneath us, each song having the capacity to move me to despair or exhilaration. I clutched the small white purse I'd brought, which I was beginning to detest as too ugly, too small, too cheap. Then hated myself for needlessly crushing my new bolero jacket and stashing it where it would probably be stained or torn—and for standing there on display, pathetic, like an unwanted Christmas tree.

Then a hand touched my shoulder.

"I made it . . . Let's dance."

Georgie, nearly immobilized against the wall, gave up watching us after an hour. And when we fled the dance floor and ran fast and high over the sand (like laughing forest deer) toward the lockers and shelters that adorned the tip of the lake, I was counting on him, counting on my cousin, to return the loyalty I had more than once accorded him.

The bench in the shelter was wet from the damp air.

"Well," he said in a smoky voice, "here we are."

"Actually," I whispered, "I'm not quite seventeen."

He said, "Nobody knows you're here. You can do whatever you want. Nobody'll ever know."

"More like fifteen," I said softly.

Those were still the days of seduction. When a girl's wavering voice constituted an invitation to continue. When a boy expected to run a finger along your collarbone, then stop; your arms, then stop.

"You're very mature for your age, Michelle."

My arms, my neck, my face, my back. The zipper that my mother struggled to insert flat into the back of my dress opening without a snag, as she had originally intended.

The next morning, Situe and my father left. Aunt Eva and I had planned our hike to Heart Rock for that day because the day after we would be packing and cleaning, and the day after that, leaving.

We left the cabin at eleven o'clock. As usual I trailed behind, over mountain dirt that hadn't felt rain in weeks, that hardly registered our footprints. Through clouds of starving mosquitoes taking to the air as we passed by.

"They prefer cows," Aunt Eva said, "but we're the only game in town."

It was warm and getting warmer. The usual assortment of lizards darted over rocks, while milky white moths favored the yellow flames at the ends of weed stems.

For about two hours we trekked without incident—I wrestling with my thoughts on the night before, reliving every word, every touch; Aunt Eva humming to herself. Once she said, "Good girl, Michelle," for no apparent reason. Steadily, competently, we walked up easy grades. Had the trail not become suddenly steep, had the realities of trying to get over it not pulled me out of my reverie, I could have been unaware of my surroundings for the duration of the hike.

The rocks on either side closed in and we fought for stable footing on the rising path. We pushed ourselves up, scraping our palms. Aunt Eva's hanging canvas bag bounced against her back when she leaned forward. We strained and laughed. Fortunately, before our legs became too tired, the trail flattened out again.

"We'll be proud of ourselves after this," said Aunt Eva. "We'll earn first showers," referring to the vacation rule that the dirtiest among us, regardless of age or status, got the first shower—in deference to the waning water pressure at the cabin. Except for Situe, of course, who was always given first place.

"Aunt Eva," I panted. "I have to sit down. I'm dying of thirst. Did you bring any water?"

"I brought something better." She pulled her bag to the front. "Cucumbers. I learned this in the old country." I doubted her, but I had no choice. I ate two large, juicy cucumbers and felt better. Then a candy bar for quick energy.

We renewed our steady pace. Aunt Eva and I walked side by side along the gully, Aunt Eva's level of exertion recorded only by a thin mustache of perspiration. I was amazed that she never complained about being tired or sore. "This?" she'd say. "A piece of cake."

For some time the path alternated between shade and sun.

"Are you sure we're going the right way?" I asked.

"Keep going, We're the tortoises."

"It was a race between a tortoise and a hare," I said.

"No hares here," she answered.

Then: "Water!"

I ran toward what was simultaneously the beginning of an underground spring (over which we'd been walking, unaware) and the end of the stream that we hoped was the precursor of the waterfall. Of Heart Rock. The water trickled downstream as we traveled up. We moved to one side of the gully to accommodate its thickening ribbon. After a while, the stream was ten feet wide and seven or eight inches deep, moving at its summer speed.

"Do you think I could take a drink from it?"

Aunt Eva shook her head. "No."

"Do you think many people have been here before?"

"Yes."

I walked faster now, energized by the water's coolness in the air, the hope that we were close to our destination, the uphill portion of the trip apparently over. At one point, because of the indifferent placement of gigantic boulders, the path narrowed and we again walked single file overlooking the stream.

Ahead, a couple approached, the woman first, enormously pregnant; I could hardly take my eyes off her stomach. We barely squeezed by each other. Then a thin man. They said "Hello," with a foreign accent. The woman said to my aunt, "Eight and a half months." How had she done this hike? Was she crazy? When they were out of sight, my aunt said, "They said it's only another ten minutes."

Finally, we reached the pool of water, surrounded by a grotto of rocks. Down one wrinkled and indented face ran a trickle of water, two or three inches wide, edged and underlaid with a feathery green moss. The shriveled waterfall, the silent waterfall, dropped into the lap of a rock below.

I waded into the pool to examine the rock more closely. So that when later my brother and sister said, "Are you sure you found it?" and my younger cousins asked, "Was it really in the shape of a heart?" I could give my best, my clearest answer. No doubt Georgie would take me aside with more skeptical questions about its dimensions, its origins, its distance from the road, but what he would really be asking was whether we actually saw it. Whether we made it up.

The water in the pool was up to my knees when I spotted a green snake abandon the bank and slither in. "A snake! A snake! Snake!" I screamed and waded to the edge as fast as the water would let me. "Snake!"

What a pleasure to scream and scream. What a pleasure to be rescued by Aunt Eva's calm, firm hand.

We found a dry place that Aunt Eva assured me was snakeless and sat there and had lunch. Afterward, I lay back, while Aunt Eva explored the area above the fall.

Years later, Aunt Eva would gather me in again and ask, "Do you remember the hike to Heart Rock?" I'd say, "Of course." Or my mother would come across an old picture of all of us standing in front of the cabin—its newly washed and stamped-down earth the subject of continuing critical comment from the locals who'd stop their trucks to remind us that water was scarce that year—and she'd ask, "Michelle, do you remember this picture?" "Of course," I'd say again. I'd think—that picture was taken right before the dance . . . or after the dance.

I had no one to tell about the dance for a number of years afterward. So its memory burned, or smoldered or warmed faintly, like molten rock at the center of the earth, depending on my distance from it.

What came after the hike? The ride home with its attendant minor miseries. More dances. And distances. Away from, toward; farther and closer; the forest, the trees. Events clustering like a stand of pines and, in between, the clearings. And later, when I was tall enough to see more from above (or merely imagined that I could), I'd measure the distances and arrange them, allocating time and feeling to some of them, ignoring others.

I returned to those mountains once as an adult and found the cabin. It wasn't smaller or larger than I'd remembered. It hadn't changed, except for the tennis court, which was gone without a trace—abandoned to a miniature forest of pine trees. Some were already taller than I, others were on their way.

THE AMERICAN WAY

FRANCES KHIRALLAH NOBLE

Mansour Malouf had a nagging wife. On a presser's salary, she wanted a brocade couch and a chandelier that looked like a shooting star. They already had a daughter with a half-blind eye. Mansour's wife called their daughter "Linda" in defiance of the expectation that the first girl in two generations and the child they never expected would be named after her grandmother, her *situe,* Mansour's mother, who lived and moved in their house like a shadow.

"Why do you come up behind me like that?" snapped Lena to her mother-in-law. The bewildered old woman pushed her open hands into her apron. "I was going to make lunch. For all of us. Mansour will be home soon." Indeed, as she spoke, the city bus roared away from their corner, two houses down. One o'clock on Saturday. In a few minutes, Mansour would walk through the front door, humming the melody from a favorite aria, carrying a folded newspaper under his arm. With him would be Linda. In her hands, ragged necklaces of jacaranda she'd made from the twigs and flowers that littered the summer sidewalk in front of their house.

Linda waited every Saturday for her father to return from his brother's clothing factory, where he pressed women's suits into commercial shape. By the time he stepped down from the bus, the only remains of his overheated morning were the pink blotches in his fair cheeks and his dampened hair, smoothed back.

"*Tameen,* my precious," Mansour said to Linda, as she half skipped to meet him. He always stopped when he saw her, to give her the chance to travel the distance herself, under his approving eye. When she arrived at his side, she looked up for a kiss, and he smiled into her uneven face and wondered whether the clipped eyelashes which lined her left eye like the blunt-cut bristles of two tiny brushes would grow back before her next surgery. Together they traveled the squares of sidewalk, then turned up the walkway to their front door.

Lena heard her husband and daughter come in. "Mansour, why are you singing when lunch is almost ready?" she called out. Dutifully, Linda went to the kitchen where the protein drink her mother daily prepared for her to enhance her strength swirled about in the blender. Mansour showered, singing, this time, from Puccini. Situe scurried from the stove to the table; the refrigerator to the table; the counter to the table, setting out the meal of grilled lamb with onions, Syrian bread and cheese, cucumbers and tomatoes in olive oil and lemon juice and hummus tahini (with garbanzos skinned, mashed and thinned into a dippable consistency that very morning).

The final member of the household waited in bed for his food. Lena's brother, Jimmy. Crippled in a warehouse accident before the war. Elevated in his white hospital bed, like an invalid king on his throne, an elaborate array of bars and rings hanging above him from the ceiling. Linda knew not to enter his room if the sliding wooden door had been pulled shut—even though the only television set in the house was in there, mounted high on the wall directly in her uncle's line of vision, so that when the rest of the family congregated to watch a show, they looked heavenward as though waiting for an angel to appear; even though their only other bathroom was tucked in a corner inside. "Your uncle needs his privacy," said her mother. "God knows he's suffered enough." No one knocked, no one called out to Jimmy, no one asked to retrieve a magazine or toy, unless that door was open. Then the room filled with people as naturally as it filled with air. For Jimmy's jokes, his card tricks, his willing ear. Jimmy took all his meals in his bed, on a metal tray that clamped over his lap.

After lunch, Lena called Mansour to the living room.

"This is where I want it to go," she announced as she pointed to a bare pink plaster wall.

"We can't afford it," Mansour answered.

"You say that every time we need something. Linda's last operation—"

"—That was different. I could borrow money from my brother for that. And he'll probably help us again if we need it. But I could never ask him for money for a couch."

"Mansour, we're sliding into squalor. Look around you."

Mansour's eyes told him that his wife exaggerated. From the upright piano in the corner (old and a bargain, yes, but a piano, nonetheless) to the overstuffed chairs, slightly worn; to a large side table (his mother's from the days before she divided her furniture among her children and moved, like a bride without a dowry, into Mansour's house); to a lamp table laden with family pictures; to a solitary couch opposite the wall where Lena stood accusing. If she were a reasonable woman, he'd have pointed out the sturdiness of their furniture, its lineage and dignity.

Lena said, "I found the perfect one downtown."

She left the living room and returned with the kitchen broom in such a short time that Mansour knew the discussion was not over. Vigorously she swept the baseboards at the bottom of the blank wall and dusted the windowsills, although there was no visible dust, as if preparing a nest for a new arrival.

"I've put a down payment on it, Mansour."

"On what?" he asked with hopeful innocence.

"The couch. One hundred dollars. Nonrefundable. The balance is COD. When we have the money. Unless someone else buys it first."

"How much COD?"

"Thirteen hundred and ninety-nine dollars."

"For one couch? No, Lena. No."

"You always managed to get money before—when we got the piano, when we all went to Las Vegas . . ."

"No."

"Mansour?"

There followed a period of resentful days. Next to his wife in the dark, Mansour noted that each age had its compensations; at least now he didn't burn with a fire that wouldn't let him sleep, reduced to running his finger down the middle of her narrow back or rubbing himself against her covered behind. He thought: how different she is from her brother, Jimmy. She thought: how different Mansour is from *his* brother. Each night they slept leaving a strip of cool sheet between them.

They needed more money than Lena knew. Their extended household could have been supported on a presser's pay, supplemented as it was by occasional contributions from Mansour's brother to assuage the guilt of a wealthy son whose mother didn't live under his roof—could have been, that is, but for Mansour's weakness.

Like his father and grandfather before him, Mansour loved to gamble. Anything would do. The horses, a football pool, the heavyweight championship of the world. His friends would say, "Mansour, here's five dollars for me. Put it on anything Valenzuela's riding . . ." and "You're calling your guy to bet? Ten dollars on New York." They relied on Mansour to make their clusters of small bets, to pick up their winnings and carry their money to pay off their debts. For a few intimates, he managed their small wagers at his sole discretion: win, place or show; football; the World Series; a technical knockout.

But then Mansour's luck turned.

His sure winners dissolved. Those nimble choices at the racetrack that allowed him an occasional strut around his steamy floor at the factory—gone. The loyal cards that he ruled like a king during lunch hour—turned like traitors against him.

At the moment of Lena's request for a new couch, Mansour was sitting, quite uncomfortably, on a small mountain of lost bets. And being needled for payment. ("Mansour, is that you? You know what this is about. I don't have to remind you, do I? When, Mansour?")

The collector's voice, distorted and threatening, floated in Mansour's dreams. In the mornings, Situe asked him, "Mansour, why are you so pale?" Lena said, "No opera? You must be sick." Thank God, he thought, for Linda, who rubbed his back and played with his thinning hair, side parting it, center parting it, combing it completely forward until he gently dozed.

Finally, Mansour had no choice. He made his way through the cutting rooms to the sewing rooms, past the presser's floor, to the factory offices and his brother's door.

"I don't manufacture money, Mansour," his brother responded to his request. "Only women's clothes." And he thought, what a foolish man, he sings opera with the Saturday broadcasts so the whole neighborhood can hear him and he lives with a shrew.

"What does Lena say?"

"She doesn't know."

"Mansour, you surprise me. For the good." He gave him the money. Then he asked, "How did it happen?"

Mansour spoke sadly. "My luck turned."

That night Mansour sat with Jimmy.

"I need more money," Mansour said. They talked into their pasts, their futures, looked quizzically around the details of the room as though the answer lay there.

"My brother was always the smart one," Mansour said.

"Bullshit," answered Jimmy.

Forward and backward they went, over their years of acquaintance, and before that, to when Lena and Jimmy moved into the neighborhood down the street from the Maloufs ("Lena loved it when I sang then"), to the days at the factory, to the few old Syrian men who'd survived their wives and seemed to twinkle, unbothered, like fading stars. Mansour talked about Linda's eyes, the couch, his mother's awkward presence—"though I've never minded having you in this house, Jimmy, never"—and Lena, Lena, Lena. They turned these problems over and over between them, like dough they were working into shape.

"You need a sideline," said Jimmy as he leaned on his elbow, reaching over to the high table between them for a cigarette.

"Think, Mansour. Everybody knows but you." Mansour looked at him expectantly. "You know the betting world inside and out. Why should you pay someone to take your bets? Why should you make bets for friends and get nothing out of it?" Jimmy paused for his words to take effect. "I'll help you run it from here. I don't have anything to do all day except exercise my goddamn arms. And I'm 100 percent loyal."

Over the next several days, Mansour's resistance began to erode like loose dirt under a steady rain. When Mansour objected, Jimmy insisted: "It's easy money," and "Of course you can handle it," and "Well, what do I know. I'm just a goddamn cripple."

Finally, Mansour said, "What about Lena?"

"Lena? Lena will be grabbing for your pants—excuse me. I know she's my sister, but I know how these things work."

In the middle of the night, each followed his own twisting, thoughtful path. Jimmy, shirtless because of the heat. Sleepless. His hand drifting down under the single white sheet to feel the disembodied presence below his waist, shriveled in every way, it seemed to him. He felt nothing except what he touched with his hand, the reciprocal sensation in limbs and groin, nonexistent. He imagined himself a seducer, stroking an innocent partner, still as death and as cold. He began a midnight rendition of his exercise routine—pull-ups and lifts, stretches—so that blood surged through his face and neck and arms, his veins protruding like long, slender balloons; his grabs for breath and the jangle of chains muffled by his closed door. When he finished, he collapsed on his pillows.

Mansour, aware that some ordeal was over for Jimmy, closed his eyes in bed next to Lena.

Jimmy lay on his back, his head resting on his folded arms while some of the rings continued their pendulum dance above him.

One morning Mansour said: "I need money to get started."

"Ask your brother," said Jimmy. "The more money you make, the faster you can pay him back."

"I need a place to collect."

"Ask your brother."

And so Mansour returned to his brother's office, facing a man who regarded him with a mixture of love, impatience and amusement, until Mansour sputtered out his plan. His brother thought, "A man at last." Then he asked, "What about the competition? Are you making any enemies with this?"

"I'm a little fish. I'm nobody's competition. We'll keep it among the Syrian boys."

"I can think of dozens of men offhand who'll be happy to place an honest bet with an honest man, Mansour." And he reached for his address book, began calling out names: "Abdenour, Abdullah" ("He's always at the track," said Mansour) "Ayoub, Buttras, Courey, Elias" ("He asked me yesterday to handicap a race for him") "Feres, Habib, Halaby, Hitti, Ibrahim, Karma, Khirallah, Malouf. Everything can be worked out."

His brother had a friend who had a nephew at the phone company who could install the phone lines; they'd work out a time for payoffs and collections ("Not at home," Mansour insisted, "not in front of Linda"). Jimmy would answer the phones during the day, keep most of the books, help keep track of the odds. They adjourned the meeting to Mansour's house.

Lena, upon hearing the front door open, approached the living room like a general. Mansour spoke first: "Lena. Look who's here for a visit. Tell my mother we're home." Before descending to her usual tone with Mansour, Lena reconsidered—something in the brothers' joint presence required it—Mansour, energized in a way she didn't yet understand; her brother-in-law, her natural enemy.

Instead, she said, "You must be hungry. I'll get dinner."

"We'll have drinks," said her husband.

Behind the closed sliding door, the planning continued: Mansour, his brother, and Jimmy.

"We need a code word."

"Keefak" was discarded from the beginning because everyone said *"Keefak"* when he answered the phone.

"What about *'burakee'*?"

"Blessing?"

"After all, the money will be a blessing . . . A happier household will be a blessing . . . Giving our friends this useful service will be a blessing."

Burakee. Yes. Definitely the right word.

"But what if I get caught?"

"Mansour," his brother answered. "This country rewards ingenuity. And hard work. I know. I started with nothing. And look where I am now. I seized the opportunity in front of me. Now you do the same. It's the American way."

Within a week a wire ran from the back of one standard black phone to an outlaw hookup in the backyard. Jimmy could reach the phone without lifting himself up. When he wasn't answering *"Burakee,"* he was reviewing his list of authorized bettors, the gambling events of the week, and getting the odds from the local papers.

At first Jimmy was nervous. *"Burakee,"* he whispered. Anton

Abdenour barked into the receiver after his third call in four days, "For Christ's sake, Jimmy, speak up. I can't tell whether it's you or not." This calmed Jimmy down.

Where was Lena during all this? Quivering with shame and pride, the former drying like a dot of water in the sun with each completed phone call. She could hardly stop herself: "More coffee, Mansour?" "What can I bring you, Jimmy?" At night she faced her husband in bed: "Mansour, let me touch you. You touch me . . . here." Lena relaxed as soon as she realized it was going to work. As soon as her cousin who read her fortune in the tea leaves told her, "I see many blessings ahead for you, my lucky Lena."

As for Linda, her father, mother and grandmother warned her, "You must never, never answer the black phone in Uncle Jimmy's room." When she started to ask why, they countered, "Because it's not for children." Her mother intoned, "Even if it rings and rings and rings and you're home alone, you must not touch it."

At this, Situe snorted to herself: home alone. "Home alone" applied to that short interval between the death of a husband, God bless him, and the date of moving in with a grown child, if you were lucky. Being home alone was the province of crippled uncles or men whose families went to church, but not young girls, or wives or widows. Situe said to Linda, "Don't worry. It won't come up," which the child heard with relief.

The first heart-stopping rings of the phone occurred on Sunday morning before nine o'clock. Uncle Jimmy was in the bathroom, had lifted himself down from his bed to his wheelchair to tend to his daily routine. The sliding wooden door to his room was closed so that the ring of the phone barely seeped through the cracks to the kitchen, where the family ate breakfast.

One ring. Mansour cocked his head. Two rings. Lena stared wildly at him from across the table. Situe—because she was the grandmother and saw herself as the anchor—continued to pour Linda's cereal into a bowl. At three rings, Mansour bolted; he shoved aside the sliding door with such force that the china plates hanging on a nearby wall shook in their elastic hangers.

"*Burakee?*"

"Burakee."

A baptism by fire, survived.

From the street, the Maloufs' house looked no different. A modest white stucco bungalow with a cement porch stretched across its front. On each end, an ancient marble planter holding an equally ancient jade plant that required neither love nor water to survive. The most curious of the neighbors, however, might have noticed a minor change in Mansour's comings and goings. On Monday nights, after dinner, his brother cruised up to the curb in his midnight blue Chrysler and Mansour left the house, careful to latch the screen door, carrying a small brown satchel. They drove at a stately pace, primarily because Mansour's brother was a very poor driver, cutting wide arcs around corners, allowing impatient seconds to elapse at the change of every light: over the side streets of Boyle Heights and Lincoln Heights to the office at the factory. To settle accounts.

Behind his brother's desk sat Mansour, increasingly jovial as he became less astounded that the operation had come together so well; on the other side, a parade of old friends come to collect or pay out. Mansour's brother occupied a corner of the room, quietly estimating his cut. More than one man there thought—if Mansour has been able to pull this off, mild Mansour—I should have been, too; look at him, smiling and raking it in; Mansour (with the ferocious wife and the half-blind daughter and the crippled brother-in-law) humming opera as he handled the money. Charlie Buttras, George Saleeby, Arthur Boulous, surprised at their desire to be acknowledged by Mansour in a way they never previously imagined.

A hot card game burned in the corner. This in contrast to the built-in temperance of the group. For most of them their winnings and losses, small amounts of money that flowed regularly in and out of the game, were merely dues in a club. Part of the price of admission. Not counted upon to produce a pot of gold, not the means to a financial hilltop or a dangerous ride to the bottom. The flow of their dollars toward Mansour's satchel was just enough to elevate him, steadily, to the top end of the group without pushing him out of it. The really serious gamblers (and they personally knew of only one, the infamous Harry Shibley, who had no visible means of support and who, twenty years before, hit it big one day at the track and used all his winnings to buy his wife a house and woke up the next day, broke again)—the big bettors went after bigger bait.

Of course, as Jimmy warned, the problem with a small-time bettor who claimed he knew you as a brother was that he sometimes forgot that he had to bear his own losses. He whined. He cursed. He asked you to forgive his debt. Mansour, inexperienced, and after all, a man who loved opera, absolved one such man, two, three, four times. He thought sympathetically of the man's wife, of the man himself, then crossed him off the list anyway. Later he asked Jimmy, "Do you think he'll make trouble?"

"And lose every friend he has?" Jimmy answered, from what had become his bed-top office, with a new shelf to the left on the wall and teacup hooks screwed in below, on which hung notebooks, lists, pencils on chains.

And yet the specter of trouble hovered over the carnival of phoning and answering and betting, collecting and paying, like a ghost at a wedding. One Monday night, a police car drawn to the after-hours activity at the factory—the lights downstairs, the small herd of cars at one end of the loading dock—cruised into the small parking lot, its high beams arrogantly pressing against the milk-glass windows.

"Open up. Police."

The taller of the two officers rattled the locked door. The closest man inside admitted them to a room whose silence was parted by the creaking of leather and holsters. Two tall, armed, tow-headed men. Fair-eyed.

"Just a friendly game of cards, officers," Mansour's brother said. He'd moved to the front. "I'm the owner of this factory. We get together on Monday nights. Just a group of friends."

The satchel, the receipts, the monies had been sucked into crevices before the policemen entered. But the card game, with its scatter of coins and bills, disported itself like an indecent lover before five eager men.

"How about joining us for a hand of poker, officers?" laughed Mansour's brother. "For fun."

The officers looked at the table. "You know the laws about gambling? Even playing cards for money among friends, it's illegal. Sometimes the games start innocently enough, but they can grow into something requiring police attention. Do you understand what I mean?"

The policemen looked at Mansour, who sat alone behind the desk. "You don't play?"

"We were just breaking up," said Mansour, refusing to acknowledge their sarcasm. "It's time to go home."

The men stirred, hoping to leave, their dark eyes resting on the intruders—but gently—so as not to provoke. "We speak English here and pay taxes in English and work in English"—their eyes said—"but we're different from you, you sons of bitches, and we want you to get the hell out!"

"Well, " one of the policemen began, "everything seems to be under control here. " Before he turned to leave, he said, "Say . . . you guys Italian . . . or what?"

In a few moments the police car glided from the premises, low to the ground, carrying with it the sporadic snaps and crackles of its radio. Inside the office, the men breathed. *"Burakee,"* whispered Mansour.

Burakee.

Lena's couch came packaged and paid for. "No, ma'am. No COD. It's all taken care of. This your anniversary?" She directed the placement of the couch against the wall she had long ago prepared for it. She called to Linda, she called to Situe, to come look. She called her cousin, the fortune teller, to congratulate her on her vision. She made Mansour's favorite dinner. She washed her hair. She rubbed Mansour's back, his front.

Was it the deep rose of the textured brocade that so stirred her? The wooden lion paws on either side of the front? Or the ebony coffee table she intended to ask for next? No matter. The couple's mutual pleasure suffused the house. In deference to the couch that had brought a smile to her daughter-in-law's face, Situe caressed its back, its arms, with the palest pink crocheted doilies of her own creation.

A series of minor indulgences followed. Glass ballerinas and porcelain birds in a lighted china cabinet in the living room; four gold ashtrays which fit neatly one inside the other; a framed oil painting of Linda with postsurgical eyes. Linda's piano teacher took note of the increasing opulence, and, as soon as it was tasteful, raised her rates.

All this is not to say that the enterprise did not require some adjustments. For one thing, old friends sometimes forgot to use the betting line and called on the home phone, saying *"Burakee,"* and launching into a jargon which infuriated Lena ("Two on number five in the sixth, H.P."). "They have no manners," Lena protested angrily, in keeping with her sense of her rising position in life. But Mansour said, "Lena, it was your cousin, George Anton. He made a mistake."

A little notebook appeared in the drawer under the family phone. "We're in business, Lena. We don't turn people away. Besides, if they accidentally call on this number, they're probably relatives."

There was also the matter of the Monday-night visitors who, because they couldn't stay for the card game (which, after all, would have required them to abandon their posts, to be out of reach of their radio urgencies, leaving unprotected a certain portion of the city), sought other means of participation. They bet, but with different odds. They got paid, whether they won or not. It was good for business; essential for business. Mansour said to Jimmy, "You never know when the ripples will stop when you drop a pebble in a pool."

"They can all go to hell," was Jimmy's reply.

For Lena, her upward progress continued. She became a patron at the church. Thanks were recorded to "Lena and Mansour Malouf" on a tiny brass plaque nailed to a pew. Whereas before, Lena had hated the patrons, hungering for evidence of listlessness or poverty or dyed hair among them, now, as one herself, she hurried to the dressmaker to commission the creation of four new dresses for church: one for each Sunday of the month.

At about the same time, Situe began to assert herself. Whether it was as the mother of two successful sons or as the former owner of furniture of quality was difficult to ascertain. She probably didn't know herself. What is known is that on the day of the delivery of Lena's couch, one of the servicemen saw Situe's old sideboard, her chairs, the field of elegant inlaid wood picture frames: "Now this is furniture," he raved and called the others to see. He left Lena's new couch in the middle of the room while paying his respects. From then on, Situe dusted with new vigor. Her joy spilled over to the new couch, whose only wooden parts—its feet—shone like polished rocks.

Uncle Jimmy died two years after he took the first bet. It was swift and somehow painless. A blessing, everyone said. One night in his hand-wanderings, he felt a lump—either grown so fast he hadn't had time to notice it or, having once been noticed, pushed behind the joyous and distracting screen of taking bets and arguing with bettors and counting the take.

After his death, the family was reluctant to remove his bed. Lena changed the sheets once a week. They watched television in his room next to where he had lain. Finally, the bed was sold to make room for a new Zenith television console, which brought their television viewing to ground level. The hats of Jimmy's favorite teams, which he'd hung on his rack on the wall, were packed in a box and put in the garage.

Burakee. Lena discovered a continuing fondness for Mansour. He had money in the bank. He had the air of a comfortable man. He called the doctor to talk about Linda's eye. He asked where, how much, and said, as soon as possible.

And Linda, beloved and encircled, grew up knowing her father was a bookie, despite the protections of her family.

Mansour? He flinched each month when the phone bills arrived. He still pored over the phone numbers, hoping they wouldn't yield their purpose to an investigating eye. He worried about the occasional breathing, nonspeaking caller who refused to say *"Burakee,"* or anything, yet who called just the same. A siren in the neighborhood jarred him momentarily. He had less time for opera and enjoyed it more.

In their closest moments, Lena and Mansour asked each other what they'd do if their world began to unravel like one of Situe's balls of thread fallen from her lap to the floor as she snored. If a loser's bitterness turned to revenge. If they foolishly betrayed themselves by forgetting to flatter, to pay off. They could take a trip,

Mansour suggested. They had family in Chile, Argentina, Australia: descendants, like them, of the generations that explored new worlds and took their chances.

"But, for now," Mansour always concluded, "let's enjoy it, Lena. Let's have a good time. All things come to an end. We'll knock at that door when we come to it."

MY ELIZABETH

DIANA ABU-JABER

I tipped my forehead to the window and watched as we passed another Indian, black-bronze in the sun, thumb in the air.

I was twelve and Uncle Orson was six years older. We'd started our trip in New York City, and I hadn't paid much attention until about two days in, when we began passing long wings of pivot irrigation and the sky started to look like it had been scoured with salt water.

We passed power lines that stood like square-shouldered figures at attention, past grain and silo storage bins, glowing aluminum with pointed tops. At the time I didn't know the names of any of those things; I'd never known that America unraveled as you moved west, until it ran straight as a pulled strand and the trees shrank back into acres of sorghum, beans, corn, and wheat. I stared through the truck window at things mysterious as letters in a foreign language.

My uncle's name had been Omar Bin Nader, but when he first pulled up to my father's apartment on Central Park, he introduced himself to me as Orson. For the rest of the ride out to Wyoming, he cursed his luck, having to transport this newly orphaned niece and all of her father's worldly goods. Then he would stop himself and apologize, saying, nothing personal, and hold my head against his chest.

I slept curled on the wide front seat of the cab. The sound of the engine went on and on. It reminded me of my toy train, an electric engine that had run a two-tiered figure eight around the hall outside our bathroom. It chugged and was painted red with "X & Y Railroad" in white on both sides. I used to watch it with Baba when I'd come home from school and he'd be waiting for me in his bathrobe and slippers and smelling of wrinkle-your-nose. He said to me, "Someday we will climb on to this train and I'll drive us home."

We passed square hay bales, plumes of irrigation water, torn tires, more trucks: Peterbilt, Kenworth, Mack, Fruehauf, Great Dane. Orson pointed out shacks with tires on the roof, sunflowers pointed toward dusk, the road ringing like an anvil.

Near dawn a train horn woke me, mournful and steady. My father had gone away to work on the train; he told me so just before he left. That was why Orson had to come to get me. Baba would be spending his days on the tracks, cross-stitching the same country that Orson and I covered.

New York was not a place to raise children, Umptie Nabila said. Umptie Nabila had become "Great Aunt Winifred" since five Easters ago when we'd last met. What's more, she'd thought it over, and it seemed my name was now Estelle.

"Estelle," I said, turning the name before me. In the following days I often could not remember to answer to it. I put the name on in the morning like a wig. Before long, though, I became accustomed to it. My former name grew faint, then fell from memory.

The land around us was spiced with yellow wildflowers. There were men crawling the construction troughs along the highway, veils of dust and diesel smoke, and grasslands bearing distant ships of mountains. A sign said, "Welcome to Maybell, pop. 437."

My aunt and cousin lived beside a freight yard; all evening long it rang metal on metal. There were yellow-sided Union Pacific cars, railroad ties, pallets, and stacks of lumber. Past the yard was a field of horses where the colts slept on the ground under their mothers' gazes.

By day, I could look out my window and see the train on the horizon, vanishing into the earth and spilling out the other side. Sometimes the mountains were gray, red lightning scratched the sky. I walked past sandstone hills dusted with sage, rows of snow fences, bikers, vans with MIA/POW bumper stickers. The grass gave way to quills of prairie brush, desert green, and downy cows. It was the top of the world, mountains curling at the edges of basin plains like the ocean.

Aunt Nabila-Winifred, her two-year-old son, and her grown-up nephew—my father—came to America in 1954. My father stayed in New York while she kept traveling, she said, until she felt "at home." She and Orson settled in the Wallabee Acres Trailer Court in a double-wide trailer, three bedrooms and two and a half baths, fourteen hundred square feet.

Now Orson was going to work as a wrangler on a dude ranch thirty miles north of Maybell. Aunt Winifred worked for the oil company, which took her out of the house all day. She fretted over leaving me alone and gave me a lot of advice on how to attract friends, changes involving dress, hair, and speech.

"Never, *ever*, speak Arabic," she told me. "Wipe it out of your brain. It's clutter, you won't need it anymore. And if anyone asks—" she said, then paused a moment, sighing over my brown skin, "—you say you're Mexican—no, no—*Italian,* or Greek, anything but Palestinian."

Wyoming was a perfect place for forgetting. The mountains and snow fences repeated like a four-note melody and chased thoughts from my head.

The week before Orson left he took me driving around in his pickup. My favorite road signs were for the Rifleman Hotel, Bad Boys B.B.Q., Indian Clem's Trading Post, and the Buckaroo Lodge. At a gas station a trucker in a white tee hung his arm out the window and asked, "What kind mileage you get?" From far away the highway glistened like a snail's trail. At Gay Pearson's Stops, a driver said, "Indians told the white man not to build their highway through here, said there were evil spirits laying all over Elk Mountains. But the white man goes on anyway, and sure enough every winter twenty, thirty drivers get dumped in some blizzard."

Outside the Pies & Eats, a black man pulled up with a little boy beside him in the front seat. The man opened his door and swung his legs out to face us, but didn't get out. "Hey bud," he yelled to Orson.

"Hey buddy." He was wearing a striped train-conductor cap. Orson walked over to him. "Hey buddy, could you help a guy? I'm out of gas, I got to get to Colorado Springs. Could you help me fill 'er up, buddy?"

Orson pulled a dollar and some change from his pocket.

"Aw, buddy, thank you, man," the man said as he took it. "But I don't think that'll fill her. I mean, I don't think that'll do the job."

"That's all I got."

"Well, how many miles *is* it to Colorado Springs?"

"Two-seventy-five," Orson said, his hand on the door handle to the pickup.

"Well, OK then," the man said, got in his car and drove away.

Wallabee Acres Trailer Court and most of the town of Maybell was inside the Sequoya Reservation. On my fifth day there I met Elizabeth Medicine Bow; she was pushing an empty cargo dolly in the freight yard and singing, "Oh the coffee in the army."

Orson and I had seen Indians on the highways and truckstops, their cars pulled over, white rags tied to the antennas. There was something about their eyes which reminded me of the full-hearted Arabs. Elizabeth and I saw each other and started off, "What are you doing?"

"I don't know. What do you want to do?"

Trains pulled away from my window toward south, sometimes coal trains, black as their cargo. Beyond the tracks were green-blanketed pyramids, stone mountains hooked with gaps like piles of skulls, mountains like thunderheads at evening, mountains soft as mirages in morning, sandy backed, oceans of silty land, cinder fields.

The longer Elizabeth and I knew each other the more certain we felt that we were twins separated at birth. There were many similarities between us: we both had secret names—mine already fading and Elizabeth's used only by her grandmother and great-granny; we both had doubled languages, a public one we spoke in common, and a private language that haunted us. When Elizabeth's mother was angry, she called Elizabeth inside using the other language. Elizabeth always marched in saying, "Speak *American!*"

Also, neither of us knew where our fathers were. We were descended from nations that no map had names or boundaries for.

Elizabeth's mother was twenty-five years old; she was named Shoshona and she looked like a movie star. She worked for the oil company, but unlike my aunt who was higher up, Shoshona said she was always "getting laid off and laid on—like all the fool Indians there."

She would send us out to Bill Dee's—a mile and a half walk into town—for a new tube of lipstick or bottle of nail polish, and always a flask of something called Yippie Tonic that Bill Dee kept behind the counter. On the laid-off days Shoshona and her girlfriends—the girls, Elizabeth called them—sat around the TV, drinking Yippie Tonic out of sewing thimbles.

Elizabeth's grandmother and great-granny preferred the TV reception in the bars downtown, at the Buckaroo. "The girls getting fancy again?" Grandmother said, sticking out her fingers to show how you drink from a thimble. Great-granny was sleeping, stretched out in a booth.

From Elizabeth's window we could see wheat like pink velvet, white floors of grain, and telephone poles going on and on like crucifixes.

"Just wait," she said as we knelt on her bed, elbows propped on her sill. "When we get out of here we'll go where *people* live."

I'd gotten used to the speckled hills and basin. When Elizabeth ran ahead of me through the fields, the sun darkened her skin to eggplant, her hair a whip against the air. In town we played That's-my-father. We would try to be hidden, and pick from the men we saw the gentlest, the sweetest, the tallest, the strongest: a man who inspired us.

The game sometimes made Elizabeth, who'd never seen her own father, very sad. I knew what mine looked like; I knew he was thrumming along the plains, rails singing under the sky, watching from the tracks that would take us back.

Sometimes Elizabeth stayed overnight and shared my bed. Aunt Winifred would tuck us in and give us a cup of tea.

"When I get big I'm gonna go find him," Elizabeth said. "I got a lot of stuff to ask him about. I plan to have money; you'll get equal half. I also plan to get muscles, so nobody will mess with us. After I get my father, we'll go get yours."

"Oh, mine's coming back, though," I said and closed my eyes. The lights were out and we could hear the freight yard; the bed trembled as a boxcar got hitched and rolled out. "Pretty soon. No question about that, dearie," I said.

Elizabeth threw one leg over mine. We were both tall and bony and traded our clothes. She left her toothbrush in our bathroom, and we woke at the same time in the morning.

That year when school started and Elizabeth and I turned thirteen, we began playing That's-your-boyfriend. We chose the most ridiculous boys in the school, poked each other, and said, "That's yours."

We watched the boys in senior high practice football on the field that connected our schools; we thought they looked like soldiers and each claimed one.

The schools were owned by the Sequoya Reservation, seventh to ninth grade and tenth to twelfth, about fifty kids each. The buildings were corrugated aluminum works, "Halleluja! Church of Christ," still fading off the junior high. Elementary school shared with the Grange. Sometimes we heard singing from Grange meetings float beyond the building.

That winter Frank Atchison, a white history teacher at the junior high, took Elizabeth aside and said she had great potential, and he would work on "cultivating" her. She would have to stay after school for lessons. After the first lesson, Elizabeth came rushing home: Mr Atchison had proclaimed a "great love" for her, and she had decided she was interested. They would see each other as long as his wife didn't find out.

Why, I brooded, had Elizabeth been selected and not me? Mr. Atchison might have preferred Sequoyans, but my skin was so dark that no one seemed to notice my difference. I was jealous that while once we had shared everything, Elizabeth hadn't offered Mr. Atchison. More than anything else, though, I was jealous of Mr. Atchison taking Elizabeth away. As it turned out, Elizabeth didn't go anywhere, and her sharing stopped just short of bringing him to sleep over.

We went to school, cut out after attendance, and walked back to the flat rocks over at the freight yard. Elizabeth told me everything in detail so small and perfect, we could sink into it, the white sun careening past us, the rails flashing like a trail of coins. Listening was like being hypnotized:

> "And then he left me this note—
> "And then we went for this ride—
> "And then he pulled up my shirt—"

It was February and a snowy wind filled the basin, flicking off the sides of the mountains, whirling like the Milky Way. When it got too bad out we went to my trailer and huddled in bed. Elizabeth said she spent most of the time she was with him figuring out how to describe it to me later. I knew about the chip in his incisor, the mole behind his ear, the pressure of his body as he flattened against her. We drifted on stories, Elizabeth floating free while I stayed moored by ordinary life.

After two months of it Elizabeth decided to stop seeing him. Everything ceased as abruptly as it had started. The only reminder was Mr. Atchison staring at Elizabeth in the hall, all the kids grinning. Everybody knew what had happened. "It's time to get on with my life," she said. "I don't have time for these men. The grandmothers need me to come for them after school."

Winter churned into something like spring. Clouds became mountains, steam, and rain. In the freight yard there were boxes of bawling calves again, hissing cargo brakes, and metal wheels heated like branding irons.

In spring assembly we watched *West Side Story* and Elizabeth and I saw that Shoshona looked like Natalie Wood. She was what Natalie Wood might look like if you took a cloth to her and polished her bronze, so her cheekbones and the wings of her nose gleamed like a statue's.

Shoshona taught us about life. She said Elizabeth wouldn't ever have any brothers or sisters as long as it was a so-called free country.

The doctor at the clinic where she had Elizabeth gave her what she called her favorite toys:

"I tell the boys, 'you gotta put on your raincoat in heavy weather.' I say to them, 'No glove, no love.'"

Shoshona usually brought one of her men home when the tonic was gone and she was laid off. Elizabeth would come over to spend the night with me. One morning after we decided that Shoshona looked like Natalie Wood, Elizabeth and I walked back to her trailer and found Shoshona sitting at the table with her eyes ringed purple, blue, and black, a crust of blood along one nostril.

"Never let a drunken Indian hit you," she told us as we walked in. "He hits you, you crack him back in the jaw hard as you can." She showed us how to make a fist, with the thumb on the outside of our fingers. She displayed a broken tooth in a baby jar that she'd extracted the evening before, and clenching her hand, showed us how.

"That was Fred Go Slow's. So's this." She showed us a wallet with what looked like a lot of money in it. "The sad thing is when he finally comes to, he won't even remember who did it to him."

About three weeks later, Shoshona walked through Aunt Winifred's door, sat down on the sofa and started crying. Elizabeth and I peeked in from the kitchen door.

"I can't believe it. Is this my life? Is this really my life?" she kept saying, while Aunt Winifred tried to get her to drink tea. "Not another one! A smelling, snot-nosed, screaming . . . oh God the screaming. I don't even care about the black eyes, but this—those goddamn rubber things break!"

That was how we found out Elizabeth was going to get a baby to play with after all.

The school yard was quiet and cows wandered across the playground. We stood behind the school, saw a ripple of antelope, the remains of brushfire, puffs of tumbleweed, a skinned possum, its tongue poking out.

Elizabeth didn't want to go to her trailer much anymore. When Shoshona got through with vomiting in the morning she started taking long pulls on the tonic bottle. The girls, some of whom were also pregnant, kept right up with Shoshona, drinking.

Fred Go Slow, who now had a big hole in his teeth, came around the house looking guilty and nervous until Shoshona's friends chased him away. He tried to give Elizabeth and me little toys and candies, but Elizabeth threw them to the ground, saying, "I'm a woman now, I don't play with baby things."

Summer flared like a match; the freight tracks groaned. Linemen stood against the dusk in overalls, swinging lanterns, coal trains sliding in behind them.

Orson came home from the dude ranch and convinced Aunt Winifred to sell my father's possessions. For a year, furniture, books, and clothing had filled her extra bedroom. Bit by bit, Winifred cleared the room, weeping over every piece she sold, getting remarkable prices in the process. She held back a few things: portraits my father had painted, a sandalwood carving, a brass-topped table, and a small prayer rug. She stored a trunk in my room with a few of my baby toys and some odds and ends.

Elizabeth wanted to investigate the trunk, but it proved disappointing: rigid Barbie dolls, Matchbox racecars, books smelly with dust, and a shotglass with the words "Monticello Raceway." At the bottom, Elizabeth found a big, white cotton square checked with black.

"Oh. Oh yeah," I said. Words and faces I hadn't thought about for a year rushed back. My hands remembered things my mind didn't know about. Elizabeth sat before my bureau mirror and I began arranging the *hutta* around her head and neck. She looked like Elizabeth Taylor in *Cleopatra*.

Aunt Winifred was just back from work. She glanced in the doorway, stopped and said, "Oh, children!" Her eyes were bright and her fist knotted against the base of her throat. Elizabeth looked like royalty.

"Keep it," I said. "It's yours, it was made for you."

"Wait," she said and stood up. First I thought she was going out to show her mother, but minutes later she came running back with something in her hand. A long, tufted feather, deeply colored as the earth, strung on a loop of leather.

"A man who said he was my father gave this to me when I was

a kid," she said, the feather covering the palms of both of our hands. "I knew he wasn't any more my father than the rest, but I like to think it came from my real father anyway. He told me it was golden eagle, a warrior's feather. It's for you, my sister Estelle." She slid the leather piece down on my head. It was too big for me and rested on my ears, but the feather glowed like a flame against the black of my hair, brushing my shoulder, lighting my face.

"I love it," I whispered, afraid to move inches to see it. "It's the most beautiful thing."

Elizabeth put her face next to mine. "Remember the Indian girl we saw last week on the late-night movie?"

"Pocahontas," Aunt Winifred said.

Not long after Elizabeth and I traded headdresses, a woman came to Aunt Winifred's door. She was known around the town as the Social Welfare Lady. She had dark eyebrows and a powdered face. Elizabeth and I spied from the doorway as she talked to Aunt Winifred and rubbed her matchstick legs together. Aunt Winifred talked to the woman in a pleading voice, but the woman kept talking straight ahead, with her gray gaze and her rubbing legs. Finally Aunt Winifred turned around to where she knew we were watching, and we saw the lady's eyes lift up, following.

Shoshona had gone drinking the night before. We had heard her outside making the mewing sounds when she wasn't feeling right and the earth was moving beneath her, and she couldn't find her front door key. She'd shown up for work the next morning around the time the lunch whistle was blowing and her boss, Sammy Hudson, who was a cousin of Fred Go Slow, up and reported her to the Bureau. The Bureau had started a new program on the Sequoya Reservation: cash reward for anyone reporting willful endangerment of the unborn through alcohol abuse. All willful endangerers would be imprisoned, length of sentence determined by their due date. They had decided to make an example of Shoshona.

The Welfare Lady said that Elizabeth had to stay with her Aunt Shyela on the other side of the reservation, ten miles away. She led Elizabeth to a big green station wagon and they drove off. That night Elizabeth came back to our trailer on her aunt's bicycle. Her hair was blowing around her face and she looked like a beautiful witch who had climbed out of the sky.

"I promise you, I'm gonna help her escape," Elizabeth whispered as we were falling asleep. "There's no way they're gonna keep my mother in their trap."

"No. I know it," I said.

The train crossed my dreams; I saw my father's eyes, clear as the moon. Voices floated through the dawn, filling me, speaking my other language, words I recognized, forget, don't forget, forget.

Orson drove us to town that day, the air humming with insects. We passed pickups in dust clouds, drivers' fingers off the steering wheels, howdy, rifles shaking in the gunracks. We watched land rising away from us, turning transparent in the light, brown and yellow as the desert.

The day before, Shoshona's pregnancy had looked like nothing more than a held breath, but it seemed to have grown overnight. She was held in a building with the words "Maybell Prison" painted on a water tower on the roof, a small reservation jail. Shoshona sat on a narrow bed in a windowless room, facing away from us. I had never been inside the building before, although we'd passed it plenty of times while searching for grandmothers. Iron bars were a shock. I had imagined a kind of special prison for pregnant women.

"Mom?" Elizabeth said. I had never heard her call her anything but Shoshona. Her voice got inside me, gathering tears behind my eyes, and all I wanted to do was get on my knees and beg Shoshona, come out, come out. Elizabeth and I started crying and Shoshona wouldn't face us. A guard came back and said, "What are you girls doing here? You're not supposed to be back here."

Shoshona stood. "Leave them alone. I'm allowed to have visitors!" Her face was puffy and she was shaking. "Now, kids, be good and go get me some of my medicine tonic," she said in a wobbling voice.

"Sorry, little mama," the man said. "These girls ain't bringing you nothing."

As soon as we got out of the prison we ran to Bill Dee's. Some of the girls were inside sitting at the counter, and they quieted fast. Their eyes slid toward us; I heard a whispered mix of languages. Elizabeth refused to look at anyone as we went to the cash register, then we realized neither of us had any money. We stood there, staring at the gun case, as if that was that we'd come in for. Then two of the girls were standing behind us and one of them said, "Bill Dee, we need some Yippie Tonic and we need it on credit and you know what for."

We walked back to the jail, past the Last Chance, "Girls Girls Girls," past scrub, weeds, and alleyways. The guard who'd sent us away was at the front desk. I had a bottle of tonic tucked inside a jacket that was zipped to the neck, though it was already ninety outside. The man fanned himself with a handful of mimeographed sheets and stared at us. We all stood looking at each other, then he sighed and said, "Girls, you know I can't let you back there."

"Please, officer," Elizabeth said, stepping toward him. "I've got to get back there. Maybe—if there's something you want—anything you want—"

He was shaking his head, eyes closed. Elizabeth started to cry, speaking in her other language, blood sounds that made him open his eyes. But he wouldn't stop shaking his head, and then Elizabeth started to scream, and he got up from the desk to grab her. He'd forgotten me—all I had to do was turn down the corridor and find the right bars.

When I got to her, Shoshona was standing, holding the bars. I pulled the bottle out of my jacket and passed it to her. She was shaking so hard she almost dropped it, so I set it on the ground.

"Estelle," she said, her eyes on the bottle, "what's happening to Elizabeth?"

"They won't let her in," I said. "She tried to come in."

Shoshona nodded. "Tell her to keep trying." Then she looked at me and said, "I can kill this baby any time any way I want to. I can hold my breath and starve off its air. I can think evil down into it so it rots before its fifth month. It's my own heart, this baby. They think they can hold onto my heart for me?"

I had to leave before they found me. Shoshona's hot voice echoed up the corridor, "What did I do? Just tell me, who says I did wrong?"

I walked back alone, past bottles of rubbing alcohol, Lysol, cooking spray, past huddles of black-haired men and women outside the plasma donor center, cigarette butts smashed on the sidewalk.

Elizabeth didn't come over that night or the next. Voices began to fill my sleep. I dreamed of the toy train running its figure eight, a man's hands, white as marble, going to it, and I woke gasping.

I didn't look for Elizabeth; I knew if I found her, I would come to the end of our world, that it would be an outdated, useless place. Weeks went by. Aunt Winifred looked at me, but didn't ask about Elizabeth. Orson returned to the dude ranch. A few days later he called to say there was an opening for a chef's assistant—mine, if I wanted it. There was a tutor at the ranch, so I wouldn't need to return to the reservation school.

One week before I was supposed to join Orson, Aunt Winifred came home carrying two bags of groceries and said she had something to tell me. She put down the bags and said, "Your friend Elizabeth has been seen in town. On the arm of a prison officer."

I moved my hands to the edge of the table. "What? Where in town? What officer?"

Aunt Winifred moved some of the cans of food around on the counter. "She's trying to help her mother, I guess," she said. "Poor baby."

I went to the door and Aunt Winifred said, "Estelle, you be careful. You are not to stay out late."

It was mid-August; at five thirty P.M. the reservation was bright and hot as midday. The shadows had barely begun sliding toward evening, things looked blurred, windows and doors shut to the sun. I walked into town, down Main Street, with its line of bars, neon lassos, and dancing girls. Elizabeth and I had gone into all of these places looking for her grandmothers.

I walked to the door of the Tally Ho and tried to will Elizabeth out to me. I slid my hands in my pockets and prayed, oh please come out, Elizabeth, please, please come out.

The door opened, but there was just an old woman with a mouthful of gold teeth and long, red-black hair. I backed up, walking away as quickly as I could. I saw people coming out of the Three Cheers down the block and I walked toward them looking for Elizabeth. It was two men and a woman. They saw me and moved closer.

"Hey, what's this?" one of the men said. "Want to party, youngster?"

"Ain't you Shoshona Medicine Bow's girl?" the woman asked. She stood with her back to the sun, her face in shadows.

"That's my sister. I mean, Elizabeth is," I said, trying to steady my voice. "Have you seen her?"

"No. You want us to help you look?" the other man said in a way that wasn't offering help. I tried to back away, but they moved toward me, so I stood still, arms clasped around my sides.

"She ain't no Indian," one of the men said, reaching out and tipping my face to the sun. "Not much. Look at her, that ain't no kind of Sequoyan *I* know about. What type mixed breed *are* you?"

I remembered Aunt Winifred's warning: never, never tell. I tried to think of other nationalities she'd offered me, but they vanished from my mind. The only countries I could remember were from the unit on Northern Europe we'd done that year: Belgian chocolate and Swiss clocks.

"Swiss," I said. "I'm Swiss."

They started laughing.

"You're Swiss and I'm the Pope's grandfather," the other man said. But they were already losing interest, walking away. I shivered in the heat, wanting to run after them and ask what they knew about Elizabeth.

I heard Shoshona's voice in my dream that night, mixed with other voices, her cry, banging like a hammer, "What did I do, who says I did wrong . . ." I dreamed cargo doors, Cottonbelt, Union Pacific, Hydro-lite, satellite dishes, tilting trees, the white face of a church minding the plain.

I went into town every evening for a week, becoming bolder, entering bars, asking everyone if they had seen Elizabeth Medicine Bow. I went to the building with the water tower on top; Elizabeth wasn't there. I tried the school, I tried Bill Dee's, I tried at the houses of Elizabeth's family and friends.

I'd worked down the street of bars and by Friday I was back at the Tally Ho again. It was late in the evening, getting dark, and the edge had come off the heat. Maybell hummed with the neon, insects swarming to the lights. I stopped on the sidewalk outside the bar, saying my prayer, please come out, Elizabeth, oh please, please come.

The bar door opened then and a Sequoyan man walked out. He had big rounded shoulders and hair that fell down over his back. I glanced at him and looked away. Then he was beside me suddenly, whispering, "Little one, what are you doing here?"

Then he said, "Elizabeth Medicine Bow lives with her new lover. Why don't you come with me instead?" It was too dark to see him clearly; that might have been why his words were so persuasive. I followed him away from the strip. It was dream-walking, following this bear-quiet figure.

We went through the sleeping neighborhoods, to where the land got steep and sharp. We walked up. At times he took my hand to help me, the rest of the time I followed, listening to the flow of his breath, his foot on the stones. The earth became soft, as if we were walking in powder. Then we stopped and the man was bent over, looking around in the dirt. "I always lose my house key," he said. "So I keep it hidden outside. Then I have to find it again."

He pulled and opened a rectangle of yellow out of the night. It was a small cottage, filled with skins and bones, an old sofa, kitchen table, chamber pot, and freezer. He led me, identifying the skeletons and skulls he had collected. He'd found some bones already sun-washed, others came from carcasses he'd found, and skinned, and sometimes eaten: deer, antelope, tiny bones of raccoon hands, cow and coyote skulls, chicken, cat, dog and the perfect knobs of snake spines. There were various feathers, some small, stitched together, some curling and striped. One, glowing like brown mineral, rested on a pile of books; I touched it. "Golden eagle," I said.

"That's right," he said. "Apparently you know a few things." That was the first time I looked at him directly. He was heavy and strong, and his hair fell all the way down his back, a bed of black, like his eyes.

"See here." He stood at a small nightstand by the bed. "I made these." He showed me a polished comb and brush. "From bear bor s and pig bristles. Very valuable, like elk and mountain lions and rattlers."

This was the way he lived, he told me: scavenging, keeping an ear to the ground, sometimes teaching a class in nature appreciation, or sculpture, or taxidermy. Night moved on a slow tide, the house sailing on his voice. We sat on his couch. I picked up his bone brush and began running it down the length of his black hair, over and over, enchanting myself with the repetition, the way it polished. He sat still until I had fallen asleep.

I woke later, drooling a little on his shoulder. His arms were soft around me, his breath deep and regular. I lay still for a few minutes. It was still dark outside, but I could tell morning was coming from the blue sheen in his window and the way my breath made a mist. It must have dropped forty degrees overnight.

He sat up and pulled a knitted shawl off a chair, then lay back and draped it over us. "What did you dream last night?"

"How do you know that I dreamed?"

He propped up on one arm. "You were talking in your sleep, your dreams speaking—"

It came in flashes: Elizabeth running, the blue of her hair melting into black sky. She was telling me, "I've found my father, he's right over there," and I looked, but it was too dark. The little train was running through its circuit on the floor of the trailer house, speeding up and slowing down; the tiny boxcars were trembling; I thought it was an earthquake. Then there were drops of water on me, red drops. I went to turn off the bathtub; it was overflowing, red as velvet, red wine. Then I saw the white shank of my father's leg and his forearm; I tried to ask why he was bathing in wine, but the words wouldn't come.

I realized that I wasn't dreaming anymore, but remembering, and my tongue got thick as if the dream-story was choking me. I stopped speaking and sat opening and closing my eyes slowly. Beyond the window I could see the prairie beneath the hill, divided by tracks, a scroll of light.

"Your dream has more than one meaning," he said.

I was shivering, arms wrapped around myself, trying to press fear back into my ribs. I remembered my father, swallowed by pain, like a drop of bitter wine, his red wrists against the white enamel. Outside the train was passing. I thought, I was weak; I wasn't enough to save him. I put down my head and my tears were light as air.

My friend went into the other room and then returned, giving me the eagle feather. He said, "You won't believe me now, but the feelings you have will dry up after a while. Like everything else, like tears. Your father went where he needed to; some people can't live on this earth. You should prize this pain of yours. This is what will make you human all the way through. Nothing less will do that."

The feather, he told me, was a warrior's prize. At the time, I only cared about my dream, but later I remembered its glow in my hands, softness where he touched me on the face.

I walked down to our trailer later that morning, the path clear in the light. Aunt Winifred was quiet when she saw my changed face. I had decided to join Orson at the dude ranch.

Four years later the owner of the ranch sent me through college, a private school back East. I came back to the reservation for just one Christmas break in all those years. Shoshona and Elizabeth had gone away; their trailer stood empty. I walked through the hills, but couldn't find my friend's cottage.

Not until I'd graduated and was working in New York did my memories become insistent, nudging me in the street or the office, making me wonder what had become of Shoshona and her baby. And of Elizabeth. When I called, Aunt Winifred never talked about the reservation. She said to me, "Your life is *there* now, in New York, out in the world. Forget about what's past."

I took an apartment not far from the one where I'd lived with my father. I imagined my father's ghost waiting there, watching over memories. My walk to work led past the old place, and its brownstone windows moved with shadows.

I began to see Elizabeth too, in stores and restaurants, her blue-black hair in crowds of brown and blond. I would get closer and see it wasn't her. Sometimes I would talk to these women anyway, my wish for her was so strong. Often, they were from other tribes, Iroquois, Tillamuck, Cherokee. Once I stopped someone from the Sioux Pine Reservation who said she knew Elizabeth Medicine Bow. She told me Elizabeth was now Mrs. Jeffrey Harrison, that she had two sons, and lived in South Dakota. Twice I stopped black-haired women from Korea, once a woman from Bombay, and once a Palestinian.

Orson settled in Denver; Aunt Winifred retired and moved to Florida. Nothing could summon Elizabeth back but imagination.

I'd been in New York for several years when I found a book in the library that described how the American Indian population was being killed off through alcohol abuse. When I finished reading I walked to the fire escape outside my apartment and wanted to shout *Elizabeth*, as loud as I could. I didn't believe the story about her and the South Dakota rancher. My Elizabeth would still be wandering, I thought, pushing open church doors and saloon gates, finding her father.

I stood on the fire escape and noticed how the city hooked itself into crags and canyons, rooftops high enough to snag a singing bird. I went back into the apartment.

I saw the way native people wandered in New York, displaced persons. I thought about the way homes, cities, and whole countries disappeared, the faces of your neighbors and the people you loved, the grass of your home, and the name of the place you lived and played were all gone, incredibly, gone.

My artifacts: a feather or two, a name, the image of a toy train that ran in circles. Sometimes in the mornings before I opened my eyes, a moment and space would come to me, an opening in the past that Elizabeth and I had shared: we are standing together, holding hands, and everywhere we look we see crops of dirt, spouts of smoke and grain, dust-devils, plumes of topsoil, burning crops, and the farmers' hay bales stacked like dominoes. And the land goes on across the wide earth, across our separate lives, our futures silent as the buffalo. We are left with the precious, mysterious past.

CONTRIBUTORS' NOTES

NABEEL ABRAHAM was born in Charlotte, North Carolina. He has a Ph.D. in anthropology from the University of Michigan (Ann Arbor) and is currently director of the honors program at Henry Ford Community College (Dearborn, Michigan). He has coedited (with Andrew Shryock) *Arab Detroit: From Margin to Mainstream* (Wayne State University Press, 2000), which received an award of merit from the Historical Society of Michigan. Abraham has also published (with Sameer Abraham) *Arabs in the New World* (Wayne State University Press, 1983) and *The Arab World and Arab-Americans* (Wayne State University Press, 1981).

DIANA ABU-JABER was born in Syracuse, New York, to a Jordanian father and Irish American mother. Her first novel, *Arabian Jazz,* won the Oregon Book Award in 1995. Her new novel, *Crescent,* was published recently in the United States by W. W. Norton and will be published in Italy, Britain, Spain, the Netherlands, and Sweden. A recipient of a National Endowment for the Arts fiction writing grant, Abu-Jaber received her Ph.D. from SUNY-Binghamton and has taught creative writing, film studies, and contemporary literature at the University of Nebraska, the University of Michigan, UCLA, and the University of Oregon. She's currently writer-in-residence at Portland State University.

SUSAN MUADDI DARRAJ earned an M.A. in English literature from Rutgers University. Her work has appeared or is forthcoming in *New York Stories,* the *Orchid Literary Review, Mizna,* the *Christian Science Monitor, Sojourner,* and other forums. She is the editor of the *Baltimore Review,* a national journal of poetry, fiction, and creative nonfiction, and she is currently editing a collection of essays by Arab women writers entitled *"Direct My Pen Eastward": Women of Arab Descent on Writing* (Praeger Publishers). Her collection of short stories, *The Inheritance of Exile: Stories from South Philly,* was a finalist in the 2003 AWP Book Award Series in Short Fiction.

YUSSEF EL GUINDI is primarily a playwright, currently living in Seattle. Originally from Egypt, he was a playwright-in-residence at Duke University and is now literary manager for Golden Thread Productions. His plays have been performed at various theaters around the country. "Stage Directions for an Extended Conversation" originally appeared in *Mizna*.

JOSEPH GEHA was born in Zahle, Lebanon, and grew up in Toledo, Ohio. He is the author of *Through and Through: Toledo Stories* (Graywolf, 1990). His stories, poems, and essays have appeared widely in periodicals and anthologies such as the *Quarterly*, the *Iowa Review*, the *Northwest Review*, the *New York Times*, *Epoch*, *Big City Cool*, and *Growing Up Ethnic in America*. He is a recipient of a National Endowment for the Arts fellowship grant and a Pushcart Prize. His work has been included in the permanent collection of the Smithsonian Institution's Arab American Archive. He is professor emeritus of English at Iowa State University.

RAWI HAGE was born in Beirut, Lebanon, and immigrated to Canada in 1992. He is a writer and a visual artist. His writings have appeared in *Fuse Magazine*, *Mizna*, *Jouvert*, the *Toronto Review*, *Al-Jadid*, *Montreal Serai*, and *Memory and Creation*. His visual works have been shown in various galleries and museums. He is also a recipient of the Canada Council for the Arts Creative Writing and Residency Program and the Conseil des arts et des letteres du Quebec grant program for professional writers. He resides in Montreal, Canada.

LAILA HALABY was born in Lebanon to a Jordanian father and an American mother. Her novel, *West of the Jordan*, was published by Beacon Press (2003). She also writes poems, short stories, and children's fiction, some of which has been published in anthologies and literary journals. Her education includes a B.A. in Italian and Arabic from Washington University, a Fulbright scholarship to Jordan, an M.A. in Near Eastern languages and cultures from UCLA, and an M.A. in school counseling from Loyola Marymount University. She currently lives in Tucson, Arizona.

RANDA JARRAR was born in Chicago in 1978 and grew up in Kuwait. She moved back to the United States after the Gulf War. She has a B.A. from Sarah Lawrence College and an M.A. in Middle Eastern studies from the University of Texas, Austin. She has just completed her first novel and lives in Austin with her son.

MOHJA KAHF was born in Damascus and grew up in the United States. She is an associate professor at the University of Arkansas in Fayetteville, where she lives with her husband and three children. Her poetry and fiction have been published in the *Paris Review,* the *Atlanta Review,* the *Paterson Literary Review, Mizna, Aljadid, Banipal,* and *Flyway.* She was a 2002 winner of the Arkansas Arts Council Fellowship for her poetry. Her first book of poems, *E-mails from Scheherazad,* was released by the University Press of Florida in 2003.

PAULINE KALDAS was born in Egypt and immigrated to the United States in 1969 at the age of eight. Her work has been published in several journals, including *International Quarterly, Phoebe, So to Speak,* and *Borderlands,* as well as in the anthologies *The Poetry of Arab Women, Cultural Activisms, The Space between Our Footsteps,* and *Post Gibran: Anthology of New Arab American Writing.* In 2001, she was awarded a fellowship from the Virginia Commission for the Arts in fiction. She received her Ph.D. from SUNY-Binghamton and is currently teaching at Hollins University in Roanoke, Virginia, where she lives with her husband and two daughters.

SAHAR KAYYAL is a first-generation Arab American and native of Chicago. She lived in El-Bireh, Palestine, for five years during the 1987 intifada, attending Friends' Girls School in Ramallah. Her short story "Lovely Daughters" has been featured in *Mizna,* and she is currently working on her first novel. She teaches at an Illinois high school as well as Governors State University, where she earned her M.A. in English. She lives with her husband and two daughters in a south suburb of Chicago.

KHALED MATTAWA is the author of two books of poetry, *Ismailia Eclipse* (Sheep Meadow Press, 1995) and *Zodiac of Echoes* (Ausable Press, 2003). He has translated four volumes of contemporary poetry and coedited an anthology of Arab American literature. He teaches at the University of Michigan, Ann Arbor.

D. H. MELHEM is the author of six books of poetry, including *Conversation with a Stonemason* (IKON, 2003), *Country* (Cross-Cultural Communications, 1998), *Rest in Love* (Confrontation Press, 1995), and *Poems for You* (P & Q Press, 2000). Publications also include a novel, *Blight* (Riverrun, 1995); the books *Gwendolyn Brooks* and *Heroism in the New Black Poetry* (both from the University Press of Kentucky); and a musical drama, *Children of the House Afire* (produced at Theater for the New City, 1999). Recipient of a National Endowment for the Humanities fellowship and an American Book Award, Melhem received her B.A. from New York University, her M.A. from CCNY, and her Ph.D. from the City University of New York. She is currently vice-president of the International Women's Writing Guild.

MAY MANSOOR MUNN was born in Jerusalem of Palestinian-Quaker parents. Her family lived in several towns in Palestine and Jordan, including Zerka and Ma'an. Later they lived in Beersheba, Jerusalem, and Ramallah. Munn received her B.A. in English and religion from Earlham College in Richmond, Indiana. She moved permanently to the United States in 1955 and has taught English at the Friend's School in Ramallah and high school world history in Houston. Her published writings include articles, essays, and short fiction. Her work has appeared in *The Flag of Childhood* and *Food for Our Grandmothers*. She is the mother of two adult children, a writer and an artist, and lives with her husband in Houston, Texas.

FRANCES KHIRALLAH NOBLE was born in Pasadena, California, in 1945. She presently lives in Santa Monica and Palm Desert with her husband, son, and daughter. She earned a B.A. in English in 1966 and a J.D. in 1972 from the University of Southern California. While in law school she was a Legion Lex Scholar and in 1972 was the recipient of a Reginald Heber Smith Community Lawyer Fellowship. In the early 1990s, she studied fiction writing at UCLA and USC. Khirallah Noble is the daughter of an Arab father and an Irish mother. Her publications include *The Situe Stories* (Syracuse University Press, 2000) and *Missing Her* (Mobius, 2000).

SAMIA SERAGELDIN was born and raised in Egypt, educated in Europe, and emigrated to the United States with her family in 1980. She holds an M.S. in politics from the University of London and is a writer, a political essayist, an editor, and a literary critic. Her first novel, *The Cairo House* (2000), was published by Syracuse University Press. Serageldin's second novel, *Love Is like Water*, will be published in early 2005; a chapter from it is excerpted in this anthology. Serageldin has also contributed essays to and served as consulting editor on a book on globalization and international terrorism, *In the Name of Osama Bin Laden* (Duke University Press, 2002). An instructor at Duke University, she is the author of articles on gender and Islam in Egypt, Muslims in America, and Arab American writing. Serageldin lives in Chapel Hill, North Carolina.

EVELYN SHAKIR, the daughter of Lebanese immigrants, is the author of *Bint Arab: Arab and Arab American Women in the United States* (Praeger, 1997). Her short stories have appeared in *Post Gibran: Anthology of New Arab American Writing*, the *Red Cedar Review*, *Flyway*, and the *Knight Literary Journal*. A personal essay was recently published in the *Massachusetts Review*. Her essays on Arab American literature have appeared in a number of journals and collections. She has also written and produced a public-radio documentary on Syrians/Lebanese in the Boston area. In 1999, she spent a semester as a Fulbright Fellow in Lebanon.

PATRICIA SARRAFIAN WARD was born and raised in Beirut, Lebanon, during the civil war. At the age of eighteen she moved with her family to the United States. She holds a B.A. from Sarah Lawrence College and an M.F.A. from the University of Michigan. Her first novel, *The Bullet Collection*, was published by Graywolf Press in 2003.

DAVID WILLIAMS is the author of a poetry collection, *Traveling Mercies* (Alice James Books, 1993). His work has appeared in dozens of magazines, including the *Atlantic*, the *Kenyon Review*, the *Hayden's Ferry Review*, the *Michigan Quarterly Review*, and *Sierra*, as well as in several anthologies, including *Post Gibran: Anthology of New Arab American Writing* and *A Different Path*. He has recently completed a novel and a new collection of poems. He teaches at Wheaton College in Massachusetts. All his grandparents came from Lebanon, and he still has many relatives there.

SELECTED BIBLIOGRAPHY OF
ARAB AMERICAN LITERATURE

Abinader, Elmaz. *Children of the Roojme*. New York: Norton, 1991.

———. *In the Country of My Dreams . . .* Oakland: Sufi Warrior, 1999.

Abu-Jaber, Diana. *Arabian Jazz*. New York: Harcourt, 1993.

———. *Crescent*. New York: Norton, 2003.

Adnan, Etel. *The Indian Never Had a Horse and Other Poems*. Sausalito: Post-Apollo, 1985.

———. *Sitt Marie Rose*. Trans. Georgina Kleege. Sausalito: Post-Apollo, 1982.

Ahmed, Leila. *A Border Passage*. New York: Farrar, Straus and Giroux, 1999.

Akash, Munir, and Khaled Mattawa, eds. *Post Gibran: Anthology of New Arab American Writing*. New York: Syracuse University Press, 1999.

Awad, Joseph. *The Neon Distances*. Francestown, NH: Golden Quill, 1980.

———. *Shenandoah Long Ago*. Richmond, VA: Poet's, 1990.

Bitar, Walid. *Two Guys on Holy Land*. Lebanon, NH: University Press of New England, 1993.

Blatty, William Peter. *I'll Tell Them I Remember You*. New York: Norton, 1973.

———. *Which Way to Mecca, Jack?* New York: Lancer, 1960.

Boullata, Kamal, ed. *And Not Surrender: American Poets on Lebanon*. Washington, DC: Arab-American Cultural Foundation, 1982.

Bourjaily, Vance. *Confessions of a Spent Youth*. New York: Dial, 1960.

Charara, Hayan. *The Alchemist's Diary*. New York: Hanging Loose Press, 2001.

Geha, Joseph. *Through and Through: Toledo Stories*. St. Paul: Graywolf Press, 1990.

Gibran, Gibran Kahlil. *Jesus the Son of Man*. New York: Knopf, 1928.

———. *The Madman*. New York: Knopf, 1918.

———. *The Prophet*. New York: Knopf, 1923.

Halaby, Laila. *West of the Jordan*. Boston: Beacon, 2003.

Hammad, Suheir. *Born Palestinian, Born Black*. New York: Harlem River Press, 1996.

Hamod, H. S. (Sam). *Dying with the Wrong Name: New and Selected Poems, 1968–1979*. New York: Anthe, 1980.

Handal, Nathalie. *The Neverfield Poem*. Sausalito, CA: Post-Apollo Press, 1999.

———, ed. *The Poetry of Arab Women: A Contemporary Anthology*. New York: Interlink Books, 2001.

Hazo, Samuel. *The Holy Surprise of Right Now: Selected and New Poems*. Fayetteville: University of Arkansas Press, 1996.

Joseph, Lawrence. *Before Our Eyes.* New York: Farrar, Straus and Giroux, 1993.

———. *Curriculum Vitae.* Pittsburgh: University of Pittsburgh Press, 1988.

Kadi, Joanna, ed. *Food for Our Grandmothers: Writings by Arab-American and Arab-Canadian Feminists.* Boston: South End Press, 1994.

Kahf, Mohja. *E-mails from Scheherazad.* Gainesville: University Press of Florida, 2003.

Mattawa, Khaled. *Ismailia Eclipse.* Riverdale-on-Hudson, NY: Sheep Meadow, 1995.

———. *Zodiac of Echoes.* Keene, NY: Ausable Press, 2003.

Melhem, D. H. *Blight.* New York: Riverrun Press, 2003.

———. *Conversations with a Stonemason.* San Francisco: Ikon Press, 2003.

———. *Rest in Love.* New York: Dovetail, 1975.

Melhem, D. H., and Leila Diab, eds. *A Different Path: An Anthology of the Radius of Arab American Writers.* Detroit: Ridgeway Press, 2000.

Nassar, Eugene Paul. *Wind of the Land.* Belmont, MA: Association of Arab-American University Graduates, 1979.

Nye, Naomi Shihab. *Fuel.* Rochester, NY: Boa Editions Limited, 1998.

———. *Never in a Hurry: Essays on People and Places.* Columbia: University of South Carolina Press, 1996.

———. *Red Suitcase.* Rochester, NY: Boa Editions Limited, 1994.

———. *Words under the Words.* Portland, OR: Eight Mountain Press, 1980.

———, ed. *The Space between Our Footsteps: Poems and Paintings from the Middle East.* New York: Simon and Schuster Books for Young Readers, 1998.

Orfalea, Gregory. *The Capital of Solitude.* Greenfield Center, NY: Greenfield Review, 1988.

Orfalea, Gregory, and Sharif Elmusa, eds. *Grape Leaves: A Century of Arab American Poetry.* Salt Lake City: University of Utah Press, 1988.

Rihani, Ameen. *The Book of Khalid.* 1911. Reprint, Beirut: Rihani House, 1973.

Rihbany, Abraham. *A Far Journey.* Boston: Houghton, 1914.

———. *The Syrian Christ.* Boston: Houghton, 1916.

Rizk, Saloom. *Syrian Yankee.* Garden City, NY: Doubleday, 1943.

Ward, Patricia Sarrafian. *The Bullet Collection.* St. Paul: Graywolf Press, 2003.

Williams, David. *Traveling Mercies.* Cambridge, MA: Alice James, 1993.